COLORADO GOLD

MARIAN WELLS

BETHANY HOUSE PUBLISHERS

MINNEAPOLIS, MINNESOTA 55438
A Division of Bethany Fellowship, Inc.

Manuscript edited by Penelope J. Stokes.
Cover designed by Dan Thornberg,
Bethany House Publishers staff artist.

Published by Bethany House Publishers
A Division of Bethany Fellowship, Inc.
6820 Auto Club Road, Minneapolis, Minnesota 55438

Printed in the United States of America

Library of Congress Cataloging-in-Publication Data

Wells, Marian, 1931–
    Colorado gold / Marian Wells.

    (Treasure quest ; bk. 1)
    I. Title. II. Series: Wells, Marian, 1931-
Treasure quest ; bk. 1.
PS3573.E4927C6   1988   813'.54—dc19   87-35333
ISBN 0-87123-966-3 (pbk.)

COLORADO GOLD

To My Husband

Chet

My Best Friend

Books by Marian Wells

The Wedding Dress
With This Ring

Karen

The STARLIGHT TRILOGY Series
   The Wishing Star
   Star Light, Star Bright
   Morning Star

The TREASURE QUEST Series
   Colorado Gold
   Out of the Crucible
   The Silver Highway
   Jewel of Promise

MARIAN WELLS and her husband live in Boulder, Colorado. There she has immediate access to the research and documentation of the historical surroundings of this series. Her research and background on Mormonism provided the thrust for her bestselling STARLIGHT TRILOGY, the *Wedding Dress* and *With This Ring*.

INTRODUCTION

There's gold in Pikes Peak country!" The shout was electrifying, the response immediate. The year was 1858. As quickly as they could put their affairs in order, they came— streaming into the wind, charging across the plains. Youths and middle-aged men, poor farmers, lawyers, doctors, storekeepers, outlaws, gamblers, and dance-hall girls—all had eyes shining with hope, sure of success. It was there for the taking— easy gold, ready to be picked up by the shovelful.

The would-be miners came. Some walked; others rode on horseback or in rickety wagons—they were the lucky ones. The billowing canvas tops provided at least feeble shields against sun, rain, and Indian arrows.

Many gave their lives there on that barren stretch of high, desolate prairie. Many a dream was buried beside the trail. Many turned back when they discovered that gold demanded their blood, sweat, and tears. But the survivors—the hardy, determined ones—were inclined to make their dreams come true.

Those who stayed learned to change their goals. The dream of becoming a millionaire gradually diminished into a determination to earn a living. These miners spent their lives ever hacking away at yet another mountain. Still others were willing to exchange the old dream for a new one. Some of these men became successful farmers, industrialists, shopkeepers.

Among the gold seekers, some were successful beyond wildest expectations. Gold nuggets rolled across the gambling tables, and guns roared. The wild west was reality; for a time each man was law unto himself.

Into this climate stepped the missionaries from the Methodist Episcopal church. Clad in threadbare coats, they preached in saloons and in tiny log cabins. As they walked from gold camp to gold camp, their very presence caught the men up short.

Perhaps it was a blessing that only a few of the gold seekers found riches, for the lack of treasure set men looking for a gold that didn't sift through their fingers. More than a few soberly considered the missionaries' words and measured the nuggets in their hand against eternal treasure.

But not only the miners faced this dilemma. The daughter of one such frontier preacher plunged into the middle of this restless scene. Amy, sixteen years old, is amazed, bewildered, and mystified by the life surrounding her. Face to face with her father's calling and the lure of material riches, she must choose the course her life will follow. And the decision that she ultimately makes—the choice between wealth and the will of God—will change her life forever.

CHAPTER 1

Think of Amy!" The insistent voice penetrated Amy's dream, making her eyes flutter. The voice continued. "You're bringing a young innocent girl into a rough gold camp. Eli, it's a mistake, exposing her to that element. You know our mistakes will dog us to the grave."

"Now, Maude, Amy's—" came Father's low voice.

"She's asleep."

Amy squinted at the light probing her eyes. Yesterday a sharp branch had poked a hole in the canvas stretched over the Rev. Eli Randolph's wagon, and Aunt Maude took it as a sign that Satan was marshaling his forces against them. Today a finger of light danced through the hole. With each jolt of the wagon it stabbed her, daring her to shed the dream and listen to the two bent figures as they argued on their wagon seat.

In her dream, Amy's tight braids had become a floating veil of springy yellow curls; her eyes were daring and brave. Now Amy screwed her blue eyes tight against the light and clung to her dream. A trickle of perspiration beaded on her lip and dropped to the pillow.

With a tiny sigh, Amy wiped her lip and surrendered the dream of the tall young man on horseback. He had come crashing into her life, spilling gold nuggets and sweeping aside Aunt Maude and Father with a smile as he reached for Amy.

Aunt Maude's voice caught her as it lifted beyond the discontented grumble, stacking the argument to dangerous, dizzy heights. Amy's ears strained to hear the words. It wasn't the familiar complaints, but new, strange things that made her uneasy.

"Following a dream you are—a foolish, selfish one. Why can't you forget her? Risking our lives, threatening your daughter with the very thing you should be fleeing. The taint makes it a bigger fear. Eli, you can't tempt fate this way and get by with it. We've not talked this out, but I know your secret thoughts. Everytime I see you looking toward those places, eyeing those painted faces, I know what ails you.

"'Tis one thing to convert the heathen, 'tis another to not rest easy with one's lot in life. Are you intending to ever tell her about—"

As Aunt Maude paused, Amy heard the pounding hooves, a shout. Her aunt's complaint ended in a sob. "Eli, Indians! Oh, the Lord forgive us for this foolishness!"

Amy rolled off the pillows and pushed her face between the two on the seat. Her aunt spoke automatically. "Amy, take your elbow out of my side."

The horse thundered past, leaving a cloud of dust that slowly settled down over the Randolph team and wagon. Amy coughed and rubbed her watering eyes. The rider circled back. It wasn't an Indian.

Amy grinned at the dusty young rider. "Are you a cowboy?"

"Naw, I'm heading for the gold mines." He tipped his hat at Amy's father and added, "Just wanted to say howdy and I'll see you in Denver City. Stay on this Smokey Hill road; it'll take you right into town." He wheeled his horse and left them to their plodding gait.

The color was seeping back into Aunt Maude's face. Amy stretched to look after the rider, and her aunt snapped, "And don't you practice poking your lip out like that and making your eyes like saucers. Eli, these miners will ruin a sweet-faced innocent."

The whip cracked impatiently over the backs of the team. The mules hurried their gait a bit, and Amy slanted a glance at Aunt Maude, recalling the things she overheard. *Taint. Aunt Maude, why didn't you like my mother? Deep down, you're really glad she died, aren't you?*

The ugly thoughts pressed against Amy as she settled back on the quilt. The noonday heat poured down on the prairie as the wagon swayed through the ruts. Amy peered out at the barren trail. Slowly she said, "A lonely trail, straight as an arrow to Pikes Peak country."

She waited for their reply as she studied the sparse gray-green bushes and the poor, pale soil. The heavy silence was broken only by the creaking wagon and the snort from the team. Father's shoulders moved again, but neither he nor Aunt Maude spoke.

Amy sighed and yanked off her sunbonnet. Trying to break the lonesome silence, she said, "I wish a cool breeze would come up. Just a little one." Perspiration had darkened her braids to honey color and plastered her hair into shiny corkscrews across her forehead.

She picked the curls away and rubbed her offending elbows, saying, "I wish I didn't look like a scrawny baby. And I wish I could wear my hair loose and curled."

Aunt Maude peered over her shoulder. "Tut," she said uneasily. "You'll grow up fast enough. Don't pine for what you don't have."

Amy fanned herself briskly with her sunbonnet. With a quick glance at the two, she said, "If the end of May is like this, what'll summer bring?" No answer. "Father, we've been staring at sagebrush forever."

Her aunt answered. "Not so. You can't forget the miles of grasslands." Her tart reply changed to a plaintive murmur as she sank back on the seat, "Not that it matters. It's the green pastures of Kansas Territory I'm wanting, not those rearing up lands they call the Rocky Mountains. Trying to stick in a wagon when your nose is pointed skyward is enough to scare a person humble in a hurry."

While Aunt Maude rambled on, Amy studied her father. He was a dark lump of dusty coat and limp black hat. But Amy didn't need to see his face; it was a copy of Aunt Maude's long-planed face, with a nose like finely chiseled flint.

Glancing at Aunt Maude she saw the one tear on her pale cheek, but the guilty sympathy Amy felt put her in partnership with her father. With a quick look at him, she began to think out her words carefully. "Aunt Maude, I know you don't like coming to the Pikes Peak country; I'd rather stay in Kansas too, but I'm not scared by mountains. They'll be beautiful, all green pines and mirror-like lakes, deer and bighorn sheep—"

Aunt Maude snorted, "You sound just like that guide book. The one by the fellow pushing us to get gold fever and join the wagon train." She sat up and waved her arm, crying weakly, "Pikes Peak or Bust!"

Amy blinked. Eli nodded, saying, "The pamphlet put out by William Byers. I'll admit he printed a pretty nice picture of life around Cherry Creek. Made it sound like a growing city with piles of gold in the creeks."

Straightening on the hard wagon seat, Aunt Maude snorted in disgust. "Last autumn, by snowfall, the greatest share of them had come back to Lawrence, Kansas.

"It wasn't hard for us to see that they had been humbled— creeping back into the territory and civilization, tail between their legs, their canvas all labeled *Busted by God*."

"Now, Maude," Eli's voice came from under the hat, "some quotations don't bear repeating. Besides, you've no doubt noticed, we aren't the gold-seeking crowd."

Amy knew it was best to keep silent, but the words burst out, "Since church conference time, you knew Father would come. And we knew you didn't want to come. Father tried to get you to stay with one of the uncles." Immediately she regretted the words. Aunt Maude dabbed at her eyes.

Father's shoulders moved uneasily again. Sadly Aunt Maude said, "I couldn't forget my responsibility. 'Tis bad enough for a widower to be out here alone to fend for himself, but one with a child—that's out of the question. I know my duty."

"Child!" Amy exploded. "I suppose I'll never get a figure, even by eating butter and cream. But on the inside I'm grown up. I'm fifteen. Lots of girls are getting married at sixteen. And what did you mean when you said—"

Amy's father reached out with a calming touch. Trembling, Amy settled back on the pile of quilts; she had nearly admitted to eavesdropping. She said no more, but concentrated on her keyhole view.

"Look!" Maude pointed. "Isn't that blue line a river in the patches of trees? Maybe the Platte?"

Eli shook his head. He held up the scrap of paper. "According to this map, it's Cherry Creek. That means we're almost there."

"Thank God." Aunt Maude breathed out an explosion of relief. "I can say I've been worried silly thinking we'd be done in by the Indians any minute. It was hard to see those other folks take off and head north to the Oregon Trail."

"Almost there?" Amy said slowly. "What do you mean? Those mountains look a long way off."

"Amy, daughter," Eli said gently as he continued to flick the reins and study the paper, "we'll be staying in a little town this side of the Cherry Creek. They call it Denver City. That is, we'll stay there until the missionaries assign us a place to minister."

"Missionaries?" Amy questioned. "You mean there aren't bishops and presiding elders here?"

"No. A conference hasn't yet been organized. It'll probably be several years until we're strong enough. There's just a few missionaries, come in from the Kansas-Nebraska Conference."

Studying her father's weary face, seeing the new lines and the way his shoulders sagged, she bit back the sharp bitter words she wanted to say. But it had always been this way, as far back as she could remember.

Father never had enough money or time for frolic. Amy

bitterly reflected on the last parish. They had just made the old house fit to live in before it was time to move on. There was time to make only a few friends before saying goodbye.

"Minister! I doubt there's even a decent church where we're going. Besides, what can a spindly fifteen-year-old and a maiden lady do in a mining camp—dig gold?"

He shot a half-grin at her while Aunt Maude groaned. "Eli, mark my words. In another year I'll remind you I said this would be a mistake."

He pointed toward the southwest. "That's our destination. We've about a half hour, just enough time to give you the bare facts about the place."

"I see cabins on each side of the creek," Amy said.

"Well, the east side is Denver City; on the other side is another small town they've named Auraria. I understand the two scrap like litter pups. The fella back in Lawrence told me as of last summer there was just a handful of cabins in each town. I think he said twenty-five on the Denver City side and fifty on the Auraria side. Looks to me like there's more now. Those bigger places must be hotels."

He paused, then added, "Even from here it doesn't look too bad. The line of trees along the creek gives it a homelike touch.

"There must be some pretty good-sized camps in the mountains by now. The young man in Lawrence said fifty thousand men and a few women had moved in last year."

Amy echoed, "Fifty thousand!" Aunt Maude shook her head.

"Eli, I heard you talking to that man. You didn't know, but just around the corner another fellow was saying that a good share of the men took one look around, shook a panful of gravel and then high-tailed it back to Kansas."

"I've an idea they were the ones who fell for the story that the gold was lying around waiting to be scooped up by the bucket loads," Eli replied.

"Or the rumor that you could quarry it like granite," Amy added.

"Up both branches of Clear Creek," Eli said, "they're saying there's good color showing, but the miners will have to work for it." He turned to grin at Amy. "See, I'm getting miner's jargon down pat. Color refers to the presence of gold in the ore."

In a moment his smile faded into the familiar brooding expression. Aunt Maude began to nod in her corner of the seat, and Amy strained her eyes to pick out the details of the area around the creek.

They dropped down a slight incline and the small settlement stretched out before them, a tiny smear of brown against the overwhelming mountains. For a moment Amy was uneasy. Everything seemed hazy and barren down that line of gray soil and green trees marking the way to Denver City.

Father was talking, his voice moving through the stillness, barely lifting above a murmur. Amy knew he was quoting scripture as he often did while they traveled. She turned to listen to him.

His voice rose and grew strong. " 'Therefore, behold, I will allure her, and bring her into the wilderness, and speak comfortably unto her. And I will give her her vineyards from thence, and the valley of Achor for a door of hope: and she shall sing there, as in the days of her youth, and as in the day when she came up out of the land of Egypt.' "

When he had been silent for a time, Amy asked, "What book are you quoting? It's pretty, almost like a love story."

Startled, he cleared his throat. When he spoke his voice was flat. Flipping the reins he said, "Hosea. It is a love story—in a way." In another moment he pointed. "See that? That's the south fork of the Platte River. Cuts down Nebraska way. We'll be living this side of it, but I hear there's a good ferry close hereabouts. Doesn't look safe to ford. They say in spring run-off it's seventy feet wide."

He paused then added, "One thing, don't forget, daughter. We're here to spread the Gospel. That should make us look at circumstances in a totally different light. It matters not whether people find gold, or that the towns be little and shabby. The

important part is that we establish the church regardless of anything else."

The passion in his voice made Amy move impatiently. His
words dug down in her, uncovering the uneasy, hidden guilt of
questions she felt but dared not ask. This was new—the need
to question nearly everything. She looked at him, wondering
what he would think of her questions. Did he ever wonder
about God? She saw his eyes were troubled.

For a moment she waited, then moved her shoulders impatiently—wanting to hear, yet fearful of all the unsaid things.
*Why won't you talk about my mother? Why do my questions make
you uneasy? Why do I feel it's wrong to ask the questions I wonder
about most?*

The sun was starting to slip behind the jagged peaks to the
west as Eli took his team into the streets of Denver City. Although the clamor of the town was beginning to intrude, Amy
didn't notice. She was caught, unable to tear herself away from
the view in front of her.

The setting sun outlined the snowcapped peaks with a
crown of light and tempered them with peach-hued clouds.
Amy watched as the light burst its cloud barriers and became
bars of gold slanting down through the mountain gorge.

She shivered with a strange joy as she watched distant
winds sweep the clouds. Now they rolled, spilling across the
topmost silvered slopes. At the same time the clouds picked up
new lights, changing from apricot to rose to lavender.

When Eli hauled in on the reins, Amy turned from the
mountains. She blinked and leaned forward on her elbows.
"Aunt Maude, look at those clouds! Makes me think life here
at the foot of the Rockies has a Midas touch. You know, King
Midas—gold!" Her heart quickened with the fairy tale promise.
But she buried the thought inside: *Just maybe there is something
exciting and mysterious about Pikes Peak country.* She took a deep
shaky breath and glanced at the mountains again.

The wagon stopped. Leaning across the seat, she watched
Eli climb out and head for a large structure made of pale logs.
He gingerly picked his way to the veranda as Amy murmured,

"That building looks like a ship floating on a sea of mud."

The wide veranda held a row of rail sitters. With unblinking eyes they studied her and Aunt Maude, who was just now stirring and looking around. One shifted a pipe in his mouth and readjusted his muddy boots. "Female," he said briefly, "but it's jest a tad."

Amy peered down the street stretching along the bank of the creek. Where the trees had been hacked out, a building had been erected in their place.

She found she could identify the log buildings. One was obviously a livery stable. The next, tall and rambling, must be a hotel. She watched a woman in a hoop skirt and scoop bonnet being handed from a carriage to the steps.

Beyond the hotel a covey of small cabins huddled, a mixture of sizes and shapes, but all of the same light log.

Aunt Maude fastened her hair more securely and pointed with her chin. "That place is a general store. I saw a man come out with shovel, and the fella behind was carrying a sack of flour. So at least we eat."

"Doesn't it smell nice?" Amy asked dreamily. "The fresh wet smell of the rain, the wood smoke and the sage and pine. Aunt Maude, I'm beginnng to think I'd like to live here forever. Maybe Father will stay in Denver City instead of going to the mountains."

Eli came out of the building. He was wearing a broad smile, and Maude frowned as he said, "The fellow inside pointed me in the direction of a vacant cabin. Says it's pretty snug. The owner got discouraged and just walked out on it, so it's ours for now. He also told me how to get in touch with the missionaries. Seems there's quite a group here."

The cabin was a steep climb up the next street. Aunt Maude clung to the seat and said, "At least we're spared the mud they have down below."

Amy and Aunt Maude were still gingerly stepping through the damp white clay when Eli came back to the wagon for another load. "What a view!" He picked up the table and turned. "Come see."

Amy went to the stoop and turned to look. On this street the little cabins were set at odd angles, without design or pattern, either to their dooryards or corrals. The road they traveled wound between the buildings and edged down the hill toward the business section of town.

"How come most of the cabins up here are empty?" she asked. "Those down below look full of people." The rambling log buildings along the creek vibrated with sound and activity.

When Aunt Maude stopped beside her, she added, "We can see the whole of the main street, as well as Cherry Creek and the Platte River."

Aunt Maude turned into the cabin. "The mountains are pretty tonight. Cabins? I don't know why the cabins are empty; I'd rather live up here, anyway—there's a view."

Inside, Aunt Maude inspected the bunks built into the side of the cabin. Her voice was brisk and determined. "We'll need new ticks. I'll not have those things in the house tonight."

Amy straightened the benches and asked, "Where do we get water?"

"I doubt out of Cherry Creek; looks pretty muddy to me. I'll go ask." Eli dumped another load and headed for the door.

"Do more'n ask, sir," Aunt Maude said scooping up the water pails and following him. "I saw the likes of the fellows lining the rail down there. I'll not be giving them the least chance to have a thought about our Amy." She pushed the buckets at him. "While we're here, you get the water."

Amy watched her father stride down the hill with the buckets swinging. "Aunt Maude, he'll be talking until nightfall."

"That's just fine. It'll give us a chance to be having our own little talk. Amy, this isn't Lawrence, and I don't want you to be forgetting it for a minute. Back home life was a mite smoother. Refined. There were schools and clean sheets on the lines, garden patches and good solid families.

"I've been watching since we started out on this journey. It's like nothing else I've seen. Coarse, dirty men with foul mouths and all eyes. I've been around enough to know there's no trusting that kind. You stay close to your father or me all the time. I heard that piano playing down there. At six in the afternoon, with music coming out of one of those places, there's nothing good going on."

"Aunt Maude. I know what you're hinting. I know the men are rough. I've no intention of letting them lead me astray. So please don't worry."

"I do worry." Her eyes brooded over every detail of Amy's face. "You're such an innocent, you wouldn't know a big bad wolf 'til he bit you."

Amy returned to sorting and folding the jumble of clothing on the table. "What I want isn't anything like what you are thinking. I want—" She caught sight of the dimming grandeur of the mountains. "Beauty. I want to reach out and capture beauty, something I can keep all for myself."

"Beauty? What's beauty?" Aunt Maude was looking around the cabin in the most suspicious manner.

"I don't know." Amy pressed her hand against her throat. "I only know the wanting hurts right here. I intend to find out."

"But what makes you think it's good?" For a moment they stood looking at each other. Aunt Maude's eyes were curious and strangely timid.

That expression held Amy. "It'll be good. If it's beauty, it'll be good. Look at the mountains."

CHAPTER 2

After nearly a month of living in Denver City, Amy was still trying to adjust to Pikes Peak land. It was strange, this land that stretched pancake-flat eastward, while westward it reared straight up.

Back home, every morning, the sun rose from the depths of the river and trees, and at evening time it sank into the cornfields. In this little town called Denver City, the sun seemed to rise like an egg yolk rolling across the flat plains.

Each morning Amy watched it skittering along, contoured with the ground until suddenly it leaped free. But in the evening when it dropped behind the mountains, it was all majesty, and Amy knew she would never tire of the glory of it.

As the days moved by, sandwiched between the rising and setting of the sun, events began adding variety to life. The Sabbath meetings were held at the cabin of G. W. Fisher. Fisher was one of the important persons in Denver City, the first missionary from the Methodist Episcopal Church to preach in Denver City.

That first Sunday after the Randolphs arrived in Denver City, they attended worship service at the Fishers'.

Listening to the missionaries, Amy was astonished to discover how different life was here on the frontier. She found it didn't seem to matter to anyone that the first sermon in Denver City had been delivered in a saloon.

That is, it didn't matter to anyone except Aunt Maude. Sitting in the Fishers' yard, in the meager shade of a mountain cedar, the missionaries tried to reason with Aunt Maude. As the men talked, Amy watched the play of expression on her aunt's face. She was outraged and astonished.

Amy was intrigued and delighted. She watched the men grow red in the face with the effort of convincing Aunt Maude, while her aunt grew red with indignation. Amy kept silent: she knew better than to let her feelings out around Aunt Maude.

Finally the knot of men around Aunt Maude moved away, and everyone found a seat on the cottonwood logs. Soon the worship service began.

Amy watched the missionary leading the singing. The sun struck his face, making it seem light and carefree. The wind tousled his hair and his coarse shirt billowed in the wind.

A mighty fortress is our God. For a moment Amy's heart lifted in a wild, strange joy. It made her one with the blue jay perched above the song leader's head. She wanted desperately to tell Aunt Maude she hoped they would never build a church house. But that wouldn't do. Aunt Maude's lips would tighten even more.

The miners from down the hill came to take seats on the log. She looked at the blue jay again. *Just maybe her feelings about beauty were real and important.*

Someday she might be able to talk about these things to them—Father and Aunt Maude. Maybe she could say them in such a way she would be proud to own the thoughts. Was God in beauty? She looked at Aunt Maude, desperately wishing her aunt would accept the differences out here.

Later that day Amy heard more details of that first barroom sermon. The missionaries said the fellow tending bar had hushed the clatter, while the customers pulled off their hats and listened respectfully. She tried to fit that picture to the church in Kansas. In Kansas, no good churchman would be found in a saloon for any reason!

Amy was learning, too; that on the frontier the important people didn't look any different from the miners. All the men wore ragged dungarees and slouch hats—they looked, spoke, and acted alike.

She concluded this after she met Colonel Gilpin and the sheriff of Denver City. Sheriff Tom Pollock had a rumpled mane of red hair and muddy, scuffed boots. He looked tough, like the miners did.

But the sameness of the men didn't apply to the women. Mrs. Fisher looked like Aunt Maude. Some of the ladies going into the hotel down the hill looked like Aunt Maude and Mrs. Fisher. But the rest of them looked like the pretty ladies going into the dance halls and saloons.

And only the women like Aunt Maude and Mrs. Fisher were introduced to Amy. She tried to keep her curious eyes off the ladies in the pretty frocks. *So these are the dance-hall girls we whispered about back home.*

Denver City had been settled for a year, and log saloons, hotels, and shops were rising as fast as the trees could be felled. The Methodist Episcopal Church continued to meet for worship at the Fisher home.

By June the Sabbath meetings were taking on a new flavor. Organization of the conference was uppermost in everyone's mind.

At the conclusion of worship, Amy and Aunt Maude helped prepare a simple meal for the missionaries who had come in from their circuits. After the men ate, the womenfolk sat at the far end of the one room and listened.

While flies buzzed in and out of the dim cabin, Amy watched the men. Their shoulders were moving with excitement as they nodded their heads in approval. In the end, when the missionaries got to their feet, their smiles and clasped hands made her wish for the years when she could accept, before her nagging doubts and troubling questions came to haunt her.

For a moment she smiled. In the past she had sat on Father's lap and listened to the murmur of voices until she fell asleep. Childish. Little girl desires. She shrugged impatiently. Now, each year seemed to drive the wedge deeper between her and the church. Pushing away the thoughts, Amy listened to the conversation.

Brother Fisher and Brother Kelly were appointed presiding elders of the Pikes Peak area. Brother Fisher waved the letter from the Nebraska-Kansas Conference. He explained, "It won't be long before we become a full-fledged conference. Until then we want to work with all of our hearts. Remember, it's work for the Master."

Brother Kelly was wiping his eyes, exclaiming, "Bless God, this is really living!"

Amy looked at him curiously, wondering what he meant. Brother Fisher continued, "It is going to be difficult and lonely, but exciting. I've never been on the ground floor work of building a new conference. As quickly as we can organize, the Nebraska-Kansas Conference will be sending men to labor here."

Amy was thinking of that scene the next day as she wandered up the road to the dirt bank jutting over Cherry Creek and the sprawl of log cabins along the bank. "Makes a person feel like an outsider when they can't get in on the excitement," she sighed. She sat down on the shady side of the bank. "Got to be going on ninety to be excited like they are."

Her gloom deepened as she looked at the rooftops beneath her. Somewhere in that mass there was reported to be an Episcopal pastor with a wife and daughter. "But how do you go about finding someone when Aunt Maude glares and shifts her eyebrows when a body mentions getting out of her sight?"

Relaxing against the cedar, feeling the sun warm on her face, she began to forget her mood. The earth smell was good— sharp and fresh, with the tangy scent of sage and cedar. It was only four in the afternoon, but the line of little log houses below her seemed overrun with people shouting and laughing. Amy leaned over to watch, yearning after them.

She tried to spot the saloon where Father and Brother Fisher had gone last week to preach.

Imagine, all those men with that drink they were calling Taos Lightning standing there and listening politely! Amy shook her head. "Those fellows know better than to be squandering their money and time with the card games. Father said so. I wonder what it is that makes—"

Suddenly there was a thunder of sound and a scream—a very feminine scream. Amy dropped to her knees, trembling. Crawling to the edge of the bank she leaned forward. The door on one of the cabins burst open and the screams and shouts grew louder.

A rush of people poured into the street. The shouts became a clamor of disjointed words. *"Fool! I call you out—pistols or knives. Cheat! Horse thief!"*

For a moment Amy grinned, then she caught her breath. The setting sun touched gleaming metal. Slowly the spectators backed off the street. Below her two men tensed, bent forward. While their heels dug into the dust, they circled each other in the middle of the street.

Another scream pierced the air. There was barely a flicker of emotion on the ashen faces glaring at each other. Far up the street Amy saw a flash of red billowing skirts.

At the moment her attention was diverted, the crack came. Smoke drifted from the pointing guns.

Pushing her hand against her mouth, Amy watched the men slowly change positions. The one facing Amy straightened and gripped his bloody shoulder. The other man quietly slipped onto his face in the dust.

Amy stayed crouched over the bank, watching the street. But it wasn't curiosity holding her motionless. A strange numbness made it impossible to believe the scene was real.

The woman in red finally moved. Slowly she walked forward, hesitated, then flung herself into the road beside the limp man. Miners trickled out of the buildings to circle the man clutching his shoulder.

To Amy it was like watching the final act of the school play. While the group around the injured gunman moved away without a backward glance, another group hoisted the limp body and staggered down the street. The woman in red slowly got to her feet and followed.

Amy found she was clenching her fists against her throat until she could scarcely breathe. She stumbled as she stood and ran toward the cabin. Nearly there, she slowed, tried to calm herself. The sun was sliding behind the mountain. The wash of shadow seemed cold and unfriendly.

The scene was impossible to explain until she could understand it. She closed her mind around the event, clutching one more secret to add to the things lodged in her heart. *Secrets,* she told herself, *like bricks stacked one on the other, build a wall. Sometimes I think I can't see over it.*

On the step outside the cabin, she hesitated, thinking of the other bricks. *Mother.* In dismay she thought, *I can't feel that way. It was too long ago to count.* Even as she tried to accept the thought, she was wondering, *Why won't they talk about my mother?*

Aunt Maude was a brick. Father too. Especially when he shut everybody out. But sometimes the walls made it easier to live.

By the following day exciting news crowded out that ugly scene. They learned Father was being sent up the mountain to a place called Central City on the Gregory diggings. Amy listened with excitement. Aunt Maude listened and moaned. Father explained. "The trip isn't that bad. I hear the road up through Golden Gate Canyon isn't good, but it isn't dangerous. We'll make it in a day."

Amy asked, "Tell us about the town."

"I know little. Right now it's a shack city. Lots of miners up there—fifteen thousand, I heard. They tell me the area was opened up this spring. There's good color showing. Men are panning along the creek and on up the gulch."

She started to ask and he guessed her question. He said, "No school, no females except two old ladies. But Amy, it won't be that way for long if the gold is that good."

That evening supper was early. Aunt Maude explained. "Your father has a meeting. I want to go along and find out all I can about Central City. You come or go to bed."

"It'll be late," Father added, "Might as well just stay here." She nodded.

After they left, Amy washed dishes and hung towels to dry. Standing by the bushes that lined the bluff overlooking the main street, she watched the night shadows moving up the streets. The first glow of light came from the windows of the hotel, the line of saloons, and the dance halls. The night seemed unusually quiet. Horses and wagons were darker shadows, accompanied by the gentle creak and clink of harness and wheel.

Amy had turned away when the swinging door of the dance hall threw the sound at her. She stopped. It was the tinny, syncopated sound of a piano, crashing gaily through a tune she didn't recognize. "A piano," she murmured, "a real piano. Oh, I would love to see it, to hear—"

The thought was there before her foot slipped on the edge of the incline. She sat down abruptly and watched the gravel cascading down the slope. Her heart began to thump, not from the near tumble, but instead because of the idea. A good hard slide would land her in the backyard of the dance hall.

In the end, Amy strolled casually down the hill instead. Under the cover of night, confident of the length of Methodist Episcopal Church meetings, she had nothing to fear.

Once she reached the street bordering Cherry Creek, Amy quickened her steps, fearful now of all the stories Aunt Maude had told about drunken miners. When she reached the boardwalk, she hesitated just long enough to hear shuffling feet and laughter.

Quickly she scooted around the corner and found herself behind the dance hall. Music came from the open window high above her head.

Backing slowly across the yard, straining to see, Amy collided with something. "Oh!" Whirling around she gasped in relief. The obstacle was not a drunken man; it was a woodpile, a very tall one. After another ragged breath, she scrambled up the logs and peered in the window. She could see a man sitting at the piano; behind him the swirling skirts were a rainbow wrapping around the somber garb of men.

Amy was unmindful of the dancing figures. Her eyes were focused on the fingers flying across the keys, measuring their movement with the sounds coming through the window. "More than anything," she murmured, "more even than a heap of gold. Oh, how I want—"

"More than gold?" The mocking voice came below her.

Amy caught her breath and leaned forward. "Oh, I didn't know anyone was down there." She squinted at the figure in the shadows. "You startled me!"

"Well, come down and help me." Amy slid off her perch and went to stand beside the woman seated on the log. She looked up at Amy. "I've ripped the heel off my slipper. If you'll hold it while I whack it with this piece of wood, I may get it to hold."

Amy studied the pink chiffon and lace. The woman's dress wasn't cut like Aunt Maude's. Amy blinked at the glorious display of creamy flesh. She reached for the slipper, "I'd expect you to take cold out here after dark."

"Well, I'll take something, but it won't be cold." She handed the slipper to Amy.

Slowly Amy turned it in her hands. "I've never seen a shoe like this. All silver except for the tip of the toe. Is that gold?"

"They said so. But if this flimsy heel is any indication, I have a feeling the gold will rub off by next week." She turned the slipper in Amy's hand. "Hold it this way. There, now hang on tight."

The chunk of firewood crashed against the heel and slipped. "Ouch!"

The woman dropped the wood. "I've hit you! Here, let me see. Oh, you poor baby. I'm sorry. I didn't dream it would slip. Hold this hanky against it. Oh, I'm so terribly sorry. That lousy shoe." She flung it away and bent over Amy. "Let me see. Come with me and I'll put some salve on it."

"Oh, no. It'll be fine." Amy pulled back in horror.

"No, I insist. I can't dance in this shoe anyway. Come on; I'll just hobble on down to the hotel and get another pair. We'll fix up that finger. How ridiculous! I should have known better." She tugged and Amy came.

Hurrying down the street, the woman pulled Amy

through the front door of the hotel. "I've never been in a place like this," Amy said with a catch in her voice. She stumbled in the thick carpeting as she followed. The woman's laugh was low and musical. "It isn't a bad place. I'll go apologize to your parents if you wish." She stopped on the stairs and turned to look at Amy. Touching the curls coming loose from Amy's braids, the woman said, "You've lovely hair. Mine was nearly that color when I was younger."

She cocked her head and studied Amy. "You are older than I thought. Such a bitty thing. That's fine. No sense having the fellows tagging you around until you're grown." She took Amy's arm and tugged her along.

The woman's room was crowded with frocks hanging from every hook and knob in the place. Amy stood like a wooden soldier with her eyes drinking in the loveliness. The woman dropped the ruined slippers and came back carrying a bottle.

"This will sting, but it'll help. Who knows what lurks in woodpiles." She smiled at Amy. After the sting was gone and the ointment applied, she touched Amy's cheek. "Seeing your apple freshness makes me feel like a shabby old lady."

"Oh, but you aren't!" Amy gasped, shocked into a burst of words. "You're beautiful. I suppose if I had a wish to grow up beautiful, I'd want to look like you."

The woman crossed the room and rummaged through an open valise. Taking up another pair of slippers, she said, "I hope you have higher aspirations than being a dance-hall girl. Why were you looking through the window?"

"It was the piano. I've always wanted to learn the piano. I've scarcely ever been close to one. My aunt believes they are an invention of the devil." Amy noticed the shoes. "Why, those are just like the others."

The woman smiled up at Amy as she fastened the shining straps. "All silver, even the heels. They've kind of become a trademark. They call me Silverheels." She stood up. "Now, if that finger feels okay, I'll walk with you back to the dance hall."

"I think I'd better be going home. It's getting late. I'll just climb the hill from here." Amy studied the woman's face. When the warm, merry eyes met Amy's, she was filled with strange emotion.

Amy hesitated, wondering and afraid to wonder. One part of those emotions reminded her of all the labels Aunt Maude would place on this woman. But another part of Amy was yearning to reach out to the laughing, smiling woman.

They had started out the door when the woman turned abruptly. The smiles were gone. Even in the dim lamp light, Amy could see her eyes were sad. She touched Amy's shoulder lightly, and then her fingers pressed hard.

Leaning close the woman whispered, "I saw the hunger in you. You want the pretties, the things you don't have. Don't let it lead you astray. Sometimes things are not what they seem. If you repeat this, I'll deny it. But if I had it to do over again—"

She turned and led the way down the stairs. Amy followed. A touch of the woman's sadness seemed to seep in, spoiling even the awesome marvel of the thick, soft carpet underfoot. Amy noticed it was marked with the soil from Denver City's streets.

Amy nearly bumped into the woman when they reached the door. Bending over, peering into the street, the woman muttered, "Those preachers are at it again. Down at the corner, snatching at every fellow passing." She turned with a bright smile. "I'm slipping out the back door. You're on your own, sweetie. See you around."

Amy watched the woman go down the back hall. With a sigh, Amy leaned out the door and considered. If all the exhorters from the Methodist Episcopal Church were in that crowd of singing men, then she could be in trouble. Aunt Maude would be home by now.

Taking a deep breath, Amy straightened her shoulders and stepped out the door. She mingled with the crowd on the street. In front of her a woman in a towering hat clung to the arm of a man who must have been someone important. He was wearing a boiled shirt and string tie.

The slurring speech of the man beside her caught Amy's

attention. He was saying, "Tad, yer meaning right, but I don't want to go home jest yet. Let's stop fer refreshment and then I'll go."

He swayed, stopped, and peered ahead. "That's looking like a bunch of preachers. Seems I recall yer ma a singin' that song. 'Nothing But the Blood of Jesus.' Mighty sweet."

"Pa." The tall youth paused to take the older man's arm and Amy nearly trod on their heels. He turned, "Begging your pardon—" He squinted down at her. Slowly he added. "I didn't know there was a tyke in camp. Kinda young to be out after dark. Your folks know?"

"I beg your pardon." Amy made her voice icy and lifted herself to her toes, pointing her chin at him.

"Oh, I'm sorry." He stepped aside and Amy scooted to catch up with the hat and boiled shirt.

She saw her father among the men. Aunt Maude wasn't there. The missionaries finished "Nothing But the Blood" and began "Jesus, Lover of My Soul."

When Brother Fisher began to preach, the drunk and the tall skinny youth stopped beside her. The man was swaying slightly and Amy grinned behind her hand. So the young fellow won.

As Brother Fisher warmed to his message, more of the crowd splintered away. Amy's restless gaze swept back and forth, studying the faces tilted toward the missionaries.

Brother Fisher pointed his finger and roared. "Look at the dens of iniquity surrounding you. There's not a man among you who hasn't come from a church pew back home. Why are you hiding out in the brothels and gambling halls?

"Do you think separation from the loving eyes of your wife will excuse you before the gates of heaven? Have you a guarantee that you will live to repent before you meet your Maker? Why not now?"

The drunken man turned away. The youth hesitated. When he looked beyond Amy to the man shaking his finger, she heard him sigh. But it was the strange uneasiness in his eyes that caught her attention.

For a moment the uneasiness touched a responsive chord in her and she shivered. As he turned to follow his father, the young man's shoulders were drooping. The light coming through the saloon door illuminated his face. *He looks like I feel after Aunt Maude gets through scalding my ears.*

Still wondering about that lonesome-looking fellow with the haunted eyes, Amy left the crowd and started for the hill. Father was beside her. "Amy, you ought not be wandering around after dark."

She looked up, "Would you believe, as of this moment I honestly forgot?" He shook his head as he started up the hill with Amy tagging along behind. When they reached the top, he turned to touch her shoulder.

"For the sake of peace and your aunt's nerves, say—" He paused. "Amy, I expect you to be more careful in the future."

CHAPTER 3

Amy skipped from rock to rock, climbing the side of the gulch. Swinging her water pail, she sang softly, "Lost my partner, what'll I do?" Halfway up, she stopped and turned to look back.

Gregory Gulch was lined by a tumble of rickety cabins, spindly corrals, and dirty flapping tents. As far as she could see, both up and down the narrow slit of a canyon, the crude dwellings were visible.

Wind tossed strange yellow dust into her face and she rubbed at it. "Central City, ha! Miners' dump number one. No wonder Aunt Maude can't do anything except scrub and complain. Fifteen thousand men, but not a one interested in anything except getting his gold—poor Father."

She turned to hop across the rocks again. Now her voice was mournful as she sang, "What'll I do. . . Skip to my lou, my darling. . . . I'll get another one, pretty one too. Skip to my lou, my darling." She jumped sideways, "Oops!"

"You'll do, you'll do." Came the voice nearly under her feet. The miner stood up, shook the water and gravel out of his gold pan and grinned at her. "Hey! you're not an Indian princess. Golden hair and blue eyes. I declare. They told me I must *dig* the gold out of the mountain."

Amy moved carefully away from his dripping pan while she scrambled for something witty to say. Feeling as shy as the little ground squirrels, she scooted to the top of the rock, her bare toes testing each step.

The fellow was still grinning up at her. She watched his brown hair being caught and tossed by the wind. His eyes were just as brown—like a friendly squirrel's. She guessed he was shy, according to his bashful grin.

Amy began to relax. *Aunt Maude's warned about these miners. Woman hungry, she says. But he's not cocky like the ones in town.*

He squatted down and scooped up another pan of water and gravel. Amy eased forward onto her knees and bent over to watch. There was something nagging at her, something half forgotten. He looked familiar. She shrugged and asked, "Have you found any gold today?"

"Today? No. Pa's having me try all the streams up high. Has an idea that we'll be led to a rich strike."

"Aunt Maude's not going to like that." Amy said. Seeing the curious glance she added, "She always tells me to go up high, up where the water springs fresh out of the mountain." Amy rattled the bucket.

Peering into the stream, she added, "Since coming to the diggings, she's had me get the water up here. It's so good even Aunt Maude can't fault it. Sparkles without a speck of mud. At least it did until you came along." They were both looking at the trail of cloudy water moving away from his gold pan.

She grinned at his dismay. He reached for the pail, saying, "I'll fill it upstream. Guess that's the least I can do."

She asked, "You've just come?"

"I was going to ask about you. We've been here since June. Rushed in with all the others."

June? Could he be the fellow I saw in Denver City, listening to Brother Fisher preach? "We've just come from Denver City. Had to stay until the presiding elder assigned a circuit to Father. He's Eli Randolph." She could see it all meant nothing to him; still, he seemed familiar.

"I'm Amy Randolph; my father is the preacher with the Methodist Episcopal Church. You know the Nebraska-Kansas Conference sent in missionaries."

His brown eyes were studying her. "Pleased to meet you. I'd heard there was a preacher in town." There was a question in his eyes, but she let him talk. "I'm Daniel Gerrett. There's just my pa and me. We're kinda footloose, and Pa's had a hankering to try his hand at mining."

Amy looked at the stream again, regretfully. "I didn't think a miner would waste his time messing up this trickle of water with his gold panning. It's so steep even a mule couldn't cross that stream without washing downhill. What would you do if you did find gold up here?"

"Well, I'd try to be careful. I'd also look for a mule with short legs on the mountain side of him. You'll be happy to know I'm moving on tomorrow. Not a fleck of gold dust, so there's no sense lingering. Here, I'll go after water for you. It's time to head down the mountain."

On the last steep hill, Amy moved ahead, hopping from stone to stone, working her way down the mountainside. He came right behind her, moving cautiously, guarding the precious liquid. Amy dared not take her eyes off the trail until the track ended at the road.

The young miner carefully set the pail of water at the edge of the trail. Still breathing heavily, Amy found a rock and sat down. She glanced at the fellow, seeing his shabby shirt and dusty dungarees. *Not much of a Prince Charming.*

She sighed and turned to look down the hill. "I'm obliged for the help. I can get it home easy now. I've been doing it all along." He chose a rock and sat down. Trying to think of something to say, Amy concentrated on the view of the mining town scattered out below. She pointed to the sprawl of little shacks in the distance. "I hear they call that Mountain City." He nodded, watching her curiously.

Then he said, "Have I seen you somewhere?"

She answered quickly, "Was it Denver City? But you said you'd been here since June."

"Pa and I were down there a month ago."

"That was it." Amy rushed on, "I saw you on the street, going down to listen to the preachers, didn't I?"

He studied her closely and blinked. "In the dark I'd decided—that is, until you pulled yourself up tall, I thought—" He blinked again. *Of course*, Amy thought. *You figured I was a baby. Like everyone else.*

She looked off into the distance. "Pikes Peak or bust," she muttered. She cocked her head to listen to the awesome sounds echoing up the valley—the braying of a mule team, the clatter of a heavy wagon coming up the rocky road. She could hear the strident voice of the wagonmaster cursing at his team. The words made her blush.

A new sound arose—the clang of iron against stone, and above it rose the excited voices of men. She looked toward the narrow neck of the town, down Gregory Gulch way. "Mountain City's busting with excitement. That means someone's had a good day at the diggings, and I'm guessing they'll all be heading for Joe's place to celebrate. Poor Father. A preacher's life is hard enough without having to fight gold fever as well as the devil."

Even as Amy spoke, she realized her words were empty of real pity. She glanced at the fellow and added, "It still seems like a dream, coming across the plains." She tried to visualize the little Kansas town with its serene, predictable life. As she choked off the half-lonesome sigh, she admitted to herself that even in Lawrence she had been lonesome. "I guess," she said slowly, "what all womenfolk are wishing for is just a spot where we can find the home feeling."

"Your mother is having a hard time? If mine were alive, I suppose she'd feel the same."

Amy felt the loneliness caving in upon her. Right now she didn't want to talk about mothers. She looked at the knobby wrists hanging out the fellow's shirt. He was young. Amy asked hesitantly, "Did you go to church back home?"

He was silent a moment. "No. My mother did. Seems none of us young'uns had the heart to after she died." Then he added, "Everyone's grown and got his own home now, except for me."

Shivering slightly in the crisp mountain air, Amy made her way down among the rocks and scrubby juniper. Clusters of mountain sunflowers, no taller than the span of her hand, prickled against her bare feet.

The late afternoon shadows were creeping up the sides of the hill. "Men'll begin swarming up from the creek. Bending over the sluice boxes since the earliest light of the day—they want gold pretty bad."

She shrugged, staring down at the tiny shacks below her. Night made them come to life. She watched a shabby miner enter the first shack.

Amy pointed, saying, "It's a wonder these little places hold so many." Daniel looked at the cabins and nodded.

"I'll have to admit"—she paused, wondering how he would respond—"I've been tempted to put my eye to the crack in the door to see where all those fellows sit." Daniel threw back his head and laughed.

"Sorry," he apologized, "I just didn't expect that of you." His eyes sparkled and he grinned. She grinned back, feeling nearly as if she had a friend.

Now they were walking singlefile, making room for the miners on the street. Already she could hear the rattle of dice and the crack of cards coming from the saloon shacks.

"It's not like home. There the suppertime smells hang in the air until any young'un would be glad to run home. Around here the only thing you can smell is that awful whiskey."

With a start, Amy glanced at the sky. Aunt Maude would be fussing if she delayed another minute.

Aunt Maude. At the rattle of pebbles behind Amy, she winced, wondering how her Aunt would react to the fellow carrying the water? Against the half-light of sunset, the figure striding behind her loomed straw-thin and tree-high.

Aunt Maude had warned her against speaking to miners. Amy hurried her bare feet smartly down the trail, trying to forget the sharp rocks.

"Wait up, little one."

Amy quickened her steps, and gasped, "Oh!" The rock was sharp and she blinked back tears while she stood on one foot.

He set down the pail. She heard the pleasant rumble in his voice as he asked. "Tyke, want me to look at it?" He started to bend close and then straightened. He sounded embarrassed as he said, "I keep forgetting you're not just a little one. I guess it's that tow hair all curled like a baby."

Amy straightened her slight body and looked up at him. For a moment she found herself wishing her fifteen-year-old body came nearer resembling those women who stepped daintily down the streets of Denver City. The brown eyes of the youth met hers. For a moment longer, they looked at each other. He smiled down at her. Somehow she knew he was really seeing her now.

Amy tried to deepen her voice as she said, "Thank you, but I can manage now. It was nice meeting you."

Slowly he said, "Well, I haven't been to services yet. Pa and I are keeping busy now. On weekends we're doing a little digging. But I hope I get to see you again."

She nodded. "Digging? Do you think there's lots of gold in the hills—just waiting to be found?"

"Oh, sure." His voice was careless. "But it will take a lot of work."

Amy hesitated on the dusty road, moving her toe around in circles. "Dirty place, isn't it?" He nodded. She was reluctant to leave. Almost against her will, she found herself echoing the words going around. "They say a fellow with any lick of gumption can be a millionaire."

There was a curious light in his eyes. "Is that what you want?"

She grinned, "It would be fun to find gold." When he didn't reply, she added, "Three weeks we've been here, and there's changes. Take this road. Ruts it was, and now—" She poked at the wild grasses and woody weeds. The light soil became airborne on the slightest breeze.

With a sigh she reached for the pail and he asked, "Where do you live?"

Amy pointed to the log cabin at the end of the street. "There. It's home and church building. But no grander than the rest."

"That means dirt floor and sheet metal stove."

She nodded, "Aunt Maude took one look at it all and said, "'Tis well I lived this long. Now I know what it means to suffer for the gospel.'"

The serious young giant bent down to Amy's level. "And what was the answer to that?"

"Father gave her his stern look, saying, 'Well then, dear sister, all the others are suffering for the gospel too, even the ones lining up at the bar every night, since they all have dirt floors.'"

The fellow chuckled and started away. "Miss Randolph, I'm pleased to make your acquaintance. Might be I'll see you in church."

She watched him go down the street. In the dimming light she thought his hair looked like maple leaves, frost-buffed into shining brown. "But it's on a cornstalk body, and that ruins it all," she muttered. "No Prince Charming."

She reached her own front door just as it began its creaking, groaning, thump. Abruptly it was wrenched into place and pried open.

Aunt Maude's sharp eye and sharper nose appeared around the door. "'Twill be a mercy when we get a decent door to fill this hole. Who was that?" Her eyes transferred their glare to Amy.

"A miner." Amy couldn't help gloating over the look of horror on her aunt's face as she reached for the pail and pulled Amy through the door.

"Do I have to start all over again, telling you all the reasons a young lady is to stay away from that element?"

"I don't think he had evil intentions, Aunty. He had a grip on the water bucket before he figured me to be past infancy."

Maude snorted as she carried the pail to the bench beside

the stove. "Father." Amy's voice lifted as she eased her way around the rough table centered in the middle of the cabin.

As he slowly raised his head, Amy noticed how heavily his hair was sprinkled with gray. Even the lines on his face seemed deeper. She chewed her lip. Why hadn't she noticed that he was getting old? What if something should happen to him? She trembled and glanced at Aunt Maude.

Slowly Eli straightened and lowered the black Bible, keeping his finger in the book to mark his place as he looked at her. His lips moved soundlessly while his gaze focused far beyond the room.

Amy said, "On my way to the creek for water I saw the stage coming in from Auraria and Denver City. My, you should have seen the fancy ladies on board, laughing like youngsters at a picnic."

"Daughter, be careful of the names you give out. A group of young ladies on an outing needn't be labeled. Take a lesson from our Lord and be generous with charity."

Aunt Maude turned from the stove and shook her wooden spoon at her brother. "Now, Eli, you're acting like a father, not a preacher. If she's labeled them, she's at least on guard, and there's more grace to be had clinging to the middle of the road than slipping off the edge."

"'Specially in the mountains." They didn't hear her, and Amy turned away from the pair. She was still thinking of the calm brown eyes of Daniel Gerrett as she studied the crowded cabin.

Curtains made of cheap canvas hid the line of bunks built into the side of the cabin. Most of the Randolph household goods lay still packed in the trunks and barrels lining the wall behind the little sheet metal stove.

With a wistful sigh she turned back to her father. "Is there a chance we'll be getting a regular church building soon? Back home in the little white church, we were somebody. Here we hold services out of doors or crammed in among the packing barrels when it rains. And if anyone comes to hear the preaching, it's a miner with a dirty neck. It almost seems they're all dodging us like you're giving out poison."

"It's different here." Eli's voice had dropped to its sad, reflective rumble. Amy was beginning to regret the words. Sadness always seemed to lurk just beneath the surface. He straightened in his chair and unexpectedly grinned at her. "Sometimes the best thing that can happen to a person is just moving out of the rut he's been in and learning to look at life differently."

Wonderingly Amy stepped close to her father and studied his face by the glow of fire in the little stove. She was ready to approve his words when Aunt Maude snapped, "This soup's about done."

Her father smiled and shrugged. "Remember, Amy, it's the bishop who decides where a man will best serve God and then sends him out. Perhaps it's even more than a human decision." She saw the dreamy, fleeting hope in his eyes before the sadness came again. "No matter. These mining camps need the Gospel. And get it they will. God will open their hearts. Now let's have evening prayers before that soup is ruined."

Amy stifled a sigh and dragged the crude benches into position in front of the fire.

CHAPTER 4

Aunt Maude watched as Amy and Eli worked the straw into place. Amy could feel the tension building. She pushed back on her heels. Father had the straw spread smooth, and the burlap feed bags were being stretched and nailed in place.

Aunt Maude spoke. "Only a bit better than a raw dirt floor. Biggest trial will be to keep them miners from spitting their tobacco on the burlap." Amy settled down and looked toward her father. She heard his stifled sigh as their eyes met in a fleeting glance.

Amy caught her breath. Her father's glance admitted that the gentle, quiet man also chafed under the caustic tongue of Aunt Maude.

Wistfully Amy watched her father. *How long it's been! Seems I nearly lost the belonging feeling.* She studied her father's face, looking for a deeper emotion, wondering. *Has Aunt Maude always been like this? Those tight lips, the bitter lines on her face.*

Slowly she said, "Aunt Maude, you don't like being here, do you? I'm big enough now, I can cook and care for Father. Why don't you go back to Kansas? You know how Uncle Jeffrey begged you to stay with him last spring, just before we left."

Amy's heart sank as she watched the lines on her aunt's face fill with a stream of tears. "Oh, Aunt Maude," she whispered. Scrambling to her feet, she placed a timid hand on the woman's arm. "I didn't mean to hurt you; it's just that you've been so unhappy, and I wanted to make you feel better. You've been with us since before Mother died and that's almost forever."

The silence in the room was as heavy as lead. Amy stopped and looked from her weeping aunt to her father. He was still crawling about the floor, methodically hammering the spikes into the packed earth. Was his hand trembling as he lifted the hammer?

She knew she shouldn't have referred to that terrible night. Even after all these years, the hazy memories fell over her like a gray curtain. She chewed at her lip and looked down at her hands. But she had said it. After all these years of pushing back the dark thoughts, she had said the word. She slanted a quick glance at the two of them. It had all been so long ago; perhaps they didn't think she remembered.

Father's shoulders moved awkwardly. Was he crying too? Amy shifted from one foot to the other as Maude dabbed at her eyes. "I—ah, I heard the wagon from Denver. Shall I go down to Joe's place and get the beans and molasses you ordered?" At her father's nod she scooped a shawl off the hook and tugged at the door.

The sky was sullen. As Amy lifted her face, she fancied she felt the touch of moisture against her skin. But the relief she felt made the threat of snow welcome.

Head down, she slowly walked the length of Central City, toward the shack they called Joe's store. It didn't need a sign; everyone knew Joe. Her restless eyes picked out the buildings and noted changes. Some of the shanties on the ridge above the main street were only half completed.

She passed a patched tent leaning into the mountain. Amy shivered and addressed the lowering sky, "At least we've four solid walls, even if the floor's dirt. That poor fella doesn't have time to build a house, 'cause he's so busy washing gold out of the creek."

Halfway to Joe's place Amy stopped. The trip was all too short. Abruptly she turned and took the first trail branching off the road.

When she had climbed beyond the final line of log cabins, she paused to rest. Looking down over the town, her attention was caught by the signs of life in the camp. A slow drift of smoke came from one chimney. Wind moved the golden leaves on the quaking aspen trees. She watched a leaf fall. A dog barked. In a moment the dog dashed into view and circled back to his master.

Down the way a miner was fastening a pack to his mule. She guessed he was one of the many quitters. William Byers in his newspaper, *Rocky Mountain News*, called them the go-backs. Another miner, leading his mule, headed down the mountains. Most likely he would wait out the winter on the plains.

From the gulch, down Mountain City way, she heard the cries of a teamster and the crack of a whip. Usually that sound filled her with excitement, but today she answered the challenge with a melancholy smile.

Slowly she wandered, feeling the burden of loneliness, and reviewing all the tales she had been hearing about this wild, no-man's land. Even worse than being without kin in this empty place was the frightening threat of Indians around every corner.

"Do I see the water lady?"

Amy turned as Daniel Gerrett approached. His smile was as lonely as she felt. "Not today," she answered slowly, "I'm just out for a walk. How I wish there was something to do in this place beside walk the hills!"

He looked surprised at her outburst. After hesitating he dropped his pick and shovel and lowered himself to a large boulder. "There is. Let's get acquainted. Tell me about yourself—why have you come here? Not many men brought their families here."

"And why not? If the men can survive a mining camp, then why not their families? It's lonely not having a friend my age."

He lifted an eyebrow at her and said, "I see you haven't made acquaintance with your neighbors or you'd know. These men have no intention of staying. They're doctors, lawyers and such—educated men, come only to gather up all the gold they can before heading home." He grinned as he added, "When the gold runs out, the Randolphs and others like them will be the only residents this end of Kansas Territory."

"Good; then we can go home too."

"Do you know that some of the people were expecting to rake up piles of gold? Don't know how the story started, but it sure was stretched. That's one reason many gave up that first season and went home."

She looked up at him, wondering about him. "What about you? Do you have a family? Are you married?" He shook his head, his eyes twinkling, and for a moment she was embarrassed.

She added, "You're like us."

He frowned, then asked, "Mother died?"

She nodded, "Years ago. I was only a little thing. Barely remember any of it. It happened at camp meeting and conference." She paused, admitting, "Most often it seems like a bad dream. Except for knowing there's supposed to be mothers, I'd find it easy to think I'd never had one."

She was busy poking her boot at the clod of mud when he spoke, and she was surprised at the emotion in his voice. "That's sad. I wish I could somehow give you half of what I have to remember."

After a pause he added, "It's just Pa and me now. But we're a good team." He glanced at her and added, "I'm not too crazy about prospecting, but he is, so I go along."

Amy could think of nothing to say, but the silence was comfortable as she watched dark shadows begin to cluster under the trees and bushes. Smoke began to puff from the cabins along the main road.

"I guess I should be a good missionary and invite you to

services. Pretty soon we'll have to start cramming into the cabin, but right now, on good days we meet under the trees."

His voice sounded strained, but he said slowly, "I'd like that."

She heard the mournful lowing of Joe's milk cow, followed by the clink of a pail and the sharp bark of a dog. She sighed and tried to prod herself toward home.

"You're going to freeze if you sit out here on the hillside much longer," he said.

"October's colder than I expected."

"Snow comes early in the mountains. Down on Cherry Creek, I expect they just have rain."

She studied his face. Plain and honest it seemed. He's shy, she decided, liking the way his eyes met hers just as he ducked his head. Abruptly she asked, "If you aren't sold on gold mining, what are you interested in?"

He shook his head, a closed-book expression settling down over his face. "What about you?"

"What I'd really like better'n anything else is to learn to play the piano."

"Piano?" he said slowly. "Then you have one?"

She shook her head. "A preacher's kid? No, of course not. Never could we afford one, and besides they don't believe in things like that in church. Father'd never even considered having one. But the want is like a gnawing in my bones."

"I remember you singing the day we met up on the mountain. You have a nice voice, even though I don't know much about music."

"Neither do I. But since I was little they've been having me lead out in church. It's getting so I know most of the hymns, even the new ones Father says aren't reverent. Back home they said I'm a natural with music."

She sighed heavily and added, "That just makes me ache all the more. One of these days I'll have a piano." Reluctantly she added "I can't see why—"

Abruptly she stopped. One of the shadows in the street below detached itself from a deeper shadow and moved quickly up the steep hill. It was Aunt Maude. She stopped in front of Daniel. "I know you! It was you the last time—walking her home. There'll be no shenanigans, young man—now be off! Don't you ever tarry around my niece again. I know the likes of you fellows, and I won't tolerate your leading an innocent into sin. Be off!" She brandished her umbrella and reached for Amy's arm.

"Ma'am!" Daniel leaped to his feet and snatched at his tattered cap.

"Say no more!" she ordered, turning her back and tugging at Amy's arm.

At home, Amy faced her aunt across the table. She was surprised at the expression the flickering candle exposed. Timidly she said, "Aunt Maude, that young fellow was polite, and I—"

"No more, young lady!" Amy stared at the pursed lips and flushed face as her aunt muttered, "I knew it was a mistake to come here."

The door began banging and groaning. Amy turned as her father came in. She saw the quick glance he gave Aunt Maude before he faced her. "Amy, it's dark. Where have you been?" His voice was gentle, but she saw the white line around his mouth.

"Father, don't fret. I'm a big girl now; it's been years since I've been scared of the dark or lost my way home." She tried to laugh, but her aunt's voice cut in over hers.

"Eli, I told you it would be wrong, bringing a young innocent girl into such a place. And now the other element has moved into town." She raised her palm ceilingward and cried, "Oh, Lord, what have we gotten into?"

"Maude, say no more." He turned to pace the room and then return. "I've a letter from the bishop. He has expressed a desire for me to stay situated here during the winter season. Likely there'll be little opportunity to minister to those in the settlements above Central City. I understand the snowfall in the mountains is significant. We can anticipate being snowed in sometimes, but—"

She interrupted, "Eli, what are you saying?"

"That you and Amy can move down into Auraria for the winter season. There's a hut next door to the bishop."

"That's no safety for two women. He'll be traveling about the territory. No thank you, Eli. If we leave, it will be for home."

"Father," Amy cried, "You can't stay here alone! You need someone to take care of you." She saw the relief on his face, and went to press her head against his shoulder.

Aunt Maude spoke reluctantly. "Eli, of course it's my duty to stay with you as long as you need me. Now come, let's have a bite of supper."

Amy hesitated, feeling cheapened and depressed. No doubt that young Daniel Gerrett would never come around now. She sighed and went to wash her hands.

CHAPTER 5

During the warm autumn days the aspen-ringed clearing close to the Randolph cabin was sanctuary for the Methodist Episcopal Church.

On the middle October Sunday, Amy came late into the clearing. Just inside the circle of trees she paused, unexpectedly caught by the scene. Like a golden dome, the yellow leaves arched over the clearing. To Amy their white trunks seemed like pillars of marble.

Her heart lifted in unexpected joy, even as the wind moved the leaves into a whispering reminder that the glory was temporary.

Amy shook herself with a sigh and cocked a critical ear. Father and Aunt Maude were leading the singing. The miners sitting on the log benches were trying to follow, and they were all off key.

As she hesitated, one of the miners on the far edge of the crowd moved and caught her attention. It was Daniel. His eyes were sparkling as if he shared a secret joke with her. The singing—he remembered that day!

She grinned and marched to the front. Father's furrowed brow relaxed as he beckoned to her.

When the sermon began, even the aspens lost their glow. Father read, " 'The harvest is past, the summer has ended, and we are not saved.'" She looked at that bench Father had placed in readiness. The old familiar dismay swept through her as she tried to concentrate on the words and forget that Daniel Gerrett was listening back there with the other miners.

Suddenly a golden beam of light brightened the clearing. She raised her face to the sun, as if to a promise. But what was the hope?

The sermon ended and the group stood. Amy sighed and rubbed her palms together. Father moved among the men with his hand outstretched. When Amy turned, Daniel met her eyes. Briefly he nodded, then slipped through the trees.

She pushed through the crowd and followed him. "Daniel!" He waited. "Ah—your father didn't come?"

His grin was twisted and his eyes darkened in a strange way. "Pa doesn't think much of meetings."

She hesitated, unable to get past the brooding expression on his face. It was Father's fault. "I'll walk a way with you. They'll be talking forever."

"Your Aunt Maude won't like it."

"You looked—" The words came in a rush now. "I could see you were hurt; don't let it be—"

"Amy, how do you get religion?"

"Religion?" She carefully searched his face. Those brown eyes were unhappy. More than that. Miserable. She knew the feeling. "Daniel," she whispered urgently, "don't feel that way. He's preaching to sinners—those who drink and gamble and curse and steal, not for good people like me and you."

He frowned. "You've never felt this way?"

She dropped her head, unable to face the expression in his eyes. She admitted, "I do, all the time. I don't know why. I've done like Aunt Maude and Father have said. I do believe. The Bible says Jesus Christ came to save sinners. We can't get to heaven without His help. I've confessed my sins." She paused, "Is that your problem? Haven't you?"

"Confessed? No. But if it doesn't help, why do it?"

"Then read your Bible." Her voice rose in frustration and she gulped. Amy twisted her hands and faced the misery in herself. *Why can't I understand enough to say this right?* She glanced at him, desperately wishing for the words that weren't there. *But why should it matter so much what this miner thought?*

"I don't have one." He frankly studied her face. "Do you? Read it, I mean." She nodded.

There was nothing more to say. Silently they walked along the road leading toward Eureka Gulch. Suddenly he took a deep breath, grinned. "Here I am walking with the prettiest gal I've ever seen and glooming like I didn't have good sense. But, Amy, I don't want you to get in trouble with your aunt. What will it take to get in her good graces?"

She could only stare in surprise. He was grinning now, but the dark expression was still there in his eyes.

She shrugged, still looking at the ground. "I expect Aunt Maude's never going to be much friendly to any fellow. It might help if you come to services. You'll be staying the winter?"

He nodded. They had reached the trail branching off the road. "Our claim is just over this ridge. I suppose we'd better say goodbye before I get you into more trouble. About services—I don't know." The troubled expression was still there.

Her emotions flattened. Conscious she had failed, Amy walked slowly down the hill. Deep inside, the memory of Daniel's face worked like a shovel, digging down through the layers, sifting thoughts she didn't want disturbed.

"Daniel," she whispered into the wind and the drift of golden aspen leaves, "I must admit, I know all the right answers about religion, but it doesn't work. I wish I could tell you how I really feel, but that would shock you. You'd never come back, and I want you to come again. Daniel, I know nice girls follow the rules; they don't have a desire to scream against God and tell Him that His rules are ugly and out of date."

Father and Aunt Maude were in front of the cabin. Amy sighed and smoothed her best smile into place.

When she saw the question in her Father's eyes and the frown on Aunt Maude's face, she blurted, "Father, I think you need to talk to Daniel Gerrett. He wants to know how to be a Christian."

Aunt Maude sniffed, "Most likely. It's a smart move when the pastor has a sixteen-year-old daughter and she's the only gal in camp."

With November, winter settled down on Central City. The snows came, blanketing the torn earth and pine cabins until the town seemed transformed from a sad, scarred world into a fairytale.

Many of the miners had returned to Denver City for the winter, but some stayed on. Nearly every day Amy saw dark shadows detach themselves from the log huts and miserable tents to press a trail of footprints up the gulch.

A few wagons pulled by long strings of mules were able to make their way up the canyon road to drop mining supplies and tools as well as sides of bacon and bags of flour at Joe's store.

Glad to escape the stifling cabin, Amy took solitary walks through the snow. Some days, when the kind sun released the lid of ice on the creek, she carried her water pail. Most often Aunt Maude melted snow for water.

Frequently on her walks she saw Daniel Gerrett in the distance. He hunched against the cold, walking listlessly to and from his father's diggings. She watched his dragging steps and remembered his dark eyes shadowed by the nameless fears. Several times he waved to her, but that was all. He hadn't come to services since they had moved inside the Randolph cabin. But then, none of the other miners came either.

One day as she and her father watched his lonely walk, she shook her head and said, "All that gold waiting to be dug, and Daniel doesn't seem to care a bit. How I'd like to change places with him! I'd gladly swing a pick if he would trade."

Father gave her such a sharp glance she was immediately ashamed, but for once she tilted her jaw and didn't try to make the confession sound better.

Each Sabbath when Amy looked at the empty benches, she compressed her lips to keep from saying her piece about the young miner Aunt Maude had sharpened her tongue on. Mostly the desire came when Aunt Maude complained about the indifference of the miners to the things of the Lord.

The Randolphs continued to line crude benches inside the tiny cabin. While they waited for the men to come, Maude would stand at the door and stare at the shack next to Joe's place. Amy watched, too. Early in the day men would appear, puffing and pounding their hands against the cold as they made their way down the street with nary a glance at the Randolph cabin. Soon the shack would vibrate with shouts and ribald singing.

Sometimes Father's sermon would slip past her as she strained her ears, wondering about the activities going on inside that rickety cabin. *Why does that laughter make me feel lonely?* she wondered, wistfully. There were so many *whys* in her life, but one look at Aunt Maude was enough to keep the questions unasked.

Just before Christmas Amy had her sixteenth birthday, and Father gave her a gold coin. Aunt Maude's frown made Amy quickly tuck the coin out of sight, but she spent long hours dreaming of spending it in Denver.

In the midst of a snow storm, Eli carried home the latest news. He came into the cabin with his packet of letters and the sack of beans.

Going to the little stove, he held out his hands. "It's a relief to see the men with a new interest," he said, "I've been concerned. Their cold empty hands and restless spirits have kept them in the saloons most of the winter. Now some outfit has come in with a wad of money and big plans to build up the place."

Aunt Maude moved away from the stove and asked, "I suppose it's not good."

"I don't know the facts, but I do know there's a bunch of fellows happy to have a job." After cocking her head to think, Aunt Maude nodded slowly.

By the time the snow melted the town was filled with the sound of the axe and the pounding of the hammer. On her walks, Amy breathed deeply of the new smells and admitted the streets of Central City were more fragrant with the scent of fresh cut pine. The aroma reminded Amy of Christmas back home.

But it was only the aroma. Christmas seemed out of place here in a town of spindly shacks, clinging to the sides of the gulch while the wind howled and piled snow high. Central City also lacked the fragrance of apples and cinnamon, sage, and turkey. There wasn't a single child's shout. No colorful skirts and bonnets were seen in Joe's store. Christmas passed quietly, almost unnoticed.

By January the streets halfway up the sides of the hill were being lined with tiny new cabins as quickly as the men could pound them together. Amy looked at the cabins and her excitement grew. Summer would bring more people. *"Please,"* she whispered, *"just one friend."*

She also saw one large, rambling log building spilling down the hill at the far end of Central City. Standing in the snow, Amy counted windows, whispering to herself, "It's got to be a hotel."

But Amy had to keep her guesses and excitement to herself. Around home no one seemed in the mood for the news. The weather made Aunt Maude grumpy, while Father was often morose, sunk deeply in his own thoughts as he huddled beside the fire.

Amy continued her walks breathing deeply of the crisp air, enjoying the snow. Often on her way to the store, she let her curiosity lead her down every trail in town and on the mountainsides.

Early February brought the first hint of spring. When the dark clouds fled after dumping their snow, the sun immediately reduced it to water, crashing and roaring down the canyon.

On one of the first bright days, Amy was at Joe's store when the supply wagon pulled into town. The long line of gray mules blocked the road, and Amy moved cautiously around them to watch the teamster roll barrels out of the wagon.

A bundle of clothing wedged between flour sacks moved,

and instantly Amy's attention was caught. The bulky figure backed out of the wagon. A valise and several boxes followed. When a brown arm stretched through the shawl, Amy took a few quick steps forward.

A slash of white in the dark face turned toward Amy. Bright eyes twinkled. "My chile, y'all never seen a Negress before?"

Amy remembered her manners. "No, ma'am. Not since leaving Lawrence, Kansas."

"Well now, I'll tell you so's y'all don't get the wrong idea," the dark-skinned woman shoved back the shawl and looked at the ring of men standing around the wagon. "I'm a freed woman." She continued, "My name's Clara Brown. I've got my papers here to prove I've bought my freedom."

One of the men stirred and chuckled. "Ya come up here to do a little gold mining?"

Her eyes twinkled. "Aunt Clara Brown's here to set up a laundry." There was a brief silence, then a cheer went up.

The men pressed forward and one extended a greasy sleeve. "I'll be your first customer—if you'll take gold dust in payment."

A wistful voice asked, "Do you do any cooking? I haven't had anything except fatback, beans, and flapjacks since I left Chicago."

There was a clatter behind Amy and she turned. The teamster was unloading a shiny washtub. He dropped a scrub board into it, and Clara Brown said, "Only thing I need now is a cabin close to the crick with a good stove in it."

Amy watched the men surround Clara. Telling about it at home, she said, "It was like a bunch of bees in clover. Those men wouldn't let her out of sight for a minute. Most of them, that is. Grabbed up the tub and her boxes. Last I saw of her, they were practically shoving her up the hill toward Eureka Gulch. Guess now I'll have to walk farther upstream to get good water."

"I saw some men carrying a little stove up the hill," Eli said, lowering his book. "Looked like they were headed for one of the abandoned cabins on the gulch."

Aunt Maude bent over her knitting, saying, "Well, it's starting to seem like a real town. A laundress, a former slave— she's had good training. Wonder how she could save enough to buy her freedom?"

"There was one man," Amy mused slowly, "ragged as the rest. Said he hoped she'd keep her place."

The next Sabbath, while Amy stood at the window, watching the line of men headed toward the shack, Aunt Clara Brown turned up the path toward the Randolph cabin. When she sailed into the room, Amy saw the expressions of surprise and dismay fight for control of Aunt Maude's face.

Clara eyed the line of benches and then peered out the door at the group pressing toward the shack. "My, oh my," she murmured. "I 'spect their families back home are all church people, and look at them a-goin' in that place."

She cocked her head at Eli. "Parson, what's in the heart of man that he'll forget everything he's been taught when he leaves home? My, the brawlin' and shootin' I saw while I was in Denver City. They's even taking the law in their own hands without fearin' no one. We watched two men shoot it out. One had to be carried off, and they toted the other direct to the graveyard. Didn't even git a preacher."

Aunt Maude was thawing. Amy moved closer to listen. "Now back home, in the old days," Maude said, "I remember camp meeting and how the sinners were getting saved. Night after night, they'd light the big old fires and draw the wagons up close. Sometimes we'd have a half dozen preachers going at it all at the same time." She smiled and her face softened. "If you didn't like one preacher, you'd move on to the next."

"Aw, and I remember too." Aunt Clara's face shone and she shook her head as she chuckled. "Oh, but we did look forward to those times! No work done in the evenings while the camp meetings were going on. Back to back, they'd stick up those big tall platforms. White folk on one side and the black ones on the other.

"Sometimes you'd get the feeling the preacher boys were

all trying to out-shout each other. Oh, the way those old sinners would hit the mourner's bench. We had our own men for preaching, but I watched Bishop Asbury. My, what a dignified gentleman of God he was! How he could shout and sing those hard old sinners into the fold! A saint, a true saint. Yessuh, I expect to see him in heaven."

For just a moment Amy saw a shadow cross Clara's face. "Up there I don't expect them to have a line drawn down the middle of the camp meetings, with white folk on one side and the darky straining to hear from the other."

Amy caught the wistfulness in Clara's voice, and Aunt Maude's strident tones overlapped Clara's. "I remember those camp meetings. Such sinners there were at times. Reprobates just come to sell their whiskey on the sly and cause trouble. But come altar time, they couldn't stand before the breath of the Lord."

She was chuckling and wiping at her eyes as she continued, "One time when old Peter Cartwright was the preacher, he got wind of a bunch planning no good. Sneaked up on their tent in the middle of the night. All by himself, he was. Heard them planning to beat up on all the preacher fellows right in their tents. Cartwright said he got himself pockets full of pebbles and sneaked up on them. When all was quiet, he started yelling out—like he was calling to a whole pack of men around the tent. He shouted, 'Charge 'em, get 'em, fellas!' and then he let go with his hands full of rocks, pelting that tent like an army was attacking. He said those fellows took off and weren't seen again."

Abruptly Aunt Maude was prim. "All we want is to do the Lord's work up here, ministering to the miners." She shook her head. "I'm fearin' they're a bunch of reprobates, too. Only wanting to go down to that shack."

Aunt Clara took a seat and said, "Well, let's sing. Maybe that'll help. At least with the four of us, we can make enough noise to get their attention." She was shaking her head sadly. "I'm a fearing they'll all take sick and die without the Lord. One of the fellas was coughing bad when he came after his laundry."

"The vengeance of the Lord."

Clara's eyebrows arched in surprise. "I wasn't thinking of that. I was in that saloon to deliver Joe's laundry, and I saw it all. There's one old table with a bunch of dirty cards for entertainment. Over by the stove there's a shelf stuck on the wall with a jug of whiskey and a nasty old cup. I watched. A fellow plunks down his twenty-five cents and gets a cup of something they are calling Taos Lightning. Then all the others line up and use the same cup. Never gets washed. That's the way the sickness gets passed around. Mark my words."

Amy did mark Clara's words. And she quickly decided Aunt Clara Brown was another Aunt Maude, only in a different color.

At least she thought so until the April thaw set in. The first stagecoach of the season had made its way up the canyon through the mud. When it pulled up in front of the store, Amy was at Joe's place, choosing molding bacon rather than a can of peaches, more flour instead of tins of imported sweets. When she heard the first trill of laughter, she dropped the bacon and shot through the door.

The man blocking her view was shaking his head, saying, "Ain't they lovely. Just guess I'm going to have to take my duds up to Aunty Clara and sharpen up a bit."

"Better go fish a few gold nuggets outta the crick first," grumbled the man beside him. "These pretty little fillies won't cast an eye on you unless they see the gleam of gold first."

Amy bent down to peer under his arm. The array of bright colors and flaring skirts filled her vision, enhanced by the swish of twirling parasols. Another protruding elbow blocked her view as the owner drawled, "Somebody better warn them pretty girls about the high winds hereabouts. Could swoop over the mountain and swish them right back to Denver City."

"Then you be prepared to grab an ankle as they fly over. We don't wanna lose our culture before we get to appreciate it proper-like."

Amy didn't report that conversation when she went home. She was still thinking about the pretty dresses and saucy smiles under plumed, velvet bonnets.

In the days that followed she heard more. The men around Joe's place referred to the rows of tiny new cabins as cribs. But there never seemed to be a suitable time to ask Father what that meant.

Scarcely had the ice melted on the creek when more miners descended on the town. "Thick as fleas," Aunt Maude said with distaste in her voice.

"This is going to be a good year," Father commented with a satisfied grin. "I'm thinking ahead to getting a church built before autumn."

Amy watched his face shed the worry lines. "Aunt Clara has helped lots, hasn't she?" Amy asked, recalling the hordes of miners who had suddenly decided church was a better way to spend the Sabbath. "I'm still wondering what she said to get all these men in here on Sunday."

Eli was thoughtfully tugging at his beard. "I'm guessing it's just Aunt Clara."

"Could be," Amy murmured. She thought of her trip up Eureka to get water. "Father, last week I passed Aunt Clara on the mountain. I fuss about carrying a pail of water up and down the mountainside, but she was carrying a load of laundry big enough to make a mule balk. Just as I got close to her, she sat down to rest. There she was on that rock, acting like she was in church. I was so embarrassed I almost didn't speak to her."

"What do you mean?" His eyes were surprised, then brooding with a strange expression she didn't understand. "You mean you were ashamed of what she said?"

Amy shrugged and took a moment to ponder before she answered. "Well, her face was shining like camp meeting and she was sitting there with her hands waving up in the sky, shouting, 'Glory, glory, glory!' That was all. It kinda gave me goosebumps.

"There were a couple of men coming down the hill on horseback. They stopped to listen to her for a moment. Dressed like gentlemen. I'm certain one fellow is the lawyer who comes from Denver. He stood there a minute, looking hungry-like, and then he went on down the road. The other fellow behind him seemed like he was about to laugh until that lawyer gave him a sharp look." Amy was aware that her father was giving *her* a sharp look, and before she could say more, he had taken his hat and gone.

Aunt Maude's glance was sharp, too. She was shaking her head as she bent over the needle she held. She sighed heavily and said, "Oh, for the good old days when revival really happened."

CHAPTER 6

Hello, water lady. It's been a long time since I've seen you." It was Daniel Gerrett, his eyes shining.

Amy ducked her head, "I—hello." She tried to find words. "Been a long time." She looked at the wind ruffling his hair and lifting the corner of his collar. Her heart yearned in a way she couldn't understand. She swallowed hard and said, "We've melted snow for water since the creek froze up. What you been up to?"

"Pa and I have been getting ore with good color. He's gone into Denver to have it assayed and to get some dynamite."

Amy shivered. "That's exciting—and scary. Blasting to get the gold. They've been shooting the mountain down in Black Hawk. Had big boulders rolling down the slopes."

Daniel shifted uneasily and said, "I know. There's more enthusiasm than sense. But there's good things happening. Heard a sharp-looking fellow's buying up every hole in the ground showing color." He paused, adding soberly, "Some say he's pushing too hard, that he's strong-arming his way, bullying people to sell when they shouldn't." Daniel shrugged. "I'd like to see him offer Pa a sum."

"What do you mean about him pushing?"

"Talked one fellow into digging his tunnel too deep. Final blast brought the whole thing in on him. Happened over in Russell Gulch."

Amy searched the troubled eyes before she asked, "You don't like mining, do you?"

"Not much. Pa's happy about the whole thing—has a dream of being rich." Amy was trying to find something to say when Daniel kicked at a rock and said, "Pa's having trouble with the bottle. Seems being rich is the last thing he needs. Besides, I don't think he's cautious enough."

Slowly Amy said, "You're mining just—to be with him?" He nodded.

"That's—" Amy gulped and grinned up at him. "Nice of you." She shrugged, conscious of her heart beating wildly. "Even Father would approve. A fellow going along with his pa like that."

He turned away, but Amy had seen his eyes. Daniel was worried. She whispered, "Blasting. Somehow it's exciting until it's someone you know."

"Hey, I didn't mean to get you fussed." He reached out to ruffle her hair. "How's the church business doing?"

She could only look at him, wondering if he ever thought about their last conversation. She recalled the glib way she answered his questions. *How could she admit her own dark feelings? Faith. Father preached about believing—but how did one do it so it worked?*

His question was waiting. She looked up, "Pretty good since Aunt Clara stirred up the men. The way they streamed in made Aunt Maude say she probably threatened to quit washing for them." She paused, then said, "We haven't seen you."

He shrugged, "I'm afraid your aunt would chase me out with a broom."

"Not if you were just coming to church." His grin was crooked. "I'm sorry," she added. "I didn't choose my aunt."

"But she's choosing your friends." His voice was bitter and Amy's heart lightened. "I'm not bragging about being much, but seems there's not enough people around to be that picky."

"Picky? Daniel Gerrett—" The hasty words were left hanging. How could she say what she thought—even admit the times she had strained her eyes to catch a glimpse of him? Would a nice girl say she was starting to like his bean-pole build and his eyes that seemed ready to swallow her? Amy hesitated, recalling the harsh words Aunt Maude had used on him. "Aunt Maude—doesn't have anything to take up her time, so she fusses about me." Then she added brightly, "Well, I guess what she doesn't know won't hurt her."

Daniel looked startled, and Amy felt her cheeks flush. "I didn't mean it like that. I'm not doing anything wrong. Being friends and talking with you out here on the mountainside isn't a bad thing, and if she doesn't know—" Daniel frowned and Amy shrugged again.

With a sigh, he picked up Amy's pail. "Well, come on. I'd deserve a bad name if I walk off without helping a lady get a pail of water."

Lady. Amy grinned up at him as they swung up the trail to the gulch where the stream gushed through the rocks and spilled into a basin. She could see Aunt Clara's cabin roof sticking up over the next rise.

"About Aunt Maude," Amy said slowly. "I think if it weren't for me, she'd be taking you home for dinner."

He grinned. "It isn't Aunt Maude I want to see."

"But you could talk to Father, ask the questions I bumbled over." He shot a quick glance at her, and the dark expression was back. "I'm sorry, Daniel. I never say the right things."

Awkwardly he thumped her shoulder. "Aw, Amy, don't mind me."

"Daniel, doesn't it help to know others have miseries too?"

"No, it just makes it worse." He stopped on the trail and looked down into her eyes. "My mother didn't seem to have miseries, but I was too young to ask questions back then." He walked a few steps more and Amy hurried after him. He said, "Guess I shouldn't dump my feelings. But somehow I've got a need. I'm restless; I want to understand life. Isn't God supposed to matter more'n anything?"

Amy nodded, desperate to say the important things. But more than that, she sensed Daniel was close to being a friend. "Let's go see Aunt Clara. I have a feeling she can help."

He turned to look at her with a question in his eyes. She hastily said, "Aunt Maude would approve. She thinks Aunt Clara is a wonder." She turned and pointed, "See, that's her roof poking through the trees."

He left the pail beside the stream and Amy led the way.

Aunt Clara's door was open. Amy could hear the thump of her iron and the creak of the old ironing board as they approached. They could also hear her voice, with another chiming in as Amy pounded on the door. "Amazing grace—how sweet the sound, that saved a wretch like me—"

"Come in, child, before you knock the door down."

Barney Ford was sitting at Aunt Clara's table. One foot was resting on her chair. Amy looked at the white bandage swathing his foot. "Hurt it?"

"The Lord was merciful or he'd be minus a foot."

Barney added, "Axe. Only a slight cut, but the doctor here says stay off it a day or so."

As he spoke Amy studied his face. She was surprised to see how light his skin was, while his eyes were gray. When he grinned, she blushed. "I'm sorry. This is the first time I've seen you up close. Why haven't you come to services with Aunt Clara?"

"I will. She's not only convinced me I'm welcome, but that the Lord's requested my presence."

"If I had my eyes closed, I'd think you were a white man. Are you a runaway slave?"

"Amy!" Daniel had her arm. "Don't ask that."

Slowly Amy backed away from Daniel, looked from one dark face to the other. "I'm sorry," she whispered. "That was very thoughtless of me. As usual, I said the first thing that popped into my mind."

Daniel said, "I've heard enough in Denver City to make me think Pikes Peak land isn't far enough away from what's going on in the states."

Aunt Clara returned to thumping her iron on the white shirt and Barney Ford said, "Don't fuss at the little lady. I could see her perplexity. My eyes and skin bring up questions. My mother was a slave; my father was the master."

"And he speaks like a white man because his mammy raised him so." Aunt Clara reached for another shirt. "He's also read every book this side of the Mississippi."

"Not quite, my friend," Barney grinned at Clara. "I have the advantage of a good many friends who've helped me make my way. None are any better than this good woman. She's rented me sleeping quarters in her woodshed for the price of a pile of logs."

"Barney's been telling me about some of his other friends. He's come from Pennsylvania." The man glanced quickly at Aunt Clara as she continued, "There's a host of people out there with a soul burden to help their brothers, regardless of the color of their skin."

Daniel stirred on his stool and leaned forward. Amy heard the note of excitement in his voice as he said, "Are you talking about the underground railroad? About people like Garrison, John Brown, and the Coffins?"

Barney nodded, "Others, too. The Coffins I've met. A finer couple you'll never know. Grew up in North Carolina, and know firsthand how the slaves are treated. He and his wife moved to Indiana, started a store there in Newport. Wasn't long until they were sheltering and feeding every runaway slave that came their way."

Aunt Clara added quickly, "There's others."

"A couple of years before we left Kansas," Amy said, "John Brown and his men started a fuss in Pottawotamie. There were five men killed. They said it was revenge for the attack in Lawrence. That happened before we moved there, but they still talk about it. I can't understand it all."

Aunt Clara sighed and shook her head. "Draw a line. On one side there's people who would die for another man's welfare. On the other side there's people getting rich by controlling men. 'Tain't the love of God in it."

Daniel shifted restlessly. "Some of the white men argue they've a God-given right to own slaves as long as they are responsible for their welfare—like children who'll never grow up."

"Do you agree with that?" Barney asked.

"I haven't had much education, especially in the Bible," Daniel said slowly, frowning over his words. "But it seems to me that men are men, regardless of their color or birthplace. Seems, if we have a better position in life, we're somehow obligated to make room there for anyone who wants to join us."

"That's the Christian thing," Aunt Clara nodded again.

"Is it?" Daniel asked slowly. "I've been wondering—"

"Aunt Clara," Amy broke in, "Daniel wants to be a Christian. I told him you would help."

Slowly Aunt Clara placed her iron back on the stove and came around the ironing board. With hands on her hips she looked at Amy. "How come you aren't tellin' him what it takes?" Then she shifted her attention to Daniel.

"Why do you want to be a Christian? Is it because you're intent on escaping hell fire and damnation, or is it something more?"

For a long time the room was silent. When Daniel finally lifted his head, he said, "I—I don't rightly know. There's just this big need. Sure, I've heard the street preachers giving it out about the wrath of God and hell. Sure, I'm scared of meeting God. Is there something more, some other reason?"

Aunt Clara went back to her ironing. Amy watched her shake out the starched shirt and pick up the iron. She was singing softly under her breath, "'Twas grace that taught my heart to fear, and grace my fears relieved. . . . When we've been there ten thousand years, we've no less days to sing God's praise—"

She paused and looked at Daniel. "That song was written by a former slave trader. The Lord sure made a change in him, didn't he? Seems a body needs to feel he wants change more'n anything, wants to live up to what the Lord has in mind for him."

The afternoon sun was starting to slant in Aunt Clara's

window. Amy moved restlessly on her stool, and Daniel glanced up. "I—I think I'd better go," she said softly.

Daniel stood up and said, "Thank you, Aunt Clara; you've given me something to think about."

They reached the stream and the bucket. Daniel still hadn't said a word. His heavy silence was making Amy uneasy, feeling as if something had been splintered for good.

She watched him dip the pail full of water. When he turned with a smile, Amy took a deep breath and grinned up at him. "So now you have the gospel according to Aunt Clara. Barney Ford seems interesting. I'd like to listen to him longer. Aunt Clara says he has a wife and child and that he's working hard to get them out here."

Daniel was really listening to her now, but there was still the need to bridge the distance between. He touched her arm, "Come on, it's getting late."

Desperation mounted, and she twisted her hands. "Daniel."

He turned and waited, then finally asked, "What is it you want?"

"Want?" She studied his dark eyes, conscious of the distance widening. It was new, this feeling of having to snatch at something quickly before it slipped away. What did girls do? "Daniel—" He waited, then she gulped, "Well—kiss me."

"Why?"

She was astonished at his curious question. "Because I'm sixteen. I've never had a fellow try to kiss me."

"Well, I'm not trying now. I know better." He was chuckling and Amy frowned, feeling silly and very young.

"Do you treat all the girls this way?"

"I've never had a girl. Wouldn't know how to treat her if I did. The kissing might not be so bad, but I sure can't risk another run-in with Aunt Maude."

"Oh, Daniel!" Amy wailed. "You are impossible! You call me a lady, follow me up the mountain, and carry my water. I almost thought this was important."

She saw his eyes. *It was important, too important for a mean-*

ingless kiss. They walked in silence, with Amy still choking over the lump in her throat.

Just down the road Amy saw her father marching toward them, head down, striding up the rough trail. Amy glanced at the sky, then sighed with relief. "Father!"

Eli looked up, blinked. A confused, lost look was melting out of his face as he exclaimed, "Amy!" He reached for the pail. "Here, son, I'll carry it. Good of you to rescue my daughter. I suppose the water pail is too heavy for her. Must remember." Dismay swept through Amy. It was Father's not-at-home voice and Daniel was as wooden to him as the pine trees.

Suddenly Father smiled at Daniel, and their hands came out. He said, "Join us for worship again, and bring your father." He studied Daniel's face a moment and turned to Amy. "Why don't you hurry on home. I'll bring the pail."

Once Amy was out of sight, Eli turned to Daniel. Before he could speak, the youth blurted, "Sir, I think a lot of your daughter, and if you wouldn't mind, I'd—well I'd like to see her—more."

Eli chewed the corner of his mouth. "My daughter said you wanted to talk about becoming a Christian." Daniel was nodding, not eagerly, just slowly, looking puzzled. Eli thought about Aunt Maude's appraisal of the situation.

Glancing up at the youth, Eli spoke slowly. "I wouldn't want you to get confused about all this. Sometimes a person makes a commitment to God for the wrong reasons. Seems to me it might be a good idea to go at life one step at a time.

"That way there won't be any confusion over—motives." He paused. "Later we can talk about your courting Amy."

At the end of the day, Amy still didn't know what it was like to be kissed, but without a doubt, Father liked Daniel. And there had been one second of special feeling when Daniel had looked at her. That was more important than anything else right now.

It was definitely spring. The roads had dried completely, and the supply wagon came more frequently. On a day especially warm and bright, it brought its most precious cargo yet—at least Amy thought so.

She was outside, enjoying the warmth of the sun on her head as she hung the wet towels and sheets on the line and listened to dogs barking and men shouting. Then she heard the wagon bumping slowly over the rocky road.

Aunt Maude heard it, too. She came to the door. "Sounds as if that fellow is driving like he's afraid of breaking eggs." The wagon came around the bend and they saw the towering bundle in the middle of the wagon. Two men were standing in the wagon beside straining ropes, and Aunt Maude snorted, "Like ants holding back a mountain. Don't know what it is unless it's the new stamp mill, but it's sure precious."

Amy pinned the last sheet to the line and said, "I'm going to walk down the road and watch."

She reached the wagon just as the last swaddling robe was removed. Amy gasped, "A piano! A dark, shiny, mahogany piano. Just like the one at the hotel in Kansas."

She held her breath as the men clustered around the wagon and lifted the piano across the dusty road to the new boardinghouse.

Aunt Clara came out of the store and walked up the street to stand beside her. "Piano. I see they're moving it into the boardinghouse. Well, I declare. Mighty fancy. I would like to hear it myself, but I don't suppose a flock of pretty ladies would invite an old darky to their fancy party just to listen to piano playing. I'd be willing to wash the dishes to hear a bit."

"Oh," Amy moaned, "do you suppose they would let me go see it? I've never touched a piano. Would they invite me?"

Aunt Clara glanced sharply at Amy. "Lands, you're more of a child than I thought you were. Do you see?" She pointed to the two-story log building. "That's a house of ill repute being started up here. You go in that place and I'll help your pa and aunty skin you alive."

"I don't understand."

Aunt Clara shrugged and lifted her hands sky-high. "Lord, what do I say now?" Looking at Amy she said, "My, how could they neglect your education?" She stretched out the word education; then Aunt Clara sighed and continued, "No wonder—

Aunt Maude, bless her, she's a frozen potato. Now come along, let's get off this street before we all get sucked into sin." She shoved the sack of beans into Amy's hands and picked up the towering basket of laundry.

They started up the road toward Eureka Gulch. When Aunt Clara stopped to rest, Amy remembered the time she had come upon Aunt Clara beside the road, having a shouting spell.

Now her dark face was very sober. Bending toward Amy, she began, "Child, all those pretty ladies in the ruffled dresses were here to spy out the land. Those ones you've been eyeing and envying—they can lead you astray."

"So they are ladies of the night. Dance-hall girls," Amy answered quickly. "Aunt Clara, I wasn't born yesterday. I just didn't know they were truly moving into town. You know, I'm not interested in being led astray or anywhere else.

"There's only one thing I want—to learn to play the piano. I'd be happy if I could just push those keys a few times."

There were quick steps crunching through the rocks. With dismay Amy cried, "Oh, Aunt Maude." Her aunt's face was twisted into a frown until she spied Amy's companion.

Still panting, Aunt Maude exclaimed, "Aunt Clara! I was afraid—I see she's helping you. Amy, did you satisfy your curiosity? Why didn't you come home?"

Amy shrugged and said, "It was a piano. They carried it into the new boardinghouse."

Aunt Maude rocked back on her heels. "Piano!" she cried, flinging her hands high. "Piano! Lord, what will become of us all? So that's the kind of boardinghouse it is. The devil himself has moved into town."

Aunt Clara Brown spoke heavily, "Law, Missy, it isn't the piano that's going to get your girl into trouble. I've heard some pretty music come outta one. I'm guessing one of these days we'll be seeing pianos right in the middle of church. Can't be a detriment to worship if it's teaching a body or two about singing the right notes."

Amy pleaded, "Oh, Aunt Maude, even Aunt Clara thinks a piano is a good thing. If only I could learn to play!" Amy was still pushing her case as Eli came toward them. "Oh, Father! It's a piano. They've moved it into the boardinghouse. If only I could learn to play it. Aunt Clara says—" She stopped mid-sentence. From his frown and the white line around his lips, Amy knew it didn't matter what Aunt Clara thought.

With a sigh of resignation Amy sat down on the rock beside Clara. Wearily she said, "I know all about the dance-hall girls being bad, about them showing their legs and about the dances. I've been hearing about them forever. Does being in a building with dance-hall girls make a piano bad?"

She waited, staring up at them. While the anger surged through her, she forced a smile into place.

Suddenly she straightened. "What if there was a concert? Like the one back home. Remember when that man came and played? What if—"

Father's voice was slow and weary as he said, "Come, Amy. It's getting late."

"I was helping Aunt Clara up the hill." Slowly getting to her feet, Amy felt despair like a dash of cold water. Trying to find the heart to accept, she looked at Aunt Clara. The woman was blinking tears out of her eyes. For a moment Amy was comforted. She knew Aunt Clara understood, but she also knew the ache to touch the piano wouldn't die.

"Child," Aunt Clara murmured as she stacked the beans on top of the laundry basket. "You best go home. I can make it fine; see we're nearly to the top of the hill."

As Amy started down the hill after her father and aunt, she could hear the first tinkling notes from the piano. The joyful, lilting sound drifted through the streets. For a moment Amy closed her eyes, seeing her own fingers moving over the keys. She clenched her fists to shut out the ache in the tips of her fingers.

"Coming, Amy?" Her eyes popped open. Father was waiting, holding out his hand; surprisingly, she saw regret mingled with a strange pain. She hesitated a moment before allowing him to take her hand in his.

CHAPTER 7

Amy walked along the rain-freshened street. Yesterday's dust had turned to tan liquid, while the drooping grasses and bedraggled blossoms glistened with moisture.

She stopped to examine the last of the yellow avalanche lilies and the tiny pink bitterroot. Tall woody stalks of purple, fan-shaped flowers were beginning to bloom. Lifting one blossom with her finger, she said, "It's about time. Back home—" She stopped and sighed.

Back home in Kansas, the hills would have been covered with a carpet of color since March. Here the mountain weather wasn't that kind. But it would do no good to mourn the differences. Amy tightened her grip on the newspapers and letters and cut up the rocky slope to the Randolph cabin.

Before she opened the door she stopped to admire the new, well-oiled hinges, and the way the door stood square in its frame. Looking across the street at the pile of logs, she said, "Hope it doesn't take as long to build a church as it does to put hinges on a door."

Eli came to the door and reached for the mail. "Father, they'll need to hurry if that pile of logs will become a church before Independence Day."

He lifted his head from the newspaper and said, "Independence Day? Better think toward September, unless I raise the logs myself. There's too much happening in the diggings right now." There was a touch of sadness in his voice as he added, "I can't pry a fellow away to build something as unexciting as a church. What about your friend Daniel? Their mining isn't showing much color. Would he and his father help out a bit?"

Amy studied her father's graying hair and the deep sad lines on his face. His statement about raising the logs made her see things she had been ignoring. He was getting old. *What would happen to me if he were to die?* Amy's throat tightened and she shook her head impatiently.

Eli waved his newspaper and shook his head in disgust. "The paper's full of war talk. There's a push to get this end of Kansas Territory designated a new and separate territory. And both the North and South want us to side with them." His voice was solemn. "The slave problem will pull us into war sooner or later. If Lincoln is elected President, I guess we'll be forced into action. The South's making no bones about their feelings, and Lincoln will push the slavery issue first thing."

She pondered his words. *Slavery issue.* The words sounded stuffy, but the expression in his eyes made her recall the conversation up at Clara Brown's cabin. She moved her shoulders uneasily. Somehow this summer seemed to be different. Even Father and Aunt Maude were pulling the wrappings away from her, forcing her to see life. But what was it they wanted her to see?

Eli tugged at the newspaper, continuing, "Slavery is an issue, even in this end of the territory. There's bad feelings against Aunt Clara Brown. A more gentle woman I've never known."

"And that man she's letting live in her woodshed," Amy said slowly. "Yesterday, down by Joe's store, a fellow on a horse tried to run him off the street. Called him a bad word. Father, do you think Barney Ford is a runaway slave?"

"I don't know," Eli turned to peer at Amy. "But then, does it matter? He's here, and I'll accept him at face value."

"How's that?" Aunt Maude asked.

"As a dignified man, trying hard to earn a living and reunite his family."

Their conversation still nagged at Amy the next day as she strolled through town. Thinking about the changes in Central City, she wondered if life had also changed in Kansas.

Sometimes it seemed as if most of the people in the United States had streamed into the mountains, armed with gold pans and picks. All spring she had watched them come, thinking, *Soon there won't be room for one more pair of feet in the creek, let alone room to wash a pan of gravel.*

These days, after her father's reference to the tug-of-war over the Pikes Peak area, Amy became more conscious than ever of the men trickling into the mining town.

They were dressed either like gentlemen or in the frayed, coarse garb of the miner. But there was a difference. In the conversations echoing through the streets, she heard soft southern accents slipped in beside the flat, clipped speech of the northerners. North and South, like Father said.

One thing that hadn't changed was the lack of women. Several women had joined their men, but the bright-bird foliage of the dance-hall girls was still in the majority.

Of the feminine faces, Amy had to admit, they were the most attractive. The newcomers were as stern-faced and rough-clad as their husbands. And not one was young enough to claim as friend.

Amy's wandering walks continued around the mining town. Her favorite time of day was late afternoon, before supper and after Aunt Maude had exhausted her daily store of tasks.

She grew to love the summer evening walks. With the sun behind the mountains, the yellow soil no longer threw heat into her face, and the day mellowed out like a soft sigh.

In the evening, on a high perch above town, Amy found she could keep track of all the comings and goings. Seated on her favorite rock wedged between the cedar trees, she watched the miners breaking out of the hills, heading for home. Some limped along slowly. It was easy to guess it had been another bad day for them, hacking through rough rock without the slightest promise of color.

But others moved briskly down the hill. Amy watched them swinging along, jumping the creek and heading for one of the three new saloons.

One evening as she sat on her rock, she could hear a sound coming from the boardinghouse. Someone was running fingers across the piano keys.

Amy moved restlessly on the rock and pressed her hands across her eyes as she tried to imagine being in that room. She could nearly feel the keys; could nearly guess the sound each touch would bring.

"What's wrong?" Amy raised her head and looked into the face of a girl bending over her.

Amy blinked and stared at the girl, dumbfounded. Finally she came to her senses and said, "Oh, I'm sorry. I thought I was seeing visions." The girl wore a neat calico frock, a band of black ribbon holding curls away from her face.

"Visions?"

"I mean, I've wanted to meet a person like you for so long—you know, a girl my age—I, well, I thought I was dreaming. Suddenly Amy burst into a barrage of questions. "Who are you? Did you just arrive? Is your father a miner? Where do you live?"

The faint frown and the concerned look disappeared. Now the girl chuckled and settled down beside Amy. "I guess you've been out here for some time."

Amy nodded. "Nearly a year. In all that time I haven't seen a soul my age except for dance-hall girls. I do hear there's families moving into Denver. We haven't been there since last summer, so it doesn't help me a bit. I'm looking forward to conference time." She added, "My father is the pastor of the Methodist Episcopal Church."

"Oh," the girl nodded. "I'm Elizabeth Steele. I've always been called Lizzie."

"I'm Amy Randolph. Tell me all about yourself. Where are you from? I love the way you fix your hair. It's a pretty color. Mine's so curly I can't do a thing with it."

Lizzie leaned back and looked critically. "It's not so bad. But at your age I'd expect curls instead of braids."

"My aunt."

"Oh, well, why don't you just start with a few little curls around your face? I'll show you."

Lizzie bent over Amy and began brushing curls loose from her braids. Amy said, "My mother is dead and my Aunt Maude is ancient. Poor soul, I can't yawn without shocking her."

"I know. I've aunts like that back in New York state. Our generation will just have to clear all the debris out of the tracks before we can make time."

Amy's eyes widened at the strange expression. She said, "New York. I suppose we really seem backwoodsy to you."

"You seemed so sad when I first saw you, is it—"

Amy said hastily, "I'm not sad. I was listening to someone plunking on that piano and I was wishing with all I had that I could just go down and play it. Just once." She knew she was pleading and she clenched her hands into fists.

Lizzie studied Amy. Slowly she said, "Seems if you want to play a piano that bad, there ought to be a way. Won't they get you a piano?"

"Father can't afford a piano. Besides, Aunt Maude thinks they're of the devil."

Lizzie shrugged. "You don't like to shock the older ones, but sometimes you have to. It isn't right to let someone's opinions ruin your life. Now take pianos—"

Amy frowned and then caught her breath. Lizzie was saying, ". . . free spirit. We can't let all the old people tell us how to live. After all, *they* broke the rules *their* parents made."

"We do think alike," Amy whispered. "Oh, I don't want you to think I want to be bad; it's just that I feel so stifled, and sometimes—"

"I know. Sometimes I wish I were more brave. I hear about some of the things others do and I wish—Amy, did you hear about what happened last week? Four of the girls from the boardinghouse nearly stampeded the supply wagon team."

Amy whispered, "I heard! I couldn't admit it to anyone, but for just a second I couldn't help wishing I were one of those girls racing the pony carts down the middle of town."

"It could have been dangerous," Lizzie added. "Just as the supply wagon took the corner, they came charging right at him." Lizzie snickered behind her hand. She shook her head, but her eyes sparkled with excitement. "I'm not that daring, but it sounded like high fun."

Amy nodded, whispering, "I thought so, too." Then she added, "I hear the fellow with the team was angry. He had three kegs of molasses tip and run all over his wagon. Got it in the mail bag. Ugh!"

Lizzie said, "I've seen a few shootouts since I've come west. I wonder if they shoot women for riding horses like that."

"You're teasing." Amy looked into the mocking brown eyes. "I don't shock that easy. I've seen a gun fight, too." She paused and then blurted out the words. "Somehow I think you're just like me on the inside."

Lizzie's solemn face moved closer. "Do you think so? Then tell me, what is it that you want more than anything else in the world. If you tell me, I'll tell you what I want."

Amy had to cover her face to shut out the curious eyes. She thought about the question. After sorting through everything, measuring the shabby cabin, Aunt Maude, the bottomless feeling of her life, there was only one thing.

She dropped her hands. "I don't know hardly anything about life except what I see right here. But if there's just one want, I want to have a piano and learn to make music on it. I know I could. It's like it's already inside, just waiting to come out."

"Oh, Amy Randolph!" the girl breathed softly, "You are such a child." Amy lifted her chin and Lizzie continued, "I've never had a chance to be a fairy godmother, but I can't resist it now. Come, Amy. Now before supper is over and the men come flocking in to play their games and sing their songs. Come, and I'll let you play that piano."

Amy studied her face. Lizzie wasn't teasing. "Do you know how to play a piano?"

She nodded, "I also know the woman who runs the board-inghouse. I know she won't mind if we go in and plunk a few keys. Come on." Her hand tugged at Amy. Amy hesitated only a second. There would probably never be another chance.

Together they flew down the hill, slipping and sliding, Lizzie laughing with excitement and Amy desperately deter-mined.

Wooden steps went down the hill to the back door of the boardinghouse. Amy hesitated on the steps. Through the high window, nearly on a level with her nose, she could see the piano. A cluster of candles threw flickering light across the polished wood. The ivory keys gleamed. She hurried after Lizzie.

Inside, Lizzie skipped across the long room and closed the door, but not before Amy saw the dining room and the wash of rainbow colors. She heard the muted voices and heard the clink of dishes. When Lizzie returned she asked, "Won't they wonder?"

She shook her head. "No one will pay any heed." Pulling the stool close she asked, "Can you read music?" Amy shook her head. Lizzie chewed her lip, instructed, "Watch my hands."

As her fingers rippled over the keys, Amy shivered with delight. "Oh, play something I know."

Lizzie's face was mocking and her dark eyes shadowed as the gay, tinkling melody faded away. Now the somber chords of a hymn came from her fingers. Amy bent close and sang softly, "Arise, my soul, arise. Shake off thy guilty fears. The bleeding Sacrifice in my behalf appears." She was still singing, "Before the throne my Surety stands; My name is written on His hands." when Lizzie's hands crashed down on the keys.

It was an ugly chord, and Lizzie hissed, "Hush; it sounds like camp meeting and you'll bring the house down around our ears."

Amy leaned against the piano as Lizzie swung into a rol-licking melody. She sang the words and Amy attempted to follow. Now she whispered, "Please, let me try." Lizzie got to her feet and Amy slipped onto the stool.

"Start here," Lizzie murmured pointing to the key right

under the gold-lettered name. Amy's fingers were moving, picking and she was humming. Lizzie beamed. "You're a natural. Now let's see if you can put music to my song."

She bent close and slowly sang the words. Amy fumbled with the keys, while Lizzie frowned and then beamed approval.

Abruptly Amy realized she must bend close to see the keys. The sun had set and there was only the flickering light of the candles. "Oh! Father and Aunt Maude will be searching for me. Please, Lizzie, talk your friend into letting us do this again."

Lizzie followed her to the front door. Amy had turned for one more imploring word when she heard footsteps. Light from the dining room flooded the veranda. There could be no mistaking that coiled mass of graying hair, those sharp elbows akimbo. Amy flew backwards, bundling into the row of cloaks, and Lizzie followed.

There was a thump on the door and quick steps.

"My niece is here; I heard her singing."

"Oh, you're the parson's sister." The woman's voice answering was strident. "Do you church people have a corner on singing? Is the likes of us too rare for singing the grand old music? Be off, old lady. I'll sing the songs I learned at my mother's knee, God rest her soul."

The door slammed, Lizzie grasped Amy's hand, dragging her to the back door. "I'll be in trouble if we don't get out of here!" Amy mourned. Lizzie shoved Amy through the door.

Quickly Amy fumbled her way up the wooden steps and turned to run. Her first step threw her full force into a dark warm object. The exclamation and the rough fabric under her hand sent her reeling away. "Wait!" A hard hand came down on her shoulder and her face was tilted to the light of the moon.

"Amy Randolph, what were you doing in that boardinghouse?" It was Daniel Gerrett and with a sigh of relief, Amy sagged against his arm.

"Oh, Daniel! I thought for certain that Aunt Maude had caught up with me. But let's go quick! That woman pretty nearly shoved her off the veranda, she could be coming this way."

"Now wait a minute," Daniel said slowly. "What was your aunt doing in that place?"

"She heard me. I don't think they sing many church hymns in that place."

"That was you singing something about guilty fears?" His grip loosened. "Does your father know you were in there?"

"No, he's been in Denver City since early this morning. I met a girl, Lizzie. She was trying to teach me to play the piano." In the dim light Amy could see the frown on Daniel's face. "Honest. She knows the woman who runs the place."

"Playing the piano. That's something to sneak around about?"

She winced. "I guess I was being a sneak. Daniel, I wanted desperately to just touch that piano just once. I knew I could play it and I did!"

"Why would your aunt object?"

"She thinks everything around here is of the devil."

"Well, I'm not sure it isn't. Though I don't know much about devils." He glanced around and then said, "But surely not pianos."

"Aunty believes the devil's trying to get fancy music in church just to send us all to hell."

By the light of the moon, Amy could see the puzzled but unwavering look on Daniel's face. She waited. Finally he sighed, "I don't know how to get you out of this fix without getting you into a worse one. You can't just walk home can you?" She shook her head. "If I take you home she'll tack my hide to the front door, and there goes our friendship."

He took her hand and tugged. "Well, come on. If we don't do something she'll catch us standing right here."

They moved slowly down the street, with Daniel murmuring, "I suppose I should face the lioness, but I'm chicken enough to look for an easier way out. What if I take you to Aunt Clara's? Then I'll just happen to pass your Aunt Maude while she is searching for you. I'll say I saw you up there and volunteer to fetch you home. She might even end up liking me after that kind deed!"

Daniel was still chuckling when they heard the footsteps behind them. Aunt Maude! Before Amy could come up with an excuse, her aunt dashed toward her. Amy and Daniel both saw the tears on her face as she threw her arms around Amy.

"It will never happen again," she breathed into Amy's collar, her voice so muffled that Amy could barely make out the words. "Not if I have anything to say about it!"

CHAPTER 8

Just past noon on a hot July day Amy heard the blast. Holding a wet towel in her hands, she stood ready to pin it to the clothesline when her attention was caught by the deep rumble. Overhead the parched leaves quivered in the swoosh of air one moment before the rumble became a blast. It was from Eureka Gulch.

At the moment of the blast the noonday heat had left man and beast barely moving. Every sound seemed flattened and dull, and then it came.

She turned to look up the mountainside. Dust was hanging, marking the spot. Strange and fearful as it was, she reacted by moving her shoulders uneasily.

It was a big one. She shivered, thinking, *Can't live long in a mining camp before learning the difference between the big ones and the little ones.*

The images were beginning to form in her mind as she admitted the worst. This one had started with a *feeling* born earth-deep.

Aunt Maude and Eli came spilling out of the cabin. Maude said, "Earthquake." Father shook his head. There was a sick expression on his face, just as there had been when the explosion happened in Mountain City. He said, "Think I'll wander down to the post office."

He had only taken a step when the cry came. "It's the Lucky Clover."

She knew, but he said it. "It's the Gerrett's claim."

Already there were men running up Eureka Gulch. Eli reached for her hand and she said, "No, I'd rather run."

By the time she turned up the road toward the claim, the first of the returning men met her. "Ain't no use, Missy. The mountain plumb rose and settled. There's no reason to dig."

"Both of them?"

He shook his head. "No, the young fella wasn't even there. He passed me running up the hill."

She kept on until she saw the wounded mountain and the tiny stream of smoke and dust. Men were standing around the broken timbers and tumble of rock. Amy stood uncertain, waiting, trembling.

Now the men were milling around, with the same aimlessness she felt down inside—she need not be told there was nothing to be done. She saw Daniel close to the broken tumble of rock, standing with his head drooping.

Amy climbed the slope behind the claim, found a rock in the shade and sat down before pressing her cold hands against her face. Father reached the top of the hill. She watched him walk through the crowd to Daniel's side.

As the sun crossed the sky and the rock became hot, Amy moved to the shade. The men were breaking away in clusters and heading down the mountain. Father left. Amy shifted her attention from the slumped figure of her friend and looked at the cabin close to the creek.

Good water up here. Lots of it. She recalled some saying the biggest problem to be faced in the next few years would be to get enough water for the machinery. The Gerretts had the water.

The cabin was worthless. All their time had been spent on the mine. She remembered Daniel saying how his pa wanted to work a mine. But Daniel had admitted he worked the mine just because of his pa; it wasn't important to him. She sighed.

He moved. She watched him kick at the shovel and pick lying on the ground. She knew she had to go down to him. He would be embarrassed if he knew she was watching.

Amy went down the slope, sliding in the gravel. He heard her coming. From his face she knew there wasn't anything to do but wait.

"It's cooling off a little," she said. He nodded. Finally he pointed to the logs piled close. She knew they were fresh cut, intended for shoring up the tunnel once it was blasted clear.

When he sat down beside her, she knew from the way he rubbed his hands over his face that he was pushing away the numbness and would talk.

"I asked Pa to wait on the dynamite. He was rushing it. He had an offer, a good one if he could find color today. He couldn't wait. I can't imagine why he took the whole sack of dynamite in there with him. He'd sent me to town to get some more caps for it."

It was nearly dark. Restlessly Amy went to sit on the rocks overlooking the gulch. He followed, saying, "I heard you singing at the boardinghouse. I wanted to ask you to sing that hymn for me some time. Seems I heard Ma once; it might have been the same one. Would you?"

Amy began, concentrating on the words, blocking out his face, and soon the words captured her and lifted, ". . . He owns me for His child; I can no longer fear. With confidence I now draw nigh. . . ." When the hymn ended, he came to stand below the rock where she sat. His face reminded her of a lost child's. Swallowing the lump in her throat, she put her arms around him and held his face against her shoulder. *Child, man, friend, love.*

No, not that! Amy's spirit shrank away from the thought as she felt his tears on her shoulder.

When she finally walked down the mountain, alone, in the dark, she knew it was all over. There was nothing. Even that embryo emotion was gone, lost. She should never have hugged him so shamelessly. Amy trembled and stumbled in the night. *What must he think of me?*

As she reached her own door, she stared at its blankness.
Today a door slammed in Daniel's life. Her sore heart ached for
him. Drooping with fatigue, she slumped to the threshold wondering what would happen to Daniel. *All over, like a slammed
door. For both of them.*

Early the next day she heard the news at the store. It was
from Joe. He took her money and handed over the pail of milk.
"That Gerrett fella," he said, without a flicker of emotion in his
eyes. "Saw him packing out about sunup. Had one mule and a
bundle. Didn't look back."

Amy walked slowly home. It didn't seem possible to share
the news. Memories caught up with her, and she blushed at the
thought of that silly time when she had challenged the young
miner to kiss her. Now, measured against the last dark expression she had seen on Daniel's face, she found herself wishing
she could wipe out the memory and replace it with something
he could hang on to. Something good.

But there was nothing, not one good thing in all the times
they had been together. And now, that last touch between them
had ruined it all. While she had clung to him, feeling his warmth
and aliveness, he had slipped away forever. Amy could feel only
shame for her strange embrace.

When she reached her own door, she muttered, "Seems,
Amy, you haven't got the sense of a mule. You don't deserve a
friend like Daniel. Lizzie is more the kind of friend you deserve—all froth." Amy frowned. Inside, her heart was crying,
It wasn't just a friend I wanted.

With her hand still on the latch, Amy shifted her thoughts,
trying to give herself time to mask the pain that must be in her
eyes.

She thought of Lizzie's fingers tripping over the piano keys,
playing the hymn like it was a familiar one, almost more so
than the rollicking songs. Yet there had been a scowl on her face
as she played. Why? The words slipped into her mind. *Kindred
souls.* But Lizzie hadn't revealed her secret, her deepest desire.
She was no kindred spirit.

Daniel was in no hurry to reach Denver. Taking the torturous road winding steeply down Golden Gate Canyon to the settlement called Arapahoe, he let the mule pick her way. She stopped at every succulent weed, giving him plenty of time to think. By the end of the day, Daniel was certain he wanted to be done with mining forever.

He fingered the coins in his pocket and thought of Indiana. It had been home. Once there had been a farm and a mother as well as a brother and sister.

After some more thinking, Daniel sighed and muttered, "Can't complain against the Almighty for taking off Ma and the little ones. Nearly every family in the valley lost at least one. Pa made a bad mistake. That's all there is to it. If—"

He sighed and tightened the reins on the wandering mule. For just a moment, his lips twisted in a grin as he looked at the mule's seedy gray mane. *What would Aunt Maude think of having a mule named after her?* His lips twisted. "Maude, that's enough." He tugged the reins, and the mule turned her head and bared her teeth. "You'll make yourself sick if you eat any more. And don't glare at me like that; I'm no more afraid of you than I am of the lady you were named after." The mule continued to eye him with a disapproving stare.

"Matter of fact, I'm much more afraid of Aunt Maude." He recalled Amy's sweet face, her trusting blue eyes, and lingered over the memory of her arms, her embrace. He flicked the reins, sighing heavily.

Staring at the mule he muttered, "I wouldn't trade that hug for all the gold in Pikes Peak country, but with Aunt Maude in Central City, I best hightail out of there before I cause any more trouble."

That night Daniel camped beside a stream, breaking out of the rocks at the head of the canyon. As he made camp and went after water, he found his fingers fumbling through the gravel. "Habit dies hard," he murmured, studying the swirl of mud and water. There was a brightness in the clearing water and without enthusiasm he scooped up a handful of stones and fished out the small bright nugget. He bit it, and the soft, heavy metal gave beneath his teeth. "Gold. Too bad Pa isn't here; he'd get a kick out of it." He tossed the nugget from hand to hand before slipping it into his pocket. "Buy a couple of loaves of bread."

A twig snapped behind Daniel. Without rising, he rotated on his heels and reached for a large stone. A man strode into the clearing—a white man. Daniel sighed with relief as he got to his feet.

"Saw the fire," the man was speaking as he approached. "I have some bacon and coffee; mind if I share with you? The name's Bill Kelly."

"I've heard that name," Daniel said slowly, "but I don't recollect anything else."

"Methodist missionary. I'm headed into Denver City to meet with some churchmen. You going that way?"

Daniel nodded. "I'm down from Eureka Gulch. Had a mine up that way."

"So you're mining. Central City?"

He shook his head. "Not anymore. Sold out my claim for fifty dollars." Kelly gave him a shrewd glance but said nothing as he kicked a log close to the fire and sat down. Daniel took a deep breath. "Lost my father in the mine. Dynamite."

"I'm sorry." The man's voice was deep and musical. "When did this happen?"

"Yesterday." Daniel slanted a glance at him. The man's hands were hanging limp between his knees and Daniel knew he was waiting. He blurted out the words, "I know it happens all the time, but why does it happen when things are rolling along smooth? I guess it's just that you never expect something like this until it hits you. I—"

He paused and looked into the man's face. "Go ahead, son," he said gently.

The next day the pair walked into Denver City leading the mule. Kelly pointed out a little log cabin beside Cherry Creek. "That's where I'm headed. Need to have a talk with the presiding elder. There're plans in the making for a big quarterly meeting at Mountain City."

"What is that?"

"The Methodist Episcopal Church has been organized in the area. Little and as struggling as we are, there're big plans afoot. You might as well come and get in on them."

"I know the preacher in Central City; know his daughter too."

A grin tugged at Kelly's lips as he glanced at the mule. "And Randolph's sister? That where the mule got her name?" Daniel felt his face flushing as he nodded.

Kelly said, "Better be careful about mentioning that name if you want to get better acquainted with Eli's daughter." He paused before adding, "Understand those two are mighty protective of the little girl."

"So protective I didn't dare show myself at church," Daniel answered bitterly.

"Well, come along. You'll be welcome in Denver City. There's a hotel on this side of the creek, but I have an idea you can drop your bedroll in the barn behind the Fishers' house if you want."

Later Daniel placed his belongings under the cottonwood tree beside the barn and went to sit on the edge of the crowd clustered just inside Fishers' open door.

Bill Kelly moved down on the crude bench. He was leaning forward, giving the unseen speaker all of his attention.

The man's voice was low and intense. "Brethren, this is God's harvest field. Never have I seen the need so great. The perils of the mining camp, the unexpected savage, the liquor, and the gambler are waiting to snatch the souls of the unsuspecting, unregenerate miner.

"These men have flung aside all restraint of hearth and home. Gold has become their god and liquor their comfort. The Master calls you; will you obey? Just as the apostles were called to leave comfort and safety, you must be willing to place your all on the altar for the sake of the unsaved. Rescue the perishing, snatching them from the fire."

When the man finished speaking, the congregation went outside. Daniel awkwardly joined them. The last one through the door was a woman carrying a pan of cornbread. She followed the speaker, who deposited a kettle of steaming stew on the crude bench under the tree.

Kelly had Daniel by the arm, steering him toward the couple. "Bishop, I found a friend on the byways. This here is Daniel Gerrett."

The group around the bench parted and a bowl was shoved into Daniel's hands. When he had finished eating, Daniel followed Kelly toward another cluster of men; as they walked he explained, "This gentleman's a salesman. Comes out into the territories once a year with his goods and we all take the opportunity to stock up."

The man was spreading his ware. "Books!" Daniel exclaimed in surprise. "Well, it sounds like a fine idea, but I don't have money for books."

"Most of us will be laying in stock to sell when we go into the mining camps." Kelly bent over and fingered the tracts and pamphlets. "Bart, how much are the Bibles going for this year?"

"I've a fine leather one for three dollars."

The man behind Daniel groaned. "Could be a million for all I care. I can't afford it, and a miner wouldn't buy it."

The salesman retorted, "Why don't you fellows dig a little gold before you come to quarterly meeting? A small nugget would buy the finest of the lot."

"I'd like to see you take a nugget for a Bible," shot back the man at Daniel's elbow.

Daniel's hand was already in his pocket. He was fingering the nugget, chuckling at the idea. Not that he had any need for a Bible.

He pulled out the nugget and balanced it on the tip of his finger. Abruptly he remembered his father's face the first time he'd found color in his pan of washings. Daniel winced and thrust the nugget toward the salesmen. "Well, here it is."

He watched the salesman bite into the gold before nodding. Handing the Bible to Daniel, he said, "Got yourself a deal."

The fellow behind Daniel laughed, "Up Russell Gulch, that much gold would have bought you a claim."

Daniel looked down at the dark leather cover and felt a

pang of dismay. Squinting at the circle of men around him, he said, "I don't want a claim, but I feel like I'm letting myself in for something I might not want."

In the silence, a deep, serious voice said, "You could stick it in your pack and forget all about it. That's what a lot of fellows do."

Looking at the circle of watchful eyes, he remembered Amy had told him to read the Bible. Daniel cleared his throat. "I'll see." He spotted the man who had been speaking and said, "You talk like it's mighty important to sit up and take notice before a body dies and goes off to meet his Maker. Suppose I'll find out why from reading this?" The speaker nodded, and Daniel took a deep breath, his first easy breath in a long time.

CHAPTER 9

Amy stood on the ridge. Far below, Central City stretched out like a haphazard village children might erect in the sand.

As Amy took another step toward the edge of the gulch, she felt it crumble beneath her feet. Quickly she stepped back and watched soil and rocks roll down to the road below. Gingerly she sat down under the juniper tree. Lizzie's head appeared just below her. "You throwing rocks at me?"

"Oh, Lizzie! After all the time you've spent teaching me to play the piano? I wouldn't do that."

"I don't know. The way you fussed about playing for the fellows, I expected you to roll me down the hill to get out of it."

Lizzie dropped down beside Amy and fanned herself with the straw hat she carried. Amy studied her friend's bright cheeks. "If I really wanted to get out of it, I'd just outrun you. That's a little slope to make you puff."

"Behave, or I'll push you down just to see you run up without getting red in the face."

"Lizzie, I'm scared to death about giving a piano concert for the people at the boardinghouse. It isn't the playing; I love that. It's just the risk of getting caught."

"Of your aunt and father finding out? No chance. We've been sneaking around for weeks and haven't been caught."

Amy winced. "I wish you hadn't said it that way. You don't ever seem to worry about your parents finding out. How do you—"

"I explained everything to Mrs. Arnold," Lizzie interrupted. "The audience won't even know your name. Mrs. Arnold will call you Annabell. She predicts you'll be such a success that her place will be more popular than ever!"

"It's getting pretty close to sundown. Both Father and Aunt Maude were so busy they didn't give me a second glance when I left. I wore my best dress, but it's terrible."

"I knew you would say that. I brought this scarf for you to drape around your shoulders." Lizzie pulled the length of silk out of her pocket and shook out the wrinkles.

"Oh, Lizzie, it's beautiful!" Amy jumped to her feet and draped the embroidered scarf around her shoulders. "The flowers and butterflies are enough to make anyone happy."

"Now let me brush your hair into curls, then we'll go."

They reached the boardinghouse parlor just as Mrs. Arnold came into the room with a lighted candle. Amy watched her hold the taper to the candelabrum on the stand beside the piano. As each candle flared, more of the shadowy room was revealed.

By the time Amy sat down and touched the piano keys, she had forgotten the line of faces beyond the light.

As the last rollicking chord died away, Amy stood to bow the way Lizzie had taught her. She couldn't help thinking, *One thing is certain. They're clapping harder now than they did at the beginning.* She tucked that satisfaction away inside and followed Lizzie out the back door. Amy lifted her flushed cheeks to the breeze coming down the gulch. Folding the silk scarf regretfully, she touched the embroidery again. *It's over, all over, and I didn't do so bad. If only I dared tell Father.*

She sighed and began to braid her hair. The sun had disappeared behind the mountains and the streets of Central City were layered with deepening shadows. Before Amy dared start down the street, she had to check each shadow. The fearful memory of encountering Aunt Maude still lingered.

Reluctant to go home, Amy turned to Lizzie, "It's amazing," she murmured, straining to see into the shadows, "Every day I see more miners coming into town with their jacks and picks. Even womenfolk are arriving. Not the ones that come by stage." She slanted a glance at Lizzie.

By the light coming from the window, she could see Lizzie's eyes flash. She said, "And what a bunch of women! Old hags, but they can cozy up to the bar just like the men."

"Lizzie," Amy gasped, "that's terrible! Why, Mrs. Wilson and Mrs. Ellis have both been to church services."

"Looking like butter wouldn't melt in their mouths, huh? I'll tell you another thing. I heard from a good source that Wilsons left Auraria because he caught her with a fellow."

"Lizzie, I can't listen to such gossip," Amy said indignantly. Lizzie threw back her head and laughed. "Besides," Amy continued, "how would you know what goes on in the saloons?"

"Prude!" Lizzie teased. "What will you do if it leaks out that you've been sneaking into the boardinghouse all summer? Think they'd believe it's just to learn the piano?"

Amy stopped on the steps and turned. "Lizzie, you give me the shivers just talking about it. The only reason I've come is because wanting to learn is stronger than my common sense. My father would never be able to take the shock!"

Lizzie was sober now. "I know, and you can be certain I'll never be the one to tell."

"I'll just always be grateful that you were willing to risk yourself to teach me how to play the piano."

Lizzie hugged Amy quickly. "It's worth it. Never have I seen a person learn as quickly as you. Only promise me one thing."

"What?" Amy asked cautiously.

"Someday really *study* the piano. No matter what you must do to get the opportunity, find a good teacher and really learn."

"I will, I will," Amy murmured, pressing Lizzie's hands in hers.

They moved toward the steps. For a moment light from the lamps beyond the window circled them. Amy glanced at Lizzie and continued, "I suppose I won't have any excuse to come here again. I'm going to miss this. You, too, not just the piano. But I understand. Mrs. Arnold has been good to let me in here during the dinner hour. I can't expect her kindness to last forever."

Lizzie's smile flashed, "I'm glad you finally agreed to play the piano for the men. Missy, I wouldn't have given you a passing grade without a recital." She shook her finger in mock sternness and Amy giggled.

"It was fun! Never would I dare do it again though."

Lizzie giggled. "I think Mrs. Arnold got a big kick out of it, the preacher's daughter playing her piano and nobody knew who it was."

Amy went down two steps and then turned. "I do wish you and your family would come to services. But I understand. If your folks aren't church people, I guess there's not much you can do about it. But I would like to meet them. We've been friends for weeks now, and—"

"We've been all through that, remember? They just don't hold much with religious types. Besides, you've never introduced me to your father and aunt."

"I guess I haven't, have I? But at least you've seen—"

The wooden steps creaked. Amy and Lizzie turned. By the narrow shaft of light coming from the boardinghouse they watched the man come down toward them.

He was dressed in white, and moved with a grace unknown to those parts. He stopped in front of them and raised his hat. "Ma'am—" His voice backed up Amy's first impression: he was a stranger to Central City, and he wasn't a miner. "May I compliment you on playing the piano? I've attended many concerts, but never have I enjoyed one so immensely."

Amy was still hugging the compliment to herself as she walked homeward. *Lucas Tristram.* She rolled the strange name around on her tongue; it sounded important. He was a lawyer, up from Denver City. He said he was thinking of settling in Central City.

Before he left, he pressed her hands, saying he hoped to see her again. Unlike the miners with their teasing, offhand compliments, his eyes, even in the shadows, were sincere.

Amy slipped into the cabin and paused. It took a moment to adjust to this other world. She stood just beyond the circle of light cast by the candle over her father's book and Aunt Maude's sewing. Her mind was still filled with images of shiny black and white keys and gleaming mahogany; the lilting chords of the waltz still echoed through her.

Taking a deep breath she stepped into the light. "That you, Amy?" Neither one lifted a head.

"Yes, Father."

"Nearly dark, isn't it?"

"Eli, it's been dark for over an hour!" Maude snapped. "Amy, with all the wild men in this town, I'd think you'd try to ease our minds by being home before dark."

"Aunt Clara is better than a bodyguard. Besides nobody would touch the parson's young'un."

Eli pushed aside his book. "The quarterly meeting begins next week."

"In Mountain City," Amy added quickly. "Are we going to camp out with the rest of them?"

"No, it looks like every spare section of ground will be needed for the tents. Most of the meeting will take place out in the open. I'm advised that some of the men will be arriving early to erect pine shelters.

"This is quite an honor for the town to have the Methodist Episcopal Church quarterly meeting up here. The presiding elder said he's expecting some delegates from Europe; imagine that!" He beamed and then added, "I just wanted to remind you that we'll be riding home after the meeting each night."

Maude sighed, "That's a shame. It will be late and we'll be tired. I still remember how much fun it was to stay in the tents with all the other girls. I did it often enough when I was a youngster. My, such meetings we had!"

"No girls here; there'll be just the men," Amy murmured. "Does that mean we'll be involved with the cooking?"

"You're behind times," Eli answered. "Several new men have arrived on the field and they've brought their families with them."

"What about Aunt Clara?"

Maude lifted her chin. "Of course we'll take her. If we don't give her a ride, she's bound to hike it every day."

Father chuckled, "Might be better for the meetings. Aunt Clara will buttonhole everyone she meets and haul them to the meeting with her."

Maude was shaking her head. "Don't understand how a darky can succeed where we've failed. But the fact is, since she's been here more people are coming to church services."

"She just backs them into a corner and paints them with a guilty conscience," Amy said. "I've watched her do it."

That next week, when they started down the road to Mountain City for the first meeting, Amy noticed the beginning of color in the trees. The brilliant aspens sent Amy's thoughts spinning back a year, when Daniel Gerrett had first come to worship services. In their grove the aspens had been a brilliant gold.

She sighed and wondered about him. Was he happy? Did he think about her? Most likely his memories were ones she wouldn't care to know. She felt her face grow warm as she tried to shove that last day out of her mind.

But Daniel's dark eyes intruded again. She chewed her lip and wished it were possible to roll up the past year and start over.

Amy saw Aunt Clara coming. She smiled at her beaming face, but her thoughts remained with Daniel. He wouldn't have left if he'd cared—even a little. Her heart sank. *Most likely he left because he didn't want to see me again.*

Aunt Clara nodded her approval as she climbed into the wagon, saying, "My, the Lord's decorated the cathedral. It's a sign we'll be havin' a good time!" Amy looked from the dark shining face to the red sumac and golden aspens. For a moment she wished her heart could be as light as Aunt Clara's was.

It was still early morning when the Randolph wagon

reached Mountain City. Both sides of the ravine, nearly to the top, were covered with white tents. Breakfast fires filled the gulch with smoke.

There was a new sound in Mountain City—the excited chatter of children. Father grinned and pointed. Amy noticed them coming from all directions, and as she watched them, rosy-faced women poked their heads out tent openings.

A youth stepped into the clearing by the pine-bough booth and lifted a tin horn.

"We arrived just in time," Eli murmured as he hopped down and began to unharness the horses. "I need to see a fellow; you ladies go find a place to sit. Looks like they've done a good job with the log benches."

Amy slowly followed Aunt Maude as she headed for the front row. Desperately wishing herself any place but here, Amy arranged the smile on her face. Already her hands were cold and her heart squeezing tight as she thought, *Why does the memory keep coming up like this? Doesn't camp meeting bring back bad memories for them, too? How could Father and Aunt Maude pretend to be happy?*

While the ripple of excited voices rose around her, Amy saw only the image of that crude length of log they called the mourner's bench. She stared at the peeling bark, vaguely remembering another one from her early childhood.

She squeezed her hands to stop the trembling while the questions pounded her. Sometimes, when it was particularly bad, she felt an overwhelming desire to shake her fist at heaven and scream out the question, *Why? Why did you take my mother away?*

Even now, with the question in her mind, a single sharp, painful image surfaced as clear now as the night her mother died. She only remembered one scene: the figure huddled by the wooden bench, then sprawled and limp. *Mother.*

Aunt Maude found a seat and adjusted the pillow she carried. She pointed to a group of dark-garbed men standing close to Father. "Amy, see? The one with the beard is the bishop from Nebraska." Her aunt was nodding, smiling.

But Amy saw only the contrast between the dignified black and the humble garb of the preachers from the mountains.

A young man jumped up beside the bishop and picked up a hymnal. "It isn't like back home where they had little Amy Randolph sing out the verses for the people to follow." Aunt Maude's whisper was too loud, and Amy cringed.

The young man began with the old familiar hymns, and Aunt Maude hissed, "He can't even carry a tune! I've a mind to suggest—"

"Aunt Maude!" Amy admonished.

The preaching began. The rustling, restless people became quiet.

The words were a river, alternately flowing and crashing. In the background, in the workaday world of mining, she heard the cry of teamsters and the steady, monotonous thump of the stamp mill.

The week of meetings blurred together until the last night. At the very end, while Father and Aunt Maude began to move toward the wagon, Amy saw one last seeker slip out of the shadows and move into the light of the fires.

When he knelt Amy recognized his lanky frame. "Daniel!" she whispered. On tiptoe with the need to run to him, she hesitated. But Aunt Maude's frown and Father's tired face made her turn away.

All the way home, riding in the moonlit night, Amy thought about Daniel. It hurt many different ways to consider him. That day of the blast, his bewildered face and pain-filled eyes had become a part of her.

Thinking now of the figure kneeling at the peeled log bench, bitterness rolled through her. *He could have found me, he knew we would be there. Not once did he bring himself around. Amy, what more do you need to know?*

CHAPTER 10

The log church was finished before the first snow. It was not white clapboard like back home, and not as wide as a respectable farmhouse. It boasted only benches, knee-knocking close, and a spindly pulpit. But it was perfumed with pine and had a rough plank floor.

On one of those first Sundays in the new church, Lucas Tristram came. Amy arrived late and flustered. Until she took a seat behind him, she didn't know there was a visitor. But having once spotted him, it was impossible to ignore his pleasant baritone and his square shoulders clothed in black broadcloth.

Amy saw Aunt Maude casting admiring glances his direction. At the same time, Amy began to feel the slow flutter of excitement in her own heart.

Since meeting Lucas Tristram last summer, she had been hearing his name mentioned often. A young attorney from Denver City, he was rapidly becoming an influential voice on the city council. It was whispered he was the money behind several new buildings. There was talk of his supporting a newspaper, and even more talk of the mining claims he had been acquiring. Amy studied his back and dreamed her way through the sermon.

At the conclusion of the worship service, when Lucas bent over her hand, the look they exchanged bridged the months since they first met. His slightly mocking smile promised silence about that night, and he moved on to be introduced to the Wilsons.

On the following Sunday, Amy wasn't surprised to find Lucas in church again. By the third Sunday Aunt Maude, cheeks bright and eyes sparkling, insisted he come home and share their fried chicken.

Only Father and Amy knew the significance of fried chicken in the Randolph's pot. And only Amy and Aunt Maude read Father's questioning frown that Sunday afternoon. Later Amy found herself wondering which of them had been most relieved when Father's frown changed to a grin. Most likely it was Aunt Maude.

That winter Amy had no tramps through the snow, no icy, lonely walks. Lucas was there with his shiny sleigh.

Father and Aunt Maude went along on the first ride. Amy watched Aunt Maude's knuckles turn white while Father clutched his hat. She also saw the twinkle in Lucas's eyes and guessed he had deliberately picked the steepest hill in Central City.

One Sunday afternoon while the two of them were riding, Lucas said, "Amy, let's talk about you. Tell me your plans. I can't believe with your talent you haven't decided to study music."

Amy met the question in his eyes. She was deeply conscious of the admiration she was seeing there, but there was something more intriguing. There were no dark shadows in his eyes. He wasn't like Daniel. This young man was full of the love of living, and he was bound to make exciting things happen. She guessed there was nothing she could say that would shock him.

"I have no plans. Aunt Maude would never consent to my playing the piano."

He understood and laughed. "How did you manage that concert last fall?"

"Lizzie did it all. She'd been teaching me all summer."

He let the reins go slack as he reached for her hand. "You know I'm fascinated by you. That funny innocent expression contrasts with the fact I've heard you play a polka that can set every foot to tapping. Amy Randolph, you are a deep pool, and you challenge me to discover all the hidden depths. I'll do my best to encourage you to study music. Just maybe I'll be able to persuade Aunt Maude you should have a piano."

She searched his eyes and decided to ignore the remark. His grin was half mocking as he snapped the reins across the mare's back.

The following day, Amy walked slowly down the street, thinking about Lucas. As she passed the newest dress shop on the street, she heard, "Psst! Amy."

Lizzie poked her head through the open door of the shop. "Come in, Amy. You must see all the pretties. This is Madame Florence's new dress shop. Surely Aunt Maude won't mind your looking."

Amy came. Unwinding her shawl in the warmth of the store, she said, "I'm not worried. It's amazing what a difference a seventeenth birthday makes. Yesterday I was a child; today I am grown up."

Lizzie gave Amy a curious look. "It takes more than a new frock to make a woman of a girl. What have you done to your hair?"

Amy touched the soft roll high on her head. "It's not just that. It's the way they treat me. I'm even allowed to have beaus now. Too bad you don't come to church. Lucas Tristram has been attending regularly."

She stopped and frowned at Lizzie's expression. "You're nodding. I suppose everyone in town knows. And also maybe it's not because of me, but instead because church has now become respectable." She saw her friend's puzzled expression.

Lizzie's eyes were wide. "I didn't know churches weren't always respectable."

"Oh, you know what I mean. It's the new building. Sure it's only log with a plank floor, but that's better than using our home as a church." She added, "He still hasn't put down a real floor—in our house."

"So Lucas Tristram is in church these days." Lizzie laughed and turned away. "Back home they said it was wrong to go to church for courtin'."

Amy shrugged. "Father seems to think Lucas is special. A lawyer. He's working up here filing claims, and doing other legal things. He told Father he's been buying up everything he can get. Father says he's sure to make a good strike sooner or later. Says he expects Lucas to be a millionaire as soon as any of them.

"But he's not the only new one at church," Amy continued. "Aunt Clara is still going at it. She's got a way of reminding the miners of their responsibility to God."

"And what's that?"

"Living up to their commitment. I think she means that if they joined the church back home, they'd better act like a member out here. If they don't, God will get them." Amy saw the fleeting expression on Lizzie's face. "What's wrong? Did I say something to frighten you?"

Her voice was strained. "Do you believe that way?"

Amy moved her shoulders impatiently. "I didn't come shopping for a new comb with my Bible tucked under my arm. Besides, why don't you come to church?"

They were standing at the counter and Lizzie lifted a rosy red ribbon. Madame Florence closed the door behind her customer and swept toward them. Amy eyed her pile of reddish hair and the bustle swishing from side to side as she walked. "My, this little mining camp is nearly as nice as Denver City now. At least with this shop," Amy said, her smile taking in both Lizzie and the shopkeeper.

"We intend to keep up with the latest fashions. Though if it weren't for the girls, there wouldn't be a market. I've some nice frocks if you wish to see them." She fumbled with the cameo on her collar and smiled from Amy to Lizzie.

With a regretful sigh, Amy said, "A parson's daughter can't afford luxuries like that. And the ribbon. Aunt Maude would burn it, most certainly."

The woman's eyebrows lifted in surprised arcs as she glanced quickly at Lizzie. Amy didn't understand the wink, but she was relieved when the woman hurried to the front of the shop.

At church that next Sunday, sitting two rows behind Lucas Tristam, Amy thought of the ribbons and combs, the lace collars and rich velvets. She touched the curl hanging over her ear.

The curl had been pure impulse and she was still uneasy, but she had felt brave this morning. When Aunt Maude turned her back, Amy had loosened her hair just enough to see a curl appear over each ear.

After the church services ended, Lucas Tristram bent over her hand with a look both bold and teasing. Amy tugged and blushed just as Aunt Maude appeared and invited him home for dinner.

While they walked from the edge of Eureka Gulch to the Randolph cabin, Lucas answered Aunt Maude's questions with stories of his family in New York. Amy watched his dimple appear and disappear as he talked. His hair was wavy; Daniel's was straight, but she liked the maple leaf brown of Daniel's. She stifled a sigh as she looked at Aunt Maude's rapt expression.

The unseasonable January thaw had left rivers of slush on the streets, but Lucas was too busy talking to notice the mud that clung to his shiny boots. Amy made a wry face to herself as she picked her way through the slush. *Let him think me dainty,* she decided, *better that by far than the truth!*

She grinned at Father, and he watched as she skirted a sloppy puddle. Father knew her dainty steps were due to the split in her boot. Surprisingly the look that answered her grin was very serious. Quickly he glanced at Lucas's boots.

From that day on, Lucas became a regular guest at the Randolph home. It was obvious Father was encouraging him, and Amy swallowed her surprise. Lucas seemed the direct opposite of the type of man she would have expected Father to endorse.

On Sundays, after dinner, Lucas and Father would talk while Amy and Aunt Maude cleaned up the dinner clutter. Amy listened to their rumble of words and saw the worried lines on her father's face as they talked about the possibility of war.

Both of them were in Denver City just often enough to keep the subject fresh in their minds, and their talk reflected what they heard in Denver City.

Amy began to read the newspapers they brought back from Denver City. Amy asked, "Father, what is this about slavery that is causing so much bad feeling? Why can't we let them be? Lucas said most of these people would starve without masters to care for them."

"And I say that is false thinking!" Amy recognized her father's pulpit voice as Eli said, "Slavery goes against the moral grain of man. Oppression of any kind is not to be tolerated in a free land. Amy, our country was settled by God-fearing men. From the beginning they advocated freedom for all. I believe we have the obligation to secure this right for the weak even as we strive to maintain it for ourselves."

Amy lost the import of his words. She was watching his face. It had been a long time since she had seen this glow. Was Lucas responsible? Or was it just the excitement of having someone to argue with?

Lucas continued to be a part of their life, but often Amy found herself measuring his sophistication against their humble place in the community. Secretly she expected every day to have seen the last of him.

She also measured her response to him. Even as she was arrested by the flattery in his eyes and accepted the tokens of candy, lacy handkerchiefs, and even a tiny cameo brooch, she was aware of a growing uneasiness. Too often her thoughts flitted away. *Where was Daniel? Had he found another friend? Why must she continue to think about him?*

In addition, it was some time before Amy began to understand Aunt Maude's happiness. With dismay, Amy realized Aunt Maude saw the gifts in a different light—to her they signified as much as a signed and sealed contract.

This was made clear the evening Lucas came to escort Amy to a phrenology lecture in Mountain City.

"Skull reading!" Aunt Maude scoffed as she ironed Amy's dark worsted skirt. "It's likely one excuse is as good as another," she added. "Decent church people wouldn't be caught at the likes of the entertainment they offer in a mining camp. I'm waiting for the day we get a big enough cabin to hold a molasses-candy pull like we had back home. If you're not married by that time."

"Married!" Amy exclaimed. "All I want is a waist of white linen with ruffles of real lace."

Aunt Maude snorted, "It is more likely you'll be married before that happens. That young man won't wait. Besides, a parson's salary doesn't support such fancy ideas." She peered at Amy, nodding, "You'll do well to look afield, rather'n settling for a preacher boy. Goodness knows, your father has suffered over not being able to provide for you."

That was the beginning. It wasn't too long until Amy realized her engagement to Lucas was being taken for granted.

With dismay, she tried to close her eyes to the direction it was all leading. After all, it was fun being with Lucas, being escorted to places she would never have gone otherwise. She didn't intend to give that up. But she was uneasy about the prospect of marrying him. She tried to push the thought out of her conscious mind.

Like the cameo and handkerchiefs tucked out of sight, Amy let herself forget the hope in Father's eyes, the twinkle in Aunt Maude's.

Finally Aunt Maude put it all out in the open. "People around town as well as them in the church are buzzing. They're wanting to know when you and Lucas are getting married."

"Married! He hasn't even kissed me."

"A proper young man. A lawyer, too. Can't do better," Aunt Maude said with satisfaction.

Amy looked at her aunt with dismay. She dared not admit to Aunt Maude that most often her thoughts were on Daniel, not Lucas. Only to herself could she admit her dreams of Lucas focused more on Amy in silks and velvets, living in a big house, than they did on the man who would share life with her.

When Lucas brought up the subject, it was he who made it possible for her to hold him at arm's length. They were riding in his smart new buggy. Lucas had taken the road through Eureka Gulch, and Amy caught sight of that wounded spot just above the Gerrett cabin. She noticed the cabin door was sagging open and made a mental note to walk that way and fasten it tight.

Lucas said, "Amy, you know everyone in town is waiting breathlessly for us to announce our plans. I hear there's bets we'll be married before the Independence Day celebration." His grin was cocky. Amy didn't know what to say. She tilted her head and looked at him.

He said, "When you look down your nose at me, I feel like throwing myself at your feet and begging. Please don't do it now; it's dangerous to drop the reins on this road."

"Lucas, I—"

"If you are going to refuse, I shall stop them from building our house and cast myself into Gregory Gulch."

"Silly. I didn't know you were building a house."

"And I've ordered a ring for you. Just say you'll marry me."

"If everyone expects it, then I suppose it isn't necessary for me to agree."

"Then you will?"

She held him off. "Please, Lucas. We've known each other such a short time. Marriage is a big decision. I think yes, but let's not talk about it until—"

"When?"

She hunted for a landmark and stammered, "June. Father's taking Aunt Maude and me into Denver City for camp meeting. After I return we can talk seriously."

"I didn't know camp meeting was that important to you." Surprised at the disappointment in his voice, she hesitated. Until now she had not even thought about camp meeting.

On the first of May Amy met Lizzie in Eureka Gulch. Early that morning Amy had remembered the sagging door on the

Gerrett cabin and decided to go there.

When she reached the claim, Lizzie was sitting on a rock overlooking the mine and the long slit of a valley below.

Amy waved and went to fasten the door before climbing the slope. "Lizzie! I'd begun to think you'd left Central City."

"No." Her voice was cool and she seemed sad.

"Problem?" Amy asked, sitting down to study the deep shadows under Lizzie's eyes.

"Oh, I suppose. Mostly I'm tired of this boring town." Glancing at Amy, Lizzie said, "There's gossip around town that you're thinking of marrying Lucas Tristram—is that true?"

Amy sighed. "Yes, I suppose so. Things seem to be heading that way pretty fast."

"You'll hate me, but I'm going to tell you a few things you need to know. Remember the McCormick-Fife Claim and how old man Fife was found murdered? Do you know who bought the claim from McCormick for nickels on the dollar?" When Amy shook her head impatiently, Lizzie replied, "Lucas Tristram."

"Lizzie, are you suggesting Lucas did something bad?" The two stared at each other. Amy watched the tears puddle in Lizzie's eyes. Amy lifted her chin and said, "You've always been jealous of me and Lucas. Well, I'd have been glad to see you get Lucas, fair and square. I think you could have. But this is ugly. Of course you know I don't believe you."

Slowly Lizzie got to her feet. "I didn't think you would." She turned and ran toward the road. For a moment Amy nearly called after her; then she shrugged and turned away.

At the end of the week, Father returned from Joe's store with an envelope for her. He was wearing a puzzled frown. "Amy, here's something for you. Joe would only say it had been given to him for delivery."

Amy carried the envelope to the shade of the aspen grove. The single sheet of paper read: *I think you should know the Wilsons are in trouble with the law over a claim. Question: Why would Lucas Tristram meet Mrs. Wilson up at the Cawson shanty every Thursday afternoon?*

Amy slowly folded the paper and stuffed it into her pocket. More of Lizzie's jealousy. When she went into the cabin, Amy pushed the letter into the stove. As the paper flared into flames and turned to ash, she tried to push the nagging question away. It was nonsense; Lizzie was making a mountain out of a molehill. Her thoughts churned on. *Amy, you'll never know for a fact unless you go up to that shanty. You know Lucas always goes to Russell Gulch on Thursday to record the land claims there. Every Thursday.*

On Thursday, feeling ugly inside, Amy slipped away from the cabin when the sun was noon-high. As she headed up the gulch she thought, *Everyone in Central City knows the Cawson claim—the stories, about haunts and lights and about the old man who froze to death there.*

Amy cut across the side of the mountain behind the deserted Gerrett claim. She paused at the raw rock and crushed timbers, brooding over the memory of Daniel's face the day of the accident. In an effort to shrug away her memories as she swung up the hill, she began singing, mocking the pathos of the words, "On top of Old Smoky, all covered with snow, I lost my true lover—a courtin' too slow . . ."

The Cawson shanty was below her. She could see it, shadowed and leaning, without a sign of life. Amy had nearly decided to turn back when a movement in the rocks caught her eye. That bright spot was a man's light blue shirt. Plaid. Slowly she lowered herself into the rocks behind the sage to watch.

He stood and moved slowly step by step down the slope. It was Mr. Wilson. Amy started to rise, to wave. After all, he was one of Father's flock. Now he stooped and lifted the long object. The sun caught and flashed light. Metal. It was a rifle. Must be he had a deer sighted.

Slowly the gun barrel rose. She watched it sweep the clearing, pause at the shanty. Before Amy could move, she heard an explosion. The door of the shack shuddered and sagged. Amy began to scream.

With both arms she clung to the sagebrush while the screams continued. The blue-shirted man jumped to his feet.

Amy's screams faded into a choking gasp as she watched the man leaping the sagebrush, with the gun barrel gleaming and the shirt rising and falling beyond the sage, out of sight.

She was still choking when the door to the shanty was wrenched open. It slanted and fell. Lucas appeared in the doorway. He held a gun. A woman's face appeared beyond his shoulder.

Lucas came out calling, "Hello out there! You saved our lives. Come down." Amy stood up as he ran to the slope.

"You," he said slowly. He stood below, looking up at her.

"I'd had a note telling me that you were meeting her out here. I guess Mr. Wilson had one, too." She looked at the splintered door. "Lucas, I can just walk home and forget this. What are you and Mrs. Wilson going to do?"

She began to climb the hill. "Amy!" She stopped. The shock was still there on his face. He looked as if he couldn't think. "You saved our lives."

She shrugged. "Not on purpose. I was scared. Besides, I didn't really think you were in there."

She saw him swallow hard. "I suppose your father will have to hear about this."

"No. Not unless you come around again. Of course, I don't know what Mr. Wilson is going to say." She climbed away from him and began to run.

That week the Wilsons left Central City. Father frowned at the news, his mouth pulled down in a way that indicated he didn't know what was going on. But his eyebrows slid up when three Sundays passed and Lucas wasn't in church.

Amy was aware of the questions that had been in his eyes for two weeks. Finally he asked, "You and Lucas having a spat?"

"Something like that."

"Need to talk about it?"

"No. Father; later, please."

Abruptly, crashing through the confusion that filled her, the first of June arrived. It was time to pack for the trip to Denver City, and Amy was eager to be gone. Her dreams still haunted her, nearly as much as the questions she dare not share with anyone.

The day before they were to leave, while Amy checked for loose buttons on her best dress, Aunt Maude said, "Amy, I'm of a mind to pick up some canned meat from Joe's store. I'll be back shortly."

"Aunt Maude, have you seen the little packet of sewing supplies? I can't believe I've lost it."

"Look in the case under your father's bunk." She pulled the door closed behind her and Amy went to look. She tugged at the small trunk under her father's bed.

Settling back on her heels, Amy lifted the lid and began carefully removing the articles inside. When she reached the stack of letters tied with ribbon, she hesitated.

The flamboyant signature on the envelope caught her eye. She winced. "Amelia Randolph. Oh, Father," she whispered, "these are Mother's letters." She blinked through tears. As she stroked the old, stained ribbon binding them, it fell apart in her fingers.

She picked up the first envelope. Someone had penciled a date on the envelope. "June 1852," she murmured, noting the smudged ink on the name.

Sewing packet forgotten, Amy sat down in front of the trunk and allowed the dark memories into her mind. "Oh, Mother, if only I could remember your face. Sometimes I think I remember your hands.

"Mother, Mother," she whispered, "how I wish we could talk! You would help me understand life, wouldn't you? How do I face the terrible black fears that sweep over me every camp meeting time? About Lucas—do I forgive and forget? Is that what being a Christian means?"

Carefully holding the envelope away from her face, she began wiping tears away. The door crashed. "Amy!" Aunt Maude snatched at the letters. "Halfway to the store I remembered them. Don't you ever mention seeing them!"

"But the date!" Amy fought the confusion. "Why that date? It couldn't have anything to do with the letters."

Aunt Maude's hand came down hard on Amy's shoulder. With her blazing eyes inches from Amy, she whispered, "Don't say anything to your father about this. Do you hear? It would kill him if he were to find out that—"

Jumping to her feet, Amy put the envelopes into the trunk and shoved it under the bunk. "I'm sorry," she whispered, "I didn't mean to pry—it was just an accident."

For a moment Maude's face looked as if she were about to cry. "Oh, please!" Amy exclaimed, "Aunt Maude, why is it I always do the wrong thing?" She hesitated, but there was no answer. Turning, she dashed from the cabin.

CHAPTER 11

Daniel Gerrett sat on a crude bench beside the little sheet metal stove, his hands dangling between his knees. He was silent and separated from the group, but he listened intently.

He also studied the men around the table, trying to imagine himself there. With their elbows on the table, they peered into each other's faces. The play of emotion he was seeing spoke more forcefully than their words. *They look and act like they love each other,* Daniel thought. He envied them.

Since the meeting at Mountain City, he wanted desperately to be part of their group. At times his desire brought with it a strong sense of guilt; over and over he found himself probing all the reasons behind this need to be a part of them. Listening to their conversation, Daniel was grateful they had forgotten him.

He compared the excitement and joy flitting across the faces of the men while he eyed their shabby clothing. A grin tugged at his lips. Being an itinerant preacher in the Methodist Episcopal Church wasn't a way to get rich. Nor was it easy.

Daniel's thoughts drifted. It had been nearly a year since the mine explosion in Eureka Gulch. He thought about Central City and the Randolphs. *What would Amy Randolph think of my life now?* he wondered. *Snugging up with all the preachers, learning to think like they do, to thumb through my Bible as fast as her father does. Measuring out kerosene and sacking beans at the store in Auraria wouldn't win any favor with her.*

He caught himself sighing. It didn't accomplish anything, dwelling on the touch of her hands on his face, while her blue eyes spread tears all over his shirt.

He gulped and shifted on the bench. Now was the best time to count his blessings. He looked at Brother Goode. Fine people they were to open their home to him, insisting they were as grateful for the board money he paid out of his salary as he was for the home cooked meals.

Nat Fosset shoved back his stool and got to his feet. Daniel studied the man's care-worn face and shabby coat. He reached for his hat. "Brethren, for the sake of my wife's husband, I'm going to have to start totin' a rifle when I ride out. Three times last month I had to outrun a band of Indians. One of these days, might not be so fortunate. Don't intend to fire unless there's a need. Anyway, can't afford the 'munition."

"Fosset, you were never told to leave your rifle at home. You have a hard circuit. The Arapahoes are restless this spring. You still planning to move your family into Fort Lupton?"

"As soon as the baby's born. There's a little cabin I can get cheap. It'll take some work before we can keep the rain out."

"Let's have prayer before you leave." Goode's glance included Daniel, and he went to kneel beside the others.

When the last man had saddled his horse and turned down the dusty trail toward home, the elder faced Daniel and clapped him on the shoulder. "So finishes the Sabbath. Evangeline won't be home until tomorrow, so let's fry some of that venison. There's a couple of dried ears of corn; we won't lack for sustenance."

While Goode poked wood into the little sheet metal stove, Daniel summoned his courage. "While we're alone, I need to have a talk with you."

"Sure, fella, what's on your mind?"

"I've been listening to the preachers today. Nearly all of

them are under thirty. I don't think they have too much book learning, do they?"

"No, Dan. I saw you taking it all in while we were talking."

Daniel nodded. "Since quarterly meeting in Mountain City last fall, I've been getting the feeling the Lord is wanting me to go to preaching."

"I'd guessed." The gray-haired man nodded, saying, "I believe you're showing a good spirit, and a genuine conversion. But I want to hear you say it. Tell me, lad, just give it to me in your words."

Daniel braced his feet and linked his hands behind his back. "Even before Pa died I was having this need. Just restless then, not knowing where life was taking me. It wasn't until the meeting at Mountain City that I began to understand what I was supposed to do about it all." He was silent a moment. Recalling Amy's stumbling explanation as she tried to explain salvation, he frowned. But this wasn't the time to worry that bone again. He looked at Brother Goode. "Sir, my mother had put a lot into me, reading the Bible and telling me how Jesus Christ is God, and how He came to this earth to die for our sins."

He paused and thought. "I think I could make that sound better if I wrote it out on paper."

"Fine, son, but most of the time you'll have to be doing your writing in your head."

Daniel considered the statement and nodded. "Anyway, at Mountain City, the Lord laid it on me. I wanted what all those men were preaching. At the time they were talking, I didn't understand what they meant—about commitment to God and being filled with the Holy Spirit." He paused and gulped. "Until it happened. Sir, I don't know how to say this all, but I don't have any doubts.

"I've been thinking about it and praying over it since last fall and I haven't changed my mind. Do I need to go somewhere and have some schooling before I can become a preacher?"

The bishop forked the venison out of the skillet and added corn to the plate. "It's usual. But I get the idea you don't have any money."

Daniel shook his head. "A worthless mine claim was all I ever had; I sold that for fifty dollars before I left Central City."

"We're needing men badly right now. If I come up with a man willing to tolerate your company, would you ride along with him until you get the hang of it? Like being an apprentice blacksmith? Only this is serious. It's holy work, with a divine obligation to God. On top of that, I'm asking you to hollow out your own nest."

"Sir, I'd be grateful!"

The elder was grinning at Daniel, saying, "In the meantime, preachers work like a mule at whatever comes up. Nine-tenths of the preaching work is just plain hoeing your patch. So you can start out by helping the fellows clear sagebrush and cottonwoods out of the spot we've chosen for the camp meeting site. There are fire pillars to be made for lighting and circles to be marked off for the wagons and tents. We need timber for benches and fuel—Whoa, boy, don't eat so fast. You won't need to start before daybreak!"

The following day, as soon as Daniel sold the last bag of beans and closed up shop, he crossed the Platte and headed for the mouth of the canyon. Goode said the site for the camp meeting was close to Clear Creek. As his horse loped toward the mountains, he began to see the men at work.

By the time he reached the site, burning sagebrush filled the air with smoke. He slowed his horse, listening to the snapping and popping as the brush caught fire.

Daniel had just hobbled his horse in the grassy bottom when a man walked up to him. "Name's Antes," he said with a grin as he held out his hand. "I expect you're Daniel Gerrett. Goode said to expect you. Sounds like he's going to make a preacher outta you the hard way. Well, come give us a hand."

The sun had set when the men tossed potatoes into the hot ashes. Later Antes built up a fire for the bacon and coffee. After the bacon was forked onto the plates, the men settled by the fire.

Antes came to sit beside Daniel. "You've come forward at a good time. We're hard pressed for men to fill the posts. Come winter, it's nigh impossible to make the rounds to all the camps. It sure would help to have a few more men in the field."

The fellow beside him said, "There are new camps springing up all over the area." Daniel watched him take a mouthful before continuing. "When the snows start a man can't depend on keeping his schedule. Take me, I have six different places to preach. There's no way I can get around to them all when I can't fight a horse through the snowdrifts."

Within a week the site was ready for the meetings. The evening the final log benches were placed before the crude altar, Goode came bringing a visitor.

Swinging his hand he said, "This is John L. Dyer. Seems the Lord's sent us another preacher. All the way from Wisconsin, he's come."

Daniel went forward to greet the man. As he stuck out his hand, he realized the man slipping from his horse wasn't young. The fellow had a plain face and raspy voice, but as soon as Dyer began to speak, Daniel knew this was the kind of man he could follow around for the rest of his life.

Later Daniel had a chance to talk with him. When he confessed to being the rawest kind of a beginner, Dyer clapped him on the shoulder and led him aside. "Look here, young fella. I was on the sliding side of my prime when I answered the call.

"Oh, I'd been fighting with the Lord for a long time. Just knew I wasn't equipped to preach. That was back before I knew the Lord would pour out His own particular fire on a man when He wanted him to take to preaching."

He paused to chuckle. "Sounds like I'm saying once you get the fullness of God's blessing upon you, then everything's rosy. It's not, and I'm not giving you to believe that. Fact is, the first time I got up to give a sermon, I couldn't get one single word out. Had to sit down in disgrace.

"Never did get to give my beautiful sermon that day. But I kept at it. Next time it was a whole different story! Fella, you gotta have gumption along with a call. The Bible says to be as wise as serpents and as harmless as doves."

They looked up. The presiding elder was standing in front

of them, poking at the newspaper in his hand. "See here. The whole country is stewing about this war business. There's talk of South Carolina pulling out of the Union and taking as many states with her as she can."

He began pacing off a circle in the clearing. Over his shoulder he added, "Denver City is starting to rumble. There's troublemakers who'll not rest until they have their say. God help us to be firm to a man. War is ugly enough, but this stinks to heaven."

"There's the faction who thinks only of money, not human lives," murmured Antes.

"But listen," Goode shook his newspaper. "Stephen A. Douglas says here, 'Henceforth, until national authority is restored, let there be but two parties—patriots and traitors.' "

In the silence the man behind Daniel said, "I'm not sure who's the traitor."

Goode replied, "That's the whole point. Both North and South are labeling the other as traitor. Douglas' statement came out when he was in an uproar over having his secessionist friends labeled traitors."

Antes stated, "I take it you're not telling us how to *think*, but just to think. Is the scripture you're wanting us to remember the one Dyer quoted, Matthew 10:16—'wise as serpents, harmless as doves'?"

Goode was nodding. "It behooves a man to learn to search out every situation. The days are coming when lies are going to be cast as truth, and the truth will be given a dirty smear by everyone who opposes it."

"Meanwhile," another voice added soberly, "there's talk of rushing through this business of getting us made into a separate territory. I guess it's common knowledge around the country. There's fellows in Denver City pushing their own ideas."

The young fellow they called Tony grinned up from his prone position on the ground. "Seems, after being in a secure spot under the protection of the United States government, a man can't rest easy until he starts trying to draw those nice warm Washington arms around himself, no matter how unlikely the spot he calls home."

"You're calling this place unlikely?"

He shrugged. "If the gold peters out, the whole bunch will either take off for home or move into California."

"Tony's right," Goode said. "First autumn, back in '58, men started talking about sending a delegation to Washington for the purpose of gaining territorial status. At that time everything was looking rosy, with the prospect of everyone being a millionaire within a month. They weren't wanting to be a part of Kansas any longer." He paused. "Didn't have much success."

Tony added, "A bunch of horn tootin', that's all it was. Remember in '59 the Pikes Peak bunch decided to take things into their own hands? Territory wasn't good enough. State it had to be, they set up a constitution and called the new state Jefferson."

"I understand," Antes added, "Wootton's store in Auraria was the site of all this big legislation."

"Hey, that's where I work!" Daniel exclaimed. "I didn't know he was involved. Wasn't too successful, was it?"

"Naw," Tony replied. "By the time they'd flagged down Washington's attention most of the miners had decided the gold strike was a dud and streamed back home. Then we weren't looking too perky."

"Part of the problem with the Jefferson state business," Antes continued, "was the funding. All the proposals including officers, taxes, and improvements seemed fine on paper, but it turned out no one wanted to hand over the money to pay for it all. When the miners rose up in arms, refusing to fork over their dollar, the state idea collapsed."

Goode nodded. "Your talking this way reminds me. The paper had an article saying Washington's going to work on declaring territorial status for us. The name they're leaning to is Colorado."

"Where did they come up with that?"

"Heard it had something to do with the Spaniards; in their lingo it means all this red color in the rocks."

"Don't let it get you too upset," Antes remarked. "I saw a list of names they were trying on us. There's a whole string of them that stands a better chance of being selected, including Yampa and Idahoe."

Goode got to his feet, stretched and said, "Well, fellows, regardless, it's great to be in on the ground floor. A raw, wild place it is. Between the Indians, the miners and the others, the Methodist Episcopal Church has its work cut out for it, and we gotta give it all we can for at least the next decade.

"Welcome to God's country, fellas. Only thing, we need to get out there and reclaim it for Him." He was silent for a moment, and the light-hearted expression disappeared from his face. "There'll be those thinking we have an easy job. But if it's an easy job you want, go dig gold; drudge in the mud and snow, break your back in the mines. That's easier by far than wrestling the devil's territory from him. We must cling to the Bible and pray until our knees and voices fail."

CHAPTER 12

Sandwiched between Father and Aunt Maude, Amy swayed with the wagon and listened. Father's voice was a nice rumble as he looked beyond Aunt Clara to the new family. Jake Worthy and his wife, Hannah, had just moved to Central City. Eli addressed Mr. Worthy, "I appreciate your offer to give us a ride into Denver City in your wagon, but I'll be needing mine. There's business for me to handle in the Fort Lupton area. I regret having to miss some of the services."

"This is just fine." Jake nodded and waved at the road. "Understand this road through Clear Creek canyon has just opened."

"Yes, it's still a mite rough in spots," Eli added, "but it will make it easier to get into Denver City."

In a low voice, Aunt Maude complained, "Amy, your valise is bulging like you brought everything you own. I don't have room for my feet."

"I did bring all my clothes. It still gets cool in the evening. Besides, I don't have all that much to wear."

Mrs. Worthy tapped Aunt Maude on the shoulder. "Move it back here—there's room a-plenty."

When Amy turned to hand the valise back, she found Clara

Brown looking at her. "Aunt Clara, you're frowning like you have a headache."

"No, child, I was just searching out what I've been hearing." Amy waited; finally the woman sighed and said, "They're telling me you're thinking of marryin' the lawyer man, Mr. Tristram. That a fact?"

Aunt Maude leaned back, patting Aunt Clara's knee and whispering, "Well, they haven't announced it yet, but it's in the wind." She paused to beam at Amy before adding, "We're mighty proud." But Amy was caught by the expression on Aunt Clara's face. She was still frowning.

When the wagon left Clear Creek canyon, Amy touched her father's sleeve. There was awe in her voice as she said, "Look at the dust and line of wagons. Father, is that the camp meeting site by the line of trees?"

He nodded and Aunt Clara leaned forward, "Oh, bless the Lord! That's the grandest sight I've seen in a long time. We're plumb going to cover the land with the Gospel this week."

Midafternoon, long after they had eaten the lunch of cold meat and bread, they arrived at the campgrounds.

When their wagon fell in behind the others, Aunt Maude began to fan herself vigorously. "Look, Aunt Maude," Amy exclaimed, "we're nearly there. I can see through the dust. Already there's rows of wagons and tents. Father, there's a corral out here!" She pointed to a grassy meadow filled with horses and cows.

Mrs. Worthy added, "I can see the line of tents yonder, beyond the wagons. And there's the platform and benches. Split log. Hope they're dry. That sap'll ruin the meeting."

Amy looked at her and asked, "Ruin it? Why?"

"Can't have no altar service with people stuck to their seats." She poked Aunt Maude and pointed. "Many a camp meeting I've attended, but never before have I seen those things. Looks like giant ant hills."

"Fire towers," Aunt Maude explained, "See, they've stacked logs on top. Come nightfall, they torch 'em. Keeps away the mosquitoes and gives light for the meeting. Four of them, there is, one each corner."

Aunt Maude paused and then added, "Also, they keep down the sparking that'd go on in the dark. My, I'm glad I don't have to worry about you now." She patted Amy.

Mrs. Worthy was chuckling. "Maude, I know what you mean. Back home, the peddlers would come in thick as flies. And come camp meeting time, all the young men and girls were there to do their sparking." She dropped her voice. "Sometimes more'n that. Got to be such a good crop of young'uns they had to get pretty stern. No fellas and gals were allowed out after dark, and no walking in the trees, at all."

"Oh my, oh my!" Aunt Maude was shaking her head and fanning vigorously. "These young people."

A large tent was going up. Amy watched the people milling around like ants. She saw the billowing canvas slowly rise, sag, and straighten. Aunt Maude pointed. "There goes the cook tent and dining hall. It's starting to look like camp meeting."

It was evening before Amy carried her bedroll to the tent set aside for the unmarried girls. As she smoothed blankets over the mound of pine boughs, Amy recalled Aunt Maude's whispered conversation to Aunt Clara about Lucas. She muttered in irritation, "I wish she wouldn't talk. It would be nice to have a chance to answer for myself."

"I didn't ask a question." Amy turned toward the voice just as the bedroll was thumped down beside her own. The owner of the voice beamed out from under a scoop bonnet trimmed in blue silk flowers. The girl was saying, "I'm Belle Myers. We've just come here from Ohio, and I've been told you're the only respectable female my own age in the whole city."

"Well, I doubt that's true now," Amy said slowly. "I've been hearing about how Denver City's growing. Besides, I don't live here. I'm from Central City. These others"—she waved toward the piles of hastily discarded possessions—"I haven't become acquainted with them yet."

Belle eyed the luggage. Some of it was as shabby as Amy's valise. Thoughtfully she said, "From what Mother and I have seen, we're under the impression that it's terribly wild. Not camp meeting—Denver City. But then, I haven't been to camp meeting before."

Belle paused to clasp her arms in a shiver. "Denver City! Last week, out driving, our buggy went past a grove of trees. Right in front of us, there was a dead man! He was just swinging out there, no one else was around. Papa found out later that the man was a criminal. He'd cheated at cards and stolen money at gunpoint. I suppose that makes it all right, but I don't like seeing dead men like that."

She paused and studied Amy. "Matter of fact, there's not much I like out here. And there's nothing I want so much as to go home."

While Amy hunted for words, Belle's face cleared and she said, "I understand your father is a parson. Well, mine isn't. We've come out here so's Papa can investigate the gold mining business. I doubt we'll stay long. At least Mama doesn't like it any better than I do. It's a sad day when the most exciting thing to do is go to revival services.

"But Papa said it was the best way to get acquainted. We're staying at the Follett Hotel, and I'm afraid to step out of the room at night. My, the carryings on! I don't think there's been a night yet but that we've heard someone firing a gun." She shivered again, but Amy's interest had drifted to the frocks Belle was carefully hanging from the tent ropes.

"Your gowns are beautiful," Amy said wistfully as she mentally reversed her decision to hang her own clothing.

"We shop at the best stores back home. Mama says quality pays in the long run. There's not a single shop in Denver City with anything worth having. I can't imagine where the women go for clothing." Belle cocked her head to listen to the tinny blast of a horn. "That must be the dinner signal. At least we aren't expected to cook for ourselves.

"Mama has been telling me about old-time camp meetings. To say the least, I'm intrigued. Do you suppose they'll be having the jerks and such?"

Amy slowly shook her head. "Jerks? I've never heard of

that, so I don't think so." She was studying Belle's curious, excited expression and sparkling eyes. For a moment she felt as if she were stepping outside of herself, looking down at a new and strange spectacle called camp meeting. Seeing it through Belle's eyes made her nod. Camp meeting was a strange place to look for entertainment.

That first evening at camp meeting, Daniel Gerrett met the new man, Dyer, outside the dining tent. With Dyer were Adamson and Kenworth, two young missionaries.

When Daniel approached, the men were deep in conversation. Adamson was saying, "Father Dyer, are you expecting those fellows to ride out here for services?"

There was a note of disbelief in Adamson's voice. Recalling the incident, Daniel couldn't help grinning. "Do you by chance mean those miners at the Cherry Creek saloon?" Adamson nodded and Daniel said, "That was something. I'd never have dared light into those men the way you did, sir." He added hastily, "Not that they didn't need to be brought up short and be reminded of eternal things."

Kenworth chuckled as he said, "Had some effect, too. Tough hombres they were until John Dyer started talking. I got the impression you put your finger on a sore spot."

Dyer was scowling. "Not a matter of winning an argument or besting the crowd. Fellas, we're here to remind these men of their responsibilities. Back home these fellows have wives and mothers praying for them. I feel a responsibility to snatch up the wandering sheep before they're caught in a snare."

"Can't quite figure out what it is about the mining camps that sends a good fella running from all he's been taught," Adamson said slowly.

"I'll tell you," Dyer poked a finger in the middle of Adamson's chest. "They're following the crowd. Trying to be tough, just like the others, who are also trying to appear tough. Everything's different here. No family, no home. Only a miner's pick and the chance to be a millionaire tomorrow." His voice dropped to a brooding note, "More likely they have a chance of never seeing the light of another day. That's what we need to remind them of."

"Well—Daniel Gerrett!"

Daniel turned and saw Eli Randolph. "Sir!" he exclaimed. "I'm glad to see you." He tried to hold back his eagerness as he asked, "Did Amy come?"

Eli nodded, saying, "She's with her aunt. We'd never find them in this crowd, so I'll go with you."

The two fell into step together and Eli scrutinized Daniel. "Goode's been telling me the Lord's pressed a call on you to preach the Gospel. My, that's something. Also, they tell me you'll be working with the young parson out Fort Lupton way for a time. That's a rough circuit. I'm certain he'll appreciate the help." He grinned and clapped Daniel on the shoulder. "I'm mighty proud of you, son. I knew there was good stuff in you."

Daniel ducked his head and then asked, "How's Amy? I would sure like—" A frown jumped to Eli's face when Elder Kelly stepped between them and linked his arms through theirs.

It was nearly dark before everyone had been served. As he ate, Daniel tried to concentrate on the conversation while he searched the tables for Amy. The people began to leave the dining tent and move toward the lines of benches.

Daniel listened to the excited voices around him. Lost in the mass of people who seemed to be on the best of terms with everyone there, Daniel was sharply aware of his isolation. But the feeling lasted only briefly. The setting sun had already blanketed the benches with shadow, and that meant he had a task to do.

Daniel turned to squint toward the melon-tinted rays bathing the mountains in stripes of color. Then he studied the dense grove of cottonwoods lining Clear Creek. Waving toward the pillars of earth supporting the firewood, he said to Tony, "We'd better torch those woodpiles or we're going to be in the dark."

When he returned to his seat beside Eli, the evening speakers were taking their places on the wooden platform. Adamson jumped to the platform. Eli said, "Looks like he's privileged with the task of lining out the hymns. Hope he's using the familiar ones tonight. Nothing worse than dragging out new ones and stumbling over words nobody knows on the first night. Gets things off to a slow start." Daniel gave an absent-minded nod. He was still searching the crowd for Amy.

The hymns were familiar, and Daniel joined in with the others as he watched the crowds move in close. He spotted a flock of bright colors and slender figures and searched for Amy in the group as he sang:

Eternal Paraclete, descend,
Thou Gift and Promise of our Lord;
To every soul, till time shall end,
Thy succor and thyself afford.
Convince, convert us, and inspire;
Come and baptize the world with fire.

When the final hymn was finished, the last of the sky's color had disappeared. The area before the speaker's platform was lighted only by the blazing fire altars.

Far back in the shadows, Amy sat between Aunt Maude and Belle Myers. Belle's mother was on the far side of Aunt Maude and the two women were nodding, keeping time with the rhythm of the singing.

Down in front she could see Father. Then with a shock of glad surprise, she saw he was sitting with Daniel Gerrett. When the sermon began, Amy blanked out the words and concentrated on the two men, wondering why they were together and why they seemed to be nodding and smiling at the same time.

From the beginning, lost in her own thoughts, Amy was unaware of the speaker and the tide of unrest moving through the crowd. But later, when the congregation began to respond to the lifted hand, the familiar churning began in Amy's heart.

They were standing now. The hymns were whispered, hummed, and then sifted like burning coals over them all.

Late that night, when the tent was dark and quiet, Belle spoke. Her whispers were designed only for Amy's ears. "You've been to these meetings before; what does all this mean?"

"Mean?" Amy asked slowly, still focused on the churning she felt inside. "I suppose you're talking about the sermon."

"Back home," Belle continued, "we go to a different

church and there's not all this kind of talk. It's scary. I've heard sermons all my life, but not talk about hell and such. That man said we're all sinners deserving hell." Belle's whisper was rising in indignation. "That was bad enough, but talk about people having the smell of sulphur clinging to them and how the flames lick around them, lapping up their whiskey and fancy clothes, Amy, that's just terrible!"

"Does it seem so?" she asked in a faraway voice. "I've heard it all my life. I suppose now I only half listen to it." In a moment she added, "Doesn't seem terrible to me. I know it's in the Bible, but I don't know where. You get used to it."

"Then it doesn't frighten you?"

Amy caught her breath. "No, but that's because I'm sorta numb."

"Why?"

Amy tried to analyze her answer amid shadowy pictures and fearsome feelings. Amy shrugged, "I guess you can walk across a high bridge so many times that finally you forget how scary it really is."

Much later, when Amy was nearly asleep, Belle's sober voice came again. "Just the same, it was scary. Do you think God sends people to hell for things like, oh, say kissing a fellow?" Her words came in a rush. "See I wasn't suppose to be at this party. But I was, and—oh, this is all so silly. We don't believe this way. Church is dignified, not all this crying and feeling scary. Why were those people rushing down in front to pray? I can't believe God expects such actions."

Amy had been thinking of Belle's pretty frocks. She couldn't resist the urge to make her squirm. "I guess if you're around camp meeting very long, pretty soon you get the feeling you'd go through anything just to have an easy heart about yourself and God. That's why they run down front. Either that, or you'll stay away from the place. But that doesn't settle the problem of hell."

Again, after a long time, Belle's voice came in a whisper, "Amy, are you saved?" And then, "Amy, are you asleep?"

CHAPTER 13

On the second day of camp meeting, just after the morning service Eli found Amy. "Daughter, I'm leaving now. I'll be back by tomorrow evening." He squeezed her hand.

Leaning back to look into his face, Amy saw the familiar sad expression in his eyes. Again, as so many times in the past, she found herself wondering what lay behind the dark shadows.

For one lonely moment she put her face against his coat sleeve. His arm was unyielding. Amy pressed her lips together to keep from begging to go with him. How could she explain the churning need to be gone from here?

"Goodbye, Father."

"Mind your aunty."

She nodded, then asked, "Does this trip mean we'll be moving again?"

"No. The bishop has expansion plans in mind, and I'm being sent to spy out the land—like Joshua." He was smiling as he turned away.

Amy spent the afternoon strolling through the trees and along the bank of Clear Creek with Belle and the other girls from their tent. When they sat down under the willows, Belle resumed her prying questions. "Do you believe it is wrong to let a fellow kiss you? All this talk about sin and stuff. Why, I know a girl back home who—" She tilted her saucy face toward Amy and said, "You tell us. Your Aunt Maude said you're engaged. What is he like? A Prince Charming, tall and handsome, strong and brave?"

Amy didn't answer, but it wasn't necessary. The conversation moved on without her. Listening to the chatter and trying to smile, her thoughts drifted to the last time she had seen Lucas. While the laughter circled around her, she bent to pick the tiny blossoms growing in the grass.

At dinner, the conversation of the older women became a gentle hum in her ears, while Amy found herself thinking of the afternoon. Her lips twisted in a mocking smile. What a contrast—innocent girlish laughter, and Lucas.

Amy shifted the uninteresting pile of food on her plate, wishing the images would disappear from her mind, especially the one of Lucas coming out of the shack with that woman beside him. *I am seriously considering marrying him! Forgive— that is Christian.* But there was another image: Amy dressed in silk with hands poised over the grand piano, applause, people jumping to their feet, cheering.

Amy caught her breath and looked around. Aunt Maude was talking. Her words pounded into Amy and she began to dread the evening service. Fluttering her hand, Maude exclaimed, "Oh, those were the good old days—but it will happen again! I tell you, no one can stand before the power of the Lord. It's no secret we've spent all afternoon praying the Lord would visit us in the same old-fashioned way.

"You girls should have been there!" She pointed toward Amy and Belle. "These young ladies have no idea what it was like. People falling under the power of the Spirit, right and left. I've seen old drunkards crawling in on hands and knees, and they stayed that way until the glory came down."

Belle was watching Amy and her eyes were widening. Hastily Amy rose, saying, "Aunt Maude, I believe I'll go lie down. My head is starting to throb terribly. If I feel better I'll join you later. Do you want to save a seat for me?"

Aunt Maude's hand dropped. "Headache? Amy, you'll be just as well off right with me. You know what they said last night. There's to be no missing meetings or moving off in the trees. Those are rules, and they are made to keep things moral around here." Amy felt as if those eyes were seeing clear through her and Aunt Maude added, "Not that I don't trust an engaged girl, but still, you'll have to sacrifice for the good of the others."

Belle's eyes brightened. "Amy, you never did tell us what it's like to be engaged!" Dismayed, Amy looked up at the circle of eyes studying her. She glanced at the firm line of Aunt Maude's lips. It simply was a waste of time to fuss when Aunt Maude put her foot down. She shrugged.

Daniel had begun looking for Amy before dinner, but it was late, nearly the close of service, when he saw her.

The moon was high in the sky and the fires on the earthen pillars had burned to bright embers. The last altar call had been given and the last hymn sung. Daniel joined the elders moving among the people kneeling at the mourner's bench.

At the first shout he looked up. "Glory! Lord, lay 'em out like you've done in the past. Glory!" When the woman turned, he saw her uplifted face. It was Amy's Aunt Maude. Immediately behind her he saw Amy's bright hair.

At Aunt Maude's second shout, he watched Amy slip from her seat and flee through the night, into the line of cottonwoods. Daniel jumped to his feet and followed.

Amy plunged through the trees, unthinking, wanting only to escape. When she stubbed her toe and flew headlong into the grassy bank, she lay there, too exhausted to rise.

The picture of the woman at the altar again flashed across her mind, and she trembled. "God," she cried, "why are you doing this to me? What have I done to deserve this? I said I would forgive him!"

Then the words died on her lips, and she gasped. It wasn't the old nightmare. That wasn't Mother lying beside the wooden bench. In horror she cried, "That's me! Why did I see me like that?"

Amy flung herself against the ground, trying to escape.

The tears came, wrenching her, tearing every inch of her mind and heart. The good and bad of herself mixed together until it was impossible to know anything except the awful finger of God pointing to the ugliness.

Finally she rolled over in the grass and faced the pale sky. She screamed her defiance, "Then you do it! I can't. Rescue me if you care."

She trembled herself into a ball, shivering against the damp soil, conscious only of mud and grass. Part of the earth. *Mother is part of the earth. And I will be too. I have screamed at God.*

"Amy!" She covered her ears, but the voice was insistent. "Amy, I know you are there. Answer me!"

It took him a long time to search through the dense grove of trees along the creek, but the strange fear in his heart kept him going. Finally he heard her crying. He plunged through the bushes, crying, "Amy!"

She jumped and turned to run. He called, "It's Daniel. Wait! I must see you."

"Oh, Daniel! I am glad you are here!" She rubbed the tears out of her eyes and reached for him.

Clasping her hands, he drew her out into the full light of the moon. "Oh, how good it is to see you again! I've missed you so much. Let me look at you. You've been crying!" He hesitated, watching her shrink away. He gulped and carefully said, "I met your father yesterday and since then I've been trying to find you. Tell me all about yourself. You're crying—why?"

She was shaking her head, trying to deny the tears; then abruptly she sank down on the ground. Huddled with her back against a cottonwood, she gulped and scrubbed at her face. "I'm sorry. It's just the way these services affect me." He knelt beside her and waited.

Amy caught her breath and looked at Daniel. Even by the dim light of the moon his brown eyes were familiar and tender. They nearly pushed away Lucas's laughing, mocking eyes. Lucas, the piano, and the silk dress.

He doesn't know about Lucas. He couldn't, acting like this. For a moment he hugged me, like a beau. The old sore spot in her heart disappeared. Maybe he had forgotten her shameless hug on that terrible day. She realized she wasn't listening to Daniel, yet the soothing murmur of his voice reached her.

As she looked up at him, she found herself desperately wishing she could tell him everything—all the frightening things that didn't seem to fit words. The impulse had her hand reaching, the words nearly there.

"Amy?" Those honest brown eyes were close. For a moment she closed her eyes. *To let him know would be to lose a friend forever.* She dropped her hand in her lap and her heart sank. His hand was warm on her shoulder. "If there's something you need to pray about—"

Never, never, never. She looked up at him. "It's just that this brings back terrible memories. We were at camp meeting when Mother died."

"I had forgotten that," he said slowly. Shoving a log against the tree, he said, "Come sit here with me. I'd like you to tell me about it, if you don't mind. Sometimes it helps to talk." Unexpectedly he grinned, "Besides, now that I've found you, I want to hang on to you."

She sat down, gulped and tried to hide the fears that sent her fleeing. Taking a deep breath, she said brightly, "Honest, Daniel, there's not much to recall. I remember only the next day. Everyone looked terrible and Aunt Maude kept crying. Father was sick and he couldn't talk. See, that's about all I remember. They still don't talk about it. I've tried to bring it up, but it's so bad that then Father won't look at me for days."

"You say it happened a long time ago?"

"Yes." She sighed and rubbed her face. "I was just four when she died."

"And you were at camp meeting." He reached for her hand and Amy was grateful for the darkness. She hesitated a moment and then snuggled her hand into his. He asked, "What caused her death?"

"I don't know. I was never told. We were living in Missouri. Shortly after that we moved. I don't remember my mother's kin," she finished sadly.

For a time they sat in silence. Reluctantly he spoke again, "Amy, there's something else, isn't there? It just doesn't seem—"

She was shaking her head, "Daniel, there's nothing, honest."

He added, "I was angry and scared after my pa died."

"Why scared?"

He took a deep breath. "Well, I suppose it's silly, but I'd never thought about death in this way before. When my mother died I was younger. We were lonely and not knowing what to do. But this was different, I guess because I'm grown now. I started thinking about God. Mostly how foolish it was to try to run my life without Him.

"Amy, after I left Central City, the Lord got hold of me. I guess what I mean is, I really started listening to Him." He was quiet; finally he added, "Somehow I expected life to go the way I planned. I never realized it could be shut down as quickly as it happened to Pa."

Suddenly she understood his direction. Abruptly she said, "Well, if you think I'm worried about dying, I—"

"Amy!" They both heard Aunt Maude at the same time. Jumping to their feet, they watched the figures crashing through the underbrush toward them. Aunt Maude had the presiding elder with her.

Amy heard Daniel groan as he said, "Brother Goode!"

Aunt Maude's voice cut through, rising hysterically. "Belle had to be the one to tell me! She says 'Amy's gone!' This is what you were planning all along! Headache? Oh, what will Eli think; what will Lucas think?" She was crying, lifting a beseeching hand to Elder Goode. "Bad blood. I trusted her. That fellow, it isn't the first time he's—"

Amy looked at the man facing Daniel and she pushed herself between the two. "Please, don't blame Daniel. I ran away and he was trying to help me. I didn't think. I knew the rule—"

"Her father will never live through this," Aunt Maude said sadly.

"Father!" Amy's voice broke. The immediate horror became coupled with that long-ago time. She imagined his stricken face. She winced, said softly, "I love my father; never would I disgrace him, make him suffer again, like—"

"How can we make it right?" Daniel was asking in a despairing voice.

Aunt Maude whirled. "This mustn't touch him. I won't have my brother hurt. Not again. This must be hushed." Her fingers were picking at the elder's sleeve. "Please, sir, I can't believe this ugliness. Make it right. For the sake of us all, will you marry them right now? This evening."

"Marry!" Amy gasped. "Aunt Maude! This is non—" The word died on Amy's lips. *Nonsense?* She saw an image of Lucas, the secret dream. She trembled. *I prayed, I shouted at God; could this be the answer?* Abruptly the heaviness slid off her heart.

Daniel paced the clearing. "Look, we've broken a rule. But you're implying we've been— I think too much of Amy to even let you hint this."

The presiding elder answered slowly, thoughtfuly. "For the sake of Daniel's future that would best quiet things down. However, this must be their choice." He added, "They're not the first young couple to be caught."

Elder Goode and Daniel were standing face-to-face and Amy heard Daniel's gasp. Quickly he turned to Amy. "You know I would never force such a situation on you."

"Disgraced forever!" Aunt Maude exclaimed. "I knew he would come to no good end. I'm not surprised he's refusing to make an honest woman out of her. It'll kill her father."

"I didn't say I didn't *want* to marry Amy. It's just that you aren't giving me a chance. I don't want a bride who's been forced to marry me. I—"

Amy closed her eyes briefly and then looked at Daniel before she turned to her aunt. "Aunt Maude," she pointed to Elder Goode, "he says it will be best. For Father's sake, too." She gave Daniel a quick glance. "You aren't forcing me. Yes, Daniel, I'll marry you."

The moment the words were out, Amy wanted to pull them back. Daniel was looking at her as if she had hit him with a log. *I backed him into the corner,* Amy thought. *He's a gentleman; what did I expect? He no more wanted to marry me than anything.*

"Come along." He avoided her eyes as they walked back into the silent campground. She could see the empty benches, the feeble glow of the fires, even that peeled-log mourner's bench. Aunt Clara Brown called it an anxious seat.

Feeling as if she were caught in a strange dream, Amy followed Elder Goode as he led the way to his tent. When he took Daniel aside, Amy could see their troubled faces illuminated by the candle beside the black, bound Bible.

There was a question she couldn't hear, but she saw the exchange of words brought relief to both faces. Moving slowly they took their places. Looking up at Daniel, Amy thought, *It's like the words are wrapping us in cotton. We're even separated away from Aunt Maude.* The thought made her straighten her shoulders.

When Brother Goode carried his Bible forward and began to carefully record their names on the paper he held, she was surprised to see a faint half-smile on his face.

Then came the unbelievable words. "Daniel Gerrett, do you take this woman to be your lawfully wedded wife? In the sight of God, do you covenant to love and cling to her only as long as you both shall live? Amy Amelia Randolph, do you—"

And now Amy was surprised by the flash of a smile on Daniel's face as he took her hand.

She was still studying that smile when Elder Goode said, "I advise you, since there are no honeymoon cottages around, be off now, before daybreak."

Amy had only begun to recover from the shock when Aunt Maude pressed the valise and the bedroll into her hands. Also, Amy saw that Aunt Maude carefully avoided looking at the two of them.

Elder Goode said, "I needed to get this horse back to Denver City. You'll do me a favor if you take it in. Daniel, I want to see you next week. Come to the house."

The moon had crossed the sky by the time Amy and Daniel left the tent. When they had led the horses beyond the camp, Amy gave a deep sigh of relief.

"Why the sigh?" Daniel asked. He was tying the bedroll behind the elder's saddle. Amy shrugged in answer to the question, grateful the darkness hid her face. She was pondering the sigh herself when Daniel said, "I hope you can stick on this horse."

"I'll manage. Back home I rode bareback when just the cousins were around."

"How little I know about you!" he murmured. Placing his hands on her waist, he lifted her into the saddle.

Silent now, they rode the horses away from the creek, heading for the arid plains and the distant huddle of dark shapes marking Denver City and Auraria. Amy was full of questions. She looked at the dark shape of her silent bridegroom and her heart cried, *Daniel, do you regret this? What happens now?*

They had nearly reached the Platte River when Daniel pulled even with Amy's horse. "It'll be daylight before we get to the Goode's cabin. I think we need to do some talking first."

His voice cut through her bemused state. She tried to fight off fatigue as she straightened in the saddle. She couldn't see Daniel's face, but his voice was melancholy. Suddenly the whole, strange night became real and she felt her heart thudding into her stomach.

Daniel slipped off his horse and dropped his saddle on the ground. He spread a blanket for her and went to water the horses.

When he came back, the dream-like quality of the evening had disappeared completely and she murmured, "Oh, Daniel, what do we do now?" For just a moment he hesitated. When he sat down beside her, she said, "I really messed things up, didn't I? How could I ever let Aunt Maude make me think like that? We'd done nothing wrong. What ever possessed me? What will Father say?"

"Well, probably less than he would if I'd just taken off. Let's face it. We were breaking rules. I honestly didn't even think of them," he muttered. "Gettin' so high and mighty with my position, I forgot everybody sees me as just another young'un."

He doesn't sound the least bit happy. Amy remained silent as the sky slowly lightened. Now with the passing of night, with the hard facts before them, it all seemed impossible.

Daniel raised his head. With a grin he said, "Hey, don't look like that! It isn't the end of the world—or is it?" Then his grin faded. "Well, I guess it isn't the best way to start a marriage. You said your father has gone to Fort Lupton. I suggest we head that way first thing tomorrow." His voice was very dry. "Might be to our advantage to have a talk with him before Aunt Maude does."

Amy winced. "I don't think that will help much. She's—"

"Amy," he began, then hastily added, "Oh, never mind. Let's go into town and then decide how we're going to handle getting to Fort Lupton tomorrow."

"I am so tired," she murmured. "Daniel, it's the first time in my life that I've stayed awake all night."

"Same here. Let's nap for a few minutes."

When Amy awakened, Daniel had gone after the horses and had them saddled. "Sleepy head," he murmured, "it's getting near noon, and we need to find something to eat. Let's take this horse home first."

When they reached the Goode's cabin, they saw a wagon by the door and several horses tethered to the tree in the front yard.

Amy waited until Daniel took the saddle off the horse and turned it into the pasture close to the house. While they stood by the barn, Amy heard a voice behind her. "All right, you two, don't you go sneaking off to the barn."

Amy turned as Daniel said, "Mrs. Goode, this is—"

"I know all about her." With hands on hips, the woman beamed down at them. "The Adriances have just come from meeting this morning. The whole place is buzzing. Supposed to be pretty romantic, getting married at midnight, huh? If it were anyone but my husband tying the knot, I'd be questioning his judgment."

She stood aside. "Now just come in here and have some dinner. There's no cake to celebrate, and it's as crowded as can be, but come along."

The table had just been spread when there was a pounding on the door. Mrs. Goode went after more plates while Mrs. Adriance opened the door to another couple. The woman, April Taylor, ducked her head shyly, even as her eyes sparkled at Amy. "We've had to leave meeting early. James is feeling poorly and this is his week to ride into Sunset for meeting."

"Will you make it by Sunday?" Daniel asked in surprise.

James was shaking his head. "The distance between the camps is too much. I just hold meetings any day of the week and any time of the day. Got into Gold Hill at breakfast time once. The fellows had just shouldered their picks, but they dropped them at once.

"There's a bad stretch through there. Nearly every time I go that route, I find a couple of Indians lurking around. They've done me no harm, but I prefer to meet them in the daytime."

Amy led April to the table. The young woman's dress strained over her pregnancy, but her thin cheeks and shadowed eyes were saying discomforting things to Amy.

She asked, "What do you do while he's gone so much?"

With a wan smile, April replied, "Feed the cow and hope and pray he makes it home alive, with a few dollars to buy more flour."

"It's not easy being the wife of a parson, is it?" Amy asked. She thought of her own mother as she finished. "It's bad anywhere, but the mountains in winter!" Amy shuddered.

April straightened. Two red spots brightened her cheeks. "I'm not complaining; it's his calling. An honor it is, to be a man of God."

There was an awkward pause and Amy hastily said, "I know. My father is parson at Central City. But the life would never be of my choosing."

Daniel coughed and moved uneasily on his stool. "Amy, a person's got to be open to the leading of the Lord."

Mr. Adriance placed his fork on the table and leaned forward to study Amy. Turning to Daniel he said, "Brother, I hope you haven't been too hasty."

CHAPTER 14

After the dishes were washed, Mrs. Goode carried a candle to the table. Stepping over the men's feet, she apologized. "Night's fallen. This is poor shelter for a houseful. I've nothing except a patch of floor for you to spread out your blankets."

" 'Tis enough," Adriance spoke for them all. "We've had a good meal and space to stretch our legs; what more could we ask?"

Daniel added, "We fellows will carry our blankets to the barn. I've been doing it for quite some time myself."

When he carried Amy's bedroll into the cabin, he met her solemn eyes and tried to smile. Nearly a whole day they had been married. *How little I know about this child wife! That's enough to scare a man. Matter of fact, what does she know of me?*

In the barn Adriance was sitting on his blankets. He pointed to the mound of straw beside him. "Saved for you."

Taylor was asleep when Daniel stretched out on his blankets. Adriance said, "I didn't know you were planning on getting married."

"We weren't," Daniel said tersely, miserable with his need for silence. Adriance waited, his eyes dark spots in the paleness of his face. Daniel added, "I guess I don't really want to talk about it."

"That's all right. Your gal's remark kinda gave me a start. Had the idea you two hadn't discussed things."

Daniel surrendered with a sigh. "Marriage was one of them. Last night after the altar call, Amy took off like she was being chased. I went right after her. Didn't use my head. Big hero. I was thinking about seeing her and helping. Since Central City days I've got this feeling she's struggling."

"Spiritually?"

He nodded.

Adriance mused, "Marriage, huh? For a preacher, marrying in haste and repenting at leisure isn't the way it's done."

Daniel chewed at the corner of his mouth and Adriance waited. Moonlight marked bars of light on the straw. The gentle breathing of Taylor and Adriance's watchful eyes brought Daniel up. "Since I first met her. She's—Do you think God works in things like this? I mean, somehow I just felt like this was the Lord's planning for us. Not getting married like this. But us together."

Daniel searched for words to explain. "Aunt Maude and Brother Goode came looking for us. That made a mess of everything. Aunt Maude lit on marryin' as a solution to our problem, and I guess I acted foolishly. Amy looked miserable. I had this idea I would be rescuing her from that woman."

Adriance chuckled, "And that's the only reason you married her?"

"No. I love her!"

"And like a young'un around molasses candy, you snatched."

"Sounds pretty bad. I didn't think it all through. I snatched, thinking I'd never get another chance. I hadn't as much as heard a word from her for nearly a year."

Finally Adriance spoke again. "Seems she doesn't know about your call to preach. I get the idea she's not much interested in being a preacher's wife. What you going to do about that?"

"I don't know. I thought a preacher's daughter was about the ideal choice for a wife."

"You know God's called you to preach the Gospel in the territory," Adriance said slowly. "Also you know marriage isn't to be taken lightly. You've pledged yourself to her. You say you think God is guiding; do you have the ability to trust Him to work it all out?"

"I'm not certain I understand."

"Two things you've pledged. To preach, and to be Amy Randolph's husband. Can you hang on to both and ride out the storm?"

"Storm?"

"You didn't think it would be easy, did you? I've lived with a woman long enough to know they have a mind to get their own way, especially when it seems right to them. Might be you'll even have to compromise some of your special dreams."

"I can't compromise where God is concerned."

"Just be sensitive to His voice. Daniel, I'll pray for you. I've been caught by you since we first met. I think God has His hand on you. Only time will tell whether this is all part of His plan. I hope it is."

"Did you know about Dyer's marriage?"

Adriance nodded. "I respect the man for doing what was right, also for being brave enough to face his shame. But then his wife was devious from the beginning. Amy's young, and if she loves you, she'll follow along until the Lord makes your calling her joy."

Daniel turned to sleep. *Love:* the word echoed through his head and he trembled at what he had done. It was a mighty big word. *Where did I get the crazy idea that Amy loves me?*

April shared the bed with Mrs. Goode, and Amy unrolled her blankets beside Mrs. Adriance. The woman settled herself to sleep, saying, "I hope my husband didn't upset you. It takes a while to settle into life together. To solve all the differences and learn the give and take of marriage.

"I also know"—her smile was arched—"young couples don't spend much time discussing the practical parts of living in the beginning. It was a quick marriage, but that's sometimes the way it must be out here. Folks don't get to visit around much. Not much time for courting."

Mrs. Adriance turned over and Amy studied her back. Mrs. Adriance was referring to her remark. It had raised all their eyebrows and turned heads toward Daniel. *Do these people know something I don't know? These preachers think every young man must become a preacher of the Gospel. I've got different thoughts on the matter.*

Amy yawned as Mrs. Adriance said, "If you can talk him out of preaching the Gospel, then I suppose his calling was just a summer itch."

"Calling?" Amy's heart sank.

In the morning, Mrs. Goode pressed them to take the horse. "Now, Daniel, you know yourself Brother Goode would have urged it on you. You'll be seeing him next week; besides, the mare needs the exercise."

The morning was still dewy fresh when Amy and Daniel started for the fort. Both were silent as they left Denver City, Amy wondering how her father would react to their news.

At noon they stopped beside the Platte River. Eyeing the dark line of the fort against the horizon, Daniel said, "Let's eat lunch. We need to do some talking."

Gratefully Amy dismounted. Daniel led the horses to water. While he hobbled them in the grass, Amy chewed her lip and thought about Mrs. Adriance's statement. *Call. Daniel a preacher!* She shook her head in dismay.

Daniel brought up the subject as they ate. He swallowed the last of his sandwich, saying, "Amy, I just didn't get around to telling you all that has been happening. I was headed that way night before last, when, well everything else—" Finally, with a sigh, he said, "See, I've known for some time now that the Lord wants me to be a preacher."

Amy crumbled her bread. She was sharply aware of the miserable lump in her throat. She recalled the shabby frock strained over April Taylor's pregnancy. *Without a doubt, I'm going to talk Daniel out of that summer itch, no matter what it takes!*

She heard Daniel saying, "I didn't mean to deceive you or anything. I know being a preacher's wife is mighty hard if your heart isn't in it. I'm not just guessing that, am I? But Amy, we're in this together now. I know the Lord can change how you feel."

"Daniel, it's impossible!" Amy cried. "Besides, you've no idea what you're getting into. I do. All my life I've lived with it. I've gone to bed hungry; I've seen my father, tired and cold, turn right around and go out when a knock came on the door. I've seen him preaching when the opposition was bigger than the offering. I've—"

She saw his steady brown eyes. *Of course, reason won't work; he's just like Father.* As she turned away she brought up that other subject. "What are you going to tell my father?" He winced.

Amy recalled the horrified eyes of Aunt Maude and that strange expression on the presiding elder's face. "Daniel," she whispered, "they think the very worst of us. How can you even consider being a preacher? There'll be those stories going around."

"I guess the best way is to just ignore it all."

She sighed. "What is it?" he asked. Amy looked up. Not for anything would she admit the plan she had. Just thinking the thoughts made her face warm. *Thanks to the piano lessons, there's hope. I learned lots at the boardinghouse. Those girls knew how to get what they wanted. I noticed they had all the men flocking after them. The gifts, the adoring looks of the men.* Amy shifted uneasily. Somehow the idea of using the tactics of the dance-hall girls left a bitter taste in her mouth.

Daniel sighed and glanced up. His voice was subdued. "One thing is certain. We're married, and that's that. We'll just have to make the best of our hasty decision. And another thing is certain. I'm going to preach the Gospel."

The unqualified determination in his voice stunned Amy. Before she could think she cried, "You're saying talk is useless. We're married; don't you care what I think?"

Ashamed of her outburst, she picked at the lint on her dress, nearly threadbare across the cuffs. The sun had faded the blue into a dismal gray.

What a contrast to the frocks Belle had hung on the tent rope! One by one, she had put them out so that Amy could appreciate each of the brightly colored garments, decked with ribbon and lace. The old dream surfaced. Lucas. Amy winced. *Just two nights ago I ran away from him. Surely God—*

Amy slanted a glance at Daniel. He still had his back against the tree while the leaves sprinkled shadows and coolness over them. His face was thoughtful and sad. She watched him fold his arms across his chest. His shoulder muscles bunched against his shirt, straining it tight. Unexpectedly she found herself wanting to touch that shoulder. She examined the emotion in astonishment.

He was watching her. She caught her breath, wondering. Abruptly she scooted closer and leaned toward him. "Do you remember the time I tried to get you to kiss me?"

He grinned. "I'm not afraid of Aunt Maude now." Their eyes met and his grin disappeared. "Amy, is it possible—"

Slowly he leaned forward. She saw the expression in his eyes. Carefully she placed her hands on his arms, feeling the wonder of his warmth, the muscles hard under her hands. She caught her breath, suddenly shy as he smiled at her. *But I can't act shy if I'm going to be like the girls.*

Amy wrapped her arms around his neck and smiled. She lifted her face, felt his lips against hers, but couldn't understand those words he murmured against her hair.

His arms were insistent. She pushed away. "Daniel, we're going to miss Father if we linger much longer."

He reluctantly released her and stood up. As he walked toward the horses, Amy smiled again, "Seems," she whispered, "this being married is much more pleasant than I suspected."

By the time they were back on the trail to Fort Lupton, Amy had in her mind the firm, clear picture of how it would be. *Most certainly not Kansas Territory. Maybe Indiana, Illinois, or even Ohio, but not this terrible place.* Being the wife of the pastor in one of those places wouldn't be so bad.

The Platte was running smooth and shallow. Just across the river they could see Fort Lupton.

When Amy's horse ran up the sloping bank, Daniel smiled and pointed. "Look at that fort. It's adobe—mud brick. I hear it was built by an Indian trader in 1836. It won't hold all the settlers now. See." He pointed toward the line of new cabins between the fort and the river.

"Let's go into the fort. If your father isn't there, they'll point us in the right direction."

Amy shook her head. "See that wagon? I'm certain it's ours. Let's go there."

Eli Randolph stepped out of the cabin just as they rode up. Shading his eyes against the sun, he exclaimed, "Amy!" He looked from Amy to Daniel. She saw the puzzled frown on his face as he came toward them.

Daniel slipped off the horse. "Sir, I'm guessing there's folks in there," he jerked his head toward the cabin. "Could you walk apart with us? I need to tell you what has happened."

Eli's face slowly paled. "Father!" Amy exclaimed, "it's not bad news. Please!" She slipped from the horse and ran to him.

Eli turned to Daniel. "There's no one here; come in." He waited until Daniel tethered the horses before leading the way. For a moment Amy watched his weary stride; then she noticed that Daniel's face was nearly as white as Eli's.

Like wax figures we all are. In a museum, Amy added to herself, as she watched the men slump over the crude table and face each other. *They act as if I don't exist.*

When Daniel was through explaining it all, she heard him insist once again, "Sir, it was our decision. Done honorably, but in a hurry without your permission because it seemed difficult to go against Aunt Maude without causing—problems. I promise you, I'll do my best to make your daughter happy."

Father's face was getting its color back. Amy saw the lines ease and then he smiled. Reaching across the table he clasped Daniel's hand. "Son, for a moment I thought I'd had another burden too big to carry. Welcome to the family. You've made me happy." There was one quick, silent glance at Amy before he said, "I could wish for nothing better."

Burden? *What does that mean?* she wondered. *And what*

about Lucas? Has Father forgotten? She watched the two men smiling at each other. Forgotten or not, obviously Lucas was no longer important to Father.

Amy heaved a shaky sigh of relief and went to prepare the evening meal. As she worked, she dreamed over the picture of a white-frame cottage, with wallpaper and a Brussels carpet on the floor of the parlor.

While waiting for the potatoes to cook, she looked around. The poor surroundings didn't touch her; inside she was secretly exalting in the contrasts. The new dream was bright. *Not for long, this place.*

Then she caught herself and sighed. In this terrible cabin there wasn't even a sheet metal stove such as they had in Central City. A blackened adobe fireplace yawned across one wall, serving both for cooking and heating.

On the opposite wall a crude, narrow bunk was built into the logs. Pegs pounded between logs supported a line of greasy clothing, while a bench held a pail of water and a battered basin for washing.

As she went about preparing the evening meal, she heard the clink of harness and the creak of wheels. Eli got to his feet. "Better throw in some more potatoes. Morgan is coming. This is his cabin."

He opened the door and said, "Morgan, we've got company. Come meet my daughter and her husband."

Later, while Daniel was spreading their blankets on the floor, Morgan chuckled and said, "One more bunch tonight and we'll have to stand upright to sleep."

"I'll be leaving early in the morning," Eli said to his host as he stretched himself out beside Daniel. "I've got to take a swing south before going back to Denver City. I don't know what these two will be doing."

Morgan turned over in the bunk, making the poles creak and groan against the walls of the cabin. "Far as I am concerned, they can stay here for the rest of the summer. I'm heading for the high country tomorrow. Might be Daniel can get a job helping the farmers hereabouts. It's getting about time to haul a load of hay into Denver City."

Eli rumbled, "Sure didn't take long for the men around here to realize there's more to be gained from growing feed than digging for gold."

Silence fell on the cabin, but Amy lay wide-eyed, wondering what the morning would hold. Recalling the stubborn set of Daniel's jaw, Amy nearly lost her courage. It might take more than kisses to get Daniel headed east.

In the morning, just before Father snapped the reins over the backs of his team, he thawed. There was a hint of a smile on his face as he looked down at Amy. "Daughter, I think you've done yourself well. Maybe best."

After Morgan told them about the men apt to be hiring and pointed out the best place to buy milk and eggs, he picked up his rifle and mounted his horse.

Together Amy and Daniel walked slowly back to the cabin. Because Amy couldn't think of anything else to say, she asked, "What are we going to do with those smelly old clothes hanging on the wall?" She wrinkled her nose and led the way inside.

Daniel closed the door. With a shrug, he said, "We won't stay in this cabin long. I didn't get to tell you this yesterday. The presiding elder is assigning me to one of the fellows."

"What does that mean?" Amy asked slowly.

"That I have a job. We'll be staying here and I'll be riding circuit. I'll be called an exhorter until I learn my job. Next summer, if my work is approved, I'll be appointed my own circuit. Amy, I'm just guessing this. But after watching the way the gold camps are settling right and left, I expect we'll be sent off up into the mountains for a couple of years."

"Mountains? I would hate that!" she said passionately. "Daniel, I'm your wife. Please listen to me."

"Well, of course," he said slowly with a puzzled frown. "I'll do everything within my power to make you happy. But Amy, I can't choose where we'll live. Surely you won't want me to give up my calling."

"No, of course not," she said breathlessly. She hesitated, then walked around the table and faced him. "Circuit—does that mean you'll be gone much of the time, like April's husband?

That you'll leave me in a mining camp with those rough miners? I've heard tales."

"You know they'll treat you with respect. Furthermore, they'll be looking out for your welfare."

She shivered. "I suppose it wouldn't be unbearable—but that first year!" She placed her hand on his shoulder. "Please, Daniel, I would be so lonesome."

"What do you have in mind?" he asked cautiously.

"There's plenty of churches in Illinois, Ohio—even Indiana. Please—any place but here!"

He was studying her face, and she was glad she'd pushed curls down around her ears this morning. She made a pout of her lips just as the dance-hall girls did. His glance slid off somewhere around her ear and she pressed close to him.

"Amy." His voice was muffled. "I won't let you try these games on me. Right now you remind me of the—the girls in Central City."

As Amy retreated across the room, there was a knock on the door. She saw the relief on Daniel's face as he went to open it.

"Daniel Gerrett?" The fellow came into the room. "I was just ready to ride out when I heard you were here. Didn't get a chance to talk with you at meeting, but Goode has asked me to take you on my circuit. I'm leaving right now and thought this would be as good a time as any to get acquainted with you and show you the territory."

He paused, embarrassed, "Guess I should introduce myself. I'm Silas Jeffry. Wife and I live in the fort. It's cheap living and a little more secure for her while I'm gone." He nodded at Amy. "We ought to start before nightfall; it's a ways to our first stop. We ride the trails straight west from here. Doesn't sound like much, but there's close to a hundred settlers scattered across the plains. Not what you'd call a regular town, but anywhere I go, I'm finding the people willing to drop what they are doing and come listen to a preacher. Dan, they're hungry people out there, hungry to hear the Gospel."

Amy was watching the change on Daniel's face. His shoulders straightened. By the time the fellow finished, Daniel was grinning with delight.

The stranger turned to Amy. "Begging your pardon. Ma'am, I'd heard you were new wedded, but—"

"She understands," Daniel interrupted. "I'll gather my things together and meet you at the fort in a couple of minutes."

"Daniel!" she cried as the door closed, "just like that, you'll ride out of here and leave me alone?"

He dropped his Bible on the table and came to her. "Oh, Amy," he groaned, "don't make it harder than it is. I don't want to leave you. But after that scene at camp meeting, for both our sakes, I'd better toe the line. We'll be back within a week. There's plenty of food."

He tried to smile. "Besides, you'll have a whole week to decide what to do with the clothes." Studying her face, he frowned. "I'll admit I don't know much about womenfolk, but you'll be safe here. I'll be back before you know it."

Speechless she stared up at him. Catching her close, he pressed his lips to hers, murmuring, "Don't look like that. I can't take it. Amy, I don't want to go. But I'd feel like a rotter if I didn't."

She pushed away. "Obviously your calling is more important than your wife." She hesitated, but the words came despite her resolve. "If you love me, you won't go."

"Amy," he cried, "you can't say that! Are you insisting I choose between God and you?"

She couldn't answer. He waited a moment while she refused to meet his eyes. She heard his step and the door closed behind him.

Slowly Amy sat down, gulping and blinking at the tears. *It won't matter. I won't let it matter to me. First Lucas and now Daniel.* She shivered beside the dark cold fireplace.

When she finally stood up, she picked up the plate Daniel had left on the table. Turning it slowly, she spoke the unbelievable words. "Just wed, and Daniel walks out leaving me alone. That hurts, more'n I'll ever let on."

She stared down at the plate. Instead of the plain clay surface, she saw a picture of the agony on Daniel's face. Abruptly she turned and flung the plate against the wall. "There, Mr. Daniel Gerrett."

She was still breathing heavily, clenching her fist, when the mental image of the white house with the Brussels carpet rose to taunt her. She threw herself on the bunk and wept.

When Amy finally went to wash her swollen eyes, she faced the squalor of the cabin. "This is my life now? Not if I can help it!" Shuddering, she picked the greasy trousers and shirt off the wooden pegs and carried them out the door, marching with the garments held at arms length.

She found a wooden barrel under a tree and dropped the clothing in it. When she heard the sodden splash she winced, then smiled. "Mr. What's-his-name, they'll be clean when you come back from the mountains."

Still trembling with anger, she scrubbed the furniture and replaced the pine boughs on the crude bunk. While cleaning the litter from the shelf, she found a pen, ink, and crumpled paper. Slowly she sat down.

Toying with the items, she thought of the letter she would write. But to whom? Who would care about her life now? Father?

Putting aside the paper she took the little milk pail and started for the cabin at the end of the road. With a sigh, she considered the night and the days to follow. "What am I to do? Amy, how could you get yourself into such a mess?" she said out loud. *Love, honor—forever, as long as we both shall live.* The tears rolled down her cheeks.

Amy was nearly home with her pail of milk when she heard the shouting. Wondering at the commotion, she stopped and turned. An old man coming down the road toward her lifted his hat. "Ma'am." He stopped beside her and shoved his hat back on his forehead, saying, "That there is the stage coming through. Seein's you're a-standing in the road, you could get hit."

Amy backed into the weeds lining the road. "Stage?" She backed farther. "A stage out here? Where's it going?"

"Denver City." He came closer. "Comes through here every two days. Comes direct from Julesburg, where the big ferry is. Sure puts us on the map. It's pretty important, a stage stop. Some of us, who don't have nothin' better to do, aren't above standing out to watch it come through."

There were more shouts and the cloud of dust drifted away as the bouncing coach slowed for the curve. It stopped in front of the fort, and the people spilled out.

"Oh, some fancy-looking ladies," chuckled the old man. "Times are right good when the gals come into town all decked out in their finery."

"Where are they going?" Amy asked as she studied the parasols and bright dresses billowing out of the stage.

"The mining camps, probably. Not much going on in Denver City since the gold petered out in the cricks. Besides, I heard Ada LaMont about has the business sewed up in Denver City." He chuckled and shook his head.

It was the next day before the idea of leaving came to Amy. In the midst of unpacking her valise, she found the coin. It was the gold birthday coin Father had given her, wrapped in the lacy handkerchief from Lucas.

Instantly the idea of getting on that stage presented itself full blown in her mind. She gasped and said, "Amy Gerrett, you are out of your mind. What is getting into you?"

It was past noon when she looked at the flour and thought of making bread. But there was only the iron kettle to serve as an oven. Shaking her head she muttered, "I'm not that old-fashioned. I need a stove if I'm to bake."

As the day wore on, gloomy rainclouds drifted in over the river, pelting the front yard with a heavy, cold rain. Amy huddled beside the fireplace and tried to coax the smoking fire into a blaze.

Hugging her arms about herself, she winked back the tears, but couldn't brush away the thoughts Daniel's abrupt departure spelled out in her mind. And as the fire began to flicker into a steady flame, anger kindled in her again.

At suppertime, she addressed the smoking fire, "Just

maybe the best lesson Mr. Daniel Gerrett could get would be to come home and find an empty cabin."

Still nursing the anger, she took the ink well and the pile of crumpled paper to the table. As she ate her supper, she thought, *It could be a lark*. If she were to take the stage to Denver City and meet Father, he most certainly would have things to say about Daniel going off and leaving her alone.

And Daniel. When he found the cabin empty, he would have second thoughts about staying in this dismal place. She murmured, "More'n kissing, and it sure could help!"

In the morning, after choosing her skirt and white shirt-waist for traveling, Amy packed her valise. She looked at the pen and paper. "Might as well give him time to do some proper worrying," she murmured, pulling the paper toward herself.

Dear Daniel, she wrote, *I've gone to be with Father. I'm wondering if this isn't all a big mistake. It seems best to go now, before*—She stopped and crossed out the last word. She was still sitting there, wondering what to write when she heard the distant shouts.

Rushing to the window, she saw the cloud of dust. "Oh, no!" she cried. "My foolin' will cause me to miss that stage." She picked up her valise and dashed through the door.

CHAPTER 15

Daniel and Silas Jeffry, homeward bound, forded the Platte that next Tuesday. As they dismounted in front of the fort, a woman came running out to meet them.

"My wife," Silas murmured, lifting his hand, "and she looks anxious."

"Oh, Silas," she threw herself at him. "It's so terrible. I really meant to go, but it was raining hard, and then the next day she was gone. Old man Morton told me she took the stage."

"What are you saying?" Silas asked as the woman glanced fearfully at Daniel.

Daniel's heart sank as he guessed. "Mrs. Jeffry, are you talking about Amy?" She nodded while she stared at the ground and poked her foot against the clump of weeds Daniel's mare was nosing.

"Does anyone know why?" Silas's voice was flat.

"It was just too soon," Daniel answered. "She begged me to stay with her."

Silas spoke slowly while he studied Daniel under frowning brows. "Being a preacher's daughter, I'd have guessed her to be tougher than that." He looked at his wife. "Did she tell anyone where she was going?"

Mrs. Jeffry was shaking her head. "We all talked about it, and seems the only ones she spoke to were the Barts, where she bought milk, and old Morton."

Daniel turned away. "I need to go think this out. I'll probably be heading for Central City for a talk with her father. She'll be there."

Daniel saw the note as soon as he walked into the cabin. He read it and when he reached the crossed-out word, he winced. "Before," he muttered. "Before she's in any deeper? Before our marriage had a chance, or did she mean before God could catch up with her? My poor little darling, I've failed you before we've begun. And you've left before I understood the dark places in your heart."

Daniel had plenty of time for thinking as he rode. For two days he tried to recall everything he could about Amy. There were pictures long past and others he had begun to see the night of their wedding. *Was I misreading it all? Love? Dear Lord, have I run ahead of you again? Guess this foolish heart was presuming when it shouldn't have. My guesses about Amy were wrong.*

In Denver City he returned the Goodes' horse. The presiding elder wasn't at home, and he breathed a sigh of relief. At least he was spared an explanation. As soon as he left the Goodes' cabin, he headed up Clear Creek canyon. That night he camped beside the trail and thought some more.

One picture stayed sharp and clear—Amy, silent and waiting beside the ruins of the mine. He saw the tears in her eyes as he thought through the words of the song she had sung.

Eli Randolph wasn't at home when Daniel arrived. The door of the cabin was latched and the film of dust on the log step sent him searching at the general store.

"Parson?" the young fellow said, "Why he's been gone for two days. Went to put his sister on the stage. You know, Randolph's daughter got married sudden-like, and his sister's going back to live with her brother in eastern Kansas."

He was watching Daniel's face curiously as he added, "Seems things are in an uproar. The daughter was promised to marry a young fella by the name of Tristram. Then she up and eloped with another guy. Don't know his name. Seems strange for the daughter of a preacher. All the town's a-buzzing. You could go see Aunt Clara Brown. Seems she's the only one not upset by it all."

He continued. "That young lady turned down a pack of money and easy living. The guy was doing right well." He paused to sigh wistfully before adding, "They're saying Tristram threatened to torch the new house he's been building for her. Come to think, he might could give you some information. Seemed pretty close to the family."

"No." Daniel backed toward the door. "I'll just head for Denver City; I'll probably'll meet up with Mr. Randolph."

"If you want to leave your name, I'll tell him about you."

Daniel studied the curious eyes and shook his head. "Never mind. I'll go looking for him."

On the outskirts of Black Hawk, Daniel crossed Clear Creek. While he was still trying to decide which road to take, he heard the wagon rumbling and thumping over the rocky surface.

It was Eli. Until he recognized Daniel, Eli was grinning as if he hadn't a care in the world. And Daniel stood in the road, trying to swallow the lump in his throat as he waited for the man to look up.

When Eli hauled back on the reins, Daniel came close. With a heavy sigh, he said, "I'll follow you home."

Eli asked, "Amy?"

All the way back up the gulch, Daniel picked through facts and wondered what he would say. One thing was certain. Amy hadn't come home, and Eli knew nothing about her.

When they faced each other across the table, by the dim west light, Daniel could see the change. The carefree expression was gone and the man's eyes were shadowed in a way he couldn't understand.

Daniel began. "The day you left, Silas Jeffry came after me to travel the circuit with him. It was my job, sir. I had to go." Eli was nodding and suddenly he looked like a feeble old man.

Daniel finally stirred. "When we returned Silas's wife met

us. The whole town was buzzing with the story of Amy's leaving. She just got on the stage and left without saying a word to anyone."

He waited a moment longer before adding, "There was a note saying it was a mistake. Sir, before I left she tried to get me to leave the territory. Wanted to go back east. She talked about my taking a church back there. I didn't take her too seriously. Guess I should have spent the time telling her how I would have to go to school to learn to be a preacher back in those fancy churches."

Eli's eyes seemed to pierce the gloom, "Is that the kind of life you're wanting? To be a fancy preacher with a big church?"

"No, sir. I know what the Lord has done for me, and that's the way I want to preach it to others. Don't have too much confidence in religion that's only a membership in church. Sir, I believe in the same kind of religion those fellows in Acts had. A walk with God through the Holy Spirit. Isn't that what it takes to make a fellow go craving after all the Lord has in store for him?"

Eli was silent for a long time. When he finally spoke, the room was completely dark. "All?" he asked. "That's a big word. Daniel, do you want all?"

"Yes, sir, I really mean it. I've realized there's no other way to live and be content with myself."

"Then take my advice. Do what the Lord wants you to do and forget about Amy."

Finally Daniel cleared his throat. "Forget? Sir, I guess I didn't make it clear. I love Amy. She's my wife and I want to spend my life making her happy."

His voice was bitter. "It hasn't occurred to you that you can't have both?"

"What do you mean?" he asked slowly.

"It's Jesus Christ or Amy, not both."

"It sounds like you're saying being married to your daughter and being a preacher is impossible."

There was silence for a long time. Daniel was conscious only of numbness growing inside. His mind was still busy thinking of Amy and that new side he had begun to see. He was also thinking of those things the fellow in the store had talked about—Amy being engaged. She hadn't mentioned Tristram. Finally he sighed and asked, "Is it because you don't want us to be married?"

"Son," Eli sounded as if he were choking, "I don't want to talk about this, but it's bad blood. I should have guessed it would come to this sooner or later. Just don't ask. Go and be the kind of man God wants you to be."

In the dark, Daniel stumbled against the table as he got to his feet. He asked, "Is it possible now? It was pushing things mighty far for Brother Goode to accept me after Aunt Maude got to him. Now, well, I might just have to go back to mining."

"I'll come with you, son. I'll put in a word for you with Goode."

"Why don't you just let me have my talk first. Maybe he considers me to be bad preacher material. If he doesn't, well, I'll ask him to come see you."

As Daniel got back on his horse and headed down the road, he was aware of something he hadn't heeded before. Eli *was* an old man.

The following day, Daniel again stood on the steps of the Goodes' cabin. The presiding elder was at home.

Goode looked at him and said, "I'm guessing the preaching business is a mite difficult."

"It isn't that, Brother Goode, but I need to have a talk with you."

"Then come with me to the church."

Silently Daniel followed the man's long strides across the field toward the new building. When Goode paused to admire his church, Daniel stopped beside him and squinted up at the log cross fastened to the eaves.

"Looks mighty nice," Brother Goode said with satisfaction in his voice. "I'm glad they got the sawmill operating before we finished building; otherwise there'd have been a soddy roof. Advantage to the logs over the planed lumber is it's warmer in winter. It's good-sized for a log building."

Goode continued to nod. "First decent looking church building in the whole of Denver City."

Inside they sat side by side on the pine pew. Daniel look a deep breath and said, "I don't rightly know where to begin. By getting married, I thought we'd done the only thing that would make things right. Seems it didn't. We'd hardly left Denver City before Amy started talking about leaving the territory and going east. I never realized she wasn't happy here."

He glanced at Goode, saw the curious, kind eyes and blurted out, "Fact is, Brother Goode, I guess I've been taken with Amy since I first met her. Being pressured by Aunt Maude started seeming pretty good after I got over being mad about the implications."

"You mean you wanted to marry Amy?" the presiding elder was chuckling and shaking his head. "You young people. So, now what's the problem?"

"When I came back from the first circuit, Amy was gone. Silas's wife saw her getting on the stage. We thought she'd gone home, but her pa hasn't seen her."

Daniel watched the last sign of merriment disappear from Goode's face, and when his chin came to rest on his collar, Daniel knew it was over. All of it. The dreams of Amy by his side, the dreams of a church like this.

Carefully Daniel rested his head in his cupped hands and waited.

"And the Lord's deserted you too?" Daniel lifted his head and studied Goode's expression.

"I haven't thought of it like that. I was just thinking of the present. How can I be serving as a parson when there's all this about Amy being aired?"

"What's the Lord done for you?"

Daniel wondered where to start. Carefully he said, "Brother Goode, I've said it before, and it's the same now."

"Say it again."

As he started to speak, he tried to clear his voice of the emotion that was coming through. "It's the same. The Lord reached down and rescued me. I asked Him for help. He forgave my sins and just plain changed me completely. I didn't know getting religion would do that for a fellow. Everything is different. All I had sense enough to ask for was to quit being afraid of dying, and He's made me glad to be living. Mighty glad. I wanted to be free of the ugliness of my past, and He's made me want to help others in the same way. I—"

Daniel saw Brother Goode nodding and smiling, "Go on."

He was grinning as he finished. "Why, nothing's changed about my call. He's still asking me to do the work."

"Do you trust the Lord in this matter with Amy?" Daniel nodded, and Goode added, "Even if you never see her again?"

Slowly Daniel said, "Brother Adriance and I had a talk. He said I had two obligations now: to God in fulfilling my call and to my wife. He said I had to trust God with both. That means putting everything in His hands and believing He'll work things out just the way He purposes to. The only thing, I don't know where to begin. Does that mean I'm just to sit here and wait until I get some help from the Lord? An understanding about the next step?"

The presiding elder's face wrinkled into unhappy lines. "Son, I don't know any better advice to give you. Just wait. But don't let your hands be idle while you're waiting."

"I'm certain she's gone east. I know there's family back there. She'll be with them. But how will it be for me here? Is there any room for a guy who's gained and lost a wife all in one week?" He paused for a moment, then said, "And I can't forget what her pa said just as I left him."

"What was that?"

Daniel lowered his head as he continued, "He said, 'Forget you ever knew Amy; it's the only way you'll be able to handle it.' Sir, his voice was bitter when he said that. And I know I won't be able to do that."

Daniel got to his feet. "One thing bothers me about being a Christian—I don't feel I've really learned to pray. Those old-fashioned prayers the men talk about, where a man gets to the end of himself and throws himself completely on God's mercy—I guess now is the time."

"Prayin's important, Daniel. But there's a saying in the church: The Lord expects his men to put feet to their prayers."

Daniel thought a moment, then nodded. "I guess I'd better tell you. If I ever find out where she is, I'll go to her. Then if it's possible to make things right with her, I'll try my best, short of disobeying the Lord."

CHAPTER 16

Late afternoon shadows were rolling across the foothills when the stagecoach stopped at the little station nestled in the sagebrush and piñon pine. Amy was the last one to be handed down the steep step.

Looking over the barren hillside to the towering mountains behind, she hesitated. "I thought we'd be in Denver City by now." She studied the lengthening shadows. "We're nearly in the mountains; it just doesn't seem like Denver City."

The graying gentlemen who helped her out of the stagecoach turned to study her with keen eyes. "My dear young lady, this stage isn't going to Denver City."

Amy searched the amused eyes, "Sir, you're teasing!"

"I'm not. Didn't you realize we were traveling nearly straight west from the fort? To the east of here is Golden City." He turned to point out the mountains behind them. "That cut through there is the route we'll take. We should be in Fairplay late tonight."

"I've never heard of Fairplay," Amy said flatly, still not believing him.

"Or Buckskin Joe?" The saucy face peered at Amy from under the straw bonnet loaded with birds and silk blossoms.

The gentleman's amused eyes twinkled at them both. "Then you two must get acquainted, for I think you'll be neighbors—at least until another stage comes through."

"You mean it, don't you?" Amy cried.

"Of course," the straw bonnet bobbed. "You've just taken the wrong stage. It's happened before. Don't worry, if you dislike Buckskin Joe, then take the stage back to Denver City."

"I have no more money for fare," Amy said dismally as she visualized the sight of her gold piece disappearing into the driver's pouch.

"Haw there, old Mac!" She turned at the shout. Fresh horses were being led to the stage. The driver was standing in the doorway of the station. "Hurry now, folks. We want to be in Buckskin Joe by midnight."

Amy ran toward him. "Please, I've taken the wrong stage. Can't someone take me into Denver City?"

He eyed her, shrugged, and turned toward the stagecoach. "Suppose you could sit and wait; sooner or later someone will be going into Denver City. Could be a long wait, and can't guarantee the charge—could be considerable. Want me to haul your baggage down?"

"No, I can't afford more." Slowly Amy climbed back into the stagecoach and took her place. Since her early morning dash to the stagecoach, she had been on edge with excitement. Now she sank back in a miserable heap. As the stagecoach pulled out of the station, the pebbles of the road pounded against the bottom of the coach, Amy winced.

Her "lark" had turned into a nightmare. The high tide of emotion was gone. She stared out the window. *What have I done?* She needn't be reminded that the hasty steps she had taken couldn't be undone.

Trying to compose herself, Amy tugged at the tiny money bag she carried and found her hands were trembling. With a wry smile, she realized that for the first time in her life she was completely on her own.

The straw bonnet noticed her hands. "Don't worry; it won't be that bad. The Tabors run the store and post office.

They also have a boardinghouse. I have an idea they'll be glad to put you up. I'll tell them you can't afford the boardinghouse and just maybe they'll find work for you."

The gait of the horses slowed and Amy could feel the shuddering strain run through the stagecoach as they started up the steep grade.

Amy caught the insolent grin of the young man in stained broadcloth who had been watching all the occupants of the stage. "Ya don't like this?" he directed his question to her. "Wait'll we start down the other side; that'll give you a thrill—'specially in the dark."

"I've been this route several times," said the woman in the straw bonnet. "It isn't bad at all. These drivers are good."

The youth was not to be outdone. "Ever been on a stage when it was held up?"

"Are you talking about that miner they've been accusing of holding up stages—his name's Jim Reynolds. I hear he's polite to the ladies, so I won't worry." She paused for a moment and added, "You deal faro at Jake's place, don't you? I'm sure I've seen you."

The stage slowed. There was a crack of the whip and a shout. Peering through the gloom beyond the window, Amy guessed they had reached the top of the mountain. As they rumbled into the descent, Amy grasped the leather strap above her head. Conversation was forgotten as the stagecoach swayed from side to side, bouncing the occupants back and forth.

The darkness deepened and Amy was forced to forget her troubles. All of life seemed to be suspended in the dipping, swaying coach as they rattled over stones, forded shallow creeks, and strained up yet another slope.

At the point when it seemed she couldn't stand another sharp plunge in the blackness, the road leveled and became a smooth, arrow-straight path through the night.

Amy relaxed and the old gentlemen's white dot of a face turned toward her. "They call this South Park," he explained. "It's flat meadow land as far as the eye can see, and it's tucked nice and secure between the mountain ranges." He was chuckling as he added, "It would be an idyllic haven, except for one thing—the Indians seem to like it, too."

"Are there many settlements around here?" she asked.

He shrugged, "Depends on what you mean. There's a few cabins around all the diggings, but most don't rate the designation yet. Up this route there's a handful."

Amy dozed. She awakened to watch them roll through a series of little hamlets. The first was Fairplay with its cluster of buildings throwing streams of light through open shutters. Then came Alma, and abruptly the stage veered left and climbed a short steep hill.

Within minutes, the driver shouted, "Buckskin Joe!" and began to slow the stage. As he clambered down off the seat, Amy knew it was time for her to get off. Slowly she retrieved her belongings and miserably stared at the dim blobs of light piercing the gloom of the street.

The straw bonnet stopped beside her, and the girl's hand was gentle as she placed it on Amy's shoulder. "See there? That's the Tabor's place. Let's go see if they won't put you up until the stage comes back this way. Augusta has a soft heart—that is, unless you bat your eyes at her husband."

Augusta was willing. Without question she led Amy to a tiny bedroom under the eaves. She explained, "We've a vacancy. Had a fellow helping out in the store and such, but he's just left to try his hand at mining. There's a claim that's starting to show a real good color. They're calling it the Phillips Lode, and it's promising to be the best in the country." She continued to chatter on, "The vein of quartz they've uncovered is running from twenty-five to sixty feet wide."

She eyed Amy as she talked. Finally she asked, "You said you're a married lady. Could it be you're out here to look over the mining? Usually there's only two kind of women coming into the camps. You don't look like a camp follower to me."

Amy was still struggling with an answer as she watched the woman pat the quilts into place. "If you don't feel like going down the street for a proper dinner with the other passengers, come down to the kitchen and I'll give you tea and biscuits."

"I would like that," Amy murmured. As the door closed behind Augusta, Amy stared at it. A new feeling was taking possession of her. *I'm a stranger in a whole sea of strangers. There's no one who knows me, no one cares what I do or say.* Her next thought made her grin. *But also, there are no eyes to frown, no challenges to be made or actions to be defended, no questions to answer.*

In the morning the thought was still there. It was like suddenly being in another world, secreted away from the prying, demanding eyes.

But Augusta Tabor couldn't be ignored, Amy realized that first day. She watched Augusta fly about her many tasks and went to help. "You could use extra hands," Amy said. The woman's grateful smile nearly brought tears to Amy's eyes. Just being needed by the gentle, sad-eyed woman lent sureness to Amy's fingers and feet.

By noon that first day, Amy discovered that Buckskin Joe was another bustling mining town. The clamor was much like Central City, although the dull thud of the stamp mill was missing. Augusta pointed out the tumble of machinery and the cluster of men down stream. "That's the stamp mill. They've been working at getting it together for two weeks now. It'll be a steam one, about the fanciest hereabouts."

Together they walked down Buckskin Joe's one main street. As Augusta talked, Amy studied the town. The road wound through the area, with buildings clustered on each side. All the buildings were of log or crudely planed lumber, unpainted and stark.

The largest building on the road was called the Grand Hotel. Amy recognized it as the building she had seen from the stagecoach, the one to which the passengers had streamed last night.

Buckskin Joe was situated in a saddle, slashed by a wide, shallow river. At noon this early July day, scorching heat seared the town. Amy tugged at her collar and wiped at the perspiration on her nose. Augusta seemed unmindful of the heat as she strolled the length of town pointing out the buildings. Amy hurried to keep up with her.

"You see, we operate the largest store," she said. "We also have the post office." She sighed. "It's enough to keep a body busy. Mr. Tabor is involved in politics, and that's a demand that won't let the poor man hardly finish a meal."

Amy reflected on the note in Augusta's voice, guessing she was both proud and sad. Glancing at Amy, Augusta continued, "There's this new problem over slavery come up. I suppose he'll be spending too much time on that. It's making people in Buck-skin uneasy to have the only newspaper pushing southern sym-pathy. Right now Tabor's in Denver City." She dropped her voice, as she continued. "He confided to me that there's big worries in Denver City, too. The factions are pulling the place to pieces."

"Factions?" Amy murmured uncertainly.

"The North and South. Those for slavery and those against," she added impatiently. "Doesn't help there's so much talk about the states seceding from the Union right now. The bad feelings are rising. He's saying there's going to be terrible pressure brought to bear on people to side with the South. Right now there's a push to get a good strong militia."

"That seems strange," Amy said slowly. "We're awfully far away from the southern states. Surely there'll never be war here."

"Don't count on that," Augusta added; "my husband says the state of Texas is mighty close and those Texas Rangers won't rest until they get their thumbs on us."

They had reached the edge of the settlement; as Augusta led the way through the meadow toward the river, she pointed out the wild flowers. "There's Indian paint brush; see the wild columbine?"

With a deep sigh she paused, hands on hips. "Have you ever seen anything as pretty as the wild iris in bloom? There, close to the marshy section. You know, I love this country. Didn't think I would, but the beauty of the place stole my heart. Look at that white cap on the mountain. Stays covered with snow all summer."

She started toward the bank of the river. "Come look.

They don't use these things much anymore, but it's interesting."
She stopped and pointed. "That's an arrastra. The Spanish ex-
plorers brought them in over a hundred years ago when they
first found gold here. There's several hereabouts, and some of
the men still use them."

Amy stopped to watch the ragged miner walking around
a large rock on the edge of the creek. Augusta added, "See the
depression in the rock and the shaft sticking up? He's putting
ore into the depression, and that rock chained to the pole will
be pulled around and around. It pulverizes the ore; then the
worthless waste floats out while the gold sinks to the bottom."

They started back toward the post office. Augusta said,
"Well, you've seen it all now, even the new nine-stamp mill
going up for the Phillips Lode."

"Does Mr. Tabor have a claim hereabouts?" Amy asked.

"Oh, my yes," Augusta answered quickly. "That's why
we came." She sighed heavily and added, "Not that I'm crazy
about the whole idea. Running the grocery and even boarding
a few men is all right with me, but I don't have any desire to
get rich. I wish he could be happy with what he has. He keeps
telling me, 'Augusta, we're going to be rich,' and just as often
I say, 'I wouldn't give a nickel's worth of my time for all the
diggings. We'll be happier if you forget the whole foolish
dream.' Of course he won't."

Again she sighed heavily. Watching the weary lines settle
over the woman's face, Amy wondered why the idea of having
all that gold made her unhappy.

CHAPTER 17

Aweek had passed since Amy's arrival in Buckskin Joe. Away from the sheltering influence of home, she saw life stripped down to the crude, raw essentials.

On the first day she saw a gun fight over a woman, the wife of one of the men. *She isn't even pretty,* Amy thought. She looked from the coarse face of the woman to the bloody arm of her lover and walked away, shaking her head.

Amy fingered the cotton curtains and watched the bevy of dance-hall girls promenading down the street. With arms linked, they built a playful barrier in front of the tired, dirty miners returning home to barren rooms or silent shacks behind the hotel.

Amy had been watching the girls since she had arrived. Initially she had searched for the girl in the straw bonnet, but now every bright-frocked woman caught her attention. She found herself admiring the saucy, daring demeanor of the girls on the street. Brashly they thrust themselves before the men, and there was no rejection here. Smiles of delight signaled their acceptance. Amy sighed and turned away from the window.

"Seems," she murmured, "there are some meant to sail through life on clouds of ease and others . . ." Her voice trailed away as she looked at her reflection in the sliver of mirror on the shelf.

Without taking time to think, she pulled down the severe knot of hair and reached for the hairbrush. Brushing curls around her fingers she pushed them high off her neck. Turning before the mirror, she studied the cascade of curls, wishing the reflection revealed more of the bright yellow lights in her hair. "Oh well," she muttered, "faded calico doesn't do much for settin' off curls."

She had just reached for the brush when she heard the stairs creak, and Augusta pushed at her half-open door. Amy saw the frown as Augusta said, "Looking like the dance-hall girls. I don't abide a girl of mine seeking to attract men, especially when she says she's married."

"Oh, Mrs. Tabor, I don't intend to wear it this way downstairs. I just saw the girls and I wanted to prove I could look as saucy as they. But the curls are strange on me, with this dress."

Augusta's frown deepened. Amy explained, "I was looking out the window, watching the girls and men. Feeling all pleased with myself for seeing when they didn't know I was up here. I suddenly realized that life isn't all we want it to be. Sometimes it feels like it's going to crash down on top of you."

The frown on Augusta's face cleared. "And yours is crashing down? Why are you here, Amy? You aren't really married, are you? Where did you come from? Why did you avoid going down the street to the post office the other day? Did it have something to do with that preacher out on the street preaching about repentance and hell?"

"Oh, Mrs. Tabor!" Amy gasped, putting her hands on her warm cheeks. "I think I need to do some explaining."

Augusta sat down on the edge of the cot and waited. Looking into her eyes, Amy thought of Aunt Maude; but there was a difference; this woman waited patiently. "I know what it is to pull your heart out for a man and have him refuse it," Augusta said.

"No, it isn't that at all!" Amy protested. "We are married, but see—even before we had a chance to—settle in, well, he just took off. Being a preacher was more important than anything. He didn't want to go back to the states and have a decent life. There's just this crazy dream he has about being a pastor to a bunch of miners."

"Then you know Father Dyer?"

"That man preaching on the street? I didn't know his name, but I saw him with—my husband." For a moment Amy was lost in contemplation. *Husband.* It seemed odd to be using that word for the tall brown-eyed stranger.

Augusta added, "So you ran away. Where were you going?"

"Well, I didn't really intend to run away. I was going to Denver City to meet my father. I figured by the time Daniel caught up with me, he would be glad to go back to the states."

Augusta was shaking her head sadly. "Where did you get the idea you could treat a man like that? Amy, women are supposed to follow their husbands, trying to make life pleasant for them. It's called being a helpmate, until death parts." She sighed. A faraway look crept into her eyes, and Amy was glad to be forgotten.

At last Augusta got to her feet and reached for the door, then paused. "What are you going to do now?"

Amy lifted her chin. "Well, seems he's not going to come looking. All he would have had to do is just ask about the stagecoach. He could have come after me. Besides," she added, "I don't have money to go back, so I'd better get a job and earn some money or I'll be here the rest of my life."

"Is that why you were fixing your hair fancy?"

Amy blinked, but as she gasped, her protest came out rather feeble. "You thought I'd be a dance-hall girl? Oh my, Mrs. Tabor! I've been raised to believe that's sinful. Aunt Maude doesn't even approve of pianos; she'd have a stroke if she ever finds out I've learned to play one." As Amy finished her protest, she was left with an uneasy feeling that there was some unplumbed depth in her that was threatening to make itself known.

Augusta got up with a sigh. "You're an innocent. Well, I

can offer you a job in the post office if you wish. The pay isn't good, but you can live here and help out. With Mr. Tabor gone much of the time, I'm about worked to pieces. Hardly have time for the little one."

Amy's duties behind the wire cage of the post office began immediately. The post office had been started on the corner of a desk at the Tabor's grocery. Now occupying its own milled lumber building next door, Amy became the sole employee, and the only person on the premises most of the time.

But she was happy in her new domain and took pride in keeping the mud swept from the plank floor and the plants watered. There was cactus by the spittoon, while the cold pot-belly stove at the far end of the building was topped with a drooping geranium.

Across the front of the building was a window nearly as large as the one in the Tabors' store. When there was nothing to do, Amy could watch the traffic move up and down the street.

The plain lumber walls had been decorated with posters and notices, mostly about men who were wanted for commit-ting crimes in the area. She read the brief horror stories and shivered. One Ben Ames was wanted for shooting his partner and leaving the country with all the gold from their diggings. Another was a description of Jim Reynolds, con artist and lately a highway man, wanted for holding up the Denver City-Cali-fornia stagecoach.

When there were customers, Amy retreated behind the wire enclosure where the cubbyholes held the mail. Three times a week heavy canvas bags of mail were dropped from the stage-coach. It was Amy's job to sort the mail into the proper slots.

She also read the newspapers from Denver City and learned to know which of the townspeople were apt to receive mail. After a week it was easy to guess which miners were married and eager for news from home.

She had been behind the desk for nearly three weeks before she realized that one segment of Buckskin Joe's society almost never came into the post office—the dance-hall girls.

As the summer waned, more men with families began moving into the area. The number of children grew, and soon there was talk of a school.

Amy learned to call the newcomers by name, and kept up on the gossip. She could guess by the faces just who was prospering and who would be leaving town before the first snows.

As the days passed, she also watched Augusta's face become deeply lined and sad. Was it related to the activities of her husband?

H. A. W. Tabor seemed to be everywhere at once—in the newspaper office, on the street with a cluster of men around him. By chance Amy discovered that in the mining claim office, he was frequently the center of a group, and when the discouraged miners filed out of Buckskin, H. A. W. was left holding their claims.

Amy needn't be told that the Tabors were prospering; it was evident in the trail of expensive merchandise that moved through the store. In addition to Augusta's new black silk gowns and H. A. W.'s fawn suits and tall hats, a shiny new carriage was housed in the log barn.

Another group in town seemed to be prospering—the dance-hall girls across the meadow. Amy was well aware of them, and she knew how frequently their rambling two-story boardinghouse vibrated with light and laughter.

She also noticed the line of girls going into the Tabors' shop was directly proportionate to the number of new claims discovered and how much gold the Phillip Lode was producing.

That information was easy to come by. Hardly a week passed without a ragged, dirty miner riding his jack into town with a broad smile and a sack of ore. Frequently his find was announced with a wild shout and a race down main street while his buddies celebrated by discharging their pistols into the air.

After the first few times it happened, Amy stopped running into the street. Now like the rest of the town, she merely smiled and nodded. Buckskin Joe was doing very well.

In late August a ponderous wagon crepted slowly across

the meadow toward the boardinghouse. When all the respect-able citizens in town lined the street to watch, Amy joined them.

There were awed exclamations when it stopped in front of the boardinghouse, but Mrs. Dickens said it all. "A piano! Would have been nice if it could have come to rest in a church instead of in that place. Sometimes it doesn't seem the Lord is dealing things out right. Here our men are working their fingers to the bone and we're a-goin' to church; while all the time *they* are the ones getting the pretties and the piano."

Amy agreed with Mrs. Dickens. Still, thinking of Aunt Maude, she had to retort, "Seems to be a worldly thinking, having a piano in a church, don't you think?"

"Times are changing," replied the short, cheerful miner's wife standing beside Amy. "I was raised with that thinking, but do you know Father Dyer has a little portable organ? Seems to be the coming thing. I hear a church in Denver City's going to get a piano, too."

Amy turned back into the post office. For the remainder of the afternoon she was thinking about it all. So the girls across the way had a piano, and Father Dyer had an organ. For a few minutes Amy toyed with idea of going to church on Sunday morning.

The next day when Lizzie appeared in the post office, Amy could do nothing but stare at the girl. "Lizzie! I'm so flabber-gasted I don't know what to say. You're the last person I'd expect to see. I didn't even know you had moved from Central City."

Lizzie smiled, but her voice was dry. As she talked, Amy studied her friend's face. It was easy to see that Lizzie wasn't the lighthearted girl she had been in Central City. She said, "There's not many places in the Pikes Peak land that'll support the likes of us. You want to find a gal, you go to Denver City, Central City, Fairplay, or Buckskin. I'm hearing they're en-forcing some old ordinance in Central City that could move all the girls outta the place."

Amy saw the shadows deep in Lizzie's eyes. There was a cynical twist to her lips. She was saying, "I hear you got married. I pulled out of Central City right after that. You were crazy to have tossed over that Tristram fella. He could have put you on easy street for the rest of your life."

Slowly Amy said, "Lizzie, what's wrong? Aren't things going well for you? You seem so strange now."

Lizzie blinked and turned, but Amy saw the tears. "You're having it rough? Can't we be friends again?"

Lizzie had her money out and was moving away from the counter. "I don't suppose your man will want us to be friends."

"Lizzie, I need to talk to you." Amy spoke slowly, wondering how much she should say. The door opened to admit a miner and Lizzie left the building. Amy went back to sorting mail, but for some reason Lizzie's sad face stayed with her.

The next day when Amy went to meet the stagecoach and pick up the mail, Father Dyer was there. As he turned from the stage, she saw that he recognized her.

Taking the heavy mail sack from her, he said, "I'll carry that for you; it's too heavy for a woman." There was nothing for her to do except follow him back to the post office.

Inside she took the sack and went behind the barricade, hoping that he would leave. But he leaned on the counter and asked, "I don't suppose there's mail for John L. Dyer?"

"Not from the last batch. I won't have the new one done for a couple hours." The question slipped out unintentionally. "How come they call you Father?"

"I guess because that's the way some of the fellows see me—not authority, just pa." He was still watching her as he said, "I'm a preacher, Methodist Episcopal. I've seen you around town, but I believe I've seen you somewhere else. Could it have been at the quarterly meeting in Denver? It'd be nice to have you come to services on the Sabbath."

She shrugged lightly. "Maybe sometime."

He waited; then finally he asked, "Mind if I inquire about your name?"

She had expected it. Shuffling the letters, she kept her head down and pondered the question. He might know Father. Lifting her head she said, "I'm Mrs. Gerrett. I think you're mistaken. I'm certain we've never met."

He waited a moment more and then in an easy conversational tone he said, "I'm trying to get the job of carrying the mail over Mosquito Pass. Seems a waste to walk over for preaching without having my hands full of the mail those people are waiting for."

Late that afternoon, as Amy locked the post office and started toward the boardinghouse, her thoughts were full of the past. Seeing Lizzie and Father Dyer had plunged her backward, filling her with lonesome feelings.

And finally, when all the thoughts had trooped past with their images of Father, Aunt Maude and Daniel Gerrett, she sighed and shook her head. "There's not a thing I can do about it all. I'm here, and my wages barely pay my keep. It'll be a long time before I can afford to take the stage back to Central City."

And then the thought came, solid and undeniable: *You could write*. Her mind protested. *Someday, but not yet. How could she justify that thought? At what point had isolation become so precious?*

CHAPTER 18

Amy decided working in the post office was better than watching life through the bedroom window. There was little to do beyond sweeping the floor and reading the newspapers coming in from Denver City.

The newspapers played a double role in Buckskin Joe. Before long, Amy became the source of information in Buckskin Joe for those who didn't read the *Rocky Mountain News*.

One day, with her head deep in the newspaper, Amy muttered, "I was getting to the place where I thought I knew everything happening around the territory. Here it is September; we've been a territory since last February, and I didn't know they had decided the official name was Colorado. I'd thought we were stuck with Jefferson for a name."

Feet shuffled and she raised her head. A miner waited for his mail. "Name's Murphy," he said gruffly, "and I don't care about the shenanigans Congress has put us through. I just want to know if there's a letter for me." He took his letter and headed for the door, saying, "The sooner I clear out of this place the better I'll like it." But Amy wasn't listening to him; she stared instead at the girl walking through the door.

Lizzie's smile was apprehensive as Amy came from behind

the barricade to give her a quick hug. "It's been so long since I've seen you! I've been wanting to visit, but I didn't know where to come looking for you. I thought Mrs. Tabor knew everyone in town, but she didn't know your whereabouts."

Lizzie's smile became bitter. Amy asked, "What's happened with you? You're unhappy, that's clear. And why did you fly out of here the last time you were here?"

"Look, Amy, I don't need to hear this line about friendship. Just drop the talk. Let me get this letter sent and I'll be on my way."

"Lizzie, I don't understand. We were best of friends last spring. Why—"

The expression in her eyes was changing. For a moment Amy expected Lizzie to laugh. Abruptly she turned away. "You haven't talked to Clara Brown? I supposed you'd found me out, that's all."

"What do you mean by that?"

"Your precious Aunt Clara Brown pinned me to the wall. Saw me once when I wished she hadn't. From the talking she gave me, I supposed you knew it all."

"Lizzie, I'm afraid I don't understand."

"You want me to spell it out? Amy, use your head. Why do you think I had an in with Mrs. Arnold at the boarding-house?"

Finally Amy said, "Are you trying to tell me you were one of her girls? Well, Lizzie, that does surprise me. But I can forget the past."

"Past? What do you think I'm doing now—scrubbing floors?"

In the silence the clock on the wall gonged out the hour. Amy watched the bronze pendulum sweeping back and forth behind the glass. *All nice and neatly ordered. But Aunt Maude isn't here to put me in a box like that.* Her eyes slanted toward Lizzie. Keeping her voice level she said, "Lizzie, if you don't criticize how I earn my living, then I won't criticize you. Seems to me we both need a friend mighty badly."

Lizzie blinked her eyes just as the door opened. She looked

up. The woman who had walked into their conversation was glaring at Lizzie. "Yer one of those fancy gals. Didn't know the likes of you addressed decent people." Amy dropped her paper and jumped to her feet.

The door banged behind Lizzie. Going to the window Amy watched Lizzie swishing down the road. Turning to the woman waiting for her mail, she said, "You hurt her feelings."

"Jest a dance-hall gal. Seems they're uppity enough without encouraging them." She reached for the letter Amy held out to her. Fingering the letter, the woman said, "You best be careful who you line up with around here. A young lady like you could get a bad reputation."

Amy chewed her finger and watched the customer leave the building. Staring at the vacant spot where Lizzie had stood, she picked up the paper and folded it with a sigh. "Poor President Lincoln. He's in for a rough time."

The miner who had just entered said, "Why's Lincoln in for a rough time?"

She tapped the newspaper. "Can't read it without getting the feeling that what happened at Fort Sumter in April is just the beginning of big problems." She looked at the miner. We're in war now. Our own country is fighting among themselves. A family fight. That's bad." The man was gnawing at a big plug of tobacco. Hastily she said, "Don't spit on the floor; I just got it swept." She held out her hand for his letter and watched him go out the door.

The afternoon was slipping toward dusk, and people hurried on past the post office, heading for home.

Amy sat down on her stool and reached for the *Rocky Mountain News*. As she thumbed to the back of the paper, a name caught her attention. She turned to the beginning of the article. It was about a Methodist Episcopal elder who had left his church at California Gulch and had accepted a commission to head the First Colorado Regiment. The article said his church had been taken over by a supply pastor, a newcomer.

Slowly Amy said, "So presiding elder John Chivington is going to be an army officer defending our territory against the

Texans." She read more. "It appears that a Daniel Gerrett has been appointed to fill his pulpit as the new pastor."

As time came to lock the post office, Amy slowly got to her feet. Dusk shadowed the streets making them look as dismal as she felt. Locking the door, Amy started down the street to her barren attic room. The article had opened up the hidden place in her mind, and now her thoughts churned.

She whispered to the autumn sky, "I'm feeling like I've been yanked out of my covering. Left here in the cold." Amy shivered and tried to find a nice warm anger to shove down between Daniel and her. It seemed the only way to handle the loneliness that unexpectedly invaded her isolation.

Daniel studied the line of books on the shelf built into the supporting cedar posts of his new home. "Mighty fine. Better library than I ever expected to have." As he spoke, he realized the one-way conversations were becoming commonplace.

But he continued. "But these books that John Chivington left are going to be no more important to me than they were to him."

He rubbed his unruly thatch of dark hair and sighed. Taking a quick pace around the one small room of his cabin he surveyed it all. The distance from the bunks built into the far wall to the fireplace was only three hard strides. Between the sheet metal cookstove to the table set in the middle of the room was another stride.

He turned around. The end wall by the door was covered with more shelves and pegs for clothing. Benches lined each side of the table, and a few cooking utensils and dishes were on shelves. But that was the extent of his newly inherited possessions. It was a church as poor as the new diggings they called California Gulch.

"Doesn't look like there's ever been a woman's touch here, but I can't blame his wife for not wanting to live here," he muttered, trying to avoid thinking about Amy. His two windows were bare and black against the night. Their blank panes stared like curious eyes, and Daniel vaguely remembered that women did something about curtains.

He turned toward the stove just as a hearty thump resounded from the door. A voice shouted, "Open up, Parson, I know you're there. I saw you through the window."

With a grin Daniel yanked at the door, saying, "I recognize your sweet, gentle voice, Father Dyer. Come in!"

The stocky man marched in. Dumping his gear on the floor, he said, "Heard you'd been given the mission at California. Decided I'd drop past and see how you're doing."

He clapped Daniel on the shoulder. "Am glad to see you again! Since quarterly meeting I've been wondering about you. How are you getting along? Surprised me to hear you've been given an assignment so soon. That speaks well."

Daniel winced. "I think it's by default, Father Dyer. Many of the fellows have gone to soldiering with Chivington. It makes the preaching ranks mighty thin."

Dyer sat down on a bench. "Mind if I drop here tonight? I'm pretty tired. Hiked over from Fairplay."

"I'd be more than disappointed if you didn't," Daniel answered soberly. "I haven't had a soul to talk to since leaving Fort Lupton. Hiked? Can't the circuit support a horse?"

"Naw, I'd rather eat. Besides there's snow stacking up on Mosquito Pass early this year. I've made myself some snowshoes." He paused to chuckle, "You'd have had a good laugh watching me learn to use them. But I'll trust the snowshoes before a horse. That's some trail in the snow."

"So you intend to keep up the circuit during the winter months?"

"My conscience won't allow otherwise. There's only a handful of people across the camps, but they'll see me as often as possible." He paused and added, "You say you're lonely? Don't you even have a congregation yet?"

Daniel grinned. "Not much of one."

"Daniel boy, I'm tempted to hang around and make sure you get some fire into you. These miners need to be stirred up. I'm finding out that most of them have a background of good, God-fearing families. But there's an indifference to the Lord like

I've never seen back home. It's the latest in golden-calf worship, and a handful of gold is the start. We need to encourage these men to be getting into church. The real fire will come later."

Daniel pulled forward a skillet and began cutting bacon into it as Dyer continued to talk. "A month or so ago I was over in Washington Gulch. 'Twas the Sabbath when I walked into a settlement called Minersville. You'd never have known it was any day except a workday. At sunup men were cutting wood and building cabins. They had a tent set up for a grocery store and men were going at it, cutting beef and selling it. I stretched my lungs."

He paused to chuckle, saying, "Now, Daniel, I don't want you to think I always do this, but it seemed they needed my attention. So I cupped my hands around my mouth and yelled, 'We're having services! There's to be preaching at the grocery tent.' Well, they came and we had a good service. I tell you, I was as surprised as they were.

"Forty men came, leading their jacks and ponies. Some customers were continuing to do business at the meat counter, even while we were singing, so I called for prayer."

Daniel stirred the beans and shifted the skillet to the back of the stove. "Did you preach?"

"Yes, and it went along fine until a mule stuck his head through the tent and made off with a loaf of bread. That was a little distracting."

While Daniel served up the bacon and beans, Dyer said, "Later that night we had revival meeting around a campfire. There's about a hundred men up there, but only one woman. The territory is a lonely place at best, and for womenfolk it's worse." Daniel saw his quizzical look but said nothing.

Dyer lingered on for another day, and Daniel apologized, "I know I've about twisted your ear off and nearly wrung you dry of words. But I need all the help you can give. It's been good having you, come back again, Father Dyer."

"Seems to me, listening to you talk, you needn't worry. Just stay on your knees and don't be afraid of laying it on the line. The Bible's our only sure textbook and the Lord is our only Teacher." He clapped Daniel on the shoulder. "We all have to learn the hard way. Remember, you preach soft and you'll see men lose their souls. You preach hard and all you'll lose is the kind of friends you can get along without anyway."

Later while Dyer was tightening his pack, getting ready to leave he said, "Fella, I've done most of the talking. But I want to tell you, if you need a friendly ear, I'm willing to do some listening."

He was adjusting the straps on his pack. Daniel studied his face, sensing more behind the words. His glib reply stuck in his throat. When Dyer lifted his head, Daniel said, "Father Dyer, what do you mean?"

"Over in Buckskin Joe there's a pretty little blonde woman who says her name is Mrs. Gerrett. I thought I saw her at quarterly meeting."

Daniel could think of only one thing and it filled his heart with a rush of gladness: Amy was using his name!

Dyer waited. Looking into his troubled eyes, Daniel said, "Think you can stay another night? I'd like to tell you about it."

They settled around the table. Daniel started at the beginning, telling Dyer about Central City and the events that had led up to the night at quarterly meeting when Aunt Maude had confronted Amy and himself.

After he finished the story, Daniel stared at his folded hands and added, "When I went to see Amy's father, he seemed to think she had headed for home—back to Kansas. Eli said he gave Amy a gold piece for her birthday. He thought it might be enough for her to travel home. Her Aunt Maude is there now so she'd have a place to go."

Daniel shrugged and looked at the table. "Didn't seem to be anything I could do about the whole situation." He looked up. "I prayed, asked for guidance—for the next step."

Father Dyer waited. Daniel wiped his hands over his face. "I have no idea why she would go to Buckskin Joe. I can hardly believe she's still in the territory and hasn't contacted her father."

He dropped his hands and looked at Dyer, hoping the questions didn't show in his eyes. John Dyer shook his head, "Daniel, I can't offer you much, but I do know she's working in the post office and living with the Tabors.

"From talking to her I get the feeling she's a lonely, confused girl with a big problem. Tried to get her to come to services." He reluctantly added, "Somehow I have the feeling your little lady is afraid of meetings. Is that possible?"

Daniel nodded. "It seems, from the little talking we've done about the past, that the fear goes back to her mother's death. Father Dyer!" he cried out against his will, "she could have written a letter if she wanted to have anything to do with me."

"Seems that way," John Dyer said soberly.

"I need help. What do you think I should do? I don't want her to feel I'm pressuring her to come back. I don't want an unwilling wife."

"Seems she needs to have a visit with you. Daniel, your marriage puts you in a new situation. You realize as her husband, you hold a special responsibility for Amy's salvation. Right off, I'd say that's so until she indicates she doesn't want to continue with the marriage."

"Isn't that what she's saying by leaving?"

"That's for you to decide, Daniel."

CHAPTER 19

Late one afternoon, when the evening shadows were stretching across the street and Amy got up to light the lamps in the post office, Lizzie came again.

She breezed in with a wave and a smile. Amy nodded and went to count out money for postage charges. She handed the letter to her customer and watched him leave, but her thoughts were on Lizzie. *That girl isn't looking for a letter. Could it be she's forgotten the slight that sent her flying out of here last time?*

Amy turned with a brisk smile. "Now, Lizzie, what can I do for you? A letter?"

She looked directly at Amy, the expression in her eyes was frank, unwavering. Amy caught her breath. Their eyes met, and Amy couldn't turn away. Lizzie was using some unseen scale to measure her. *What does she see and why are Lizzie's thoughts important to me?* The woman had called her *only a dance-hall girl.*

Lizzie's gaze still held Amy's. Her voice was flat as she said, "The letters come care of the madame, if they come at all. Most of the ones we write stay unanswered. And most of us don't peddle our last names for a good reason."

Amy winced at the girl's twisted smile. "Lizzie, I'm sorry.

So you didn't come to talk about the mail. What can I do for you?"

"You really mean that? You want to do something for me—us?"

"Well—" Amy hedged, beginning to regret the direction her impulse was leading.

Lizzie's laughter was as clear and sharp as a bell. "Don't worry! I don't intend to put you on the spot. But I do have an idea, and you'll be the one to benefit. Did you hear the Grand Hotel has a piano now? Just today it was delivered."

"Oh, was that the commotion down the street? I wondered about all the excitement. I heard the wagon and saw people heading out like they were going to a fire."

She paused, as the facts caught up with her, "Oh, Lizzie! A piano! How wonderful; will you be playing it?" She saw the shadow in her eyes and wished the words back.

Dryly Lizzie replied, "I don't think I'll be asked. But that's the reason I've come. I hear they're looking for a piano player among the respectable people in town. There was a fellow, but he's left for California Gulch."

She continued, "Amy, up Central City way you were anxious to play the piano—and running scared your aunt and pa would catch you at it. Aren't you free to do as you please now? How about coming over to the boardinghouse and letting me teach you a couple of snappy tunes. A gal with a natural talent like yours shouldn't be hiding it under a bushel." She paused and added, "That's Scripture."

Amy leaned across the counter and thrust her fingers through the wire mesh of the cubicle, "Oh, Lizzie, don't do this to me! You know I would love it more than anything, but I can't. I don't know enough."

"You do. More'n once I've heard you sit down and pick out a tune after hearing it just once. You've got a rhythm too, a real good beat. That's important. And you can sing. Learning the words will be harder than learning the notes of the music."

Amy was still clinging to the enclosure, feeling as if her heart would burst with longing. Lizzie's eyes were gentle now, and she patted Amy's hand. "Come on. Let me teach you what I know; then if you keep your nose clean and stay away from the likes of us, you'll make it in big time. Who knows? The way Denver City is booming, in another year or so, you could be earning your keep in a respectable hotel."

Amy forced the words. "You're forgetting my husband."

"I know you're here alone. Word gets around. I thought you'd already forgotten him." Her smile was mocking. "Come on, Amy, you aren't the first gal who's had a change of heart."

Amy watched Lizzie turn quickly and head for the door. Her voice was muffled as she called out. "Come up; I'll teach you. Just ask for Lizzie."

During the days that followed, Lizzie's voice continued to ring in Amy's ears. It wasn't just the words. It was the mocking challenge in her eyes. *Could Lizzie be lonely too? Was this a test? Is she asking me to prove my friendship by going up to that place?*

One day, while musing over the invitation, Amy watched the new grandfather clock in the Tabor parlor. Deeply conscious of the measured ticking, it seemed every swing of the pendulum gave a secret message. *Act now while there is time.*

Amy knew she had decided. No matter what, this was her opportunity; it was the secret dream come to life. *Secret dream? I threw that away that night when I married Daniel. Or did I?*

Amy shivered. *Just this, just the piano. Father can't be hurt— he won't know.*

Later that week Amy realized the advantage of the fast-approaching winter. In the evenings when she locked the post office, darkness had cloaked the town of Buckskin Joe.

Safe from the probing of curious eyes, Amy could cut through the dry brown grasses of the meadow leading to the boardinghouse snugged at the base of the mountain.

These evenings Lizzie would be waiting in the parlor with a plate of pastry or a bit of meat and bread. While Amy ate, Lizzie would sit at the piano and pound out the notes and explain the curious signs and words on the sheet of music.

Soon after the sessions began, Amy made several new discoveries. The first was that often she detected the odor of liquor on Lizzie's breath. She wondered, *Why, Lizzie? You've always been the happy and carefree one. Why drink?* There was no answer to the unasked question, but Amy continued to watch Lizzie, trying to dig out a deeper understanding of the girl.

She also discovered that in this house it was impossible to keep her secret. The dance-hall girls were there to grin through the doorway and cheer her on as she played the piano. She was the stranger, the outsider, but they accepted her without question.

As time passed, Amy began to realize those secret sessions at the boardinghouse in Central City had only whet her appetite. Piano became her passion. She plunged in, studying everything Lizzie could teach her.

Soon she began to feel confident. Lizzie was right—for her it *was* easy. Her fingers rippled across the keys as if they were born to produce music. Now before the evenings ended, the dance-hall girls began slipping into the room. Amy was only vaguely conscious of them dancing, swaying, and singing in the darkened parlor behind her.

After several weeks, on an evening when Amy had played until she felt her fingers would drop off, Lizzie brushed her hands away from the keys and cried, "Enough! Amy, you've about worn out this piano. The girls have waited patiently, and you shan't have my job. Be off now, go down to that hotel and tell them you'll play. Do it quickly before someone moves to town and snatches up the job."

Amy took a deep breath and said, "I'm just now realizing that there's something I need to do before I can go looking for that job."

"What is it?"

"I've never told Augusta Tabor about the lessons, nor my desire to play the piano at the hotel."

Lizzie followed Amy to the hall as Amy wrapped herself in a shawl. In the dimness she peered at Lizzie's face. Her friend shuddered. "I know what you're thinking. No one dares do something like this behind Mrs. Tabor's back. Yes, go tell her immediately."

"I'd like to thank"—Amy stumbled over the title and all it implied—"the—your madame for letting me use the piano."

"Never mind. You needn't; she's—"

"Lizzie, on the contrary," a voice interrupted. "I would like to meet your friend. Dear child, you do have a talent. It makes me happy to see you use it." Amy turned toward the open door behind her. Through the shadows she watched the woman beside the fireplace rise and come toward her. Amy could see the woman was tall and slender—beautiful. By the light of the fire she could see the pale gleam of hair, piled high and cascading in curls.

Even in the shadowy room there was something familiar about the woman. Amy frowned, trying to dig back into her memory. Then she shook her head and said, "You've been good to let me use the piano. I—" Amy hesitated, "I'm sorry, I don't know your name."

"Well, I'm not called *madame*." She gave a derisive twist to the words and added a low throaty chuckle before saying, "I'd answer more quickly if you call me Silverheels."

"Silverheels—I thought you looked familiar! I met you in Denver City. Remember the woodpile?"

The woman's smile thawed slightly. "I do. You've changed. Such a skinny little thing you were; now you've the marks of being a beautiful woman." Her smile was mocking and her eyes dancing with glee. For a moment Amy expected the woman to offer her a job. Feeling awkward, she headed for the door.

As Amy left the boardinghouse, the men and the girls were trooping into the parlor. She stood on the steps and drew on her mittens, listening critically. Lizzie was back on the piano stool, playing a polka. *Lizzie is good, but now I'm better*, she thought.

The day she walked into the Grand Hotel, Amy bolstered her courage by clinging to that memory. But as soon as she entered the parlor, nothing existed beyond the beautiful piano.

Swishing up to the front desk, just as Lizzie had instructed, Amy asked for Mr. Mayer. While she waited, Amy smoothed the silk frock she wore and wondered how much of her confidence was due to Augusta's gown.

Unbidden came the memory of that conversation with Mrs. Tabor. As she mulled over it, Amy wondered why it seemed so necessary to hide Lizzie's part in the affair. Why had Augusta asked those probing questions, and why had she wanted to know *what* she could play?

She had thrust Lizzie's borrowed music into Augusta's hands, and had given answers to clear the troubled frown from Augusta's face. Later Augusta had given her the gown—gray, not a bird of paradise color. Augusta had stamped the word *respectable* on it all.

Now Amy followed Mr. Mayer to the ballroom, its bare floors and peeled log walls warmed by a scrap of carpet, deep wine velvet draperies, china lamps decorated with gilt and painted roses—and that piano. Amy stroked the shiny dark mahogany and reverently touched the gleaming keys. She forgot all else. Now this was *her* piano, nothing else could be important.

Soon, nearly as often as Amy played, Mr. Mayer came, bearing piles of sheet music clutched in his pudgy fist.

By the first week of October the peaks surrounding Buckskin Joe were pristine white with the first heavy snow of the season. But in town, the same storm had merely dusted a fine powder. The snow that hung on the brown meadow grasses like garlands of tinsel disappeared as soon as the sun touched it.

The day after the storm, Daniel Gerrett walked into Buckskin Joe with Father Dyer's snowshoes hanging from his shoulders. He looked around at the fast disappearing snow. Recalling his hike across Mosquito Pass, while Father Dyer rode his mare toward Denver City, Daniel had to grin.

The first miner he met inquired of the grin and the snowshoes. He pointed to the glistening white mountains and explained, "Too deep to take a horse across."

With a frown the man replied, "Horses' legs are longer than yours."

"But when I wear these I have bigger feet."

The fellow was still frowning as Daniel headed for Father Dyer's cabin. As he leaned the snowshoes against the cabin, he was thinking he should have made some inquiries—but on the other hand, maybe not.

Restlessly Daniel moved around the cabin. He started a fire, checked out the supply of beans and cornmeal in the tin lard pails, and thumped the straw mattress covering the bunk. By the time he had finished settling in and preparing his evening meal, it was dark.

"Chicken," he muttered, "just like a stupid chicken running from the ducks." But he couldn't deny the reluctance he felt. "Dyer advised the trip. You were willing to go clawing your way over the pass. Now you haven't the gumption to walk down to the post office and say hello."

He decided to go to the Tabors' place. Dyer had said it was close to the store, and that it was a two-story building. It shouldn't be hard to find.

When he left the cabin the moon was topping the snow-covered peaks. The town lay on the hill below Dyer's cabin. As he walked, Daniel could make out the bulk of the stamp mill. The glow of lamplight identified the scattering of cabins and made it easy to guess the direction the road took. In the distance, close to the shadow of the mountain, stood a large structure, lights streaming from every window.

"Must be the Tabors' boardinghouse over that way," Daniel muttered. Changing direction he headed across the meadow. As he walked along, he mused aloud, "Strange to stick a boardinghouse so far out of town." With a shrug he headed up the path.

When Daniel opened the front door, he hesitated. A long blank hallway stretched in front of him. There were two closed doors, one on each side of the hall. From behind one door came the low murmur of voices. Just as he started toward the door, the one behind him opened with a crash and a woman surged through.

Daniel stepped backward just in time to collide with the woman. She murmured, "Oh, I'm sorry. I didn't see you. I'll find someone to dance with you."

She turned to go and Daniel stretched out his hand, but just as abruptly he dropped it. That sleeve he had nearly touched was as fragile and transparent as the wings of a moth. He felt his face warm as he began to understand. "I—uh, I'm looking for Amy Randolph Gerrett. I suppose I've come to the wrong place."

The woman turned slowly. There was something changing in her face. As he watched, he realized she wasn't young.

The words came slowly. "Amy Randolph Gerrett." Abruptly she tossed her head and looked him in the eyes. "I know her. Mister, I have an idea you can find your young lady in town at the Grand Hotel." She turned with a swish and Daniel saw the impudent flash of black stockings and dancing shoes spiked with shining silver heels. The rainbow gauze of her skirts settled as she opened the door and disappeared.

Daniel's face was still burning as he hurried back through the meadow and turned toward the row of lights marking the road through Buckskin Joe. Tramping down the road, he discovered his thoughts were moving in a troubling circle. That woman said the Grand Hotel. Dyer had said the Tabors' boardinghouse.

The music from the hotel attracted his attention. Daniel stopped in the middle of the street and caught his breath. She had sung for him just that one time, but the memory of her voice was still with him. This was Amy singing.

Slowly he walked through the door, wondering at the song he was hearing. Daniel hesitated in the lobby, looked at the man behind the counter, and then turned to follow the voice.

"Down in the valley, the valley so low. . . . If you don't love me, love whom you please. . . . Angels in heaven know I love you."

The last plaintive phrases were fading away when Daniel stepped into the room. The woman at the piano played another melancholy chord, paused, then swung into a polka.

Later he watched her toss her head at the applause. He saw the flash of her smile as she bent over the keyboard. He continued to study her. The smooth, blonde braid he remembered had become a cascade of curls that moved with the music. Her frock was soft gray, of a fabric that seemed to have become part of her body.

Daniel sighed with regret as he watched. He stood there in the doorway a moment longer before he turned slowly and went back the way he had come.

CHAPTER 20

You went all that way and didn't speak to her, why?" Father Dyer frowned.

Daniel was stunned. "What should I say? That I'd found out a dance-hall gal knew her. Remember, I saw my wife dressed in a way I couldn't afford, singing and playing worldly songs for a dance. I don't know what to think, except she's—Dyer, I've got a call to preach the Gospel, I can't have a wife like that."

Dyer winced. "You've heard me enough to know I'm convinced dancing is something the devil stayed up all night inventing. This old preacher may not have enough education to pick the minds of great men, but I know sin when I see it."

Daniel watched Dyer close his mouth into a tight line. For a long time he sat with his chin resting on his chest. When he lifted his head, he asked, "Do I detect a bit of pride? Talking about your call?"

Daniel wilted in his chair and thought about it. Dyer cleared his throat. His keen eyes bored into Daniel. "Another thing. I thought you sounded like a jealous husband, huffing outta there without even a kiss."

Daniel rubbed his neck and muttered. "I guess I was fussed about a couple of things. She seemed to be doing fine without me. And she was dressed pretty fancy for a poor girl."

"Maybe she's digging gold. Maybe she's rich. Were you expecting a hungry barefoot gal to come running back to your arms? Is that what you want, a defeated wife without a place to go? Maybe Amy took off because she's trying to grow up."

Daniel digested Dyer's words in silence. When he took a deep breath and looked at Dyer, the man said, "One thing I can't get away from is the Spirit urging caution." He glanced at Daniel. "Sometimes I feel the Lord doesn't judge nearly as harshly as we do. On the other hand, He's the only one seeing the true picture. Son, give the Lord time to work. Don't make a hasty decision."

Daniel slowly said, "Eli told me to forget about her."

"Her father?" John's voice sounded strained. "I—oh, never mind." Finally he got to his feet. "Daniel, there's missionary meeting in Denver City next week. Let's go. I've had something in mind for several weeks now. Right now, I'm reluctant to broach the subject. Could be if we have a week together riding the trails and going to services, I may be able to persuade you."

"About what?"

"Coming to Buckskin Joe with me the first of November and holding a revival service. That's a tough district and I need help. My idea is while you preach, I pray and then while I preach you pray. By the way, this isn't the first I've thought of it. Felt the Spirit urge before—"

Daniel was shaking his head as he got to his feet. "After being there this past week, I can't face it again."

"Even for her sake? Boy, I don't know what the Lord has in mind. I just feel this is right."

When Daniel looked at Dyer, he felt his face twist. He asked, "You'll be preaching the whole Book of Hosea to me, huh, John?"

"Maybe so. The prophet forgave his wife and took her back."

Daniel's head jerked. "I'm not accusing her of anything— it's just that there doesn't seem to be room in her life for me."

They borrowed a horse for Dyer and started for Denver City in a driving snowstorm. When they came down out of the storm, Dyer shook the snow from his collar and straightened in the saddle.

"I have this little portable organ," Dyer said. "Knowing my thoughts about the dance, how do you think I felt when I discovered some of my best folk were borrowing the organ while I was outta town and playing it at their dances?"

"I guess you felt like dumping them."

"Somehow, I didn't think that was what the Lord wanted."

When they reached the outskirts of Denver City, Dyer pulled on the reins and turned to Daniel. "They called it log city for a time. It's sprucing up now. See that fancy place over there? That belongs to a woman named Ada LaMont. Ever heard of her?"

Daniel shook his head. "I was told the story of her last year by a fellow who knew Ada and her husband well back east," Dyer said. "First off, the fellow said Ada was the most beautiful woman he'd ever seen. She was only seventeen when she married a young preacher. Seems, the fellow said, that Ada was a good woman, happy with being the parson's wife.

"Well, Parson LaMont felt the call to come out here in '59 when all the miners were following the rush. They started out, but somewhere out in Nebraska, one night the parson just disappeared. His bride had no idea what had happened. The wagon train spent the next day looking for him. Seems, too, that there was a female in the train with a pretty shady reputation. She also was missing."

Dyer was silent for a moment before he said, "Mrs. LaMont finished the trip in a state of terrible depression, but on the day they arrived in Denver City, she stood herself up in the wagon and yelled to the people: 'You see me now as a God-fearing lady: I tell you, take a good look, because from this time on I intend to run a pleasure palace. Any of you men looking for a good time, my tent flap is always open.' " Dyer paused and pointed to the imposing house. "Seems she did well in her new occupation. But I shudder everytime I think of her. She threw her defiance in God's face, and I'm fearful she'll be broken in the end."

The two of them rode in silence until finally Dyer raised

his head and shook it. Daniel watched him curiously, wondering at the sad expression on Dyer's face. "Something about the gold fever. Makes the worst come out in a man. God hasn't given up. He's sending us out to pick up the men and dust 'em off, give 'em another chance."

"We're getting close to the Elephant Corral, aren't we?" Daniel asked. "I've been studying out that bunch up ahead. See them milling around that store?"

Dyer squinted. "If I'm not mistaken, that's a Confederate flag hanging across the front of the store. Let's go see what's happening."

They reached the store as the crowd erupted into catcalls, a quick scuffle, and then a cheer. A man was hoisted onto a barrel.

"Well at least there's no shooting," Dyer remarked.

"Looks only half serious," Daniel added. They were close enough to hear the man on the barrel. Daniel reined in his horse.

"There'll be no rebel flag flown in Colorado Territory," the man was saying. "The majority wins, and that's a vote for the Union. If you fellows want to fly your flag, head for Missouri. We might can get up an escort for you." There were good-natured boos and catcalls and Daniel guided his horse away from the crowd.

"Guess that's the end of the war in Colorado Territory," Daniel said with a chuckle.

Dyer's face was serious. "Let's hope so. Lad, there's a great deal of fear that southern sympathies will get a foothold."

"You mean there'd be fighting here?"

"Possibly. Right now Colorado is a powder keg. The Texas Rangers are pushing on one door and the Indians are getting restless. We need every man to defend the territory."

Daniel nodded. "I can't help being uneasy about the Indian problems. Been here long enough to know the settlers and Washington aren't living up to the promises they've been making to the Indians.

"We were the intruders. I can't buy that idea of Manifest Destiny. They're God's creation too, and we're not a bit better than they are. If we don't do some giving pretty soon, we'll all be killing each other off."

"I'm hoping for an opening to move south to minister to the Mexicans," Dyer said. "Likewise, perhaps someday there'll be an opening for honest work among the Indians."

He added, "Well, there's the church just ahead. Seems to be a good crowd moving in already."

"I see Eli Randolph," Daniel replied. "I need to do some talking with him." As he slipped from his horse and started after the man, Daniel saw the quick flash of sympathy in Dyer's eyes.

Eli was just walking away from the corral when Daniel caught up with him. With a sharp pang of regret, Daniel noticed how the man's shoulders drooped.

"Sir," Daniel wrapped the reins around his hand and waited until Eli turned. "I need to talk to you. Should it be now or later?" He saw the man hesitate. A shadow dulled his eyes as he studied Daniel's face.

He turned away, saying, "Better make it now. I don't know what I'll be doing once meeting starts."

Daniel corralled his horse and followed Eli through the grounds to the line of cottonwoods beside the creek. Abruptly he started, "It's about Amy. I've found her, and I don't know what to think."

When he finished with his story, Eli sat down on a stump and stared at his clasped hands. *If I'd expected to find hope,* Daniel thought, *just looking at him ruins it all.*

Slowly Daniel hauled forward a stump of firewood and sat down. Eli lifted his head but he didn't meet Daniel's eyes. "Son, I think I've done you a disservice by not telling you the whole story. I gave you good advice; now I'm just sorry you found her. I'm supposing you'll not be able to forget her until you hear the whole thing."

Daniel flung himself off the stump and grasped Eli's shoulder. "Forget! Sir, I don't want to hear anything bad about Amy. Even if things can't be straightened out, I still love her and I don't want to know anything to change it all. There might be a time in the future—"

"You don't understand." Eli was looking him in the eyes now. "I'm not talking about Amy. It's her mother."

Slowly Daniel sat on the stump. As Eli began to talk, Daniel felt as if he had slipped through a closed door. Seeing the pain in the man's eyes, he wished the door had never been forced.

"Amy's mother was the prettiest little girl I've ever seen in my life. She was the daughter of a couple who attended the first church I ever pastored, back in Arkansas Territory. Folks are dead now, and her brothers drifted off, went west years ago." Daniel knew he was rambling and waited patiently.

Eli lifted his head. "I was more'n twice her age. You'd think I'd had better sense. She was a little child in a woman's body. I didn't know that until we were married. I don't think she'd had a childhood, and Amy was her doll." He was silent. Daniel saw the faraway expression in his eyes was tender.

He sighed and took up his story, his face marked by a new bleakness. "She was only fifteen when Amy was born. We were happy, if a grown man can be happy with a little girl who sometimes tires of playing house. She was pretty all right, and I spoiled her—petting her along when I should have known there was a limit to it all. When the money was gone and there were no more pretty trinkets coming in, when the hard realities of parsonage life began to come in the front door—well, we had troubles."

Daniel spoke. "Amy's talked about her mother. She seems to remember nothing but the good. I know she still grieves deeply over her death. Sir, I believe that's why Amy's so unhappy at camp meeting. I think there's shadowy things she remembers, buried deep inside."

Eli raised his head and interrupted. "Son. Amy's mother isn't dead. It was Maude who started that story. She just plain couldn't face the disgrace of it all. See, Maude had come to live with us. She was mother to both Amy and Amelia."

"That's her name," Daniel spoke automatically, as if reviewing the facts. "Does Amy know?"

Eli shook his head. "Amelia left me at camp meeting time. She just couldn't take the pressure."

"What do you mean?"

"The old struggle—old as Adam and Eve. At the time I'd only an inkling of how bad it was.

"During the meeting I watched Amelia running forward to fall on the altar, and I thought there was hope. Later she stood and walked away, saying she'd never go back."

"She left then?"

Eli nodded. "She made her choice, but it's been a hard one for me to live with. Some of the men saw her go. Left with a fellow who'd been hanging around the meeting all that week. I've had letters from her. No address, just notes saying she was sorry for it all.

"Once in a while tales drifted back, people saying they'd seen her. Always the tales came from the west. When I was sent out by the Nebraska conference, I wasn't too reluctant. I was moving west. Guess a person never gives up hope. I'd be more content if I knew how it had all turned out with her."

"You sound—" Daniel coughed, "I guess it's hard to quit loving." Eli didn't answer. Finally Daniel stood up.

Eli looked him in the eye. "See, son? I've done you a disservice. Like mother, like daughter. They say it's bad blood; maybe it is. When I heard you were married, it was like a load of fear slid off me. I kept thinking she'd be safe, now—"

Daniel was surprised by the wooden stiffness of his lips as he forced the words. "She's probably dead. Amy need never know about this."

"That doesn't change the situation now."

"Except that I know where Amy is. Father Dyer and I'll be holding revival services in Buckskin Joe during November. Sir, pray for us, and for Amy. I'm beginning to see something I didn't recognize before—I thought being a preacher's daughter, she knew."

Eli looked at him, puzzled. "I want Amy to know Jesus Christ as her Savior." Eli started to protest, and then shrugged in silence. Daniel looked at the bewildered expression on Eli's face and regretted his words. *I shouldn't have said it to him. God, what pain, to preach over the heads of those we love most. It's too late for her mother, but not for Amy. I understand now. Amy doesn't know about love. Only fear. Wrath, hell fire. And I want to be the one to help her learn that you run after God because you love Him.*

CHAPTER 21

It was nearly ten o'clock—church time. That made Amy uneasy. She glanced at the sun. It was shining brightly; everyone could see she wasn't going to church. She hurried along, taking hasty gulps of the morning air; she turned off the road to cross the meadow.

Having been there before made it easier now. After another quick glance at the sun, Amy marched across the frozen expanse of brown grass, trying to not care about what people were thinking.

She walked up the steps and into the boardinghouse. This Sunday morning, her footsteps were the only ones creaking across the rough-timbered floor. She paused and closed the door again, hard this time. A tousled head appeared over the banister, sleepy eyes widened. "Is the place on fire?"

"No," Amy said slowly, "Where is everyone? It's nearly noon."

The rest of the girl appeared. She came down the stairs hugging her skimpy gown about her. Shivering she said, "Ugh, it's cold. What do you want?"

"I'm looking for Lizzie."

"In the middle of the night? Come back this afternoon!

None of us get up this early." The scorn in her voice ended the conversation and she headed upstairs.

The door opposite the parlor opened. Amy exclaimed, "Silverheels!" She studied the face above the blue velvet robe. The question in the blue eyes changed to anger. "Oh, I'm sorry," Amy whispered. "I didn't mean to disturb you. I've today off and I just thought—"

"You'd come visiting." The woman sighed and Amy was surprised to see lines creasing the smooth face into a pattern that was both sad and lonely.

The blue eyes softened. Amy couldn't turn away. The woman's face, free now of the bright dabs of color and the strained smile, was beginning to seem warm and attractive.

Amy blurted out, "You have such beautiful skin; it's a shame to—"

"Cover it with rouge? Spoken like a true daughter of a clergyman."

Astonishment made Amy's jaw drop. "How did you know about Father? Oh, I know—Lizzie must have told you all about Central City."

Amy rushed on. "That's why I've come. It's been so long since I've seen Lizzie. And because of what she said, I dared not wait another day."

"And what did she say?"

"Well—she thought I was uppity. Too good for her."

The woman's mocking smile burst through. "You're sure it isn't because of the piano, of feeling obligated? Lizzie hasn't been well."

"Oh dear, I was afraid of that. I thought she looked peaked the last time I saw her."

"Come back to the kitchen; I'll start coffee and see if Lizzie can come down." Amy followed Silverheels down the hall, looking curiously about as she went through the dining room and into the kitchen.

The big cookstove still cradled warm embers. Silverheels poked around inside, and then crushed in paper and kindling. When the flames settled, she pulled the coffeepot forward and ladled in the fragrant coffee. "I'll get her," she murmured, heading for the door.

Amy paced about the room, examining everything. *Abundance—more of everything than I've ever seen,* she thought. Her eyes took in the stacks of dishes, the big oven, the mammoth table and the heaps of potatoes, onions, and squash piled beside the back door. A pantry door stood open. She could see mounds of pastry and covered tins stacked high.

The floorboards creaked behind Amy. She turned around as Silverheels came into the room. "No wonder you like living here—no danger of going hungry."

A line appeared between Silverheels' eyebrows, "You've gone hungry?"

"Oh, not really. But a parson sure doesn't live like this."

Silverheels hesitated, then glanced at Amy. "I'll get you some coffee. I've called one of the girls to go after Lizzie."

They settled down at the table with their mugs. While Silverheels sipped coffee, Amy studied the mug. "This is pretty!"

Giving her a pleased smile, the woman leaned forward, "You appreciate fine things, too bad—" There was the quick slap of heels coming down the hall. "Oh, Silver," wailed the girl as she came into the room. "Lizzie is throwing up again. She says she can't come yet."

The girl stopped. "Oh, begging your pardon." Her voice was prim but her eyes were wickedly gleeful. "Now the other half'll know how we live." She bobbed a mock curtsey and backed toward the door, clutching the shawl over her thin gown.

Amy got to her feet, "Oh, dear. I didn't realize she's that sick. Is it something catching?"

Silverheels sipped her coffee and smiled. "I don't think so. Mrs. Gerrett, you should know all about these little problems. It is Mrs., isn't it?" There was a glint in her eyes, and with a sinking heart Amy understood.

That girl. What did she mean 'other half'? Was she talking about life here in the boardinghouse? Strange, how easy it was to ignore the ugly part. The girl had drawn the line with her mocking voice. For another moment, Amy played with the handle on her mug. Father had hinted about these kind of things. Dance-hall girls.

"You mean she's pregnant, don't you?" Amy sighed. "Poor Lizzie. I guess I was thinking she had better—sense."

Silverheels' face was growing hard, cold. Impatiently she got to her feet. "It's a risk the girls have to take!" she snapped. "Also, you notice they aren't starving. I'll go take care of Lizzie."

"Then I'd better leave."

The woman paused and turned. Her face was completely expressionless. "Aren't you fearful of what she'll think?"

"Tell her I'll be back."

"Maybe she should just come see you—at the post office."

Amy walked back to Tabors' boardinghouse, feeling guilty. *Friend! I'm nearly glad I couldn't see her. What do you say to a person like that?*

Amy was nearly home before she could examine her other emotion. Silverheels' eyes had been scornful. "She's thinking I'm a silly little baby because I was shocked." Her steps dragged. Amy tried to understand her reaction. *Why should I care how the madame feels?*

Then with astonishment Amy said, "Maybe I've just been pretending I don't know what's going on in these places. It's easier, because Lizzie has been so nice to me. But Aunt Maude says nice girls don't let boys touch them." She moved her shoulders impatiently even as she imagined the thin, disapproving droop to Aunt Maude's lips. "Aunt Maude would say Lizzie has all the marks of hell on her. So now I know, I'm obligated to stay away from Lizzie." Rebellion boiled up—against Aunt Maude, against the mockery in Silverheels' eyes.

Augusta, leading her little boy by the hand, met her at the door. "We've been to services. Mighty barren it was. Folks don't seem to have much enthusiasm for worship on the Sabbath." She sighed heavily and then brightened as she said, "Father Dyer is going to be holding revival services starting the first part of November. I happen to know he's looking about for a person to play his little portable organ. If you're interested, I'll tell him."

Amy couldn't control the shudder. She rubbed her arms and said, "My, I hope I haven't taken a chill."

Later that week, while Amy was sitting behind the wire mesh cage enclosing her desk, the first of the compelling hands reached out to her.

A woman marched into the post office carrying a sheet of paper advertising the revival meetings. The woman's appearance was familiar: a calico was hidden under a dark shawl, steel-gray hair twisted so tight her eyebrows were stretched into an expression of surprise.

She pulled a hammer and a nail out of her bag. Amy's mouth twitched with amusement as she watched her attempts to hold the paper, lift the hammer and pound the nail. The woman's face was red from effort when the door opened.

The girl in yellow taffeta grinned under her fur-trimmed bonnet. Flashing a mischievous smile at Amy, she stepped forward. "Here, I'll help you." She held up the poster while the woman pounded the nails. "So we're going to have a revival meeting, starting November 6, 1861?"

The woman backed up and looked at the fur-trimmed bonnet and the yellow frock. "Thank you for the help. Yes, we'll be having meetings." She paused and slowly added, "You're welcome. Bring your friends."

With a saucy smile, while the bonnet bobbed, the girl said, "It would cut competition, wouldn't it?"

During the week, Amy watched as the wall in the post office was decorated with more posters. The boardinghouse across the way was having a grand ball on the night of November ninth. And the Grand Hotel was holding a ball in their ballroom on the twelfth.

Another poster announced the opening of the new dancing school for the miners to come and perfect their ballroom skills. The battle lines were drawn.

The next week Amy was pulled into the middle of it all. She had heard Father Dyer was in town, no doubt to prepare for the revival. He was going to be surprised. Amy had been cataloging the buildings in town. Between the balls and the dancing classes, there wasn't one building spacious enough for a revival meeting.

She also knew that sooner or later Father Dyer would be in the post office, and she was prepared. Before that day came, Mr. Mayer made a special visit to the post office to inform Amy that she was to play with the band being brought up from Denver City.

"A band from Denver City?" Amy exclaimed. "What's wrong with the band from Buckskin Joe?"

His expression was scornful. "That's small time. I hear these fellows from Denver are good. We want the best for the ball."

He handed her the sheaf of music. "There will be a practice session." He chuckled, "Those gals think they can outdo us. We'll show them. After all, we have a better pianist."

She didn't have time to be nervous before Father Dyer's visit. When he came to the cage, she saw his measuring eye, but his first words totally disarmed her.

"I need you to play the organ. Thank God there's a clergyman's daughter here who knows all the hymns. It's a blessing that you play by ear."

His words had slipped past her, catching her off guard. As he waited she remembered the speech she had prepared for him. "Where are you going to have services? Haven't you heard? The only place big enough is being used by the dancing school that has just started up."

He turned to go. "Don't worry about that. Your landlady, Mrs. Tabor, has volunteered her parlor. If the crowd is too big, we'll talk H.A.W. into letting us meet in the grocery store. Won't be the first time I've preached with hams swinging around my head."

Feeling trapped, Amy could only stare at him. "I'll count on you, Mrs. Gerrett."

CHAPTER 22

Amy stood in front of her mirror, trying to twist her curly locks into the latest style. Augusta tapped on the open door. Amy turned. "Augusta, will you please help me? I'm trying to make one of those fancy double knots."

"Like that hussy Silverheels was wearing when she came into the store yesterday?" Augusta snorted, but she came to peer at Amy. "Your hair's too curly. No, that can't be the reason. Silverheels has hair just as curly as yours. But hers is faded-looking. I suppose in another year or so she'll be smearing on the henna."

"Then what is the problem?"

"I—oh! Amy, I came to tell you there's a gentleman waiting to see you in the parlor."

"Gentleman?" Amy laughed. "Are you talking about the old man with the whiskers who's been following me around? He's a miner."

"No, this is a young man. Looks more like a preacher than a miner. So, twist your hair up quick, and I'll tell him you'll be right down."

Amy turned back to the mirror and shook her head. "If I dared, I'd cut all this off; wouldn't that shock Aunt Maude?"

She rolled it into a soft knot and thrust in the pins before she started for the stairs.

Halfway down she stopped. *What'll I do if one of those men from the hotel has come calling?* She cringed, thinking of the implications. Married, but without a husband. *It's no wonder I have difficulty convincing people—men. I could get a reputation as bad as Silverheels'.* Shaking her head, Amy ran down the last steps.

At first glance the parlor seemed empty; then she turned slowly, and saw him closing the door behind her. Amy's hand moved to the tiny white collar of her frock and then to the wad of hair.

He gestured toward the rocking chair and she said, "I— my pins are falling out." But she sat and he pulled a chair close.

His brown eyes seemed distant, but they took in everything, from the new dark calico frock to the slipping hair. For a moment she was grateful that she wasn't wearing Augusta's gray silk.

"Amy—" he began.

She interrupted, "Daniel, how did you find me?"

"Does that matter?" His eyes continued to probe as he said, "I've business here in town and it didn't seem fair to let you bump into me on the street." While she tried to find something to say, he added, "You've changed. Grown up. Before, I guess I didn't spend much time looking for changes." He cleared his throat and took a deep breath.

"Daniel—" She stopped. The necessary words would do nothing except hurt those brown eyes. She could see he was waiting out the silence and she must say something. "All that happened was so foolish. Please, just let's forget about it, about—each other." Now the words rushed out. "I just can't be a preacher's wife."

The frown deepened. "I'm not here to force you to come back. I'll not put pressure on you of any kind. I want to know that you're happy, and that you're not needing anything." He stretched out his hand and then pulled it back.

That gesture hurt, and Amy spoke over the tightness in her throat. "I am happy." She hesitated; now she couldn't see his eyes in the dim room. Abruptly he got to his feet and wandered around the room with his hands in his pockets.

Searching for something to say, she asked, "Why did you come?" *Anything, Daniel—just say something. I feel so guilty—I suppose I should say I'm sorry.*

"John Dyer has asked me to help with revival services." He hesitated a moment and then moved toward the door. "I hear he's asked you to play the organ." She nodded and he said, "I'd like that." His voice sounded muffled as he spoke in a rush. "I hope we'll get some time together while I'm here. We mustn't have bad feelings over this." His eyes were imploring.

"Of course." She kept her voice level. But at the door she touched his arm. "Are you well? You seem—thin."

She could see the shadows in his eyes. He started to speak and then slowly nodded and smiled. Silently he pulled on his hat and hunched into his old coat. Just before he walked out the door, he touched her cheek lightly.

Amy walked up the stairs, trying to keep her footsteps slow and even. She was also trying to swallow the lump in her throat.

When she closed the door of her room, she leaned against it and looked at the reflection the mirror threw back. Her hair was slipping. With trembling fingers she fumbled with the pins.

"Getting married is sure one way to ruin a good friendship," she murmured. She turned away from the mirrored sight of the tears on her face. "Why does it hurt so much? I was going to be angry—I didn't expect to feel so sorry," she mourned, holding her hand against the cheek he touched.

At noon the next day, Amy was still thinking about Daniel as she walked to the post office. The sun beat down on her back, and she moved her shoulders, realizing that the impersonal warmth heightened her loneliness.

Down by the river's edge the stamp mill was thumping out its monotonous message. She turned to look at the hulking object. Beyond, barely visible from where she stood, stretched the jagged, raw furrows that were the Phillips Lode.

Some were expressing fears about the Lode. The surface gold was gone, they were saying. Now, as if the earth were reluctant with her bounty, the content of the ore.had changed.

Just yesterday a discouraged-looking miner had come in with a letter to send. He leaned on the counter and explained the rumbles of discontent. The sulfides in the ore, couldn't be broken down by the stamp mill, so they would have the expense of shipping ore to the smelter.

A miner coming down the street seemed to have lost his jaunty walk. She noticed the man's dirty, tired face, the tattered clothing, the discouraged stride.

A trio of girls marched down the street. Arms linked, they were singing softly under their breaths. But their rouged cheeks didn't disguise the dark shadows under their eyes. Their shrill laughter startled the jack in front of Tabors' store and drew a half-smile from the miner.

Surprisingly, Amy found herself feeling sorry for the girls. She watched them continue down the street.

As she fumbled with the heavy post office key, Amy saw the man coming down the street. It was easy to guess the stocky figure dressed in brown was Father Dyer. She watched the girls stop on the edge of the road and cluster around him.

Amy leaned against the doorjamb, feeling the sunshine on her face. Glancing down the street, she watched the group move closer together. Father Dyer was talking earnestly. Then the laughter came, and like butterflies in the wind, the girls spun away from him.

Amy had the door open now. She scooted inside, flipping her shawl to the hook as she dashed behind the counter. Father Dyer walked into the post office. His first words revealed he had seen her. "Like pasteboard pretties," he said, jerking his head in the direction the girls had taken. "Paint and froth. Gets your attention like a poster, but that's all."

"Some don't think so." Amy couldn't resist the urge to push the words at him. "I was in the store the other day and H.A.W. Tabor was holding court around the stove. He was saying that while the girls had been criticized, they've also done some good. He mentioned the miners being more prone to shave and clean up when the girls are in town."

He shoved her words aside impatiently. "You going to play the organ for us?"

She pointed to the posters on the wall. "One night I'll have to practice with the band and the next night is the ball. Other than that, I'll come play."

He watched her with eyes that didn't tell her a thing. But when he finally began talking, he didn't leave room for questions. "Mrs. Gerrett, I know your father. He's a God-fearing man of the cloth and I know for a certainty that he's raised you to know right from wrong. If you can't see anything wrong with playing for ballroom dancing, well, I'll be praying for you.

"You know the Bible teaching; you know we must all stand before the judgment throne of God. With that choice on your conscience, will you be able to look Him in the eyes and say your life is measuring up to the fullness of His will for you?"

After he left the post office, Amy thought of a question. Did he know about that marriage ceremony at last quarterly meeting?

But after she quit shaking with anger, she addressed the vacant spot where he had stood. "John Dyer, thundering prophet, self-styled oracle, you know not one whit better than I do about what the Lord's thinking. I don't like old men who chase away pretty girls and frighten Christian women into smelling burning sulphur from the pit, just to get them to think like you. I'm as good a Christian as you, and I'm a lot less judgmental."

"Atta girl." There was applause behind Amy and she turned to the door. Lizzie was standing there, laughing and clapping.

"Oh, Lizzie!" Amy rushed across the room and hugged the girl. "I didn't know I had an audience. I do think I will go on the stage. Don't you think I have a good speech?"

"Yes, and I dare you to go down to the saloon and hop up on a table. If you can make those men clap, then you'll be a star for certain."

"Lizzie, that's silly. You know those men will clap for anything in skirts, and I was teasing. I'm just so angry."

"I gathered that," Lizzie replied. Amy looked at her friend. She was pale and the sparkle was gone.

"You don't look well."

Lizzie winced and a shadow came into her eyes. "You do know how to make a person feel good."

"Sorry. Did you know I was up there to see you three weeks ago?"

"Silverheels told me so." Her eyes were measuring Amy.

"Yes," she nodded, "they told me that you are—"

The door opened and Amy scooted behind the counter. After the miner collected his letter and counted out the money for the charges, Amy turned back to Lizzie.

The girl's bright smile was forced, but it was there. "Don't you fret. Everything will be fine. You know it takes more'n something like this to put us down."

"What do you mean by that?"

"Just that you look like you feel sorry for me. Amy, don't you realize we're getting out of life just exactly what we want? And I've a sneaking hunch that if most of the women were brave enough, they'd admit they want the same. We're buying pretty clothes and fun, a place to stay and plenty to eat." Her lips twisted in scorn as she added, "Most either don't have the courage to go after their desires, or they don't have the looks to carry it off. I happen to have both."

Amy was still pondering the remark and wondering at the the feelings she was having. One moment there was a strange thrill over Lizzie's brave, independent words and the next minute the churning she felt inside made her want to run.

Lizzie was talking again and Amy lifted her head, "What was that?"

"I said, that other preacher man has the same last name as you. Is that a coincidence?" Her curious eyes held Amy's.

Amy turned and paced the floor.

"He's my husband." Amy told Lizzie the whole story, and when she finished, Lizzie was looking at her with a strange expression.

Slowly she said, "That's the weirdest thing I've ever heard.

You marry a man and he hardly passes you a kiss before you're both taking off in different directions. So you didn't get what you wanted the first time you tried to talk him into leaving the territory; is that any reason to give up? If a gal can't vamp her own husband, how's she supposed to get anywhere in life? Amy, I got news for you. I think you flunked the first test of being a woman."

"It was just a dumb thing to do. I was thinking more of escaping that Lucas Tristram than I was of marrying Daniel Gerrett."

"You wanted to get away from that fellow? He's got money." She shook her head. "I got more news for you. I think you're in love with your husband."

"I'm not."

Lizzie sighed patiently. "Amy, once I thought I was in love. He was just a farm boy and I was scared to death of being a farmer's wife. I didn't stick around long enough to find out if I loved him. Funny, but I still think of him."

CHAPTER 23

John Dyer carried his portable organ into Augusta Tabor's parlor. He turned to Amy, his expression very sober. "Now I want you to remember, you play only hymns on this. It's sacred. Besides, if you play anything very fast, it'll fall apart."

Amy's carefully built wall fell apart and she threw her head back and laughed. Touching her eyes, she said, "You know, you're almost human. I may even enjoy this."

He set up the organ, saying, "Daniel will be preaching tonight. I'll be praying. Tomorrow we'll switch roles."

She shrugged as she leaned over and brushed her fingers across the keys of the organ. Sitting down on the stool, she said, "Show me how to run this thing. I've never seen such a contraption."

Augusta whisked into the room, saying, "Parson, you two men might just as well have your dinners here. A couple more won't make a difference around the table."

"Thank you, ma'am," Father Dyer said carefully, "but I doubt Daniel will eat before preaching."

Augusta's face lengthened, and she said softly, "Well then, you just tell him to stay for a bite afterwards."

After several false starts, Amy finally hit the rhythm of

pumping and playing. Father Dyer placed the hymnbook in front of her. She shook her head, saying, "Just tell me what and then start singing."

"You know them that well?"

She shrugged. "I don't know what you call it, but I can play it if you can sing it."

After dinner Amy came back to the organ. She began playing through everything she could remember. Later she opened the hymnal Father Dyer left. When the shadows nearly hid the book, Augusta came with a lamp.

As she played, Amy discovered the music was releasing a flood of memories. Lost in the mood of the music, Amy began singing as she played. "God moves in a mysterious way His wonders to perform. . . . Behind a frowning providence, He hides a smiling face."

She was still singing her way through the book when Augusta came with more lamps. Now she saw the people quietly filing into the parlor.

When John Dyer stopped beside her, Amy looked up. Her heart sank. This was revival. The room was packed. Daniel was there. For one brief moment their eyes met. In the next minute she knew he had forgotten her.

When the last prayer had been heard and the final hymn sung, she fled upstairs. Burying her face in her pillow, she wondered miserably how she could endure the two weeks.

Rolling over, she addressed the ceiling. "It will be a happy day when people will not have to be wrung to pieces, pounded to mash—all in the name of God."

One thought remained about Daniel. *It's the first time I've heard him, standing up in front of people, giving out just like Father.*

This was a new Daniel. She reviewed the feeling of wonder she felt as he spoke. Strange it seemed, to hear those old thoughts come out in a new way—not stern, not scorching, but strong, with complete conviction.

Daniel believed what he said. For a moment she wanted to ask him to say it again.

Amy settled against her pillow, recalling the expression on

Daniel's face, the sight of his strong hands holding that black Bible. Yesterday his hand had brushed against her cheek. She touched her face, but she was thinking about all she had heard him say.

Daniel had snatched at her unwilling attention when he said, "God is the author of love. His greatest expression of love has been given through Jesus Christ. Both God and man, both human and divine, Jesus Christ died because of love. But you will never know His love until you stretch out your accepting hand."

Did it seem to strike a gong within her simply because it was Daniel speaking? This Daniel, the youth from Central City, was no awkward miner. Amy marveled at the differences. Something about those firm lips and steady eyes set her heart to trembling.

Amy moved restlessly on her bed and thought about the music she had played: *"Just as I am, without one plea, but that Thy blood was shed for me . . . waiting not. . ."*

Amy sat up on her bed and frowned. For the first time in all the years she had heard the music, she was filled with wonder. *Daniel, what has happened? You're not the same, not timid. I sense a sureness I didn't see before.*

"Amy." The tap and the voice came at the same time. Augusta pushed the door open. "Everyone has gone. Won't you come down and have something to eat with Father and Daniel—" She paused, and Amy saw her eyebrows arch toward her hairline. She had guessed. Amy's refusal died instantly.

Getting off the bed, she said, "Yes, I'll come. I'm very tired, but I do need to tell Father Dyer I won't be here tomorrow night."

She followed Augusta downstairs. The house was quiet except for the murmur of voices from the dining room. The two men were facing each other across the table. The kerosene lamp cast a puddle of light that neatly enclosed them. Amy hesitated; deeply conscious of being an outsider, she slowly walked into the room.

Augusta bustled into the kitchen while Amy waited beside

the table. She saw the two had shoved the pie and the plate of meat and bread off to one side. With arms folded on the table and noses within inches of each other, they were deep in conversation.

Augusta came back carrying the coffeepot and more plates. She said, "Now you men, just start in on that food. I know you're both hungry. Besides, if we get a word in edgewise, it'll be when your mouths are full."

Both men looked at Amy and got to their feet. Glancing at each other both began to speak at once, and Father Dyer said, "Oh, pardon!"

And Daniel muttered, "Of course you know Amy." He pulled out a chair for her, still avoiding her eyes.

When Augusta over-filled the coffee mug, her sharp exclamation caught their attention. Father Dyer reached for the mug. "That's all right, I don't like cream."

Augusta cut the pie, and the awkward silence stretched. Impatiently Amy said, "Go on with your conversation, I've only come for the pie and to remind you both that I won't be here to play tomorrow."

"Possibly, could you play before your practice?" Father Dyer asked wistfully. "I can't do much more than thump on that thing." Daniel watched her. The lamplight made his dark eyes darker still, increasing her discomfort.

Finally, with a sigh, she said, "I suppose I could stay long enough to get things started." She finished her pie.

Daniel was still pushing the meat around on his plate. "No wonder you are thin!" she said impatiently. "But then did any man alone ever eat properly?"

The words were coming out all wrong. In the silence she searched for something to say. Finally Father Dyer rescued them. "Daniel was telling me about some of the people he's met at California Gulch." She looked at Daniel. So he was living at California Gulch now. He really did take Chivington's circuit.

Dyer added, "He's thinking the area is going to boom within the next few years. I hear the gold's peaked."

"No matter what," Daniel said slowly, "there're people

living heedlessly. I can't get away from the urgency I feel to warn—"

Augusta leaned forward, asking breathlessly, "Then you think the Second Coming will be soon?"

Daniel threw her a sharp glance. "I haven't spent too much time thinking that way. I'm more concerned with life rising up and giving these people a swift smack."

She settled back with a frown. "But this is the age of reason. We can perfect ourselves, and that's important. But, in addition, don't you believe a God of love will make certain everyone goes to heaven?"

Daniel was frowning. "There's nothing to support that idea in the Holy Scriptures. If that is so, there're a lot of people who've misunderstood the Lord. Some of us are mighty convinced you live life God's way or live with the consequences."

"Hellfire and brimstone," Amy murmured.

"Can't get away from that part either," Father Dyer said soberly. He pointed his fork at her, "Don't forget, young lady, some things can't be ignored out of existence. Justice doesn't make sense if the Author of justice looks the other way to keep from offending His creation." He paused and then slowly added, "There's not a one of us who wouldn't choose a different occupation if hellfire and brimstone weren't in God's Word. But we can't avoid it. We've got to live God's way."

"What's God's way?" All eyes shifted toward Augusta's small voice.

The silence lasted long enough for all to hear the measured gonging of the grandfather clock. Father Dyer's voice was tired, heavy. "It's all there in the Bible. First you accept the atonement for sin, Jesus' death. Then you read the Word, day by day. You'll stack up a lifetime of knowing what God wants. In the days when the Word wasn't available, you'd have listened to a preacher say, 'Get down on your knees and beg God's forgiveness for ignoring what He's said through the mouth of some poor donkey or written on the wall of a palace.' It's a better idea to settle down before the Lord with Book in hand and start taking instruction." There was a slight grin on his face. "Seems that's better by far."

Amy looked at Daniel. When he met her eyes, she asked. "Is that what you did?"

He nodded with a smile. "It was your advice." He continued to look at her and Amy knew they were sharing the memory of that time.

The next morning Amy was still pondering Father Dyer's fragmented statements. Could it be his way of warning her?

A storm had blown through Buckskin Joe last night. Amy had felt the cold and heard the wind. This morning, as she left the boardinghouse and turned down the street toward the post office, she discovered a dusting of snow on the ground. The wind was biting through her shawl.

"Please, ma'am." Amy looked up into the woman's face and blinked. The stranger was the color of Augusta's good coffee with cream. She was shivering in a thin shawl.

Her lips trembled with cold as she tried to speak. "Could you point me the way of the Tabors' boardinghouse?"

Amy turned to point. "Just right there, the two-story building. Are you looking for someone? Mrs. Tabor is probably busy right now."

The woman hesitated, sighed and said, "I'm looking for work. Spent my last dime getting up here on the stage, thinking I'd get a job over at the other boardinghouse."

Amy said, "You're cold. I'll walk back with you and find Mrs. Tabor. I don't know that she's been looking for help, but she certainly needs some."

As they hurried down the street, the woman continued bitterly. "Right sad when the sisters can't look out for each other."

"Sisters?" They were inside the parlor now, and Amy led the way through the long dining room toward the kitchen. "You're related to someone there?" she asked curiously as she pushed the door open.

The woman shook her head and her face split in a grin, revealing even white teeth. "You call us soiled doves; we call each other sisters."

Augusta was wiping her hands as she came toward them. Amy explained. "I found—"

She gestured and the woman said, "I'm Crystal Thomas. I had a promise of a job, but now it's fallen through. Amelia— that's the madame—I've known her for ten, fifteen years, thereabouts. She's had to go back on her word. Said she'd give me a job. Now times are bad." She paused, pondered a moment and continued. "When I told her I wanted to get out of the business, she promised to help. Seems I can't get work in Denver, and I thought—"

Augusta's nose was twitching. "What kind of work are you looking for?"

"Kitchen. I keep a neat, clean place. Cook good and won't mind working."

Augusta straightened up. "Well, I don't know—"

"Oh, ma'am," Crystal said, "I see yer question. I'm clean. Never had the problem."

Curious about the woman, Amy continued to study her. She looked from her sad eyes to her trim figure. Her clothes were shabby but clean. "Augusta, you've said you need help. Why can't you try her, at least until H.A.W. gets back from Denver next week." Augusta nodded. The two women were still talking as Amy hurried out of the house.

The icy blast of wind struck her, sending Amy shivering deeper into her shawl as she hurried toward the post office. Recalling the conversation, something caught Amy's attention. *Silverheels. She called her Amelia; that's my middle name. Strange coincidence.*

CHAPTER 24

Late the next evening, after Amy had finished the practice session with the band, she found Daniel waiting for her. Amy was frowning in frustration over the dismal evening as she left the piano. Her heels made staccato exclamations of anger on the plank floor as she crossed the ballroom to find her shawl.

Chewing her lip and fuming, she paid scant attention to the tall man unfolding himself from one of the deep velvet chairs. Flipping her shawl from the rack and thinking of the miserable evening, she glanced up as he stopped beside her and took the shawl. "Daniel! I didn't know you were here." She paused, "Shouldn't you be at revival service?"

"It's long finshed. I've come to walk you home."

She swallowed hard. Last night's hurts surfaced. He wrapped the shawl about her shoulders, adding, "You should have a heavier wrap; but then I shouldn't meddle." His lips twisted in a wry grin, "Certainly you're earning more than I ever shall."

Outside the steps were icy, and he took her arm. She could feel his warmth coming through the thin shawl. Without willing it, Lizzie's word popped into her mind. *Vamp*. Lizzie had told her to vamp him. Amy's face burned.

"I was hoping it would be warm enough to walk for a while." His voice was muffled, making her wonder at the note of regret she was hearing.

With a touch of malice, she said, "We could go to Augusta's for pie."

"I've had enough pie for a couple days." He tightened his grip on her arm, pulling her closer.

Slowly he asked, "Mind telling me why you left Fort Lupton?"

She shrugged. "I intended to go home. Took the wrong stage and didn't have money to leave here."

"That isn't *why*." He waited. Finally he asked, "Why didn't you write to your father or me?

"Because I discovered freedom. I like it." She lifted her chin, and saw his eyes. He seemed miles away. She thought back over their conversation. Why did he mention her earnings?

Now could be the right time, she mused, especially if he feels the lack of money. Her pulse quickened as she reviewed the dream of the little white church back east. The two of them together. *Funny, I'd nearly forgotten that dream. It's becoming more attractive*.

Glancing sideways at him as they walked, she spoke, finding her words stiff and uncomfortable. "Daniel, you're different; I hardly know you. Grown up. We're strangers." She paused and rushed on. "How can I say it? Is it the preaching?"

"Preaching? Amy, it's more what God's doing in me."

She found herself liking the new maturity. *The confidence and dignity—surely he'd be able to get a church back east*. "Daniel," she said slowly, "you mentioned money. I'm certain the churches back in the states pay more—" she stopped when he frowned.

They continued to stroll down the road, first silent and strained, then abruptly spilling unimportant words. Amy felt the tension growing between them.

At last he said, "I didn't realize you played the piano like that."

"Thanks to Lizzie I do." She looked up at him, wanting to

say all the other things, about how music was a need digging into the deepest part of her. A craving. But it didn't seem to be the time.

When they reached the boardinghouse she protested, "You know it isn't necessary to escort me. Buckskin Joe is perfectly respectable. I'm not afraid to be on the streets at night."

"I didn't think you were." He waited, and Amy shivered. Finally she swung the door open and he followed her in. The parlor was dimly lighted by one lamp. The round iron stove still radiated heat and Daniel pulled chairs toward it.

Augusta passed through the hall from the kitchen. She looked around the door and smiled. "Night, children."

Amy murmured, "Night," and listened to the whisper of her slippers on the stairs.

"Nice woman," Amy nodded. He hesitated, shifted uneasily on his chair and then asked, "Where do we go from here?"

"What do you have in mind?" Her voice was flat. "I walked out."

"I can forget that." He leaned forward and took her hand. "You're still my wife. I realize I'd be asking you to give up more than I can offer; you have a good job and an opportunity to play the piano here."

"Doesn't it bother you that I play for dances?" He winced, and she pressed on. "I do so because I don't happen to feel the same way you, my father, and John Dyer feel." She hesitated. Feeling compelled, she added, "Daniel, I am what I am. To deny how I feel inside is to be false to myself. You must accept this."

When he didn't reply, she leaned forward, speaking earnestly and quickly, "There was a girl at quarterly meeting last summer who told me how it was back east. Big cities. I've never been to a large city. For me it's always been a poor little town and a poorer church.

"I would like going to a church where they preach about good and beautiful things. About love and honesty and self-respect. Not all the things that make people fearful."

Daniel leaned back in his chair and the brooding expression

on his face made her heart beat faster. He was thinking, considering. Maybe it wasn't foolish to dream.

Amy continued, "She said they go to concerts and have dances. She's—"

Daniel looked up, "Amy, please. I think you know how I feel; I also know how you've been raised." He hesitated, as if about to say more; then taking a deep breath he said, "You know how important this is—" He gestured toward the line of benches in Augusta's parlor and the little organ by the makeshift pulpit. He took a deep breath. "Right now, I think it's best to put off this talk. I want to discuss our future when the revival services have ended."

"Because you think I will be changed?" Amy leaned forward to look into his eyes. "Daniel, I feel just as strongly. Don't forget, I've been in the church much longer than you, and I see it as hopelessly out-of-date."

"What replaces a personal commitment to God? What's better than learning to follow after Him with all your heart?"

"I still believe that," she said quickly. "But—

He looked at her for a moment, hesitated. Finally he said, "We're both tired. Now I don't think either of us would give an inch." His grin was crooked as he reached for his hat and stood up.

He went after his coat and Amy followed. While he stood beside the door, she saw the twisted grin. She whispered, "Last night hurt you, too. Oh, Daniel, what is wrong with us? We were such good friends before—" She couldn't finish the sentence, but it was easy to lift her arms to the hunger on his face.

Between kisses he admitted, "Amy, I want you so badly. Do you understand? I love you." When he held her away and looked into her face, Amy's throat tightened.

She reached for him again. *Love? Whatever it is, Daniel, I want you.* She dropped her arms, remembering those words— *One of us must give.* "Daniel, you said one of us must give. You meant me, didn't you?" She studied the hunger on his face. *Right now,* she thought, *I am afraid it will be me, and I'll spend the rest of my life regretting.*

By morning Amy was able to think clearly, without emotion. At the post office while she worked, she firmly lectured herself: *Amy, you get control of the situation and worry about love later.* She relaxed and smiled. "All it takes is a plan," she murmured, feeling pleased with herself.

Now there were other things to think about. This was the evening of the ball at the Grand Hotel, and the band Mr. Mayer had brought from Denver was terrible.

Late that afternoon, sorting mail and stacking newspapers impatiently, Amy chafed in her solitude. The last customer had left the building when she allowed her fingers to rest among the letters. Too bad Lizzie couldn't make an appearance now; it would be nice to have a talk with her.

She flipped through the letters still wondering about Lizzie. The last time she had been in the post office her sunny smile had not hidden the shadows in her eyes. Lizzie was afraid.

Slowly Amy sat down on the stool behind the counter and thought. What would it be like to be a Lizzie? She shuddered. Somehow the pretty dresses and the gay, laughing girls didn't seem as attractive since she'd begun to see the shadows in their eyes. *What had Father Dyer called them? Pasteboard pretties.*

Amy got down off the stool and walked toward the door. Storm clouds were rolling in over the peaks. She watched them drop lower, until one by one the white-capped mountains disappeared from view and the sun was only a lighter circle in the clouds. Slowly the afternoon flattened out into a wash of shadow gray. Amy shivered and rubbed her chilled arms.

While she was still looking out the door, she saw clusters of people on the street pause, turn, and wait.

There was something sad about those motionless figures and Amy's attention was caught. She watched drooping shoulders sag even more.

In unison, the figures began to turn slowly. The undertaker's long black wagon slowly passed the post office, and idly Amy wondered where the mortician found a pair of perfectly matched jet black horses.

One of the pedestrians broke away from the group and

came into the post office. It was a miner clad in grimy buck-
skins, dirty from the mine. He carried his hat in his hand and
his face was still marked with sadness.

She asked, "Who died?"

"Don't know." He grinned at her with a white slash of
teeth in his dirty, tired face. "Us young ones don't care as long
as it's an old, worn-out one. But if it's a miner or one of the
pretty little girls from the boardinghouse across the way, it gets
scary. Makes a body fearful."

"Why?"

"You oughta listen to the preacher. After death comes the
judgment. It's enough to make a person straighten up his life,
seeing that wagon and thinking of someone being hauled off,
someone like you."

"You don't think a loving God is going to take everybody
to heaven, no matter what?" she asked curiously.

He scratched his head. "I'd like to think that. But deep
down inside I know better'n that."

He leaned against the counter and folded his arms, a frown
on his face. "There's something you can't ignore. If that kind
of thinking is right, then how come people never get over the
fear of dying? Seems that'd be the first place God would start
changing things for a body."

He paused and then slowly said, "Might be a nice idea if
it were so. At times this earth seems about all the hell a body
ought to have to face."

As he left the building, Amy couldn't keep her thoughts
away from Lizzie. The afternoon wore on, and Amy's fear
grew. That miner had talked about a young person dying.

The moment the big clock pointed to five, Amy was at
the door. Turning the key in the lock, she wound the shawl
tight and flew down the street and across the meadow.

It had been a long time since she had come this way—to
the boardinghouse. The madame, Silverheels, had seen her as a
meddler. But no matter what Silverheels would think of her
meddling now, she must relieve her guilty conscience by finding
Lizzie. *Lizzie needs to know about God, judgment.*

When she stepped into the hall of the boardinghouse, Amy was met by a blast of warmth and delicious food smells. There was the clink of silverware and soft laughter. She followed the sounds and went to stand in the doorway of the dining room, searching the crowd for Lizzie.

Silverheels saw her and hastily crossed the room.

"What is it?" There was an impatient frown on her face, and Amy found herself stammering.

"Lizzie? I saw the hearse and couldn't help—"

Silverheels' face cleared and she laughed, "Quite a crush you have on that gal! Lizzie's all right. She's out right now. I'll tell her she's not to neglect you again."

The woman's playful air and gentle smile swept Amy and the room. Those watching turned back to their plates.

Silverheels took her arm. Leading her into the hall, she said, "My dear Mrs. Gerrett, I can't have you disturbing the whole place. My clients mustn't—"

Seeing Amy's face, she sighed wearily and her lips drooped. "Do I have to stand here and defend myself?"

"No, no. It's just that I'm fearful."

"I heard it was a girl—not from here. She was a coward, tired of living. She couldn't face the future. Some say she had a lover who'd jilted her." She shrugged, "Who knows? She probably took laudanum." Her voice mocked as she added, "The fruit of the poppy has stolen her away."

Impatiently Silverheels spun away from her. Fascinated, Amy watched the bright full skirts swish around her body, drawing tightly across her thighs and hips. Just before they settled back into place, Amy saw the quick flash of silver dancing slippers.

Amy went home, with Silverheels' mocking smile and gentle laugh following her. When she reached the boardwalk, her steps slowed as Amy mulled over the strange, fascinating woman.

She looked up. It was dark. "The ball!" She ran into the Tabors' parlor and stopped. She had forgotten the revival meeting. Feeling as if she had dropped into a different world, Amy stood looking at the sober crowd pushing into the parlor before she dashed toward the stairs.

Late that night, when the ball was over, the events of the afternoon rose to trouble her.

Now Amy crashed her final chord and turned around on the piano stool. Exhausted by the effort needed to follow the bumbling musicians, she rested, watching them put away their instruments.

The group—two violinists, a short fat man playing the French horn with one sticky key, and a saxophone player still puffing from the high altitude—were joking and laughing, full of their success and wine. Shaking her head as she reviewed the evening, Amy got to her feet and discovered Father Dyer.

"I'm here to escort you home." He eyed the clinging gray silk and she detected a note of reproach in his voice as he said, "We've had a good service tonight." His grin was twisted as he added, "For making people do some serious thinking, there's nothing more effective than a tragic death." He paused. "You know we've had one today."

She nodded, wishing desperately for his total silence. "Daniel's still with some of the seekers."

"So he sent you."

His eyes were twinkling as he patted his thick hair. "I might be an old fogey to you, but at least I don't go barefoot on the top of my head." While she laughed, he added, "And I'm not so old that I don't recognize a tug-of-war. Good luck, my dear."

She blinked up at him. "You want me to *win*?"

"Only if you get what you want."

At the Tabors' she left Dyer in the parlor with Daniel and the crowd of people kneeling beside the benches. As she hesitated in the hallway, Amy was conscious of the seekers. She moved her shoulders uneasily as she walked up the stairs. In her room she pulled the pins out of her hair, admitting she could feel only scorn.

But with the silk dress half off, she paused. The miner in the post office had talked about being afraid of dying. Curiously she probed the things he had said.

That miner must think about death every day, she mused. *With every stick of dynamite he handles, every time he walks into those dank, dark mines.* She shivered.

And those people downstairs—why did they come to listen to a man who frightened them? What sent them running to fall before that crude bench in an agony sometimes lasting for hours?

Just before she slipped between the sheets, Amy looked at the dusty Bible lying beside the lamp. Ironic, that she had suggested to Daniel that he read it for answers to his questions. Now he talked about how important it was to be reading it all the time. With eyes wide, staring at the ceiling, Amy thought of Daniel's beliefs and a tiny twinge of misgiving touched her. But then, if he really loved her, he would change.

CHAPTER 25

John lumbered about the cabin, banging kettles and sloshing water. When he dragged the dishcloth across the table, Daniel straightened, sighed and rescued his Bible from John's soggy cloth.

"I hear you, Brother John," he said dryly. "You've been thumping around all morning."

Father Dyer's expression was guileless. "I wasn't intending to interrupt you; it just seems to me that you ought to be up and taking nourishment. It's your turn to preach tonight and I've a feeling you need all the strength you can get."

"Amy?" Daniel asked, paused and shook his head. "She plays that organ oblivious to everything else. It's as if she's not hearing a thing that's being said. I can't figure it out."

John dropped the cloth back into the dishpan. Sitting down to face Daniel, he folded his arms and waited. Daniel lifted his head again. "I suppose I'm pushing my will against God. Not content to wait. But, John, I'm fearful for what could happen to Amy, especially in a place like Buckskin Joe."

"Remember Hosea. He took his wife back after she'd been living the life of a prostitute."

Daniel winced and said, "Don't talk that way."

"Oh, son, I didn't mean to imply your Amy is like that. I'm certain the Lord will protect her while we're waiting to see His will accomplished. But people are willful."

"John, how can I be so bold as to think He wants us together?"

"Don't ask me. I've messed mine up; I can't give out advice about another man's marriage." He paused and added. "You married her, and that's a solemn covenant you two have made before God. Seems He doesn't ignore any serious promises we make."

In a moment, after studying the man's face, Daniel said slowly, "You said 'messed yours up.' Is that why you aren't married?"

"Yes. I'll tell you about it some time; right now let's get you on your feet. When I mentioned Amy was in Buckskin Joe, you had it all decided she was a poor little lonesome gal, just waiting to drop in your arms and surrender to Jesus, all in one fell swoop, didn't you?"

"I suppose that was my dearest dream," Daniel admitted, feeling his grin twist. "Why didn't you tell me before that she was doing fine, that—"

"First off, I didn't know about her piano playing. But then, our ways aren't God's ways. His are higher and past finding out. I thought you'd read it."

"I have. I just didn't think I'd have to prove it in my own life."

"We all do at some point. It's called testing our faith." John fiddled with the pencil lying on the table; finally he looked at Daniel. "I wonder if I can try a thought on you." When Daniel nodded, Dyer continued. "Well, it all started when I got to hearing so much criticism of our ways of revival. Some were saying revival doesn't last. It's a fact. Once the emotional pressure is off, people backslide. I'm inclined to agree. But, Daniel, we can't quit revival either because of criticism or backsliding.

"With this in mind, I recently read an interesting statement by a fella I have a lot of respect for—name's Charles Finney. He said something that made me sit up and think." He paused and added, "This is one of those ideas to chew on for now. I'm not so certain there's a need to start making changes, but here goes: Talking about revival, Finney said there's never been a real reformation except by new measures. The key word here is *reformation*. Then he went on to say whenever the church gets settled into a rut—he called it a form of doing things—there's trouble.

"People rely on the *human*. They hang on to a form of religion while they lose all the real substance. He said it becomes impossible to arouse these people to real soul-deep revival by pursuing the old established forms. Finney gave us hope, though; he said at this point God will bring in a new way to reach the people."

Head down, Dyer played with the pencil. When he looked at Daniel he said, "I've been thinking about this the whole two weeks we've been here. Oh, don't get me wrong. There's been results and people have come, but it isn't like it used to be. The ones that have tumbled at our altar aren't the old hardened sinners in need of religion; they're the repeaters. These are the fellas I've been preaching to ever since I came. I brought this up because of Amy.

"Seems the Lord's got something in store that we can't guess yet. Who knows what's in her heart? Be patient, son, and don't be surprised if the Lord doesn't do something new and different."

He got to his feet. "Daniel, I'm going over to the Tabors' and then wander the streets and do a little talking to people. We're down to the last few days, and I feel the pressure to see something happen."

After the door closed behind John, Daniel continued to sit at the table, fingering the pencil and staring at the open Bible.

The words in front of him said: "If my people, which are called by my name, shall humble themselves, and pray, and seek my face, and turn from their wicked ways; then will I hear from heaven, and will forgive. . . ." Daniel saw Amy's face and thought of the pleading he had done on his knees.

Amy bent over to lock the post office door. She heard the footsteps behind her and straightened as Father John Dyer stopped beside her. He looked from Amy to the napkin-covered dish he held, and his face brightened.

"Mrs. Tabor gave me some stew to carry up to Daniel. He hasn't eaten anything today. I've things to do—would you?—"

"Hasn't eaten?" Amy interrupted. "Is he ill?"

"No, but he will be if this keeps up. I need to walk down to the newspaper office—here."

This time she heard him. Slowly taking the dish she said, "I suppose so. I have nothing to do until time to play the organ."

He started down the street, saying, "There's enough for two in there. Better bring the dish back with you. I'm afraid Daniel will forget."

When she reached the cabin, Amy was still pondering the things Father Dyer had said about Daniel. Slowly she mounted the step and knocked. The door was wrenched open.

"Amy!" Daniel stood blinking.

She looked at the tired lines around his eyes. Slowly she said, "I hope I'm not bothering you. I met Father Dyer and he sent me up with this. Daniel, you hadn't ought to go without eating."

He stood aside to let her enter. "I would have come down—it was just that I'm finishing tonight's sermon."

"Then I am bothering you. I'll go."

"No, stay. I'll share what's in the pot and we can have that talk. I'll be leaving soon and there seems no better time."

He went to scoop the table clear and Amy awkwardly dropped her shawl on the bunk.

"John made coffee just before he left," Daniel brought mugs to the table while Amy uncovered the bowl. He peered inside. "Looks good." For a moment the brooding expression in his eyes lightened and he smiled at her. "You're fortunate to have someone take such good care of you."

"Especially since I'm a terrible cook."

Now he was really looking at her. He asked, "You are? I wouldn't have guessed that. But then, that's one of those things that change with time, isn't it?"

Unexpectedly Amy was blinking at tears. Daniel leaned across the table to touch his finger to one. "Why?"

"I—I'm not certain. It's just that you seem so lonely and sad." He turned away to get the coffee.

"Daniel, at times I'd give anything just to go back and do last summer over. I don't like this. Do you suppose there's someway we can settle it all without—"

"Either one of us having to give in?"

She chewed her lip, wishing she could recall the words that had brought them back to the same impossible spot.

Slowly she said, "I think we could have been happy together if it weren't that you—"

"Amy, sit down and eat your dinner before it's cold. Do you care for coffee? Did you see the bread Mrs. Tabor sent?"

She stared at him, unable to believe the easy, friendly smile. He might have been talking to Augusta herself.

She sat down. In silence they ate. While Amy's throat tightened until she could scarcely swallow, Daniel seemed to be enjoying every bite.

At last Amy got up to wash the dishes. "No," she protested as he reached for the towel. "Go back to your reading; there's no need—" He was grinning down at her and suddenly she was defenseless. Frowning slightly, she looked up at him, wondering.

"So Dyer sent you here," he said. "Did you two have any words of wisdom to share with me?"

"He didn't say anything, except that you hadn't eaten."

"The fox." He wiped silently and then stacked the dishes back on their shelf. "You should see my house."

"Really all yours? Where?"

"California Gulch. Some say the camp will fold in another year; some expect a good strike. So far it's a community of discouraged miners and a couple of women—wives," he added hastily.

She grinned, "It must be a poor community if they don't have a saloon and some dance-hall girls."

"Oh, there's a saloon, but the fellow is going broke. He's taken to digging gold too. It's pretty up there," he added. "Just down the slope from my cabin there's a patch of blue columbine, with lots of wild iris down along the creek. This fall the aspens were the prettiest gold I've ever seen."

He stopped abruptly and she said, "The cabin?"

"I'm putting down a floor during my spare time. But I sure need window curtains. At least there's a little stove. Gets cold up there—it's higher than Central City."

The sadness was back and Amy's throat tightened. He turned to look at her, asking, "What about you? Where do you go from here?"

"I don't know; I hadn't thought."

"Back east? Amy, I don't have much money, but if it will help you get out of this place, I'll give you every cent I have. I'd feel better about it all if you were back with family, playing in a respectable place, having a good life."

He paused to sit down at the table and pull the Bible forward. Now his voice was low, hesitant as he said, "I suppose it'd be pretty easy to get a divorce back there. I won't oppose you." After a pause, his voice dropped even lower as he said, "This poor preacher sure can't offer you as good a life—not like the one you seem to be making for yourself."

"Daniel!" she cried. He looked at her. "Are you saying there's someone else, someone you want to marry?"

"No, there's no one."

"You'll let me go to Kansas alone, but you won't come with me?" She went around the table to him. "I thought I heard you say you love me."

"I do. More'n anything, I love you and want to be married to you. I—"

"Oh, Daniel, don't look at me like that." She threw her arms around his neck and buried his face against her.

He pulled her down to his lap and cupped her face in his hands. She didn't try to hold back the tears now and he kissed them away.

When he stood up with her in his arms, she saw his face and tightened her arms around his neck. "Oh, Daniel, I really do love you, and I am your wife." There was the sweetness of his smile and her heart began to pound.

"It is all right, isn't it?"

"What do you mean, my precious wife?"

"You will come with me, won't you—back east?"

Abruptly he released her and went to the window. With his back to her, he spoke and his voice was flat, "Amy, it's late. I'll walk you to your room. You'll want to comb your hair before services begin."

"Daniel?"

He turned, his voice was bitter. "You want to go back east and you'll do anything to get there, including pretending to love me. Amy, I can't be bought. I wasn't trying to strike a bargain. And I understand you completely. If I go east, I get a sweet little wife, who gives out her favors as rewards."

She looked at him a moment longer. She saw his lips tighten into a hard line. Scorn. She felt as if she were dying, beginning deep inside. *I could take it, Daniel, except for the scorn. Think me cheap, selling cheap love, and there's no place to go. Nothing left.*

That night, after the service she fled upstairs. *Two nights to go and then it will be over. Like all revivals, it will be forgotten.* Tonight had made one thing clear. There would be two more days of having to face herself, knowing she could never back down from the decisions she was making.

Tonight Daniel talked about wanting God. He said we must run after God, be desperate for Him. Amy mulled over that picture and sighed, *Desperate? Well, I'm desperate, but not for God.* She thought of the things she wanted. Even the white church wasn't as important as that craving hunger for the piano. *One of these days I'll have it.* She smiled, thinking of the small pile of coins tucked in her money bag.

But every night Amy's hands trembled on the organ keys as she played and sang: *"All hail the power of Jesus' name. . . . Oh, that with yonder sacred throng, We at His feet may fall. . . . And crown Him . . . crown Him Lord of all!"*

There was something else to consider. In these last two days she had discovered it as she watched Daniel and listened to him. While he preached and avoided her eyes, she listened and admitted, *If pain is love, I love him. It is agony to think I'll never see him again. How do you stamp out love?*

That night Daniel watched Amy leave the organ and walk

slowly up the stairs. She moved as if each step took all her strength. He sighed and regarded the hard, numb spot inside. *This must be what's called the death of a dream. Nothing.* He tried to feel comfortable for having made the only decision possible, but the word *self-righteous* continued to come into his mind. Daniel headed for the door, desperately needing fresh air.

With coat in hand, he hesitated. People clustered around the front door. Turning he charged through the dining room and out the kitchen door.

"Oh, I beg your pardon!" Daniel reached for the figure he had slammed against the door. "I didn't see you. Have I hurt you?"

Now he could see the woman's face, a pale circle in the moonlight. She shook her head, slowly saying, "You're the preacher, aren't you?"

The moonlight turned her face to a white mask, revealing the yearning on it. Gently he asked, "Why don't you come in?" She paused and shook her head.

"It's too late for that, years and years too late."

He had nearly brushed her off. Now he stopped. The voice was familiar and even more so, the pile of light curls above her forehead. "Did you want to see me?"

He heard her catch her breath. "I—oh no. Just curious. I came to see Mrs. Thomas and lingered on to listen." She hesitated and he peered into her face. "You were talking about God loving and forgiving if people would just ask. I'm wondering. That doesn't always apply, does it? I mean . . ." She hesitated again. "I've heard about the unpardonable sin and such."

"If you hunger for God, then it's a pretty good indication He's standing ready to accept you. Silverheels, He'll never fail to forgive. Just ask."

For a moment longer he saw the hunger. Then she sighed and straightened her shoulders. Her smile was mocking. "That'd be a feather in your cap, wouldn't it? Silverheels, the madame. Sorry. Some things are impossible." She turned and clattered down the steps, with her bright slippers flashing in the moonlight.

CHAPTER 26

The storm moved in during the night. It was the first heavy snow of the season, and it made a miracle out of the wounded mining site called Buckskin Joe. Amy awoke to find an icy trickle of white drifting across her bed.

She burrowed deeper in her pile of blankets while she examined the rim of frost lining the crack between the logs.

Her window was a seashell, gleaming first pink and then gold with the sunrise. Unsuccessfully Amy tried to pull her aching nose under the blankets while still viewing that gilded world.

Later that morning, as she trudged through drifts toward the post office, she saw the changes. Log cabins wore towering top hats of white. The stamp mill, moving sluggishly, pounded loose cascades of snow, while the river stacked up slushy waves along the bank.

Amy's mittened hand had just maneuvered the key into the lock when H.A.W. Tabor came out of his store and hailed her. "No need to waste wood heating the post office today. The stage won't be through, and I doubt a customer will sail forth on a day like this. Go home and keep warm."

Amy looked around at the unblemished blanket of snow

on the road. "Oh, what a shame to stay indoors. It's beautiful! If you're wanting to save wood though, I'll just take the day to plow around through it."

"Be careful where you walk. Stay on the trails so you don't fall down a mine shaft."

Amy fluttered a mittened hand at him and wound the shawl another turn around her shoulders. The sun, in mid-sky now, had turned the pristine snow into a thousand flashing diamonds.

Mound upon rolling mound beckoned, and Amy tried to climb them all. She passed the last cabin in Buckskin Joe and waded through the snow along the banks of the river.

Just below the waterfall she discovered the graceful branches of the willows had been encrusted with gleaming crystal. On down, away from the frozen waves, the water had taken on an intense blue, a second sky reflected against the snow below.

Above the waterfall the mountain began, and Amy began the ascent. When she stopped to rest, she looked backward toward Buckskin Joe and caught her breath at the sparkling white landscape.

There was a shout behind her—no, up and beyond. A sound distorted by distance and brittle air. She shaded her eyes and saw the dark mark against the white. It was a man striding down the side of the mountain as if he possessed wings for feet.

As his great strides brought him close, Amy could hear him clearly.

See on the mountain top
The Standard of your God:
In Jesus' name it is lifted up,
All stained with hallowed blood.
Happy, if, with my latest breath,
I may but gasp his name;
Preach him to all, and cry in death,
Behold, behold the Lamb!

It was Father Dyer, and his giant strides were bringing him

down beside her. She studied the contraptions on his feet, nearly ready to tease until she saw his face.

When he stopped beside her, she spoke in a whisper, "Father Dyer—your face looks as if you've been rubbing it in sunshine!"

"Aye," he said slowly. Even then the glow was fading. "It is Son shine. I must do that every day or the light will go out." He looked at her, explaining. "Jesus Christ. You know He's created this beauty to remind you of eternity. The everlasting, unending eternity of being with Him."

He paused and thoughtfully studied her face. "A young lady like you should know the joy of rubbing shoulders with Jesus Christ."

She moved her head impatiently. "Father, you tease."

"No, I only try to say the unsayable in little bites of understanding. Do you know Romans 8:37? 'Nay, in all these things we are more than conquerors.' I am rejoicing in the conqueror attitude today. There's not one thing in our life that He won't give us the ability to overcome."

His voice softened as he quoted, " 'For I am persuaded, that neither death, nor life, nor angels, nor principalities, nor powers, nor things present, nor things to come, nor height, nor depth, nor any other creature, shall be able to separate us from the love of God, which is in Christ Jesus our Lord.' That's the other two verses."

"Why are you telling me this?"

"Because I think there's something you need to overcome." They started back toward Buckskin Joe together.

Amy was silent until the pain became too great. "Father Dyer," she said carefully, trying for the amusing touch, "you would not quote that verse so easily if you lived with the ghosts of the past."

"You assume I don't. Come, my child, and I'll tell you the story of my past. I married young, had five beautiful children and then my sweetheart wife died very suddenly, and shortly thereafter our little daughter died.

"With four children to raise I needed a wife, and I soon

found one. At the time, Amy, I was a prosperous man, with money in the bank and good land with a clear title. Before long, that pretty-faced woman showed her true colors.

"Not only was I left penniless, but I also discovered I was third in line in her affections." Amy frowned and Father Dyer explained. "She hadn't bothered to divorce her first two husbands."

Amy fumbled for a reply. Father Dyer said, "People hurt each other; that's the ugly part of being human. But there's something even more ugly—not being able to forgive."

Her smile was full of pain. "Father Dyer, I'm sorry that you've been—"

He cut in, "You may find it hard to understand what I'm really saying, and I don't know why I told you this. There're few who know my story."

Amy looked at the ground as she said, "If you think it's about Daniel and me, well—"

"No," he answered gently, "I haven't probed, and I won't. Yesterday was only impulse. I wanted you two together just on the chance you might be able to clear the matter between you."

"It didn't work, and it won't."

"Well, let's go before you take cold. I can see your feet are wet."

When they rounded the last hill, they were back on the trail to Buckskin Joe. Before them stood Father Dyer's cabin.

As they walked around the cabin, he looked at her wet feet. "Do you want to—" They both stopped. A woman in a flowing black cloak turned.

"Silverheels!" Amy gasped, looking from the woman to Daniel standing in the doorway. Their faces were sober.

With a sigh of relief, Silverheels came to Amy. "I've been looking for you. It's Lizzie. She's—"

"I just knew something was terribly wrong!" Amy cried, reaching for the woman's velvet cloak. "Please, what is it?"

"She's very ill," Daniel spoke up. With a quick glance at Silverheels he stepped between them. "Amy, it's possible she won't live. I'll go with you, unless you'd rather have John."

"But why—" She stopped and looked at their faces. "I've never had something like this happen—Daniel, please come."

Silverheels led the way, walking rapidly down the road. The snow was now scarred by feet and split by deep brown furrows—a scene that stamped itself on Amy's mind: the ugly marks man had made.

Quickly they crossed the meadow. When they reached the boardinghouse, Silverheels veered away from the front door. Daniel and Amy followed her around the sprawling building and into the trees behind. There was a tiny log cabin nearly hidden in the trees and underbrush.

Amy saw smoke puffing from the chimney. Silverheels walked in ahead of them and spoke to the woman bending over the cot. "Mattie, you may go now and rest. Get some dinner and I'll come after you later."

The face tossing against the pillows was flushed. Amy watched, unable to believe this creature was the Lizzie she knew.

Silverheels looked at Amy. "She asked for you. Don't just stand there."

The tossing figure on the bed quieted and she opened her eyes. "Amy?"

"Lizzie, I'm here. What's happened, why—"

The cold voice came from behind Amy. "She tried to get rid of the baby. I told her no—it's always better to wait it out. But she was impatient—had to get on with life."

Over the click of her heels Silverheels said, "I'll be back later."

Daniel moved to the other side of the cot. Amy said, "Lizzie, this is—my husband, Daniel."

For a moment her eyes were clear. "So there really is a Mr. Gerrett. I've been wondering how could a married lady be so dumb about life. She—" Her eyes closed.

Timidly Amy reached for her hand. "Daniel, she's so hot!"

The minutes passed and Lizzie opened her eyes. Now Amy understood how weak she was. Lizzie whispered, "Amy, sing."

"Shall I sing Camptown Races?"

She shook her head slowly and whispered, "Hymns. About the blood."

"Blood?" Amy questioned. She started to protest, but Daniel's eyes were holding her. Settling back on her heels beside the bed, Amy began to sing softly, "What can wash away my sin? Nothing but the blood of Jesus. . . . For my pardon this I see, nothing but the blood of Jesus. For my cleansing this my plea, nothing but the blood of Jesus. Oh, precious is the flow that makes me white as snow . . ."

Lizzie opened her eyes again, tried to raise herself as she looked at Daniel. "I wish—I could undo life." She tried to smile. "Guess it's too late, isn't it? But oh, God, how scared I am!"

She looked at Amy. "I didn't want to admit it, but I used to be a nice girl like you. The religion didn't take too well."

"What do you mean?"

There was a slight shrug and Lizzie's hand touched her flushed face. "I wanted excitement."

Daniel leaned over the bed. "Lizzie, it isn't too late. His atonement is still good for you. The blood will wash—"

"I'm scared. I never thought hard enough about what I was doing. It's too late." The tears crept from under her eyelids and she seemed to doze.

Abruptly Lizzie was shaking her head. "I'd be lower than a snake to run asking now. I chose—"

Amy gasped, "Lizzie! you'd let your pride keep you from asking for forgiveness—mercy?" Daniel was watching her. She backed away.

Daniel murmured, "Lizzie, don't play games. You made a mistake once; don't do it again in the name of pride." He settled down beside her and said, "The words of that song are for every one of us. We all must come to Jesus and ask for His forgiveness. You see, He's God, come to this earth to die for our sins. By believing this, you have the privilege of being called a child of God."

She turned her head slowly on the pillow. "It's too late. I had my chance, now—"

"It isn't. It is never too late to say you're sorry, that you want to accept the atonement sacrifice for your own sins." Her eyes were open. Amy saw the expression and turned away. Behind her Daniel was still talking, bending over the girl.

Amy went to stand by the door. *That terror on Lizzie's face.* She was still shivering when Silverheels came in. Glancing at Lizzie and Daniel before turning to Amy, she said, "You're cold and wet. Go home now, before you catch something."

When Amy shrugged, Silverheels spoke more sharply. "You can't go out in that shawl; it's wet." She pulled the shawl from Amy and dropped it to the floor.

Before Amy could protest, Silverheels slipped out of the black velvet cloak she was wearing and threw it around Amy's shoulders. "There. It's a little long, but it'll do. Now go."

The black velvet smelled of Silverheels' perfume. Amy stared up at her, tongue-tied, confused. Unexpectedly, the woman kissed Amy on the cheek. "Now, go. Drink something hot and get into bed or you'll be ill."

Numb with fatigue, Amy obeyed. When she reached the Tabors', Augusta brought heated stones and hot tea. While Amy pulled her nightgown over her head, Augusta hung the black velvet cloak to dry.

"Beautiful—and costly. Just like you'd expect a woman of Silverheels' reputation to have. But she was generous—I'd not expect that of her. It's a little wet around the hem, that'll dry soon. Now get some sleep. You've got to play the organ to-night. We can't get along without you."

Those final words greeted Amy when she awakened, re-calling her to the duty of the evening. As she rolled over, she saw the black cloak hanging on the back of the door.

Slowly she pulled herself out of bed and dressed. Although she selected the dark calico designed for revival meetings, her thoughts weren't on the evening service. She was thinking of Lizzie—weak, flushed, and crying as Daniel prayed.

When Amy left the organ to sit with the others clustered in tight rows across Augusta's parlor, Father Dyer stood to preach, while Amy's thoughts were fleeing back to Lizzie.

He began his sermon, but Amy found herself unable to

escape the memory of Lizzie. *She's caught. Like a butterfly in a net, trapped. She's no longer free to choose how she will live. Lizzie can no longer choose life.*

When he opened his Bible, John Dyer looked at Amy and said, "Take hold of life. Life is there, waiting for us. But we claim our rightful heritage only through Jesus Christ. The Apostle Paul's letter to the Philippians uses the word 'apprehended.' He is saying he takes hold of life for the same purpose that Jesus Christ took hold of him. Are you aware of God's design for your life? Take hold of life."

Amy lost the thread of Father Dyer's message. Again thinking of Lizzie, she felt a moment of bitterness. *But Lizzie chose; at some point she chose. Was it Daniel who said we must live with our decisions?* She shivered.

When she looked up, it was time to play the organ. The evening was gone. It took all the discipline Amy could muster to touch those keys and sing with her leaden heart, "Almost persuaded, harvest is past. . . . Almost cannot avail. . . . Sad sad. . ."

As she fled toward the stairs, she met Daniel. With his hand on her arm and bending down to look into her face, he said, "Lizzie has gone to be with her Savior. Just after you left, she slipped into a coma."

"What makes you think she's gone to heaven?"

His expression was strange. "I would have expected you to guess. She was coming home, back to Him. A prodigal daughter. Amy, no matter what the sin, if we ask, He will take us back."

His hand was still upon her and he must have felt her trembling. They both waited, then Daniel dropped his hand and turned away.

"Amy." As she hesitated on the stairs, he came up to her. His eyes were on a level with hers as he said, "I'm leaving tomorrow. But Amy, I'll be back. I can't leave without your knowing that. I'll pray for you."

Still feeling the pressure, Amy protested, "Pray that I will change my mind and stay? Daniel, I want only—" She stopped and for a moment her heart yearned after him. She nearly said love, but she reminded herself; *then I will have lost it all.*

"Amy"—his hand rested on her arm—"I'm not talking about that. There's only one thing I have in mind. It's your relationship with the Lord Jesus Christ. Amy, you need Him, and that's my dearest desire."

She looked down the stairs to the ring of faces watching, while the disappointment welled up in her heart.

CHAPTER 27

The revival was over. Like a stone pulled from a fast-moving stream, leaving only silty depression and a placid surface, life in Buckskin Joe smoothed out now that the impediment was gone. Amy felt the difference in herself and saw her relief mirrored on the faces around her.

But there was one difference. In her life the hole was still there, and the silt trickled slowly—too slowly to hide the pain she felt. But then, the others in Buckskin Joe weren't as attached to the lanky evangelist with the brown eyes.

Within a week the snow came again. The wind howled, and drifts piled up, raking the meadow bare and stacking the snow against the cabins until sometimes only chimneys were visible.

Those miners who hadn't fled to a lower altitude found themselves without occupation. The stamp mill ceased its monotonous pounding, and Buckskin Joe was held in a quietness that amplified the braying of the jacks and the muffled gurgle of the waterfall.

The miners moved from saloon to home and back again, wallowing through the drifts as if the snow itself must be challenged.

Shortly after Daniel's departure, Father Dyer also left, snowshoeing over the mountains to minister to another flock in another mining camp.

That week of the storm, while Buckskin Joe was digging out and life was restricted to the necessary, Amy once again considered the black velvet cloak hanging from the tallest hook in her bedroom.

Just having it in the room brought back dreadful memories of the day Silverheels had wrapped it around her. She could still see Lizzie's flushed, pain-filled face even though the picture was overlapped with the memory of that bleak caravan winding down to the rocky, snow-swept cemetery.

Amy recalled the things Father Dyer had said at the graveside. As he spoke his face had turned from one to the other of the flower-bright girls. And Amy had watched them shed his words, like delicate blossoms repelling spring showers.

But Amy had left that place feeling his words heavy against her heart. Father Dyer had talked about the prostitutes Jesus had encountered, and how His word to them had changed their lives even as He forgave their sins.

As Amy turned to go, Father Dyer lifted his hand and quoted Jesus' words. Crystal Thomas was standing there, her dusky skin glowing and her lips moving as she quoted the words along with him. " 'I am the resurrection and the life; he that believeth in me, though he were dead, yet shall he live: . . . believest thou this?' "

Changed. That was Daniel's word, and it made her think of his sermon. Some of the words still bounced around in her thoughts: *How much more shall . . . the blood of Christ purge . . . to serve the living God?*

In his sermon he had talked about this kind of change. He called it being redeemed, not only for eternity but for now. And for a moment, she hoped.

The cloak continued to hang in Amy's room. Finally Augusta spurred Amy to action. On the day that the sun came out, warming and cheering all of Buckskin Joe, she peered around the doorpost at Amy. Nodding at the cloak hanging there she said, "Might as well take that back. You wear it and people'll line you up with Silverheels. Don't wear it, and she'll want it back."

"I'd better," Amy said with a sigh. "As long as the stages aren't running, I can't work at the post office; there's no want of me at the Grand Hotel. I might as well go up there."

Augusta left and Amy set aside her mending. She went to lift the cloak down from its hook. Most certainly it was too long for her. "Best be rid of it," she murmured, shuddering.

But just one more time she wanted to feel its luxury against her face. Amy slipped it around her shoulders and tried to see her reflection as she turned in front of her scrap of a mirror.

Silverheels' perfume still clung to the cloak. But all Amy's turning merited her nothing; the mirror simply wasn't large enough. With a sigh, Amy pushed her hands deep into the pockets as she turned away. A piece of paper cracked beneath her fingers.

Slowly Amy pulled out the paper and turned it over. It seemed to be a portion of a very old envelope, and it was folded over an oval object. Jewelry? Amy's curiosity prodded her to unfold the paper, even while her conscience stung.

There was writing on the envelope, but Amy's fingers were intent on lifting out the oval. Not jewelry; just a dim old photograph set in an ornate frame.

She carried the photograph to the window and held it up. With a gasp, she bent closer. Surely not another coincidence! As she fingered it, she realized a second glance wasn't necessary. The photograph was identical to the one Father had on his dresser!

Slowly she picked up the envelope and smoothed out the paper. The first words stated: Property of—the name was spread across the paper—*Amelia Randolph*. Amy's heart thumped until her whole body trembled. She sat down and tried to calm herself. When she picked up the envelope to study the curiously rounded letters, she remembered something else. Crystal, that woman Augusta hired, had referred to Silverheels as Amelia.

Studying the round bold signature, Amy murmured, "I'm nearly certain that this is the very writing I saw on the envelope in Father's trunk."

She tried to persuade herself, murmuring, "The name's common." But that writing, those rounded letters, they were uncommon. Amy picked up the photograph again. She recognized the dress. Even though the picture was dim, she could see the tucking, the rose embroidery. "It's blue with pink roses," Amy murmured. "I know; the dress is at home in the trunk, next to the letter with this same curious, rounded writing."

Amy paced the room. "I'm certain this is a copy of the photograph Father has. I've seen it often enough. This is a photograph of me when I was just three."

Clutching the oval, she went to sit on the bed, staring down at the object. She was finding it difficult to think clearly, but facts couldn't be denied.

Finally she got up. Moving quickly before she could change her mind, Amy gathered up the cloak, thrust the paper and photograph back into the pocket, and ran downstairs.

"Augusta, may I borrow your old coat while I return this cloak and pick up my shawl?" Augusta looked up from the pie crusts she was rolling and nodded.

Plunging through the snow to the road and on to the meadow, Amy nearly lost her courage. But the paper crackled in her hand. She began to walk faster.

By the time she reached the front door of the boarding-house, Amy's heart was thumping with gladness, and all the questions were being shoved to the back of her mind.

Running into the hall, Amy tapped on Silverheels' door. There was no answer. As she hesitated, disappointed and trembling, Amy heard the stairs creak.

She ran to the stairwell and stopped. It was Silverheels. Amy clung to the bannister, waiting breathlessly. It was too much, too unbelievable.

Silverheels stopped on the stairs. Her pale face was tilted, unaware of Amy. She seemed to be listening as she lingered on the steps. Watching, Amy decided she must have just awakened.

There was a strange dazed expression on her face.

Amy wanted to fly up the steps, but her trembling legs kept her there, waiting. There was a softness on Silverheels' troubled face. A mother look. Amy blinked at the tears in her eyes as the woman slowly, hesitantly, walked down the stairs.

When she reached the landing, Amy's questions were settled. It didn't matter what she was; this woman was her mother—only that was important.

She clung to the railing for support as she whispered, "You really are my mother. I know you now. So long ago. I was tiny, but I remember."

She saw Silverheels' ashen face clearly for just one moment before her tears veiled it. "Mother, oh, Mother! Did you know they told me you were dead?"

Amy could smell Silverheels' perfume. Blind from her tears, she reached and the woman's arms closed around her.

When Amy could control her sobbing, Silverheels led her down the hall to her room. Once the door was closed, they faced each other. Silverheels examined Amy's tear-streaked face. For a moment her voice broke and then became firm as she said, "Amy, you are my dear little girl, but you are forgetting—"

Amy shook her head. "Let's not talk about that. Please, just tell me what happened and why."

The woman stiffened. Leading the way to the round pink couch, she patted the cushions in place and slowly said, "I'm stunned. Of course I'd guessed, but never did I dream that you would. How—"

Amy placed the photograph on Silverheels' knee. "It was in the pocket of the cloak you gave me to wear."

"Oh, how careless. I'd been going through things."

"You mean you wouldn't have told me?"

"Amy, I didn't think you'd accept me."

Amy pressed her fingers against her eyes. "But you are my mother, and that means everything. I—I guess I can't understand, but now that I've found you, I don't intend to leave you ever."

After a long silence, Silverheels asked, "What about your husband?"

"That's not working out."

There was a twisted bitter smile on Silverheels' face, "What will your father say?" Amy stared at her. The smile was like a hand pushing them apart. Amy felt it and fought.

Moving quickly she pressed her head against the soft shoulder and felt only resistance. But after a moment their arms went around each other and Amy sobbed, "Oh, Mother, I can scarcely believe this. Why did Father tell me you were dead? Why—" She bent over, crying uncontrollably.

"Hush, my dear." Soft fingers pressed against Amy's lips and then, with a quiet moan, Silverheels lifted Amy's face with both hands. "If only you knew—"

Abruptly she stopped and pushed Amy away from her. Jumping to her feet, she paced the floor in quick, hard steps, stopping frequently to press her hands together, to wheel and come back. Amy mopped her eyes, crying softly.

Silverheels knelt in front of Amy, pressing a fresh handkerchief into her hands, "There, don't carry on so."

Amy wiped her eyes and sat up. Silverheels' smile was sunny and tender as she said, "We're big girls now, and we don't cry."

Then she frowned again, got to her feet, and paced the floor. Amy watched the quick, hard steps.

Coming back to her, Silverheels said, "Of course, my dear, it is unthinkable for you to remain. I have my career." The words were clipped and she gave her twisted smile again. "I'm certain your father will drive me out of town if he were to find out that—"

Amy exclaimed sharply, "Do you mean that—" she couldn't continue, but Silverheels nodded with a faint, sad smile. Slowly Amy said, "I didn't dream Father would be like that." She looked up and said, "And having found you, I'll never leave you."

Silverheels slumped down on the couch with her head cradled on her arm. In a moment she sat up, sighing, "You don't understand. You're grown; you don't need me. I've made my life and I know you won't understand this, but I forbid you to waste yourself on me."

She lifted her hand to stop Amy's protest, and continued, her voice growing stronger with each word, "I not only want you to deny that I'm your mother, but I want you to leave Buckskin Joe. Go, forever."

The soft note in Silverheels' voice was gone, and as Amy watched, her mother's face hardened. "I want you to catch the next stage and go home. Don't ever mention my name again."

Shaking her head in confusion, Amy pressed her fingers against her throbbing temples and caught her breath. "Leave when I've just found you? That's impossible. Mother, how can you—"

Silverheels jumped to her feet and walked to the door. For a moment she stood with her back to Amy. When she whirled around, her face was contorted into ugliness. "It is unfortunate you bumbled into this whole affair, but now I must tell you. Amy, I left because I wanted to. I wanted my freedom more than I wanted my daughter. That hasn't changed.

"I despise all that you stand for. You, your father, and your husband. Get out of my life."

"Mother," Amy pleaded, "you're judging me by their narrowness; please—I intend to be my own person, too. Doesn't that matter?"

"Let you stay and be the nice little self-sacrificing missionary? I don't convert. Can't you understand? I'm trying to be kind to you. Amy, I'm a prostitute. I'll drag you down with me.

"Amy, go!" She gave a hoarse, choked laugh. "I'll never acknowledge you as my child. It would ruin me to admit to a grown woman as my daughter. Forget about this. And don't tell your father you've found me. Do you understand? I don't want him whining at my door." She ran to the dresser. Coming back she pushed a handful of coins into Amy's hand. "Here; it's gold—enough to get you home. I'm *buying* my freedom once again."

She had her hand on Amy's shoulder, moving her toward the hall. With a sharp jerk Amy whirled away, slashing out with her hands.

Silverheels caught and flung Amy onto the couch. "Amy, stop it! You're being a good little missionary, but I'll tell you something. Given the opportunity, you'd be just like your mother. I saw the way your eyes sparkled when you came here looking at the gals and their fellows. I saw you eyeing the pretty clothes and my jewelry. I could see you nearly green with envy over it all.

"And I'll tell you something else. My passion is dancing; yours is the piano. But does it matter what it is? You'll sell your soul for the piano, just as I sold mine for the dance. See, I know how Aunt Maude feels about pianos." She leaned close to whisper, "Amy, down underneath, we're alike, and you can't escape it." She paused, forced her voice between clenched teeth, and hissed out the words, "Now go. I don't want to see you again ever. Get out of Buckskin Joe before I scratch your eyes out."

Suddenly Mattie appeared. "Yer shawl is here. She had me wash it for you." There was a man behind her. He came into the room with a lifted eyebrow and a grin.

"Theodore," Silverheels murmured. "Please—until this evening. I'll see you then. This is important."

"A new one, huh? Pretty." He chuckled and touched Amy's hair. "Nearly as pretty as yours."

Amy turned away. She was fighting the cold, sick anger welling up inside. Behind her, she heard the murmuring, the soft laughter, and the closing door.

While she waited, Amy picked up one of the china dolls from the table.

"Beautiful, isn't she?" Silverheels' brittle voice was behind her. "Just what every little girl dreams about. One of my lovers gave it to me. Take it to remember me."

"There's the cloak," Amy pointed.

"I intended you to have it. Amy, I'd like to give you a nice heavy wrap if you don't care for the cloak. I can well afford it."

Amy's emotions had flattened, and she discovered that she

could speak with indifference, overlooking the arrogant state-ment. "It isn't necessary. I need nothing more than I have."

She faced Silverheels, waiting and wondering.

"What is it, my dear?" The mocking voice shredded into pieces those precious early minutes. Amy accepted the cold, final separation. She looked around the room, seeing the luxury. A kind of deadness began taking over the new warmth.

"I was just thinking—not very many girls have their moth-ers die twice." She looped the shawl over her arm.

Silverheels' eyes were shadowed, but the smile on her face taunted Amy as she turned to go. She called, "Don't forget your dolly."

Amy turned and picked up the doll. The cold spot in her heart disappeared. She looked down at the doll. "When I was little I looked at dolls like this. They always belonged to the other children. I would have given anything to have had—" She paused, the rush of anger leaving her breathless.

One more second she stared at the beautiful, porcelain face; then Amy threw the doll with all her might, arrow straight, at Silverheels' mocking smile.

CHAPTER 28

You're lucky, young lady. Bad storm for November. A week ago the stage wouldn't have been able to make it up the canyon from Denver. One thing about Colorado Territory, you can't take the weather too seriously. Winter one day, spring the next."

The driver dropped Amy's valise on the boardwalk in front of Joe's store and lifted his hand. "Here ya are, Central City, it is."

Amy stepped gingerly through the mud and followed the driver into the store. Joe grinned at her. "Well, Miss Amy! I heard you got married. If you've come to visit, you should have written first. Your pa's off in Denver City to a church meeting."

"Denver!" Amy gasped. "I've just come from there. I didn't know." She sighed and thought of her dwindling funds.

Joe said, "If you want, I'll carry your bag to the house for you. Need any groceries?"

Amy nodded and went to select flour and eggs. "That should do for now." Handing him the coins she added, "The town's changed. So many new places built up. Coming from Mountain City I couldn't tell when we reached Central City."

Joe nodded and went after the valise. "Some are saying it'll be all one big city in another year or so. Used to be that you could spot Gregory's diggings right off; now the whole place is one big diggings, and more fellows are coming every day. Me? I think I'm getting rich quicker than most the diggers."

They reached the cabin and Joe waited until Amy found the key and opened the door. Dropping the valise, he shook his head over the coin she offered and left.

After her initial disappointment, Amy began to realize that solitude was a soothing hand, straightening out the roughness of her life, softening the memory of Silverheels' last words.

Shaking her head over her father's absent-minded housekeeping, Amy rolled up her sleeves and threw her sore heart into making order of the shambles in the cabin.

She finished housekeeping, but Eli hadn't returned. Amy mended the frayed window curtain, still brooding over the painful memories of Silverheels' rejection.

As Amy sewed, she remembered Daniel mentioned needing curtains for his windows. She sighed over him as she tried to remember all he had told her about his house and the meadow with the columbine and wild iris.

Later she rummaged through a box and found the curtain that had hung in front of Aunt Maude's bunk. "Just big enough. I'll make curtains for Daniel." Trying to avoid thinking about him, Amy measured off a length, muttering, "Knowing what I do about the mining camps, I guess Daniel's windows will be the standard, ready-framed ones, just like these." She got the scissors and began cutting.

When the last hem had been stitched, she used Aunt Maude's embroidery floss to add a touch of color to the curtains. And then she folded them away. "Silly," she chided herself. "Making curtains for Daniel, and you'll likely never see him again."

After finishing the curtains, she climbed the well-remembered hill to Clara Brown's little cabin. Amy cocked her head and smiled. Most certainly Aunt Clara was at home; the dear little cabin nearly vibrated with her singing.

Aunt Clara hugged Amy and held her off to study her.

"Land child, skin and bones, you are. Looks like you're carrying the whole world on your shoulders. Did you come to tell Aunt Clara about it?" She shoved a stool forward, poured coffee for Amy, and then returned to her ironing.

"Where's Barney Ford?"

"Got himself a claim over the ridge. He keeps so busy I don't see much of him anymore. Comes over for church sometimes."

Amy sipped coffee and murmured, "It's good to be back. I suppose you know Father is in Denver."

Clara nodded as she swished her iron briskly over a white shirt. Slanting a mischievous glance at Amy, she said, "This here is Lucas Tristram's shirt. Wanna deliver it for me?"

Amy's eyes widened, and Aunt Clara hastily said, "Jest joking with you." She chuckled silently and her whole round frame shook. Rubbing a palm over her eyes, she grinned at Amy, saying, "I never expected that turn of events. Right out from under Tristram's nose. That's what he gets for being too uppity for camp meeting. Shore 'fraid you were going to hitch up your wagon to that fella's, and I was prayin' nearly night and day that God would break it up.

"Didn't know He'd supply the need so abrupt-like, though. Now, that Daniel Gerrett is about the best young man around." Her iron slowed. In the silence, she asked, "Child, you happy and pregnant?"

"Neither," Amy said slowly, pushing her mug round the table. "Daniel and I can't agree on anything."

"Like your piano playing?"

"How did you find out?"

"Think those dance-hall girls could keep anything like that under their hat? Pretty good joke, the preacher's young'un sneaking off to play the piano honky-tonk when her pa's not looking. Guess everyone in town knew except Aunt Maude."

Amy winced. "Father?"

"Oh, sure." Her keen eyes were studying Amy. "Takes a mite of growing up before a young'un can appreciate older folks, 'specially if she's related to 'em."

Amy continued to study the burned mark on the table. "But you talk about Lucas like you haven't heard any gossip concerning him."

Aunt Clara picked up the iron. She studied Amy. "I don't know what you're referring to. There's always a little rumbling on about him, but—"

"Then it's obvious it's been hushed up."

"Child, did he mistreat you?"

Amy grinned. "No, why? Was he roughed up?"

Aunt Clara slowly shook her head, saying, "I see I ain't going to get anything outta you. That's fine. I'm happy the way it all ended." In a moment Aunt Clara said, "Seems you have a mite on your mind. I don't have anything to do except iron and listen."

Those bruising words *just like your mother* were lying hard against Amy's heart. Of all that happened that afternoon at Silverheels' house, they alone had the power to keep her trembling in the quiet times.

Maybe it wouldn't hurt to try some of the ideas on Aunt Clara. She, more than anyone, would listen and understand.

Amy took a deep breath and began. "Do you think just because a person's father was a horse thief that his children are bound to follow in his footsteps?"

" 'Course not. Bound? No. But he might take a liking to thieving if he doesn't know better."

"Then you think a person can better himself by trying?"

She nodded and her iron slowed again. "Git the feeling I'm walking myself into a trap. Amy, child, the only way you can learn to wash your face of a morning is by practice. You earn your living by doing a job better'n the fella standing behind you waitin' for you to fail. You do and do and do, but that's not going to count a penny's worth with God unless you're doing it the right way. Was that the trap you was backing me into?"

"Aunt Clara, I wasn't backing you anywhere. I am just trying to understand—life."

"God?" Aunt Clara said. Amy thought about that for a time; then she nodded. Aunt Clara looked at Amy in a way that seemed to pierce far too deep. She pushed the iron back and forth. "You gotta want God more'n anything else in this whole world. Anything less'n that won't work, 'cause in a tight place, you'll toss it all out. There's a kind of religion that gets you to sign your name on the dotted line, and then it's all forgot about. That's not the way it has to be."

She pushed the iron again and Amy thought she had forgotten her until Aunt Clara placed the iron on the stove and turned. With hands on her hips, she said soberly, "Seems more often than not, God has to let a body get in a tight spot before he sees he wasn't made to handle life without the Lord's help."

"Then why—" Amy stopped. She just couldn't bring out those words Silverheels had said. Wasn't it possible Silverheels knew better than this ignorant washer-woman the unseen forces that could twist and push a person where he didn't want to go? Amy sighed and got to her feet.

Somehow, knowing what she was inside, it seemed easier to believe Silverheels, and that was frightening.

The next day Eli Randolph returned to Central City. When he stood in the doorway and Amy looked at his ashen face, she couldn't help wondering what his reaction would be if she were to tell him about Silverheels. But she had promised.

He stepped into the house, dropped his valise, and said, "You've tidied up my mess. Looks like a home again."

"You're not going to ask where I've been or what's happening?"

"Do you want to tell me?"

Amy considered. The thought was cheering. Father was treating her like a grown-up. She didn't have to answer. She looked up at him and grinned. "Since I'm here, as you can see, well, I'll just keep quiet until I decide what to do next."

That wasn't enough. She saw the disappointment on his face and tried to smooth over the words. "Father, I know you like Daniel. But that marriage should never have happened. I've been working at the post office in Buckskin Joe, thinking and trying to decide what I do want. Maybe I should just go back east and live with Uncle Malcolm and get a job."

She turned away, saying, "I've been up to see Aunt Clara." That didn't help. She took a deep breath and said, "What would you like for your dinner?"

She saw the lost look in his eyes. For just one moment, Amy wished she were young enough to sit on his lap again. She also wished she didn't have all these problems.

November was gone. December, in typical, unpredictable mountain fashion, was warm and sunny. Amy's birthday passed without notice. All the while she chafed at her restricted, pointless life, which seemed circumvented by church, home, Aunt Clara, and the grocery store.

Except for the piano money, her tiny funds were evaporating, and still Amy lingered in Central City, uncertain and unable to decide what to do.

When her restlessness surfaced, her father looked at her over the top of his book and reminded in a mild chiding tone, "Wartime in the states doesn't make life safe in the territories. Better stay until spring at least." He seemed about to say more and thought better of it.

Amy tried to be satisfied with the thought that he needed her. But with the balmy weather, Eli began riding his circuit over the mountains to the congregations scattered from Nevada Gulch to Russell Gulch.

The Methodist Episcopal Church in Central City had changed. Amy began seeing the people in contrast to the Central City of a year ago. Now there were families with small children, young wives with shadowed eyes and young miners with restless eyes. All reflected the emotions of excitement and fear rampant in a camp promising both instant wealth and instant disaster. But the church continued to grow both in numbers and acceptance among the townspeople.

The Sunday after Amy's birthday, Lucas Tristram came to church. When he walked back into her life, Amy was struck again by differences. His tall silk hat and spotless suit marked a night and day contrast to the other members of the congregation.

She guessed, from the flutter of attention moving through the crowd, that Lucas hadn't been to services for a long time. She also noticed the dismay on her father's face in his quick glance at her.

When the service was over and the people were out on the street, Lucas came to bend over her hand. His eyes mocked her, challenged her. "You look surprised," he murmured. "I am wondering what you are thinking."

"That half the price of your finery would buy a piano for this dismal place."

He blinked. "Amy, my dear, you've changed."

She whispered, "Aren't you glad? At least I consider myself a little more sophisticated. Or would you rather I stay a little girl?"

"No," he said hastily. Examining every detail of her face, he added, "On the contrary. I can't get too fond of a timid mouse, even if she happens to be the most beautiful mouse in all of Colorado Territory."

"And you, Lucas Tristram, are capable of getting by with the most outrageous actions of any person I've met."

His eyes were wary. "Tell me what you mean by that."

She waited until she saw the uneasiness in his eyes. "I've heard of the number of mines you've acquired in the past year; I've also heard of the number you've sold at a considerable profit."

He grinned down at her. "It takes money to make money, and that seems to work in Central City."

"It helps to have a smooth tongue. Did you know that Lizzie is dead?"

His smile faded, "The girl from the dance hall? How should I know?"

"I didn't think you would, but she remembered you. I hear the Wilsons left Central City just about the time I left."

Abruptly he changed the subject. "Amy, the absence of a bridegroom makes me bold enough to ask if you care to go riding this afternoon? I've a new carriage and I'd like to try it out."

She laughed. "Oh, Lucas, you will always be the most outrageous person alive. You'll go down in history as Colorado's most famous symbol."

They went riding in the new carriage, recklessly charging through town and down the canyon road. As Amy clung to her hat, a sharp picture of the two of them flashed across her mind. It brought to mind the more ancient picture of dancehall girls, pelting through town in a wild, reckless race. They, too, had daring eyes shining with excitement.

CHAPTER 29

Amy pulled on the white kid gloves. Lucas had given them to her, saying it was a late birthday gift. Eli watched. "Father, please don't fuss. This is a stuffy old reception at the town hall. Lucas asked me to go with him because it is unpleasant for him, being the only unmarried man at these meetings. The other men bring their wives."

Eli's face was a map of his emotions, creased with valleys of pain and despair. After years of his gentle chiding, she could hardly believe her ears. He straightened and said, "Daughter, you are edging close to being more than a friend to Lucas. It disturbs me."

"You know I'm being honest about all this. Father, I know for a fact just how important Lucas is, not only in Central City, but also in church. I've watched him when the offering plate is passed."

"That's so, but may I remind you, he was an absent church member until one Mrs. Daniel Gerrett moved back to town. I don't like it." Eli's frown took on thundercloud furrows.

Hearing Lucas's carriage, Amy quickly fluttered her fingers as she backed out the door. "I won't be late."

Lucas tucked the robe around Amy, patting it close. She

battled the new irritation. Since she had accepted the gloves, she had noticed Lucas's hand lingered too long, no matter where it landed.

Smiling at her, Lucas said, "After the reception"—he maneuvered the carriage around and headed down the street—"I want to show you my new house. The last carpet is spread and the last picture hung."

"Oh, it sounds elegant for Central City."

"It isn't so unusual. There's lots of gold being pulled out right now."

It was dusk when Lucas and Amy left the reception alone. He saw her quick glance and answered it with a smile. "I won't forget your reputation. We'll be there only a few minutes."

The house was high on the hill bordering Eureka Gulch. From the veranda Amy could see lights glowing up and down the gulch. Amy paced the white frame house, measuring off its spacious rooms and elegantly appointed furnishings.

She saw Lucas's slightly mocking smile as he watched her delight. She also saw him raise one eyebrow in an undeniable question mark as they left the house.

Sunday afternoons picked up their old pattern. It started with Lucas giving Aunt Clara a ride home from church. Soon it became a weekly event, the rollicking ride in his carriage on Sunday afternoon after dropping Aunt Clara.

Making it a point to ignore Aunt Clara's frown, Amy decided: *It's fun and harmless, like a fairy tale—but that's all.*

All—until she helped Aunt Clara Brown carry a bag of flour up to her cabin. "You stay and have coffee with this old lady. It's been a long time since we've had a visit, now that you've been going places with that Tristram." Aunt Clara stowed the flour away in the battered lard pail and went to stuff wood in the stove.

She sat down in her rocking chair and fanned her perspiring face. "My, seems impossible that a body can work up a sweat in January. No matter; we'll be getting it another week or so. I feel it in my bones. It'll be the best storm of the winter."

"What else do you feel in your bones?" Amy teased.

"That you're a-playing with fire." Aunt Clara leaned over and patted Amy's knee. "Child, it burdens my heart to see you so. I know it's harmless, but most bad things start with the good getting outta hand."

"Father's frowning just like you, but he doesn't say much and that's good." Amy said with a laugh. "My intentions are totally honorable. I'm going to get Lucas to buy a piano for the church."

Clara gasped and for a moment her eyes softened. "Piano! Oh how I would love to hear the music!" But just as abruptly her expression changed. "You should be guarding your reputation a little better. You could hurt your pa and Daniel Gerrett."

"Daniel won't be around again," Amy said, and then nearly squirmed over the unexpected catch in her voice.

Aunt Clara studied her with an unwavering gaze for a long time. When she got up to fill the coffeecups with the fresh-brewed coffee, Amy thought the matter finished.

Settling back in her chair, Aunt Clara said, "This here fresh coffee smells so good, and it always brings me to mind of a scripture. Don't know why. Maybe it's 'cause I drink coffee in the mornings while I'm getting ready to have my prayer time."

Amy sipped the coffee and waited. Clara continued, "It's the part in Matthew where Jesus's talking about putting new wine in new bottles. Couldn't understand it until the word *perish* began to penetrate this thick skull. Bottles don't perish, but people do. You take the Holy Ghost. The heavenly Father can't go putting the Holy Ghost in these old petrified bottles without doing something to us first, lest we break apart under the pressure. New bottles, new wine; He's giving new treasures, even a new creation and a new covenant."

Amy waited while Aunt Clara drank coffee, rocked and chuckled. "I could go on and on—new self, new mind. Bless my soul, it's exciting to think of all the *new* in heaven, but right down on this earth—well." The delight faded from Aunt Clara's eyes and she leaned forward. "Little missy, that's what you need. I've seen it in your eyes. A girl less'n twenty with eyes like an old lady is asking for trouble."

Amy left Aunt Clara's house fuming inside. It was bad enough to have Aunt Clara preach, but it was the final straw to have her look at her with that expression—sad, or was it just plain frightened?

Amy snorted. Halfway down the hill, Amy passed the spot where she had first seen Aunt Clara, sitting at the side of the road, with her face shining, praising the Lord. Amy's angry steps slowed, and by the time she reached home she was chewing her lip.

Father was at home, submerged in the stack of books in front of him. The stew was bubbling peacefully on the stove and after a second, Amy went to find her Bible and search for the scripture. Aunt Clara had mentioned Matthew. As she turned the pages she remembered that Father Dyer had said God never asks anything of a person without providing the grace needed to accomplish His purposes.

Strange. Now it seemed important to heed the advice Daniel gave at revival meeting. Amy began reading her Bible in the evenings. But while Amy's nighttime thoughts were a goad toward improvement, they were interrupted.

Before she would sleep, the old half-formed desires would arise in her. Later the deep hours of the night brought dreams of Silverheels. Surrounded by luxury she beckoned Amy, whispering: *Like mother, like daughter.*

In rational daylight hours, Amy sighed over life and chafed at the lack of activity. "Father, I just can't stay here in Central City. It isn't fair to you. I earned my keep in Buckskin Joe, but I've failed to find any employment at all since I've come back.

"People are still thinking of me as Father's little girl, too young for a job."

His expression was strange. "More likely they're expecting you to go be with your husband. Not much sense in hiring someone ready to leave."

Amy couldn't answer. How would she dare tell Father her real desires? *Kansas, a job, a piano*—

Looking at his lined face and troubled eyes, Amy felt a pang of guilt for her selfish desires. "You are so alone. I wish Aunt Maude had stayed."

But before spring, they had more heavy snow and in the isolation and boredom Lucas was there. She began seeing him on a regular basis. She knew the flirtation was harmless, but Father's silence and his troubled eyes made her increasingly uneasy. She knew what he was thinking. Someday soon she must explain why her divorce wouldn't be wrong.

In the midst of the storms, Amy spent the largest portion of her hoarded money on a length of violet velvet. She did so ignoring the inner chiding that reminded her there was no longer money enough for the stage fare to Kansas.

The snowy days brought forth on a number of parties, and Amy knew she would be expected to attend with Lucas. As she wrestled the velvet into a dress to wear to the parties, Amy explained to Eli, "I don't like spending the money, but I'm getting very shabby. Besides, these parties are important to all of Central City.

"Father, you just have no idea what is happening—the development, the mining claims. Lucas says this town is attracting international interest. I think Lucas will be a very influential person in Central City in the future. He appreciates my going to these functions with him."

Soon she was seeing the renewed ardor in Lucas's eyes. Even while trying to keep the church piano firmly in mind, that look made Amy uneasy. But it also excited her.

Central City's first vaudeville theatrical was held in the new fire station. At the reception afterwards in the mayor's home, Lucas bent close to her as they stood in the cloak room. Glancing over his shoulder to the crowd beyond the open door, he murmured, "Amy, let's get out of here. I'm tired of all this. Come with me up to the house for a bit."

When she tilted her head to look at him, he pressed his lips to her cheek and then sought her mouth. "My darling," he murmured. Shock held her motionless for a moment, long enough for another kiss. With a gasp she moved away from his restraining hand, rubbing her lips as she wheeled around. "Lucas, I am—" She had nearly said the word she had been ignoring. How could she say *married* when her actions were denying it?

Turning, she straightened her shoulders and said, "I'm tired, too. Please take me home." The sardonic, knowing smile on his lips shocked Amy. As the anger began to gather in her, the picture of that cabin flashed across Amy's mind. Last year she ran away from Lucas after seeing him there with Mrs. Wilson. She faced his smile again. He paused and then moved to kiss her again. Going to the door, she said, "Lucas, I'll walk home; it's only a few blocks."

Through compressed lips, he said, "I'll not let that happen. Get your wrap."

The ride home was silent and swift. Amy knew nothing except the incredible sensation of being soiled deeper than it seemed possible. It was too late, she knew, to say to Lucas the things she had intended to say to Father. Too late and unnecessary.

But anger wasn't justified. By the time they reached the cabin, Amy realized she was all those things Lucas thought. She said, "Please, Lucas. I beg you, stay away. I know this seems like a farce, but I didn't intend—" She slipped out of the carriage before the tears came. It helped that he didn't follow, and that he snapped the whip over the back of his horse with an angry crack.

Night after night Amy would awaken in the midst of a dream in which she was trying to scrape filth from her apron. Though once a spotless white, the apron was reduced to a tattered, soiled rag, in spite of all her efforts.

Then with her life in limbo, Father came with a worried frown. "Aunt Clara is poorly. I heard it at the store. I've bought a chicken for you to make soup."

She prepared the soup, and Father said, "I'll go too. She'll need wood cut."

Aunt Clara threw a towel over her head, lamenting, " 'Tis a disgrace. Only the dying need a body to wait on them. I'm well enough." But she ate the soup while Eli chopped the wood and stacked it in the corner, close to the stove.

Amy brewed tea and heated the flat irons. "You stay in bed; I'll iron these shirts. I've done Father's often enough to know how these collars are to be ironed."

Aunt Clara dozed under the pile of blankets while Amy ironed and set the soup on the stove to heat. Eli dumped the last load of wood in the corner and said, "If you're finished, I'll take the shirts down to the store. Joe'll see the men get them."

After he left, Aunt Clara sat up in bed and remarked, "Overcome is as good as new."

"Oh, dear," Amy murmured, going quickly to the bed. She reached for the blankets with one hand and Aunt Clara's head with the other.

"Now, you listen to me." Aunt Clara dodged the hand. "I'm telling you more. New is good, but overcome is better."

"What ever are you talking about?" Amy asked, bending over the bed.

"Scripture. The overcoming verses. Most in the book of Revelation." Aunt Clara struggled to sit up. "I been reading them. Listen. The overcomers get to eat of the tree of life, and they won't be hurt by the second death. We get to eat of the hidden manna and have a new name. To those that overcome there'll be power over nations, whatever that means.

"I like most about having white raiment, and having my name in the book of life. Jesus himself will talk about us to the Father, giving Him our name. Can't you just see it? Jesus up there saying, 'This here is Aunt Clara Brown, she's my child.' Whoopie!" She paused to cough before adding, "Amy, child, sometimes this old earth gets tiring, but 'tis easy to struggle along when you look at heaven."

"Aunt Clara, do you want me to stay up here tonight? You're—"

"Jest fine." She leaned back against the pillows and now the shrewd old eyes were studying Amy's face. "I've been hearing things, child. Amy, do ya'll know the difference between angel men and demon men?"

"One's—"

She was nodding her head. "It's what the Lord has done in them through the blood of Jesus. You rear up and flaunt yourself, and you become like the devil. You get on your knees and plead with the Father, and He cleans out your old heart and makes it all new. That's the overcomers through the blood of the Lamb."

She settled back in bed, and Amy prepared to leave. Abruptly she spoke again. "Amy, what are you craving? I mistrust cravings a whole lot. Go home and read Ephesians, chapter two and verse three."

Amy went home without any intention of reading. But she was frowning. It was serious, Aunt Clara ranting on and on about religion.

She asked Eli, "Do you think she's dying?"

His eyebrows shot up. "Of course not. She'll be fine." He looked at Amy, frowning as he said, "If you're deciding she sounded—irrational, well, there's been few women I esteem more than Aunt Clara." After another pause he added, "A Bible scholar, yes. I do believe she has more Bible heart-knowledge than anyone I've ever known."

Before going to bed, Amy looked up Ephesians and read: *Children of disobedience . . . fulfilling the desires of the flesh and of the mind . . . by nature children of wrath . . . But God who is rich in mercy*—As she crawled into her bunk she was thinking of Lucas, of his passionate kiss, and that dream. *Like mother, like daughter.*

CHAPTER 30

The February storm was over and the sun came out. But while the tempo of life in the mountain communities picked up, snow remained packed on the streets and the breath of the horses and burros crusted frost around their muzzles. At the store they were calling it unusually cold for nearly spring.

Aunt Clara regained strength slowly. As Amy continued to make frequent trips up the hill, she discovered the old bond between the two of them had forged into a link more durable than ever. Amy was allowing Aunt Clara to say things to her that she wouldn't have allowed a year ago. And Aunt Clara's honesty was creating questions in Amy that couldn't be dealt with easily. Yet for some reason she didn't understand, she felt an inner urge for more.

On the last day Amy helped with the laundry and ironing, she asked, "Aunt Clara, you keep talking about angel people and devil people. Tell me more."

Clara was sitting at the table sewing on buttons and stitching up rips in a pile of blue woolen shirts. She looked up, and her brow wrinkled, "Amy, you're asking me to put words to things I thought you understood, being the daughter of a preacher. Don't you see the difference in people? There's some who act like the devil; Jesus told the Pharisees they'd proved the devil was their father because His word didn't have room in them."

As she pushed the iron over the shirt, Amy asked, "Then what makes a person an angel person?"

"Why the person who asks the Lord to clean him up on the inside, taking out all the old Adam so's he can live for the Lord with a pure heart."

A moment later, Aunt Clara said, "Amy, I see clear as day that you don't believe this old lady, thinking I don't know what I'm talking about." She leaned forward, "But I do. What do you see when you look at me?"

"A very sweet person," Amy said, reaching out to pat the dark hand.

"Do you think I came by it natural? How'd you feel, being taken from your family and put to work in the fields, pulled away from your loved ones and forced to go where you didn't want to go and do what you didn't want to do?"

She stitched at the rip with three short jabs of her needle. "Never knew a happy day 'til I let the Lord wash out the bitterness and set my eyes on the Lord Jesus and Him only." In another moment, after more stitches, she added softly, "You'll never be content, Amy child, 'til you want the Lord more'n anything, 'til you go running after Him with your whole heart. Seems then, even being a slave isn't important."

Aunt Clara no longer needed her. Amy's restless spirit and flattened pocketbook sent her tramping the streets of Central City, looking for work again.

Lucas had been rebuffed for the last time. In one final painful scene, she convinced him she would no longer be seen with him. Now the only reminder of that foolish time was the violet velvet hanging in her closet.

But that dress made escape to Kansas impossible. Even with her hoard of piano money, there wasn't enough.

With spring here, Central City, as well as the other high mountain mining camps, was welcomed back into the world. Freight wagons once again moved through town, dropping off the goods that had been stacked in storage all winter. And on the return trip, the wagon carried a load of the first ore from the mines.

Stage coach runs resumed, and with them came packets of mail and piles of newspapers, all dated before the storm.

Amy carried one newspaper home—a December paper; she wouldn't have bothered except for the bold headline: *BUCKSKIN JOE BATTLES SMALLPOX EPIDEMIC.* She searched the later papers but could find nothing except a brief note mentioning a telegraphed plea from Buckskin Joe for nurses.

When Eli Randolph returned from Russell Gulch, Amy showed him the newspaper. "I'd heard it too." He gave her a quick glance, "I suppose you have friends over that way."

"Yes." Her voice was low. "The Tabors; I stayed at their home. But most of the others I knew by sight. Those that came into the post office, and—" She stopped. To go on would mean she must mention Lizzie, Silverheels, and playing the piano at the Grand Hotel.

Eli hung up his coat. Looking at Amy with a worried frown, he said, "I'll be going to missionary meeting in Denver City the end of February. Come along, if you like. You might be able to make inquiries about your friends."

Amy nodded slowly. "That would be nice. I'd like to look for a job there, too. I've exhausted every possibility in Central City." She saw him wince and added, "Father, I can't continue to stay here with nothing to do."

"I suppose," he said slowly. "It's just that I'm thinking of your welfare. Denver City still isn't the place for a decent woman. For any law-abiding person. Last time I was there I saw a duel in the street, a foolish quarrel over a horse and saddle. They carted off one killed and the other wounded. He'll never be a whole man again."

But before they left for the missionary conference, Daniel came. Amy had been walking down the hill from Aunt Clara's cabin when she saw the lanky rider turn in at the Randolph cabin. She stopped in the middle of the road, wondering about the urgency she sensed as he dismounted and hurried to the cabin. He turned; with a shock Amy recognized him. She pressed her hand against her throat, feeling both elation and despair.

He had come—but why? That last night in Buckskin Joe had dashed all hopes. They had parted cool strangers despite his promise to return.

Slowly she continued down the hill, trying to compose herself. As she approached the cabin, Amy saw Daniel standing in the doorway, his hands braced against the doorposts. Although she couldn't see her father, she knew he was there.

Daniel's mare stood neglected, trailing her reins as she nibbled at the melting snow. With another perplexed glance at the house, Amy turned aside to care for the mare. She stopped when she heard Daniel talking. "Sir, I just found out. I've come as soon as I could ride out of Denver City. I knew you'd want to go with me."

Father's voice came, "Son, come in and sit down. What has upset you?"

Daniel still leaned in the doorway. His words were terse. "Just arrived in Denver City when I began hearing about Buckskin Joe. It happened in November, after Father Dyer and I left. Smallpox. They say it was like wildfire. First a dance-hall girl, then half the town coming down at once.

"The newspapers said the women and children were moved to Fairplay, but those taken with the pox stayed behind. There was a plea for help. I saw in the papers where several nurses went, but that wasn't enough. Many died." Daniel's head went down on his arm. Before Amy could speak, he straightened and added, "I wired Fairplay to check the survivors there. Amy wasn't among them. I'm going now to search for her. Thought you might want—"

"Son!" Amy could see her father prying himself out of the chair and moving across the room. In that one stunned moment, the name *Silverheels* flashed through her. So the newspaper stories weren't just rumor.

The men turned, and she heard Daniel say her name. Looking up, she saw his face ashen, his shoulders trembling.

Slowly she walked to him, unable to look away from his face. Suddenly she knew she wouldn't leave Colorado, not while Daniel was here. She lifted her hands and he caught them. For a moment his lips trembled. He pressed them together and then gasped, "Amy—I, I didn't know you'd left." He turned, gulped and looked at her again.

"I just decided to leave," she said, forcing the light words past the lump in her throat. "It seemed best. I didn't know about the smallpox until we saw a newspaper."

Daniel sighed heavily. Eli said, "Come in and close the door."

"The mare—" Amy said.

"I'll care for her." Daniel touched her arm and she looked up at him. The color seemed to be coming back into his face, but there were still lines of strain around his mouth.

Later she discovered the explosion of feeling had left its mark. When Daniel came back to the cabin, awkwardness surrounded them all. He paced the floor, answering their questions curtly. Although he was nearly reeling with fatigue, he said, "I'll just ride on tonight."

"No, son, you won't." Eli's voice was gentle. "We have an extra straw tick to put down. I think you need to rest at least tomorrow. I'll leave first thing in the morning for a meeting at Russell Gulch. But if you'll stay, I'll see you Thursday."

"Father!" Amy protested.

He looked mildly surprised. "Well, he's part of the family now. If you two plan to scrap, then you'll have the cabin to yourself, and I won't have to listen."

He clapped Daniel on the shoulder. Daniel didn't look up, but Amy had the distinct feeling there was a bond between the two that she didn't understand. Also she was aware of a new feeling. She wanted Daniel to stay.

In the morning, after Father left, Amy studied out the matter, trying to decide how to coax Daniel into remaining.

I could just say it: I love you. Please, Daniel, forgive me. While she washed the dishes, he fed and watered his mare and returned to the cabin.

"I need to get going," he said as he packed his bag. "It's a long ride over the mountains and I want to start before there's a possibility of storm. It rolls pretty fast over these peaks," he added, as if Amy didn't know.

She hung the towel over the stove to dry and took a deep breath. The light touch seemed out, and certainly begging on bended knee was ridiculous. "At least stay until I walk to the store for bread and cheese. There's spice cake and some bacon too."

Tucking his Bible into the bag he nodded. Looking up he said, "I'd appreciate that." And then his eyes were changing. Inside, Amy cried, *Why? You love me, and I am starting to find I can't live without you.*

He hesitated, touching the Bible again, he asked slowly, "Amy, if I'm not pushing where I shouldn't, would you mind telling me what you believe? This morning while we were reading Scripture I felt such wonder in your voice as you read Ephesians 3:17. Do you know the reality of Christ dwelling in your heart?"

Reluctantly she admitted, "Daniel, I joined the church when I was very young. I said, 'Yes, I believe Jesus Christ is my Savior.' Is that what you mean?"

"Ephesians?" he urged.

Slowly she replied, "I felt as if I were reading it for the first time, and I wondered at it all. Awe, I guess. It's the bigness of the love of Christ. Breadth, length, depth and height. Those words are almost a song. And what is the fullness of God?"

Daniel was quoting softly, with a light in his eyes she couldn't understand. " 'Now unto him that is able to do exceeding abundantly above all that we ask. . . . Unto him be glory . . .' " His voice was husky as he said, "Amy, read Colossians; it will tell you. It says that Jesus has all the fullness, and that He has made peace through the giving of His blood on the cross in order to reconcile us—that means to bring us back to where we belong, to God.

"Amy, do you have peace? Are you aware of being reconciled to God, complete in Jesus Christ?" He paused and then added, "Christ in you, the hope of glory."

"Glory?" she asked. "Doesn't that mean heaven?"

Daniel was nodding as he got to his feet. "Come, I'll walk with you to the store, and then I must go."

Disappointment flattened the thoughts crowding into Amy's mind. With a sigh she stood up and followed Daniel to the door. When they reached the road, Daniel took Amy's hand and pulled it through his arm. Gladly she fell into step with him, but glancing up, she was surprised by the lines of strain on his face. It seemed he had forgotten her already.

They had just stepped onto the boardwalk in front of Joe's store when Amy heard her name. She turned. Lucas Tristram came down the street, tall white hat in hand. He smiled happily as he extended his hand.

As she gave him her hand, she said, "Lucas, I'd like you to meet my husband, Daniel Gerrett."

His smile faded as he turned to Daniel. "I remember you. Lost your father a couple years ago. I was the one who bought your mine. It's doing very well—took out close to a hundred thousand last year.

"Haven't seen you since then." Tristram glanced down at Amy. "But we've been enjoying the company of your wife this winter. Central City is starting to blossom culturally, and Amy is a welcome addition. I hope you've been encouraging her to develop her talents. By next year we plan to get some theatrical groups started. She'll be my first promotional project." His possessive smile was making Amy uneasy.

She glanced at Daniel's face as Lucas's smooth voice caught her attention again. She saw him looking at Daniel's shabby jacket. His smile was patronizing as he added, "She deserves the finest, and I don't mind telling you I'll do my best to make that possible."

She felt Daniel's arm tighten and she tugged. "Lucas, please excuse us. Daniel is in a hurry to get on the road."

Meeting Lucas made a difference. Amy saw the shadows in Daniel's eyes as they returned to the cabin.

Amy chattered too much; Daniel listened and was silent.

When he accepted the lunch, Amy's hand lingered on his arm. He hesitated and she pushed her head against his shoulder, there was his light kiss on her cheek.

She followed as he mounted the mare. "I'll see you at missionary convention," he said. She nodded, her heart aching with all the other things that could have been said. *I'm sorry, Daniel, so sorry.* A moment passed. He turned to fumble with the reins.

With a twisted smile he said, "Looks like Tristram is pretty stiff competition. More'n I can take." The hot denial rose to Amy's lips; then memory caught her. Her cheeks burned. Wordlessly she looked into Daniel's face, and he turned away.

CHAPTER 31

The wheels of Eli Randolph's old wagon creaked, providing a backdrop to Amy's thoughts, emphasizing the words she wanted most to forget. *And be ye kind one to another, tender-hearted, forgiving one another, even as God for Christ's sake hath forgiven you. Be ye therefore followers of God, as dear children; And walk in love, as Christ also hath loved us, and hath given himself for us an offering and a sacrifice to God . . .*

As the wagon jogged along, Amy thought back over the past month when she would take her Bible and make the trip up the hill to Aunt Clara's. It had started the day after Daniel left, and because of his urging her to read Colossians. She had thought to please him by reading the Bible, but she was beginning to regret all those days spent with Aunt Clara.

Eli interrupted her musings, saying, "Amy, you're uncommonly quiet. Having big thoughts you want to air?"

"I'm not certain. I've been doing lots of thinking lately— about life. Father, don't you think Aunt Clara is too—" She couldn't finish the thought.

His expression made her uncomfortable. Slowly he said, "Aunt Clara enjoys the goodness of the Lord in a way we don't see too often. Is that what's bothering you?"

"She's pretty set in her ways."

"How's that?"

"Several weeks ago, we were discussing what it means to be Christian. I don't think she's convinced I'm Christian. I've started taking my Bible up to her house and we've been reading together. Father, is it possible for a person to take the Bible differently, to come out with a meaning that's altogether different? She called it distorting it."

He flipped the reins across the backs of the lagging team and pursed his mouth. "Being human, we always see what we want to see. That's the correcting value of Scripture—if we believe it's God talking to us, and if we follow instruction. Amy, it's always good to be reviewing our beliefs, making certain that what we hold in our minds is truth according to God's Word."

"Then it isn't enough to just confess you're a Christian and belong to a church that teaches the Bible?"

"Well, the Bible says we must believe in our hearts, and that belief is proven by our obedience to God." There was a perplexed frown growing on his face, and Amy was begining to regret bringing up the subject.

"Father, don't look so disapproving. I haven't thrown out all the teachings. It's just that she asked such questions. Some scripture I read makes me uneasy because I don't understand."

"Tell me."

"She's saying that being a Christian calls for change. More than that. She said surrender to God makes you become all new—in what you hold dear and how you live out your life. She said it's called being reconciled to God, brought back to the relationship He'd wanted to have with Adam and Eve.

"Then Aunt Clara said something about being a new creature. She quoted verses from John where Jesus was talking to Nicodemus. About being born of the Spirit—being born again." She added, "And what about all those other things in the Bible?"

"You mean the things He tells us we'll do if we are obedient? In the book of First John we find that if we keep His word, the love of God is perfected in us, and it proves we are really His. The reverse is true. If we hate, we are walking in darkness. No matter how much we say we're Christian, we're going to have to prove it by our actions."

His brooding voice seemed to cut her out as he said, "Even more than that, our very secret, inner cravings tell on us. Sooner or later, they reveal whether or not we belong to Jesus Christ."

Amy found she couldn't interrupt that sad monologue. She drew her shawl close, shutting out the sight of his face and the fearful words.

First Aunt Clara, now Father. It was starting to seem as if both of them felt the same way about the Bible. Funny, never before had Father made her feel uncomfortable in this way.

And now he spoke again, looking at her with a quizzical frown on his face. "Amy, ever since you've been big enough to go to church, you've been hearing these things preached. Why do you ask these questions?"

Amy couldn't answer. How could she explain? It was as if all the thoughts were new to her.

As they continued down the road leading out Clear Creek Canyon, the two of them lapsed into silence, busy with their own thoughts. Amy determined anew to seek employment in Denver City.

Once out of the mountains, the horses picked up their pace. It was midafternoon when they reached Denver City, and Father turned the team down the trail to the Cummings' house. "They've got plenty of room, and several of us will be staying there. It's within a mile of the church, so we'll be able to walk to services."

Amy discovered the Cummings had planned for Daniel to stay at their home too. But that was to be expected. They knew of the marriage. Amy saw the curiosity in their eyes as she heard their apology. There wasn't enough room and the men must bunk down on the floor in front of the fireplace.

April Taylor was there to share the bedroom with Amy. She cuddled her baby and beamed at Amy. Remembering the wan April she had met nearly a year ago, Amy was secretly and strangely relieved to see April's cheeks blooming with color and to see the peaceful contentment in her eyes.

While Amy unpacked her valise, April chatted happily, telling Amy all the details of her confinement. And when she stopped for a deep breath, Amy asked, "What is it like now? Does your husband still travel a lot? Are there Indians nearby?"

April nodded. "Yes, He still travels his circuit. And there are Indians close." When Amy shivered, she gave her a puzzled look, saying, "Amy, it isn't so bad. There's other folks around even when he's gone. And the Indians, poor things. James is trying to make friends with them too."

In a moment, as she diapered the baby, she added, "Part of the call is being willing to trust the Lord. Amy, we're in God's hands. Whether we live or die, we are the Lord's—that's Scripture." With calm, clear eyes she studied Amy.

Closing her valise, Amy went downstairs to help Mrs. Cummings prepare dinner. Daniel arrived while she was in the kitchen. She saw him ride past to the corral, and her heart went yearning after him, even as she reminded herself there would be little time to talk.

At this meeting she noticed a difference immediately. The wives of the elders welcomed her with special smiles. She had become a part of the inner circle and their friendship left her with a guilty conscience.

Later, at church, when Daniel came to sit with her, she murmured, "What have you been saying to all these women?"

He looked surprised. "Absolutely nothing. I haven't exchanged a dozen words with them. Why?"

"Mrs. Cummings, Mrs. Foster, even the Taylors have been telling me they're praying you'll get a better post this year, one in town so that I won't have to spend another season with Father."

Daniel moved uneasily on the bench and murmured, "Amy, I know this is difficult, and it will be even harder to explain when you leave. Believe me, I haven't given anyone information about us."

Then, before the pianist went to the shiny new piano, Amy asked, "Is Father Dyer here?"

"No. Some are saying they doubt he'll make it this time. I don't know why, but I'm guessing he's too far afield to get here."

The pianist began to play. Amy watched, listened, and very carefully tried to control her impulse to wince. Under the cover of her flaring skirt, Daniel searched for her hand and gave it a quick squeeze. Surprisingly, she found herself blinking back the unexpected tears. In his quick glance she saw both compliment and sympathy.

After the service ended, the people lingered, visiting with each other. Daniel came to her side again, saying, "I have something to tell you about Silverheels; will you walk with me?" Amy nodded and followed him through the crowd.

Outside he dropped her shawl over her shoulders and Amy said, "February, and it's like spring tonight. That softness in the air—am I smelling willows too?"

"I doubt it, but it is encouraging." They started down the road together with their arms linked. For a time, Amy forgot their reason for being together. Finally Daniel sighed and said, "I stopped in at the *Rocky Mountain News* today, just after I arrived. Went to ask about the epidemic scare at Buckskin Joe." He turned to look at her. "Amy, it wasn't just a scare. It was very bad. I'm fairly certain, from what I heard, that the smallpox started at Silverheels' place."

A wagon was passing and he led her off the road. "Look, let's go sit on the steps of that deserted cabin. The wagons and carriages are moving out from the church and we'll be covered with dust if we don't wait this out."

In front of the cabin they found a stoop made of split cottonwood logs. Amy pushed the partially open door and said, "Someone thought enough of his home to give it the little extra touches, the stoop and the floor. I wonder whether the family moved on to the mining camps or if they returned to the states?"

Daniel shook his head, saying, "I can't guess. But empty, it's a lonesome place. Will you be warm enough if we sit here?" She nodded and he sat down beside her. For a moment his words slipped past her. She was deeply conscious of his nearness. He bent to pick up a twig from the ground. As he flexed it, Amy studied him covertly, liking the way his nimble fingers tested the strength of the wood.

He said something. She knew it from his quick glance her direction. "I—what did you say?" And in that second before he looked away, the expression in his eyes made Amy catch her breath. Was it possible he still cared?

"I said they evacuated Buckskin Joe. All the townspeople who didn't have smallpox left. Except for Silverheels. According to the fellow at the newspaper office, she stayed behind to nurse the sick. Those who didn't die were just getting back on their feet when she was taken ill."

Amy caught her breath and pressed her hand against her throat. She had to wait for her heart to steady. "Did she die?"

"No, but she was very ill." The twig in his fingers finally snapped and he tossed away the fragments. "Amy, I can't stop thinking about that woman. Most would consider her the scum of the earth. But why did she risk her life to help others? She could have left with the other dance-hall girls."

Amy shrugged. But when she spoke, she couldn't keep the bitterness out of her voice, "Maybe she had a sweetie who had the pox."

"Could be." Daniel found another stick and as he turned it over in his fingers, Amy's thoughts were drawn unwillingly to that last encounter with Silverheels. And now she saw a new picture—Silverheels nursing the smallpox victims, while Amy, the good, proper Christian girl, was smashing the china doll against the hearth. She winced at the comparison.

She tried to recall the anger she felt that day, but the picture of Silverheels bending over a sickbed, nursing one of those poor miners kept coming back.

Daniel looked up. "Amy, I've been rattling on about California Gulch and you haven't heard a word. Is there something on your mind?"

"Well, I was thinking about Silverheels. She didn't seem like the kind of person who would care." Even as Amy made the statement, other images pushed past the anger hidden securely in her heart—Silverheels caring for Lizzie, and that light kiss she had pressed on Amy's cheek.

The day she had returned the cloak, for a few brief moments they had been in each other's arms. Amy winced and pressed her fingers against her lips. *Mother*. That word longing to be said.

Daniel said, "I forgot to tell you the townspeople took up a generous purse to present to Silverheels, but she disappeared. The fellow at the newspaper office says he's had no more information about her."

They sat in silence. Finally Daniel said, "You're tired. Shall we start for the Cummings'? I suppose it would have been wise to have ridden with the others."

"No, this is better. Just talk, please. Tell me again about California Gulch. I promise to listen this time."

He pulled her arm through his and Amy found herself wishing for more. As they walked slowly, Daniel talked. "The gulch is starting to attract more people. This time it's families moving in. There are children and they're beginning to talk about a school for them."

"Why the change?"

"I have an idea it's because the diggings have been so poor that the claims are up for grabs. Now a man with a family can afford to buy into a spot that's been dug. Might be there's more of a risk, but it's hard to say so to these folks."

For just a moment Amy thought she detected a wistful note in his voice as he added, "There are more coming to church and the women are excited about getting a sewing group going."

"California Gulch is awfully high and cold, isn't it?" Amy asked because she could think of nothing more to say.

"High, but I don't think it's worse than Buckskin Joe." For a moment there was an eagerness in his voice that fell flat as he added, "But it's terrible unless a person's heart is in it. One of the young wives has left."

"For Denver City?"

"Home, back to the states." The unspoken subject lay between them. For a moment Amy toyed with the idea of telling Daniel her new plans, but they had reached the Cummings' house. In the flood of lamplight coming through the door, Amy saw his grim face and lost her courage.

Several of the men were spreading their blankets on the floor. From the kitchen came the clatter of dishes and the rush of excited feminine voices.

Daniel's hand detained her. "Amy, I sense your heavy spirit—what is it?" She could only shake her head. "I wish I could help you. You know I do want that, don't you?" Briefly the temptation appeared. *Ohio.*

Mrs. Cummings was watching them from the kitchen doorway. Daniel glanced at her and then bent to kiss Amy's cheek. Amy started up the stairs as Mrs. Cummings addressed Daniel, "I'm right sorry I don't have more room. Sure's a crowd here this year. We've got people all over town."

CHAPTER 32

The next morning Amy lingered behind while the others hastened through breakfast and headed for the church. Even April, carrying her baby, went with her husband.

Weeks ago, Aunt Clara had insisted that Amy read the Bible with her. And then she discovered Father seemed to be siding with Aunt Clara.

But the culmination of Amy's uneasiness came with last night's sermon. During the night the words had probed her hidden thoughts. The sermon had left one clear impression—she was an old wineskin.

After the door closed behind the Taylors and Father, Amy restlessly paced the floor. She kept coming back to the final words of the presiding elder, wondering why they still rang through her thoughts. *You will know God not only as Redeemer, but also as Lord and Friend when you trust Him more than yourself; when His desires are more important than yours. The Holy Spirit will come upon you when your hunger for God exceeds everything else in life.* Daniel had used the word *desperate*.

Last night, for the first time, while she watched those people kneeling at the altar, she had been touched with a strange envy. Those people hungered and thirsted in a way she couldn't understand.

But even more, the elder had made the clear, flat statement: " 'Neither do men put new wine into old bottles, else the bottles break, and the wine runneth out and the bottles perish: but they put new wine into new bottles and both are preserved.' "

Perish or be preserved. Fearful words, just like the words Aunt Clara used. Yet it wasn't the words that struck her, but the hunger revealed on the faces of those people reaching out for that something Amy didn't understand.

Mrs. Cummings came into the room, and Amy saw she was watching her with a knowing look in her eyes. "Aw, you're feeling poorly. Well, you just rest. The morning is always worse."

She pulled her shawl across her shoulders and hurried out the door. Amy had just resumed her pacing when Daniel came back into the cabin. She saw the worried frown on his face as he said, "Mrs. Cummings tells me you're ill."

Slowly she sat down. Surprisingly her lips were stiff as she said, "No, I just wanted to be alone."

He hesitated, about to leave; then he abruptly knelt beside her chair and asked, "Wanna tell me about it?"

One part of her was crying, *You less than anyone else in the world*; at the same time she wanted to throw herself into his arms. Amy settled back and thought of the gnawing inside. The need was bigger than her pride.

"Daniel, have you ever had a problem that confused you until you didn't know what to do about it?"

"Yes, I have."

"Well, what did you do about it?"

"I had to settle it myself, but I also needed a helping hand to start me in the right direction. Amy, do you remember the day Pa died, and how you sang to me? You were that helping hand." He touched her gently. "Do you want me to help you?"

She could only nod as her tears splashed on his hand. He waited, then, "Tell me."

She took a deep breath and tried to decide where to begin.

He decided for her. "Amy, have you ever just plain, flat out told Jesus Christ that you want Him to be your Savior? I know from experience, carrying around a sin problem gets a person down. Our Lord can't do a thing about it until we believe His promise to us. His Word says that even while we were still dead in our sins, He loved us, and died for us in order that we can be alive in Him.

"See, it is God's love, grace and kindness in Christ that does all this for us. We only need to believe and accept what God is saying to us." He looked up and waited.

"You make it sound so simple!" she cried. "Daniel, it isn't that simple. Confess and get up and go on with life? I've tried it. Maybe I don't have faith."

"Why?" He waited and finally he said, "Does it go deeper? Are you trying to place limits on the Lord and what you are willing to give Him?"

"I suppose."

"Shall I help you?"

She nodded her head and slipped to her knees beside the chair. He prompted, "Remember, He is God, and He loves you so much He died in order for you to live forever. We dare not neglect a salvation so great. On top of that, He knows what's upsetting you. So the work's half done."

"Jesus Christ," she began carefully, "thank you for dying for me. Please forgive my sins. I want you to be my Savior. I—" Her body shook with sobs, but finally she could say; "I really did hate you. But now I can't. You started to rescue me. But I stopped co-operating with you. Now, I promise, it will be different—the stubborn Amy, the ugliness—my dreams."

Daniel helped her to stand. Wrapping her in his arms, he said, "Welcome, Amy. You are now my sister in the Lord. For all eternity, we'll be friends together with Him."

"Daniel, I must confess. Now I understand my dread of revival. I've blamed it all on the past, my fear, thinking it was because I saw my mother die. Now I understand. I've been fighting God. I did remember her, but I used that memory to build a wall shutting me away from God."

He nodded. "I was beginning to wonder about that. I'm grateful you understand." He hugged her again.

"That isn't all." His arms dropped.

He hesitated and then added, "If you want me to listen, I will; if you don't, that's all right, now and forever. I give you that promise."

"I do." She went to sit down beside the fire, to search through the jumble of feelings, sensing her shame, wondering if it would affect how Daniel felt about her. For a moment she looked at him. *Even that must be risked.*

"Those verses in Colossians—peace, reconciled to Him, being complete in Jesus Christ. They are things I want. I see I can't have them until I'm willing to forgive.

"It's Silverheels. I've discovered she's my mother." There was a strangled sound from Daniel, nearly a sob. She said slowly, "I know it's terrible. A dance-hall girl—worse, a madame in a place like that. I am so ashamed, yet—"

Her voice dropped to a whisper. "I went to see her and we had a terrible time over it. See, I didn't know until I found my picture in her cloak."

His arm was warm and protective now. She leaned against him, taking comfort from his nearness.

She told of finding the picture, and then, slowly, painfully, she admitted, "We said horrible things to each other. I don't know why. At first it seemed good, and then she sent me away. Ordered me out of her life. Said she didn't want to be bothered by me. I'd ruin her career. She ended up mocking me like I was a worthless, silly baby and I screamed ugly things at her."

They both were silent, alone in their thoughts. Amy's emotions had flattened, but one heavy burden remained upon her heart. Finally Daniel sighed and moved away from her. "Do you need to do something?"

Reluctantly she nodded. "It bothers me still. For a time I *tried* to stay angry with her in order to avoid thinking about it. But—" she shrugged.

"I think you'd better say it."

"I must tell her I'm sorry, ask her forgiveness, and Daniel, now there's something else. All of a sudden I feel so responsible. She may be in need. I must help her, even if she doesn't want me around."

"What do you suggest?"

"I'll go. I have enough money to take the stage to Buckskin Joe."

"I'll go with you," Daniel said in a matter-of-fact voice. "I will try to borrow a buggy from a friend and we can be up there in a few hours' time."

He was nearly to the door when he stopped. "Amy, what about your father?"

She blinked. "Well, I don't think he'll mind at all. He's been pushing us together every chance he gets." Daniel was frowning and Amy whispered, "Oh, that isn't what you meant—" A new question formed in his eyes, but she turned away from it, asking, "What did you mean?"

"Silverheels."

"You're saying I should tell him," Amy said slowly. This was something she hadn't considered. She turned from Daniel to pace the floor. "She asked me not to tell him." Amy caught her breath, added, "She told me she didn't want Father coming after her." Amy chewed at her lip and added, "Right now I don't feel inclined to talk to him about it." He waited and she added, "Yes, I've been angry about that, too. But if you insist, I'll write a note. That'll mean we must leave soon, before he comes back."

"I think it's important," Daniel said slowly. "There's a possibility she's no longer living, but if she is, your father may need to see her, too. At least, I feel this isn't something we should hide from him."

In a moment Amy nodded. "I guess that's the right thing to do."

"I'll go see Mac at the livery stable. Better pack a bag."

That question flashed in his eyes again, and Amy came to him. "Daniel, you're not beholden to me for anything. This, us, was all a bad mistake from the beginning. I won't cling to you."

"Amy, say no more." His voice was sharp. "You're not forcing this upon me. Don't forget, I've got an interest in Silverheels. She's—worthy because Christ died for her too." He paused, adding, "As for us, let's agree to just forget everything for now. Even the fact that we're married. We could pretend to be strangers, just getting to be friends."

Amy was trembling as the door closed behind Daniel. She wiped her fingers across her eyes and considered her sore heart. "Daniel's thinking I prayed like that because I was trying to get him. Never." As her voice broke in a half sob, the new realization rushed over her.

She cocked her head, beginning now to smile. It was a gentle urge. It had been there before, but she had paid no heed. It was the urge to pray. Just like the elder had said last night. He was Lord and friend now, and He wanted her prayer. Her lips were still soft with the smile as she whispered, "Lord Jesus, thank you for being with me. I really believe in your presence, and that is so good!"

With a sigh she got up to look for the paper and pencil in her bag. When she sat down to write, she had to search for words. It was difficult. The words came out stiff and stilted. *"Dear Father. It seems Daniel and I must go to Buckskin Joe immediately. We've word that the dance-hall woman they call Silverheels has disappeared. When we return, I'll tell you all about it, but for now I must say that I've discovered Silverheels is my mother. There is no doubt about it. Please don't worry; Daniel will be there to take care of me."* She signed her name; then with a touch of irony in her voice, she said, "He'll be there to take care of me—whether or not he likes it."

Daniel came in. "Ready? I'll get my bag. Where's your blanket roll? If we go to Father Dyer's, we'll need it."

"I guessed that." She picked up her bag, adding, "I've left the note on the table. Mrs. Cummings will see he gets it."

It was only ten o'clock in the morning, but the streets of Denver City were filled with people, animals, and every kind of conveyance possible. When they reached the business district, they found a group of Indians parading slowly through the center of town. Fascinated, Amy watched them, caught by their stoic dignity. She studied their colorful warbonnets and ceremonial dress, and shivered.

"Daniel," she murmured, "they act as if this parade is of deep significance to them, and look at the people around them. It's as if the settlers don't know they're here. Do you suppose they are planning a fight?"

"Arapahoes," Daniel said, shaking his head as he watched the Indians. "See the women's horses dragging the tepee poles? Those cross bars are added to carry children and baggage. The contraption is called a travois. It's an efficient way to travel if you don't have wheels."

"The beadwork on that woman's blouse is beautiful," Amy murmured.

"From the way they are dressed, and the presence of the women and children, I get the feeling they're headed up South Park, the same way we're going. Just might be there's a squabble in the making. I've heard the Utes have been drifting into the territory for several weeks."

"Is there a danger?"

"To us? I don't think so," Daniel answered. "For the most part, the Arapahoes have treated us better than we have them."

"April says her husband, James, has been attempting to make friends with them." She added, "April doesn't seem to mind being left alone, even with the Indians around."

Daniel gave her a quick glance, and Amy wondered why he smiled.

They left town and started into the foothills. The horses were pulling the light carriage easily, and Daniel was pleased. "Good team. At this rate we'll be in Fairplay before sundown." He snapped the reins across the horses' backs. "I wouldn't mind having a rig like this. It would make traveling more pleasant, but then, I don't have a need for such. Maybe someday."

Someday. Amy considered the word. There was promise, and perhaps a hint of yearning in the way he said it. She glanced at him, and he looked back with a grin.

"What makes you so happy?" She asked curiously.

"The day and having company. It's unusual. I've traveled a lot of miles in the last six months, but few spent with company. I like this."

She found herself beaming back at him, feeling as giddy as a child over the unexpected holiday. But then the burden of the trip fell and she settled into her shawl, mulling over the emotions that alternately left her curious and angry. *So the people at Buckskin tried to pay Silverheels. What could have happened to her? It seems everyone in the territory knows about Silverheels.*

She examined the situation and tried to feel proud, but all those other emotions churned. Amy looked at Daniel's relaxed grin and felt her heart sink. How badly she wished to be back in Denver City! She searched for something to say, a way to make him talk.

She toyed with the idea of telling Daniel of her experience this morning. For the first time God was a sweet, comforting presence. Good, not fearful. Would he understand? After a moment of studying his face, she was satisfied he would, yet she was caught, remembering his expression when she had foolishly misunderstood him.

Her cheeks were burning. As her hands tightened into fists, she vowed that she would never throw herself at him again.

"Daniel." She took a deep breath, disliking the timid waver in her voice. "You said something about being friends. That would help; I wouldn't feel so—"

He glanced quickly. "Amy, I've never wanted you to feel that way."

"What way?"

"Weren't you going to say *pressured*?" She nodded, and he asked, "How would you want a friend to act?"

"So friendly that he'd accept me no matter what I thought or said."

"About people like Silverheels and Lizzie? About wanting to play the piano even when Aunt Maude and the Methodists think it's the devil's invention?"

She winced. "Piano. I suppose that'll be one of the things

I'll need to give up. Surrender it at the feet of Jesus, as Aunt Clara would say."

"Would you mind?"

"Too much."

They rode in silence and then Amy added, "This is an ugly thing, from beginning to end." She looked at him and added, "Nice families just don't have mothers who are prostitutes."

He looked at her. "Prostitutes are people Jesus loves too."

In a moment she added, "I'll go. Do what must be done and then be gone forever."

"Forever? Amy, how will you feel if you find a sick woman who must have you in order to survive?"

She considered all the implications of his statement. He was testing her confession of Christianity. Yet, she looked at him, thinking, *It's as if he's testing himself. Dance-hall woman. Mother. And now, mother-in-law. That's what she would be to Daniel.*

Poor Daniel. She considered what his life had become since she had stepped into it in her bumbling, willful way. Amy sighed heavily. *I'm ashamed. How'll the mess ever be righted?*

"Say it."

"You'll have a prostitute for a mother-in-law."

He grinned at her. "You forget, we're just friends."

She leaned forward and touched his sleeve. "Be serious, Daniel. Have you considered what this will do to your future?"

"I just realized it. It would make good copy, wouldn't it? Dance-hall woman accepts Christ and admits she's the mother-in-law of the famous Colorado Territory missionary for the Methodist Episcopal Church."

Amy was still looking at Daniel as she said, "It's a good thing you said 'famous'—otherwise I would have been a friend and pushed you off the seat."

He winced. "Amy, we really don't know each other very well, do we?"

"No." The words were coming almost against her will. "And I'm afraid we'll know each other too well before this trip is over."

"Afraid? You don't like the idea?"

She considered herself. She was fearful of all the untried places in her life—untried since the decision this morning. How dare she trust herself after failing so miserably before? She felt the smile disappear from her face. *I don't trust myself. I love Daniel too much to let him see the real Amy.* "No, I don't." He looked surprised, but said no more.

CHAPTER 33

It was dark when Amy and Daniel reached Buckskin Joe. When the carriage slowed and turned, bumping up the rocky road toward Buckskin, Amy yawned and tried to push away the dreamy state of near sleep in which she had been submerged for the past hour.

She had been rearranging life into a pleasant scene where Daniel loved her passionately, and Silverheels wasn't her mother. In this dream Silverheels admitted to having stolen the picture and fabricated the whole story in order to discredit them and bring shame upon them all. It had ended with Amy and Daniel rapidly riding eastward to Ohio, just as quickly as their steeds could pull their new carriage.

She sat up and leaned forward. Buckskin didn't seem to have changed, at least in the dark. There were lights in the Tabors' boardinghouse, and the Grand Hotel fairly blazed with light. Daniel urged the horses on and quickly they headed up the incline to Father Dyer's cabin.

He was at home. Still bemused by her dream, Amy was momentarily disappointed. Father Dyer met them at the door, saying, "I heard the carriage and team. Wondered what glorious company I was having. Been a while since royalty's visited."

"Well, royalty's planning on staying a spell. I'll explain as soon as I bed down these fillies."

Amy followed Father Dyer into the cabin. Hands on her hips, he studied her and asked, "Still not sleeping together, huh?"

"How—how do you know?"

"There's two bedrolls here." Shaking his head, he went to the stove to stir the pot of beans. "Can't understand the likes of the younger generation. I'll get down some more plates."

Amy stood motionless in the middle of the cabin and reality crashed in. She looked about the dim smoky room, poorly furnished with handcrafted stools and a rickety table. There was one sagging bunk in the corner. Only a few planed boards kept the cabin from being totally floorless.

She also noticed all Father Dyer's clothes hung on three pegs, while the portable organ leaned against one wall, looking as if mice had been chewing on the straps.

This was reality; this was life for an elder in the Methodist Episcopal Church in Colorado Territory. It was the life Daniel wanted more than he wanted her.

Amy shivered and pulled her shawl tight. But there was more. Tomorrow she would have Silverheels to confront.

She sighed and turned to look at Father Dyer. His square, stocky figure embodied his no-nonsense, uncompromising attitude toward life. Without a doubt, even yet tonight, explanations must be made to him.

With an impatient movement, Father Dyer turned and shoved the chipped plates toward her. Feeling as if her feet were wooden, she tried to move in his direction. He was watching and she saw in his eyes an unexpected sympathy. Blinking, Amy turned away.

Daniel came into the cabin. He gave them both a quick glance as he walked to the stove to warm his hands.

Much as she tried to relax, Amy moved like a wooden doll, placing the forks and knives on the table before she reached for the coffee mugs. "Once the sun sets, you remember it's only February," Daniel muttered.

Father Dyer set the plate of bacon on the table and handed the knife and bread to Amy. He said, "What brings you two here?"

Amy looked at Daniel, and he said, "Let's wait a bit; don't want to ruin supper." Father Dyer's eyebrows showed his surprise, but he sat down and bowed his head.

When Amy made the second trip for the coffeepot, Daniel shoved his plate aside and looking at her asked, "Do I do the talking, or will you?"

Amy sighed and sat down. "Guess I can start. Father Dyer, the reason I left here was because Silverheels ran me out of town. Threatened to do me harm."

He looked startled. He opened his mouth to speak, and Amy blurted out, "She's my mother. I found my picture in the pocket of the cloak she had given me to wear the night Lizzie died, so I guess there's no doubt."

Just saying the words, seeing the strange expression on his face, set Amy's hands to trembling as she lifted the mug. She added, "It was like having someone come back from the dead, for a few minutes at least, but that didn't last long. She turned on me, told me to get out, saying I'd ruin her life if it was known she had a grown daughter. It was terrible."

"So why are you both back here?"

Daniel answered, "First, we're both uneasy about her. Read the newspaper stories about the epidemic here. Later I picked up information in Denver City, indicating that she'd been ill with the smallpox and then disappeared."

Father Dyer nodded his head. "That's what I'd heard. But I doubt there's a person around who can give you information about her. As far as I've been able to discover, all the girls have gone, flown the coop. I don't have much information to offer you because I was out of town when the disease flared up. They stuck a quarantine on Buckskin Joe. So I didn't get back in until later."

He sipped his coffee and added, "You said first. What's the next reason?"

Daniel waited for her to answer. Amy stared at the splintery table as she said, "We didn't part friendly. Fact is, I'm ashamed of myself. Need to apologize."

Daniel took a deep breath and leaned forward, "There's good news too—the best." When Amy heard the thread of excitement in Daniel's voice, she lifted her head. In the shadowy room she couldn't see his eyes, but as he continued, she found tears coming to her eyes. "It's Amy. This morning she prayed, asking the Lord Jesus Christ to be her Savior. I just can't think of anything better."

Suddenly shy, Amy pushed her mug around, glancing quickly from one to the other. Father Dyer's face was a study of questions, but Daniel continued to smile at her. She grinned, feeling her own spirit respond joyously.

Later she washed and dried the dishes while John Dyer talked. "Wasn't long after you left that the smallpox started up. As soon as the doctor came and the folks got wind of it, they started evacuating people. They told me all this later."

Daniel restlessly paced the room. "Many died?"

"Yes. I don't know the number. Mostly it was the single men. They're kinda hard to keep count of." In a moment he added, "Sure filled up the cemetery. Felt bad about not being here, but they were being pretty strict about keeping people out, except for the nurses coming in from Denver City. Didn't want it to spread across the whole territory."

"When we passed I noticed the Tabors' house was lighted," Amy said.

Father Dyer nodded. "But you can believe H.A.W. had his family out of here in a hurry." Abruptly he lifted his head and said, "What about Silverheels? What do you want me to do?"

"I don't know," Daniel said slowly. "I suppose we'll go up to the boardinghouse and make inquiries."

"It's closed. Far as I know there's not a soul around there."

"What about going to the Tabors' first?" Amy asked. "Augusta has probably heard something."

John Dyer stood up suddenly and stretched. "Well—nighty, night, children. This old man gets up early. Going to Mosquito Gulch tomorrow." He headed for his bunk.

Amy and Daniel unrolled their blankets on the planks close
to the stove. John had banked the fire and the warmth was
pleasant against Amy's face as she tunneled into the blankets
and turned to drop her shoes carefully on the floor.

Daniel murmured, "Guess you'll have to put up with my
quoting Scripture. Nights when there's no light I talk myself
to sleep by saying all the Scripture I can remember. This one is
for you. 'That ye would walk worthy of God, who hath called
you unto his kingdom and glory. For this cause also we thank
God without ceasing, because when ye received the word of
God which ye heard of us, ye received it not as the word of
men, but as it is in truth the word of God, which effectually
worketh also in you that believe.' Then there's one we both
need to remember when we see Silverheels. 'But the natural
man receiveth not the things of the Spirit of God: for they are
foolishness unto him: neither can he know them, because they
are spiritually discerned,' and 'That he would grant you, according to the riches of his glory, to be strengthened with might
by his Spirit in the inner man. . . . Now unto him that is able
to do exceeding abundantly above all that we ask or think . . .'"

Amy turned on her side to listen to Daniel. When he finished, she said, "Daniel you are reminding me that I have an
obligation to act like a Christian now, and a responsibility to
treat the Bible different—it is God speaking. I will, I really
intend to do so, but I'm scared."

He raised himself on one elbow and looked down at her.
"Amy, I believe you. You've taken a vow to live out your life
for God, and that is not to be taken lightly. Also, we need to
remember that Silverheels cannot be expected to act any differently than she has in the past."

"You say Silverheels, not Mother," Amy said slowly. "Is
it because you can't imagine her as my mother?"

"Possibly."

"It would be nice to have all this just disappear," Amy said
slowly, feeling guilty and miserable even as she admitted it.

"But it won't. Amy, could we pray together about it?"

Daniel reached across the mound of blankets and took her hand. "Lord, the burden of Silverheels lies between us. Please guide us to her and use us in her life. We can ask for nothing better than your will for her."

When Daniel turned away to sleep, Amy watched the faint cherry glow of the stove and wondered about her response to it all. It seemed his prayer had lifted Amy to a new position. One in which she realized she sided with him, not against. It left her feeling as if she had been drawn into an inner circle, of knowing Daniel in a new way.

She turned her head to look at him, conscious of a lonely wish to reach out and touch him; but at the same time, she felt constrained.

As she mulled over their separation, she felt the difference. Was it possible to be held at a point where spirit communion could grow to a new dimension, with a clamor that blocked out all other need? He had used the word "friends." But as she continued to think about it, she sighed. It wasn't enough; there must be more to life than linked hands.

In the morning Father Dyer looked at her rumpled frock and tumbled hair. With amusement he said, "I suppose we can take a walk until you manage a miracle with your comb and a bar of soap." Turning to Daniel, he added, "Let's go salute the dawn, and then I must be on my way."

Fresh clothing and breakfast righted Amy's world and by midmorning she and Daniel were on their way into town.

"Let's stop at the store; most likely H. A. W. will be there."

But before they reached the store, Amy and Daniel passed the squatty log cabin that served as the courthouse. Amy said, "Did you know this place was Buckskin Joe's house?"

Daniel said, "I didn't know there was such a person."

Amy nodded. "He not only found gold here, but owned part of the Phillips claim. I hear he sold out for a little bit of nothing and left the country. At least he had a town named after himself."

Daniel said, "Let's go there first. I know the clerk who is recorder of deeds."

Amy nodded. "He came often to the Grand Hotel while I played the piano there. Mick Sawyer is his name." She followed Daniel into the building. Mick got up from his desk and came to the counter.

Amy couldn't control her gasp. As Daniel shook hands with the man, Mick said, "Might as well say it. Most of us look like this, the ones that survived."

"The scars are bad now," Daniel admitted, his distress showing in his eyes. "I'm sure time will help. Meanwhile—"

"Most of us are just glad to be alive," Mick said. Now, with a twisted smile, he added, "I suppose you preachers are saying it's the mighty vengeance of the Lord on us for not heeding revival."

"Might be better to say it's the work of the Adversary. He's been known to do such things every since he first got Eve to listen to him." He paused and added, "You're not going to tell me none of the good Christian folk had the pox, are you?"

Mick grinned at Daniel and said, "Well, what can I do for you?"

"Have any idea what has happened to Silverheels? We'd settle for information about any of the girls who lived over there."

Mick shook his head. "Most of them scattered like autumn leaves soon as they heard about the pox. Not surprising when you consider their faces are their business." He paused. "Silverheels? That's one genuine lady. Stuck with us to help out in a bad time. Most of the folk can't say enough good about her. But we don't know where she is now. Some say she's left the territory. Most of us think otherwise. Maybe you should talk to the Tabors."

Daniel and Amy continued on down the street. It was nearly noon and there was a scattering of people on the street. But Amy noticed the difference, not only in the people but in the very atmosphere.

The rollicking gaiety of the town was gone. The dancing schools were silent, with gaping lifeless windows. Only one saloon had open doors, and the sober murmur of voices coming through the door seemed strange.

Continuing down the street, Daniel and Amy noticed the faces of passers-by. Few were unmarked. Amy could see many people walked with effort; their faces were white and sad.

At the store they found H.A.W. behind the counter. His shop once signaled the prosperity of the town; now there was a look of neglect. The shelves were nearly empty and dust covered the line of tinned fruit and vegetables. He apologized. "We're still trying to get things back in swing. Augusta and the boy are staying in Denver City for a while. That's one reason we just can't get a handle on life. I sure need that woman here."

He listened to their request and slowly said, "So Mick sent you to me. No one wants to be thought the strange one, and that's what the giver of this story will be called."

He paused, seeming to consider his answer. Finally he took a deep breath and said. "I'm sure I know every cabin and shanty in the area, so it's almost a fact that she's not living around here. But there's something strange going on.

"Come night, some say they see a woman dressed in black and heavily veiled. Most often it's by the light of the full moon when they see her. Seems she walks among the new graves, weeping. Now, don't you two go outta here saying H.A.W. Tabor is losing what little wits he had. 'Cause if you say I told you this story, I'll deny it."

Silently Amy and Daniel retraced their steps to Father Dyer's cabin. Halfway there, Daniel stopped suddenly. "I'm just not satisfied. Amy, let's go over to the boardinghouse and look around. There ought to be something or someone around."

CHAPTER 34

Daniel started down the road so lost in thought that he nearly forgot Amy. At last he saw she was trotting along at his side, trying to keep up with his long strides.

Frowning at himself, he stopped and turned. He took her hand and apologized. "Sorry. I was off on my own tangent. Wondering what to do next."

There was a worried expression on her face. As she looked up into his face, she caught her breath and said, "Might be we'll have to forget about the whole thing."

"Wanna sit down and rest?" He pointed to the rocks beside the road.

She nodded, "It'll give me time to get my wits together."

They found two large rocks and sat down. Daniel watched Amy point to the touch of green appearing around the base of the rock. She said, "Soon it will be spring." But he was thinking it would soon be a year since their marriage. *How much longer could they both endure this awkward situation? Friends. That was laughable, heartbreaking.* He sighed.

"Daniel, you're tired too. We've tried, can't we forget about it?"

He hesitated. "Well, I can't stay up here too long. There's

folks depending on me. Also, if you're not back in Denver City before the week is up, your Father may head for home without you."

She nodded, got to her feet and started down the trail. "I've rested enough. Let's get on with it."

As they approached the boardinghouse, Amy said, "Looks empty. It's probably locked."

"That door is ajar." He went in ahead of her, and she followed, hanging on to his coattail like a frightened child. But even he had to admit to the strange feeling it was giving him. The emptiness, the creaking of the floorboards under their feet, and the scurry of mice made the deserted building seem alien.

"That's her room over there." Her voice echoed as she pointed, "But I sense there's not a soul here." Her brave voice was too loud. Daniel tried the door that led to Silverheels' room. It seemed locked. He twisted and shoved. The door moved inches.

Amy murmured, "It's a chest against the door. I can see it. I'll squeeze past."

"Do it then." He stepped aside, adding, "No reason to force our way if there's—nothing to be seen." She slipped through. There was silence and impatiently he asked, "Amy, can you move the chest?"

"Not alone. Push on the door, and I'll push on this side." He pushed, then heard the rasp of wood against wood, and found he was able to slip through the opening.

Heavy draperies covered the windows. Amy went to pull them aside. She stood, slowly looking about the room, and he saw the sadness on her face.

He felt the weight of the room himself. As she turned away, he saw her blinking her eyes. "Amy, it's somehow pathetic, isn't it?" His voice sounded lame to him. He walked about the room, wondering how to express the sadness the empty room was making him feel.

Amy moved restlessly about. Picking up the black cloak Silverheels had given her to wear, she said, "I wonder what happened to the picture? It isn't in the pocket." He watched her go to the closet. With her toe she nudged the pair of silver-heeled slippers lying there.

"Looks as if they've just been kicked aside," he murmured. Daniel saw the sadness on Amy's face had deepened. Feeling a surge of tenderness welling up inside, he clenched his hands and turned to pace the room.

The overwhelming hopelessness of their situation swept over him. *To love and have a chance of winning was one thing, but to be committed to denying the possibility of fulfilling that love is a burden I no longer want to carry. Friendship, Amy? Dry crumbs compared to having a wife.* He rubbed his face and sighed, admitting to himself, *These days a spiritual tiredness is sapping my strength.*

He lifted his head and saw that she was standing in front of the dressing table. Her fingers moved among the line of bottles, brushes and crystal flasks.

Daniel took a deep breath and went to her side, saying, "It's as if she's just stepped out for the day. Amy, you must accept the possibility that she's—"

Amy looked up at him. "Dead? It almost gives relief. Don't feel bad. I'll never be touched by her memory again." He looked at her strangely and she continued. "It seems certain she's dead or gone forever. Obviously no one has been here for a long time."

"We haven't been upstairs yet. Come along." He headed for the stairs, glad to be free of the room and the strain of seeing the tears clumping Amy's eyelashes together.

Amy was behind him as they walked the hallway, looking into the tiny cubicles. Each roughly finished room still held the tattered remnants of the life left behind. The beds had been stripped of their blankets, but many of the open closets spilled forth color and texture.

To Daniel the abandoned marks of the trade—the costly and garish, the silks and satins—proclaimed a message more loudly than words. Their owners no longer had need of them.

Amy shuddered and turned away. "I can think of only one reason those dresses would still be here. Just like Lizzie. Left behind." She touched the spill of cheap perfume bottles on the dresser and the candle holder bearing a mouse-chewed candle and a frayed hair ribbon. "Daniel, do you know that at one time I envied these dance-hall girls with their pretty dresses and their saucy, confident ways?"

They resumed their silent march up and down the halls, checking in all the rooms for evidence of life, clues that promised hope. Daniel murmured, "This is like a wake, a silent mourning. It seems a vigil of emptiness for a froth of brightness that has lost the reality of life."

Amy looked around, "Reality of life—yes, I suppose that is so."

When they returned to the first floor, Amy stopped in the hall. With a quick glance he passed her and entered Silverheels' room again. Standing in the middle of the room, he turned slowly, studying every detail.

Amy came, saying, "The piano is gone from the parlor. I suppose it's been carried off because of its value." Her voice was wistful and he glanced at her. That note in her voice revealed a yearning he should have guessed. He wanted to promise her a piano. But that was something he couldn't say. He took a deep breath and sought the safe ground.

"Music is a part of you, isn't it—like I have brown eyes and a funny nose."

She looked up. He saw astonishment, and then her expression changed. He turned away quickly even as his heart was pounding with a new revelation. Amy had a soul-deep hunger; he could see it in her eyes. Was music a need in her life? A something as big as his need to preach the Gospel?

Now he recalled the things Lucas Tristram had to say about Amy's talent. The fellow had looked at him, saying he'd do everything in his power to see Amy got her opportunity. Well, he'd be the fellow who could afford to give her the biggest piano in the world.

Daniel paced around the room; his thoughts circled back to Amy as he felt a growing excitement. *Just maybe God was behind her soul-hunger.*

He stopped. Amy was waiting with that wistful expression in her eyes. *Maybe I can't now, but someday, my Amy.* Daniel straightened his shoulders. He also clenched one fist and smacked it into his hand. He grinned, tempted momentarily to inform his wife that after all, friendship wasn't so great, and nuts to Tristram—she was Mrs. Gerrett.

He turned to nod toward the closet door hanging open. "About Silverheels—Maybe we shouldn't give up just now. Look. There's a gap in there. I see her dancing frocks, but where are the warm, sturdy clothes?" He pointed to the half-drawn curtains around the bed. "What has happened to the blankets on that bed?"

"Perhaps someone has stolen these things," Amy murmured as she continued to walk around the room, looking into every corner. When she reached the mantel above the fireplace, she stopped.

Daniel watched her stiffen and catch her breath; she moved forward slowly, even reluctantly. Frowning now, he saw that for Amy the room had ceased being an impersonal memory. Something had touched her deeply.

"What is it?" Daniel bent over her. He saw a fragment of china on the mantel.

"Oh, Daniel!" her voice was breaking, but she persisted, pressing out the words as if they were a form of torture she deserved. "See, it's part of a china doll's head. Mother gave the doll to me. She said to remember her. I had intended to take it. But—" She gulped. "Daniel, we shouted terrible words at each other. Before I left she reminded me to take it. She said, 'Don't forget your dolly.' "

Daniel waited. He watched her clench her fists, and lift her chin. With tears streaming down her face, she admitted, "I threw it at her. Just as hard as I could throw. I was sorry it missed hitting her." He waited.

Her face crumpled as she said, "Don't you see? I hated her." Now with imploring eyes, whispering, she said, "Daniel, I am afraid!"

"Amy!" He had not intended it, but his arms were open

and with a sob she came at him. "My darling." He held her, kissing away the tears and feeling the urgency of her body against him.

But he had made a commitment to be her friend. Just a friend. He held her away. "Amy, Amy, my dear, please!" Her lips were still lifted and he kissed her once more. Then gently he put her aside and paced the cold darkening room.

When he came back to her, the approaching dusk had hidden away the expression in her eyes. Bending close, speaking softly, he said, "I promised you I'd be your friend. Do you want me to keep that promise?"

Then he said, "You're crying; why?"

She shook her head slowly from side to side. Steadying her voice she said, "It's Silverheels. I can't get away from the sense of responsibility. What if she's alive and in need?"

"I don't know what to say. I've no suggestion to offer unless we go to the cemetery after dark. It seems nearly a hysterical story."

"Do you mind going with me?"

"No, of course not. Amy, we're still in this together. If that is what you want, I'm willing."

While the minutes passed slowly, Amy considered it all. Daniel's rebuff still stung. Her tears were only partly for Silverheels; how much more deeply his rejection had wounded her pride! She thought back to yesterday. *Friendship? Daniel, I sensed you jumped at the chance to escape the trap we're in.*

"Then I think we should go tonight. It may take several days to be certain that she isn't visiting the cemetery." He paused and then added, "It's important to get you back to Denver City before your father leaves."

Important. Most certainly, otherwise he would be stuck with the task of getting her home. She considered the dismal future. Central City or Denver. Without Daniel, either one would be part of the past.

She sighed and shook her head, impatiently wondering why the need to be with him had risen to a clamor. Willful Amy. Again she blushed with shame as she thought of the way she had thrown herself into his arms.

She looked at Daniel. What would he say if she were to reveal her plans to stay in Denver City? For a moment hope flared, and then flattened. Somehow she had the feeling he would say nothing.

Daniel was holding her shawl. With one last glance at the broken doll lying on the mantel, they walked out of the boardinghouse.

That evening they told Father Dyer. As Daniel talked, Amy searched the man's face, expecting ridicule, even disbelief. But he nodded, saying, "It seems to be the only thing to do. If you're serious about this, Amy, the Lord will either make a way for you to contact her, or lift the burden to do so. I'll come with you if you wish." They both shook their heads, declining his gesture.

After supper dishes were washed and placed back on their shelf, after the embers in the stove were cherry red and Father Dyer had poked in the big chunk of wood and set the damper, Daniel said, "Let's go now."

There wasn't a full moon, but the light reflecting off the snowbanks filled the bowl of the gulch with light. When they reached the road, Daniel took her arm and pulled her close. "Will you be warm enough?"

"I've put on an extra jacket under this shawl." He nodded and moved out ahead of her. Striding quickly to the well-traveled road, they turned and headed down the cut to the cemetery.

"Hear the owl?" Daniel murmured. Amy nodded and shivered. The cemetery was a cleared space in the midst of the trees. By the light of the moon, it was a glistening expanse of white. Daniel whispered, "A mouse can't cross that without being seen."

They moved back into the shadows of the trees. She shivered and Daniel came close to wrap his arms around her.

She felt her spine stiffen in response even as she guessed he wanted to talk. "There's movement over there in the trees. It's either a doe or a coyote; I didn't want you to scream." She resisted the impulse to snuggle against him. It seemed as if they had waited forever in silence when he began to speak. She heard the strain in his voice. "Amy, please, I—" They both heard the crack of twigs.

They held their breath and waited. A buck moved into the clearing and began to paw at the snow. "Look at that set of antlers," Daniel murmured. As they watched him feed, Amy felt Daniel relax and she leaned back into his arms.

A cloud drifted across the moon and he sighed and moved. "I'm guessing we might as well forget it for the night. We're both half frozen." She waited a moment longer; finally he bent and kissed her, gently, lightly. "We better hurry before we freeze."

The next evening a swift storm moved through, filling the air with icy snow. The following night, as Daniel shrugged into his coat, he addressed John Dyer. "Might as well come along with us, unless you're too old for the game of standing in the snow."

"Maybe Amy should stay in and keep warm," Father Dyer suggested.

"It's mostly because of Amy that we're here." Daniel answered firmly. "She probably won't have another chance to talk to Silverheels."

"Daniel, do you think she'll refuse to have anything to do with us?" Amy asked.

Daniel considered, then said, "If the story is true, there are a lot of unanswered questions. A normal healthy person just doesn't wander around in cemeteries at night; neither do they hide away from people they have associated with in the past."

"I want to go with you," Amy urged.

It was very late when they saw her. The snap of breaking branches alerted them. Amy heard Daniel's whisper. "That isn't an animal."

By moonlight her dark cloak was easy to identify against the lighter wood. Soon she left the trees and began to walk slowly up and down between the line of headstones.

Amy stood transfixed, watching her slow movement. Unexpectedly she found herself responding to that lonely figure.

Wiping at her eyes, Amy tried to guess the reason for the zigzag course, the stooping, the way her hand moved to touch each stone.

The stark black and white scene, the rhythm of it all, pulled her spirit down. She was trembling now, trying to hold back the sobs.

Daniel bent close to whisper, "We're going to move around to the other side while you walk up to her. If she runs, we'll try to stop her." His flat words brought her back to reality. Shivering now with cold, she nodded.

The men started off together. When they disappeared from sight, Amy hesitantly stepped out.

She approached slowly, creeping close enough to hear the murmur of Silverheels' voice, the sobs. And then the next step plunged Amy's foot into an icy snowdrift.

At the sound the woman turned. As Amy caught her balance, the shock of that black-swathed figure held her motionless and shivering. Silverheels' face was invisible. There was nothing to be seen except the slender column of black.

For a soundless moment, they stood facing each other. Then the dark figure spun around and ran toward the trees.

It took Daniel's shout to break Amy free, and send her stumbling through the snow after them. It seemed to go on forever, the lurching, plunging, churning through snow, into trees, pitching into snags and tearing free. Only the shouts of the men in front of her marked the way.

At last, when she thought another step was impossible, Daniel and Father Dyer were beside her.

They linked their arms about her, pushing her back up to the road. She was sobbing with cold and frustration when they reached the cabin.

Daniel knelt and stripped off her soaked boots and handed her the towel. "Start rubbing those feet and legs as hard as you can or I'll do it for you." She heard him say something about frostbite, but it didn't seem to matter.

The stove was glowing nearly cherry red and Father Dyer brought hot tea while Daniel spread the blankets on the floor.

"Let Amy have my bed," Father Dyer said.

Daniel shook his head. "She'll be better off here with her feet close to the fire. I'll make certain she's warm enough."

Amy had only begun to wonder how when he carried hot stones to her and piled on some of his blankets. She shook her head but couldn't find voice to protest. He took her empty mug and pushed her down. "If you get cold, tell me." But that was the last she remembered.

CHAPTER 35

Over breakfast the next morning, Daniel said, "We're certain now that the story is true. The woman has got to be Silverheels. We also know where she is living." He paused to sip his coffee and then glanced at Amy. "By the time we reached the cabin, she had barricaded herself and wouldn't answer our shouts."

Father Dyer sat, elbows on table, cradling his mug of coffee. Slowly he said, "This whole business is getting to me. Sure, I'd heard the stories, but there was no evidence they were true. Now that I've seen her, I'm feeling my responsibility to her. Also, I'm seeing her as a needy soul. I didn't before. Something must be done."

Amy turned away from the question in his eyes, whispering, "Please, I don't know what to think about all your talk. I only know I must see her. What happens then—well, I guess that's up to you."

John Dyer looked at Daniel. "I think I'd better go with you. I'd intended to head up the gulch today, but that'll have to wait."

"If that's what you think needs to be done," Daniel said slowly. The man nodded.

By midmorning when they started out, the sun had broken through the last of the clouds, and even Amy's heart lifted in response. Again they were afoot. Father Dyer had mentioned a horse for Amy, but Daniel had shaken his head, saying, "There'll be no chance to slip up that way."

The snow had been churned into ruts on the road, but when they reached the trail leading to the cemetery, Amy looked at the unbroken expanse in dismay. Daniel pointed to the tracks cutting across the field. "That's the path we took last night."

"What a sad place it is." Amy spoke in a whisper. "When we came for Lizzie's funeral, there were only a few headstones. Now look, line upon line; those markers show how many have lost their lives."

In silence they looked across the cemetery. Father Dyer shook his head, settled his hat lower on his forehead and slowly turned.

"Seems different in daylight," he murmured. Shading his eyes, he continued, "I'm guessing the cabin is right through there, due north of where we stand now. Here's hoping she lets us in. Amy's feet can't take much more of this."

They started out single file, with Father Dyer cutting the trail and Daniel behind Amy. Amy tried to forget about Silverheels and concentrate on the beauty of the willows. Each branch offered a delicate wand of fluffy snow. Against the bright sky the whole forest seemed angel pure.

On the far edge of the clearing, she could see the buck. Antlered head high, he followed their movements.

The trail they had taken last night cut into the drifts, suddenly appearing like a canyon gouged through the snow. They stood in the snow at the side of the road while Daniel shaded his eyes. "There's plenty of tracks through here, but I'm inclined to believe it's deer and elk. Too delicate for human or bear."

Father Dyer murmured, "I smell woodsmoke now. The wind is coming down out of the north, so it isn't from Buckskin."

"Think we need to separate?" Daniel asked. Dyer shook his head and Amy sighed with relief. But she couldn't help noticing the men's faces were grim as they again moved out on the trail.

When Father Dyer stopped, Amy slid into him. Daniel's restraining arm was around her. "There it is," Daniel whispered softly. "No wonder townspeople don't know about it. The person who built the place liked solitude—see how it's hidden?"

As they looked down on the house snuggled in the cup of trees and rock, the door opened. Briefly they saw the figure of a woman and then the door was closed. "Hope she didn't see us," Daniel murmured anxiously.

Amy shifted her aching feet and said, "I've an idea. Why don't I go down alone? After all, this is for my sake."

The two considered and then shook their heads. "It just doesn't feel right," Dyer said, and Daniel's dark eyes agreed.

She shivered and said, "Then let's go—now before I turn and run." Daniel took her hand and the gesture brought tears to her eyes. Slowly and as quietly as possible, they worked their way down the incline behind the cabin.

When Father Dyer knocked, Amy discovered she was holding her breath. Their fears were all for nothing.

Silverheels simply opened the door. She studied each one in turn and grudgingly pushed the door wide open. "Never kicked a dog in my life; no sense in doing it now. I guess you're not lost, you are the ones who followed me last night."

"Begging your pardon if we frightened you." Father Dyer pulled off his hat and bobbed his head. Amy still couldn't speak. Moving like a wooden toy, she followed them, unable to look away from Silverheels.

Gone was the cascade of curls. The knot of hair on her neck was frankly middle-aged. But then that was to be expected. Amy was staring at the skin exposed above the rough collar of her dark dress. What had been porcelain perfection was now red, deeply pocked scar tissue, spreading across her neck, face and even her hands.

When they faced each other, Silverheels' eyes challenged Amy's quivering lips with contempt. Amy turned away, fighting desperately the need to express the outrage and pain she was feeling.

With only that icy look, Silverheels turned to Father Dyer. "I'm sorry I can't offer you coffee. I've been without for months. I don't go into town for supplies."

"What are you living on?" Daniel asked.

She glanced at him, quickly letting her eyes dart to another part of the room. In a moment she said, "I took all the canned goods and flour and beans from the boardinghouse. It's sufficient."

They stood awkwardly waiting. Finally she gestured toward the crude benches beside the fireplace. Amy could see Daniel looking at her, and she couldn't avoid the question in his eyes.

Father Dyer's voice was not the usual cannonball blast. Softly he said, "We've been hearing about your nursing activities during the epidemic."

"It's no more than anyone would have done. It was there in front of me. I was well, and there was no one else to do the job."

The silence became awkward under Silverheels' stoic stare. Daniel's eyes were imploring Amy. She got to her feet. It was impossible to control her trembling lips, the tears, her shaking knees. She sank down beside Silverheels' chair and reached imploringly for the hands that eluded her.

"Mother! Please, I've felt—I've come to beg your forgiveness. I'm sorry for the ugly things I said, all the—please."

"And now, like the good little pious Christian, who's been to revival meeting and had her head reamed out, you'll pour your emotions on me." The cold words slashed into Amy, making her rock back on her heels. "I want no part of it. I told you I didn't want to see you again. My situation now doesn't change any of that.

"I don't want your pity or tears. Get out of my life with your contemptible whining. I want no part of a religion that sets itself up above the common man, that sets a mealy-mouthed standard you pretenders must cling to in order to win the approval of God."

Amy jumped to her feet, sobbing as she screamed out her

rage, "What a detestable mother you are! What corruption moved you to abandon us? How dare you drag me in the dirt now! I've tramped through the snow to make things right with you. What an ugly, ugly—prostitute you are! I've suffered and suffered over you for years, and now you throw all that in my face. I—"

She stopped. Daniel saw one brief flash of horror on her face before she snatched up her shawl and fled. "John!" he begged, glancing at the woman in the chair. Father Dyer nodded and went after Amy.

Daniel knelt beside the rocking chair. The woman's head rested against the back. He saw the waxen cast to her skin, the tear sliding down. Carefully he bit back the questions. "Mother," he whispered. She was shaking her head, moving her lips.

"I'm not leaving until you sit up and answer my questions." A spot of color appeared in her cheeks, and then she opened her eyes and sat up.

"Young man, you've no right—"

"To try to keep you from sitting here until you die? Can't you understand? We are fearful for you. It's no desire to make you miserable. Amy's confession was sincere."

The tears were streaming down her face as she whispered, "You called me *Mother*, but I'm not. I've never deserved the title. I don't want it now. You're that preacher boy, her husband. I will talk to you if you'll promise me you'll go away afterwards and keep her away."

"Maybe I'll promise. If you answer my questions." She waited. Daniel hesitated. There seemed no right question. "You love her, don't you? The picture."

She nodded, weeping soundlessly, and then saying, "It was my decision; there was no turning back. Young man, you've no idea how the heart can hurt when it's all boxed in with no way to back out."

"Why did you chase her away from Buckskin Joe? Was it because of smallpox?" Her reaction gave her away. "Tell me about it."

"One of the girls. I'd just discovered it when Amy came. I was hoping to hide it, hoping we could keep it from spreading. Oh, Daniel, how badly I wanted to keep her from catching the disease! I would have cut my soul out to prevent it. Much as I wanted her love, I had to chase her away!"

He watched her shrink into brooding silence. Finally he moved, looking at the waxen face, her bloodshot eyes, he bit his lip and pondered. It seemed wrong to push at her. But how much he wanted to offer a hope.

She was speaking again. "I should never have married Eli. A mere baby myself, I made life miserable for him. I *wanted*. At least I thought I did. The church was a noose around my neck. I didn't understand then. I only wanted freedom."

She looked up now. "Always I've carried the picture of Amy. Bittersweet. Once I tried to reach out to them. After he left."

"He?"

She nodded. "There was a man who offered me freedom, money, a good time. It only lasted until he tired of me." She was rubbing her pocked hands slowly, speaking softly. He knew she was revealing the deep places in her heart.

"It's hard enough to back down from what you've chosen and admit you're wrong. It's impossible when life's squeezed you into a corner. Now it's totally out of the question." Her voice was flat, leaving no room for argument.

"Is that why you couldn't accept Amy's apology?"

She thought for a moment and then nodded.

"Pride?" he asked.

When she didn't acknowledge hearing him, he added thoughtfully. "Is it possible God allows second chances through the most difficult trials of life? Like the epidemic?"

She was still unresponsive, but he continued. "And isn't a circumstance like this redemptive?"

"What do you mean?"

"That you've proven to yourself the fiber's good."

"I don't understand. Please explain."

"If you were capable of acting in genuine love, sticking

with the fearsome ugliness of life when the others ran out, then doesn't this tell you something?"

"That all's not lost?"

"That God has poured out a grace gift—a genuine *enablement*. Just maybe His reaching out to make you strong when you wanted nothing to do with Him is the picture of the same kind of God He's always been. Reaching out, taking our insults and rejection. Being *used* by us for our purposes yet still waiting in love."

He got to his feet and paced to the fireplace and back. There were tears running down her cheeks. She sat up and leaned toward him. "Daniel Gerrett, can you answer me truthfully? Don't give me false hope. Is it possible to find some way— peace, freedom from soul ugliness? For me?"

"Why would you think otherwise? You have a Bible on that shelf; surely you know what is in it."

"I've prayed, begged," she admitted. "I'm down to the bottom of the barrel. It's a terrible place to be, and it leaves me with nothing else. I don't have anything to offer, so how can I have faith?"

"What makes you think that *any* of us have a suitable offering? After all, He's God. What does that make us? From that angle, I suppose we all look like the same lump of clay. Except He doesn't talk like that. He says He loves with an everlasting love. Enough to die for us, without a guarantee we'd ever take advantage of the grace of His suffering."

After a long moment he asked hesitantly, "Would it help if we prayed together?" She was nodding, slipping out of the chair onto the cold carpet-covered earthen floor.

It was late afternoon when Daniel reached Dyer's cabin. With a quick glance around, he asked, "Where's Amy?"

Father Dyer's expresssion was pained. "I guess I'm a bumbling idiot, but I don't know. She wouldn't have a thing to do with me; marched six feet in front of me all the way back, came into the cabin, snatched up her blankets, and all the while she was muttering something about a doll." He paused to turn his troubled eyes toward Daniel. "I'd a hung on to her if I'd guessed she'd take off."

"Doll." Daniel's fatigue began to lift and a flicker of excitement started to warm him. He remembered her statement: *Father, I don't think he'll mind; he's been pushing us together.*

He got to his feet and went after his blankets. "Have anything around to feed on?"

"Well, sure." Looking mystified, Father Dyer went to the stove. "I shot a rabbit. There's some stew cooking."

"Anything to carry it in?" Father Dyer's eyebrow lifted, and he began to grin.

As Daniel headed for the door, he stopped and turned. "Tell you what. This is all just a hunch, but if you see smoke rolling out of the chimney over at Silverheels' boardinghouse, don't come looking. Everything's under control. We'll see you in the morning."

CHAPTER 36

For a moment, when Daniel stepped into the hallway, he nearly doubted his hunch. Today it was evident the boardinghouse had begun a slow spiraling down; there was the smell of decay, the scurry of mice, the moan of creaking timbers, and silence.

Going to the door he had entered with Amy, Daniel cautiously eased it open. He could see the fireplace as only a dark hole, but in the corner of the puffy pink couch there was a darker bundle. "Amy?" He slipped through the door, deposited his blankets and the kettle of stew on the floor and went to sit beside her.

Her nose was pink and her eyelids swollen. "It's cold in here. I'm going to look for some wood." She sobbed softly but didn't answer. He looked at the tears on her face and clenched his hands in his pockets. He headed for the kitchen, grateful for the task of building a fire.

When the fire was crackling in the fireplace, he threw on an extra bundle of dry piñon. He smiled to himself and hoped Father Dyer was watching.

Then he made another trip back into the kitchen for more logs. After he had built a pile of wood on the hearth, he went after water and plates. On his last trip Amy sat up and pushed the blanket away.

Sitting down beside her, he asked, "Are your feet dry?" She thought for a moment before shaking her head. "Well then, let me pull off your boots." She unwound her legs and thrust out her feet in a trusting, childlike way that had him blinking tears.

As he unlaced her boots, he said, "I've brought plenty of blankets, so take off your stockings too."

Now she was watching him with curiosity, giving a tiny quick glance that made him smile. He resisted the impulse to kiss her forehead.

He carried her wet stockings to drape over a log on the hearth, saying with a studied calmness, "They should be dry soon."

Back beside her, Daniel asked, "Why did you come here?"

"I needed to think." That spark of interest in her eyes had dulled. She leaned her head against the back of the couch and stared into the fire. Slowly, with a strange flatness in her voice, she said, "I messed everything up again. I tried. If only she hadn't mocked me."

She raised her head and shook it slowly from side to side. "Daniel, no matter how hard I try, everything comes out wrong." Her voice dropped to a whisper and he bent close to hear. "I make up my mind to act in a certain way, but it never happens that way. I don't know why I screamed like that. I'm so ashamed I—" He watched her scrubbing at the tears on her face and carefully controlled his impulse to comfort her.

In a moment she steadied her voice and added, "She made me so angry I couldn't think clearly." She lifted a defensive chin, saying, "I know a Christian isn't supposed to act that way. But I'm positive I'll never be able to live up to those high standards. I've tried and failed so many times."

Her eyes were imploring him as she added, "I thought now it would happen since you prayed with me." Again she waited, then shrugged, "I guess it's well for both you and Father that I leave."

"Amy," Daniel replied slowly, puzzling his way through all she said, "You're trying to do something the Lord wants to do for you. You've listened to your father preach sanctification, heart purity, holiness. You know Jesus told His disciples they would be baptized with the Holy Ghost, now—"

She turned impatiently, interrupting, "Daniel, I know all that! Why are you preaching to me now?" She got to her feet and went to the hearth to check on her stockings. Abruptly Daniel jumped to his feet and followed her.

"Amy, I want to help you. God knows why you've failed to understand, but I'm determined you'll know the facts before you leave here."

"You mean you'll make me stay?" Her voice rose.

"Yes. I pushed the chest against the door, and I know you can't move it alone."

For a moment she was speechless and then, as he watched, color and excitement moved back into her face. Her voice deepened as she came to him, saying, "This could be a very interesting evening."

He grinned down at her. "I promise you it will. Now sit down." Still smiling impishly, she dropped down on the pink couch and tucked her feet under her. He pulled a stool close to the couch and sat down. "Unfortunately, I didn't think to bring my Bible, so you'll have to put up with my memory."

She reached out to smooth his hair and he clasped her hand in both of his, ignoring the twinkle in her eyes. Beginning slowly, he said, "The Bible, in both the Old Testament and the New, holds up a plan God has for a genuine relationship between men as individuals and God himself. This is what He wanted with Adam and Eve. But to make the plan work in a genuine way, there had to be complete freedom."

She was caught, and her playfulness disappeared. She leaned forward and asked, "Why? What does freedom have to do with it all?"

"God desires love from each one of us. How can love be love unless we are free to not love?" Daniel lost the train of thought as their eyes met. They were looking deep into each other, weighing, yearning, promising, then retreating.

The brooding expression settled down over Amy's face. "And we're not free to either love or not love. What a situation. We would never in a hundred years of marriage be able to decide whether or not we love simply because we don't have that freedom—to choose."

She settled back on the couch away from the light of the fire, and Daniel sighed, conscious of the moment of retreat in both of them.

He gathered his thoughts and said, "But because of Adam and Eve choosing sin, there had to be a bridge. You're familiar with the law."

"Yes, and I know all about the Children of Israel sinning and repenting throughout the whole Old Testament." Amy snapped. "You are being pompous. I also know the story of Jesus' coming and dying in the New Testament."

"But there's details in the story you haven't heeded." He saw her compressed lips and the flash in her eyes. Grinning, he said, "In Ezekiel God promises to give the Children of Israel a new spirit, to take away their stony heart and give them a heart of flesh. The purpose of this is to enable them to obey Him. In Jeremiah, God promises that when we *seek Him with all our heart*, we shall find Him. Amy, think about that; it's important."

As he talked Daniel was aware that the gentle, half-mocking smile had reappeared on her face. With a shock he realized it reminded him of the expression on Silverheels' face as she taunted Amy.

"What is it, Amy?"

"I'm thinking you must have a stony heart. Are you so much the preacher that you can do nothing except preach, even in a setting like this?"

"I didn't intend to preach," he admitted ruefully. A blush crept up his neck toward his ears. "Did you have something else in mind?"

"Yes, I want to talk about me, us." She darted a quick look at him. "Daniel, I've been doing a lot of thinking about this impossible situation."

"What's impossible?"

"You say you love me, and I think I love you, yet, we can't agree on anything."

"Like what?"

"I want to go—"

He got to his feet and paced the room. "Don't say it," he said. "Let me guess. You want me to go east and pastor a proper church. Sorry, Amy."

"I knew it." Amy shoved the blanket aside and stomped to the fireplace. She felt her stockings, sat down and began to pull them on. "Don't look!" she snapped.

"Why, you're my wife."

"Daniel, I—" Abruptly she dropped her face into her hands.

"You haven't asked about Silverheels." She dropped her hands and he watched the stillness on her face. "We had a good talk. Tomorrow we'll go back for another visit." He waited. "Come on, let's eat Father Dyer's rabbit stew. It's been keeping warm for an hour."

With a sigh she got up. "You mean we're still friends?"

"No." He was beginning to enjoy himself. "Amy, why are you so afraid of me?"

"I'm not."

"It's suddenly dawned on me that you are. Since we got married, it's been one dodge after another."

She pulled the blanket across her shoulders and sat down. Her face was suddenly thoughtful. "One thing—I've always expected life to be big and wonderful someday. Now, reality is so ordinary. I want—"

"The moon! And you wouldn't be satisfied with the moon if you got it." With a startled look, she got up and went to the fireplace.

"Yes. Let's have our dinner. Daniel, I don't know what to make of all this. I have been running, ever since I married you."

"I know you have. You said life was ordinary. What about your commitment to Jesus Christ; was that ordinary?" He watched the wonder grow in her eyes. "Has it occurred to you that God has put within our grasp the possibility of making life, even in the dailyness, something grand?"

She was still waiting when he came to her, lifted her chin. Gently he kissed her. "Amy, you reached beyond the ordinary when you fought all the obstacles to learn to play the piano. An ordinary piano, a less than admirable teacher in Lizzie, but you learned.

"Now you think because we common people don't possess a star-studded destiny that our lives will lack the spark to transform the lusterless. You don't value love, do you?"

He saw the shock on her face and pressed. "Did Central City teach you only that love is a bargaining tool? That value lies only in gold?"

"Daniel!" her voice was shocked. "I don't feel that way. I've never thought—" He saw the change, the crumbling of her defenses. "It does appear that way. I never intended it—"

"What?"

"A fairy tale. Grasping for something so far out of reach that I needn't be fearful of catching it."

She was motionless for a long time. He saw by her eyes that she examined, thought, rejected and then decided.

"Daniel, I am willing to surrender those desires. I started that yesterday. Now I know it must continue. But those things you said. About being a friend—"

"I was only providing a refuge for your fearful soul. I no more want you *only* for a friend. In addition to being my companion, my wife, my lover, I want you for a friend."

"I suppose, if I'm to grow up, I must quit hiding behind the bargaining table. Daniel, I'm sorry for all this. No *ifs*. I'll be your wife, no matter where, or what our circumstances. Just let me be with you. See, I discovered, at the point I thought I'd lost your love, that I value you more than all the gold in the territory."

"Amy, I've got to tell you something. We don't ever get to the place where the Lord doesn't have something more to tell us. Last night, He started talking to me.

"I've been stiff-necked, proud, thinking I was doing Him

a big favor, that He can't get along without me." He stopped
and gulped. "Now I understand. I had it all wrong. Pigheaded,
self-righteous. I should never have left you alone, never let you
go. Amy, will you please forgive me?"

Bewildered, she wiped the tears from her eyes and peered
up at him, "I don't understand."

He took her hand. "I was wrong, Amy. You come first—
after Christ, but before my ministry. I promise, I'll spend the
rest of my life loving you and taking care of you. As Christ
loved the church, that's the way Paul put it. First.

"He finally got it through my thick head that He'd given
you to me. You see, I didn't marry you because I was forced
to, but because I wanted you very much. I think since the first
time I saw you I felt that way.

"As soon as I can, we'll head east. I'll find a church where
I can preach the Gospel and you can play the piano—if you'll
have me after all this."

Amy was shaking her head, wiping at the tears. His voice
sounded hollow as he asked, "You won't?" Still unable to speak,
she threw herself into his arms.

He hesitated and she pressed her wet face against his.
"Love?" He nodded and bent his head. When he released her,
she wiped the tears from her eyes and smiled, even as fresh tears
were falling. Finally she wiped the last tear and took his hands.
"Daniel, you won't need to leave. Strange how long it took me
just to understand *me*. That's what I want too. We'll stay here,
and you'll go on preaching the Gospel, just exactly in the place
God wants you. Only, please, Daniel, help me. I'm fearful—"

He was smiling. "There's one more verse. 'Are ye so foolish? having begun in the Spirit, are ye now made perfect by the
flesh.' Amy, don't worry about the weak human flesh. The Holy
Spirit will be there to help you every step of the way. Both of
us. I know I can't get along without His help constantly. Sometimes I need to be reminded too. Not me—God."

He got to his feet. "Let's eat that rabbit stew."

"It's getting late!" Amy exclaimed. "Father Dyer will be
out looking for us. We'd better just take the stew and go—"

Daniel was shaking his head, grinning down at her. "No, my dear wife, we're not going anywhere. I made certain Father Dyer won't come looking, and I've brought plenty of blankets."

"Daniel?"

He nodded. "Me and you—together."

Hesitantly she said, "You decided that before you came here—how did you know?"

"That it would work out this way? I didn't. I only knew that the Lord put us together intending for us to stay together, no matter. And you dropped the hint."

"I didn't tell him where I was going."

"He said you mentioned the doll." Now he tilted her face and slowly rubbed his thumb over the last traces of tears. "It bothered you more than you admitted. That encouraged me, gave me hope. Amy, tomorrow we'll go see Silverheels. This time, I'll help and it will work out just fine. Now, I'm hungry, Wife; let's have dinner."

CHAPTER 37

Amy had been conscious of sounds, the clink of the water pail, the crackle of fire; but she snuggled down in the warm blankets, blissfully happy and comfortable.

When she heard his step and felt his touch, she opened her eyes. He kissed the end of her nose, saying, "I never guessed it would be so nice to have blue eyes peering out of my blankets."

She wrapped her arms around his neck. As he kissed her, he murmured, "It's late. I think we need to see Silverheels as soon as possible." He settled back on his heels beside the bed and added, "Also, I'm going to quit calling her by that name. That's the past."

"You sound very hopeful," Amy said slowly.

"I am. After you left yesterday, we did some talking. We even prayed together. I didn't want to get your hopes up yesterday, but I was encouraged. Time will tell."

"The fruit of the Spirit?"

He nodded, then said, "There's warm water. While you bathe I'm going to look around, see if there's something we can take to—Mother. She mentioned not having coffee. I saw a coffee grinder and, I thought, some coffee beans. I also found a towel for you."

"Did you remove the chest from in front of the door?"

"No. There's a door in the back of the closet, leading into the kitchen hallway." The strangeness of Daniel's discovery was a reminder. Amy bit her lip and looked around the room. Daniel pressed his lips against her neck and murmured, "Be back in a few minutes."

She found a bar of fragrant soap in the drawer of the washstand. A silver-backed hair brush still lay on the chest. As Amy slowly brushed her hair into softness and let the curls cluster around her face, she was thinking of the luxury Silverheels had left behind. Now she was scarred, abandoned, alone in that poor cabin. They must go to her now—quickly before she evaded them again. Fastening the final pins, she started to turn from the mirror and paused.

That face smiling back—was the soft new curve to her lips, the peace in her eyes the result of loving, or of praying?

As she set the plates and the bread on the table, Daniel came. In his face there was a reflection of the gentle peace she felt. She went to him with her face lifted for his kiss. He held her close, then tipping her head back, he kissed her tenderly, saying, "Oh, Amy, to think I could have lost you. I love you, sweetheart." Then grinning, he said, "All right, Wife, where's the breakfast?"

It was nearly noon when Amy and Daniel stood on the last slope, looking down on the little cabin. The thin stream of smoke coming from the chimney was reassuring. Daniel smiled and reached for her hand. "I'm afraid," Amy whispered.

"I'm here. We've asked God to have His hand upon this situation. Do we believe He will?" She nodded and let him lead the way.

After Daniel's knock, it seemed they waited forever. Finally the door was slowly opened. Silently she stood aside to let them enter. When the door was closed, Amy went to stand in front of her mother. For a moment Amy found herself trying to imagine this woman with her scarred face and dowdy dark dress in that pink boudoir.

She took a deep breath. "I've come to say it all over again.

This time I won't let you make me angry. Mother, please forgive me. I did say those terrible things and I am sorry. I want my mother back, regardless of who she is or what she has done."

Silverheels turned to pace around the cabin. When she stopped across the room from Amy, her face was drawn and pale. "The past can't be ignored, Amy, if it weren't—"

There was a pounding on the door. With a startled glance at Silverheels, Daniel went to open it. They heard him gasp, "Eli!"

Amy ran to the door. "Father, oh, Father!" She pulled him in, touching his white face, sobbing and tugging at his coat.

Daniel patted her back. "Amy, it's all right." He looked at Eli. "She's doing fine. It's just been a rough week."

Eli looked past them both, grief pulling furrows into his face. Moving heavily, like a very old man, he walked past them. Daniel slipped his arm around Amy as they watched him approach Silverheels.

"Amelia? Amy left a note saying she'd found you. I've come—"

The woman turned away. "Kind of you, but totally unnecessary. I'm doing well. I didn't realize you were here." The words sprang from her lips in a jerky rush as she turned, studied his face, and then turned away. "I'm sorry you've come. The past is too painful for either of us to discuss, and certainly it doesn't warrant this." Her pocked hand swept out to include them all.

His voice was weary, slow. "Amelia, I didn't come immediately. After all these years, just knowing you were in the territory, accessible, brought it all back. I would not be here if I weren't ready to take you home with me."

She gasped and whirled around. "Eli Randolph! You are crazy to consider it. You'd open yourself to the same kind of life we had in the past?"

Amy saw him wince. He straightened his shoulders and said, "If it were all your fault, I would hesitate. Both of us were too inexperienced with life then. I hope the years have added a maturity that'll see us through."

"Maturity?" Her voice was bitter. "After Jake Jenson tossed me over for a new excitement, I had nothing. Without a cent, how do you suppose a good-looking woman makes a living?"

"I know. You don't have to explain. If I'd had less pride and more sense, I would have come after you when I got your first letter."

She threw back her head and laughed. "I wouldn't have stayed. I won't come now. My pride would have had me out the door and now my pride won't let me in. Eli, I am ruined, broken. The only thing I ever owned in my whole life was my beauty. It's gone. Do you think I'll come begging now?"

"Silverheels." Daniel's voice slashed through the dialogue and they both turned. For a moment she stared at Daniel and then wearily touched her forehead. He was still silent. Finally she lifted her head.

"I know. You are going to remind me of that prayer."

"Didn't you mean it?"

"Yes, at the time." She hesitated, moved restlessly around the room, and then came to stand in front of Daniel.

"Sorry." Her mocking smile made Amy's heart break. "I guess it just didn't take. When I consider how far I would have to go—" She gestured toward them all. "I guess I know better than to trust me."

"Mother," Amy said hesitantly; then throwing herself at the woman, she cried, "Hold me; tell me you really don't love us, want us!"

That smile was bent on Amy now. "You'll introduce me as your mother, the prostitute, who earned her living by manipulating men, breaking their hearts, taking their money?

"Amy, do you have any idea what you are so easily suggesting? You can't imagine. It is out of the question to suggest that I could use my body in this manner and then casually step back into life expecting to be accepted as a decent woman." Her eyes were sad, not flashing with anger. "Some sins can't be rectified. Forgiven—"

Amy wasn't hearing; she was looking at Daniel, and his steady brown eyes told her he was recalling the scene that was passing through her own mind. She stepped close to him.

"Daniel," she whispered, shaking her head slowly from side to side. "Please forgive me. Until now, I couldn't see it that way. But now—please?"

He wrapped his arms around her. "Amy, all's forgiven. I mean it. Please, sweetheart, don't cry. It's all in the past."

But the shame and ugliness were obvious to her, and she had to say it. "I was doing that very thing, trying to get my way. Bargaining with my body. How can I ever claim to be better—"

Daniel caught her close, murmuring in her ear, reminding her of the prayers she had prayed, the promises they had made. Amy lifted her head from Daniel's shoulder and confronted the other faces. Eli and Amelia stood shoulder to shoulder, their faces stricken, waiting.

"It's just exactly what *I* did." She couldn't meet their eyes as she explained. "I wanted Daniel to leave Colorado Territory. I tried to use my body to get my way."

Eli was pacing back and forth; every jerky movement of his body proclaiming his outrage. "My daughter, sinner—"

His waving hand dropped. Slowly he sank down in Amelia's rocking chair. With head in hands he sat while Amy trembled and pressed against Daniel's shoulder.

When Eli lifted his head, it was Amelia whom he addressed. "Sinners, we all are. How can we measure sin and decide which sins to forgive, which to use as bludgeons?"

Amy caught her breath, looked at her mother. Amelia's face was impassive, pale. Daniel said, "Pride is a sin, particularly when it binds people away from us."

She began speaking slowly, hesitantly. "You don't know how impossible it is. Difficult. I'm ruined. If I had something to offer. I'm trying to see my sins as forgiven, but—" Her voice was muffled as she moved restlessly around. "I'm scarred and ugly."

"Mother." Amy's voice was strangled and it was difficult to force the words. "All we want is for you to love us. If just once you would hold me, if only I could know you really loved me—at least in the past, if not now. Do you know? I used to dream about you, wondering if you loved me when I was little."

Amelia came, and Amy saw the tears running down her face, pooling in the scars. As she opened her arms, she said, "Eli, may we have the rocking chair?"

When Amy finally sat up and looked at her mother, she gave a shaky laugh. "We're soaked with each other's tears."

Eli was standing behind the chair, patting Amelia's shoulder. Daniel was setting out the coffee grinder, filling the cabin with the aroma of roasting coffee beans. "Mother, is it possible to grind coffee beans while they are still hot?"

"You can try." She was smiling as she hugged Amy again.

"Mother—" Amy looked from Amelia to Eli. "What about—" She couldn't finish. It would be an outrage.

Silverheels pressed her face against the hand on her shoulder. "Please, Eli, will you forgive me? That's all I ask. Nothing more."

"Amelia," he said, "I never wanted you to leave, even when I knew—it was just that in the end I wanted, more than anything else, to have you happy. That wasn't happening while we were together."

Amy got up and went to Daniel, who was shaking his hand. "Burned my fingers. How do you grind hot beans?"

"You wait for them to cool." She pushed her head against his shoulder. "I have a request." Lifting her head she looked into his eyes, searching for those shadows that just might be there. There didn't seem to be any, but just in case, she said, "Could we say our vows again, in front of Father and Mother?"

"Because a father and mother should be there when a girl is married?" He was grinning, but there was a question in his eyes, too.

"I suppose that would be nice. But, no. Because of us. Daniel, my heart is so full of love for you, I feel the only way I can express how I feel properly is to stand here and say our vows and really mean them. For richer or for poorer, in sickness and health, as long as we live, I want to be your wife."

Daniel reached for Amy. When they turned they saw Eli and Silverheels standing shoulder to shoulder, nodding, with smiles just beginning in their eyes.